Abo...

Carol Marinelli rec...
was asked for her jol...
these years, to be a...
'writer'. Then it aske...
After chewing her pen for a moment Carol put down the truth—'writing'. The third question asked—'What are your hobbies?' Well, not wanting to look obsessed or, worse still, boring, she crossed the fingers on her free hand and answered 'swimming and tennis'. But, given that the chlorine in the pool does terrible things to her highlights, I'm sure you can guess the real answer!

Emily Forbes began her writing life as a partnership between two sisters who are both passionate bibliophiles. As a team Emily had ten books published, and one of her proudest moments was when her tenth book was nominated for the 2010 Australian Romantic Book of the Year Award.

If you would like to get in touch with Emily you can e-mail her at emilyforbes@internode.on.net.

Lindsay Armstrong was born in South Africa, but now lives in Australia with her New Zealand-born husband and their five children. They have lived in nearly every state of Australia, and have tried their hand at some unusual – for them – occupations, such as farming and horse-training – all grist to the mill for a writer! Lindsay started writing romances when their youngest child began school and she was left feeling at a loose end. She is still doing it and loving it.

Australian

AFFAIRS

Australian Affairs:
Seduced

CAROL MARINELLI

EMILY FORBES

LINDSAY ARMSTRONG

MILLS & BOON

All rights reserved including the right of reproduction in whole or
in part in any form. This edition is published by arrangement with
Harlequin Books S.A.
This is a work of fiction. Names, characters, places, locations and
incidents are purely fictional and bear no relationship to any real
life individuals, living or dead, or to any actual places, business
establishments, locations, events or incidents. Any resemblance is
entirely coincidental.

This book is sold subject to the condition that it shall not, by
way of trade or otherwise, be lent, resold, hired out or otherwise
circulated without the prior consent of the publisher in any form
of binding or cover other than that in which it is published and
without a similar condition including this condition being imposed
on the subsequent purchaser.

® and TM are trademarks owned and used by the trademark owner
and/or its licensee. Trademarks marked with ® are registered
with the United Kingdom Patent Office and/or the Office for
Harmonisation in the Internal Market and in other countries.

First Published in Great Britain 2019
By Mills & Boon, an imprint of HarperCollins *Publishers*
1 London Bridge Street, London, SE1 9GF

AUSTRALIAN AFFAIRS: SEDUCED © 2019 Harlequin Books
S.A.

The Accidental Romeo © 2014 Carol Marinelli
Breaking the Playboy's Rules © 2013 Emily Forbes
The Return of Her Past © 2013 Lindsay Armstrong

ISBN: 978-0-263-27528-5

0419

MIX
Paper from
responsible sources
FSC™ C007454

This book is produced from independently certified FSC™ paper
to ensure responsible forest management.

For more information visit: www.harpercollins.co.uk/green

Printed and bound in Spain
by CPI, Barcelona

THE ACCIDENTAL ROMEO

CAROL MARINELLI

With love to Fiona McArthur
I love our chats
C xxx

CHAPTER ONE

SO IT HAD been too good to be true!

Marnie Johnson drove slowly down Beach Road with a sense of mounting unease. The modern apartments and townhouses she had inspected just a couple of weeks ago were slowly giving way to dilapidated renovators' delights with sprawling, overgrown gardens. These were the type of homes that would require a whole lot of TLC for anyone to live comfortably in them—and the one thing Marnie didn't have was time to give a new home a lot of attention.

Almost certain that she had the job of nurse unit manager at the Bayside Hospital on Melbourne's Mornington Peninsula, Marnie had spent the afternoon after her interview looking at suitable homes to rent and had fallen in love with this street in particular. Yes, it was expensive but it was still a lot cheaper than her smart city apartment. She had been taken in by the sun-drenched, sparkling apartments with views that looked out over the bay and the townhouses with their balconies perfectly angled—just right for relaxing after a busy day, and Marnie certainly intended to be busy.

When the job offer had been confirmed Marnie had found herself far more stretched for time than usual, what with finishing up her old role and celebrating her sea change with friends. Yes, it had been a gamble but, after a lengthy conversation with Dave, the real estate agent who had shown her around, she had signed a month's lease on a house unseen, having been told that it was very similar to the ones she had inspected.

Similar!

The only similarity to the homes Marnie had been shown was that they each had a front door. Not that Marnie could see this particular one—it was obscured by overgrown bushes and trees, and the grass, as Marnie walked up the path, was waist high.

Never trust a real estate agent.

Marnie knew that but had been taken in when Dave had told her that this home had just come on the market and there were no photos yet. She had been so stretched that, for once, the very organised Marnie had taken her eye off the ball.

And look what happened when she did!

Pushing the door open, Marnie stepped inside and it was easily as bad as she had been expecting.

Marnie pulled out her phone and when the real estate agent's receptionist answered she asked to be put through to Dave. Marnie could hear the irritation coming through in her own voice—her usually lilting Irish accent was now sounding a touch brusque and harsh and she fought to check it.

'Dave is at an auction,' the receptionist that Marnie had collected the keys from explained. 'I'm not expecting him to come back to the office today, though I can call him and leave a message asking him to get in touch with you.'

Marnie bit back a smart response—after all, none of this was the young woman's fault. 'Yes, if you could ask him to call me as soon as possible, I'd appreciate it.'

There wasn't a hope that Dave would be calling back today, Marnie just knew it.

Tomorrow was Sunday and on Monday she started her new job and there simply wouldn't be time to arrange more inspections and shift her things again—she made sure that she led by example and she wasn't going to spend the first week in her new role trying to sort out somewhere else to live. She looked around at the grimy beige walls and told herself that once she had washed them down and cleaned the dusty windows, the place might not be so bad after all—though Marnie was sure she was fooling herself. As she wandered from room to room it grew increasingly hard to stay positive. The place didn't even have a bath—just a very mouldy-looking shower that would certainly need a good scrub before she used it. 'What is it with Australians and their showers?' Marnie asked herself out loud—she liked to have a bath in the evening to relax.

Letting out a sigh, she gave up dwelling on it—she'd been through far worse than this.

The removal truck would be arriving with her furniture at eight o'clock tomorrow, along with two of her brothers, Ronan and Brendan.

So she'd better get cleaning!

Marnie tied her thick black hair into a ponytail and headed out to her car to collect the bucket, bleach and vacuum cleaner that she had brought for the job, though she had expected it to be a far easier one. Still, if there was one thing Marnie excelled at it was organisation and cleaning. She'd have this place sorted in no time.

Men! Marnie thought as she lugged in the equipment. They took one look at her china-blue eyes and petite but curvy figure, saw her smiling face, heard her soft accent and thought that they had worked her out.

No one had ever worked her out!

Dave had no idea what he had let himself in for.

She took a call just as she was getting ready to start—
it was Matthew, a friend that she went out with now
and then.

'How's the new place?' Matthew asked.

'Grand!' Marnie lied. She certainly wasn't about to
tell Matthew her mistake. He had thought she had gone a
bit crazy when she had announced that she was leaving
the city and moving out to the bayside suburb.

'You'll be back,' Matthew had warned. 'You'll soon
be bored out of your mind.'

Marnie would like ten minutes to be bored, she
thought as she chatted to him for a few moments and
then ended the call.

It never entered her mind to ask him to come and
help. Matthew was starting to get just a bit too familiar
and Marnie didn't like that. She worked very hard at
keeping all areas of her life separate. Family, work, social life—all were neatly separated, even her sex life. At
thirty-one years old Marnie had long decided this was
the way that worked best for her. She was an independent woman and certainly didn't want Matthew coming
over to gloat about her real estate mistake and, worse,
meet her brothers—that would render her relationship
with Matthew far more than it was and Marnie had no
intention of that happening.

Marnie opened every window throughout the house
to let the sun stream in and then started her cleaning
in the kitchen, gradually working her way outwards.
She stopped occasionally for a drink and to admire
her own handiwork. She was like a mini-tornado once
she got going. Rubber gloves on, Marnie washed down
the walls and cleaned the windows. The curtains she

took down and hung out in the sun and, before putting them back, she vacuumed and mopped the floors, all the while thinking about Monday and the challenges that lay ahead.

She was looking forward to running a department. She had been an associate in a large city hospital for a few years but, realising her senior had no plans to leave and loathing having to answer to anyone, when she had seen the job at Bayside advertised she had taken the plunge. As she worked on, Marnie thought back to her interview. The place needed a strong leader, she had been told—and Marnie was certainly that. Christine, her predecessor, had apparently spent more time in the office than taking care of the department. The off-duty was a joke—the shifts dependent, it would seem, on who had brought Christine the most coffee. For now the place was being run by Cate Nicholls, who had chosen not to take the role permanently as she was soon to be married.

The emergency department was woefully short of doctors, though that, Marnie had been told, was being addressed and there were two new consultants starting soon. Another problem that had been hinted at was that one of the consultants, Harry Worthington, who hadn't been present at Marnie's interviews, was using the nursing staff as a babysitter to his twins.

'Not any more!' had been Marnie's swift response, and she had seen Lillian, the director of nursing, not only give a brief smile but write something on the notes in front of her.

It was then Marnie had known she had the job.

Harry Worthington!

As Lillian had shown her around the department Marnie had learnt a little bit more about the staffing issues and had found out that Harry was a recent widow and single father to four-year-old twins.

Marnie hadn't let on that the name was a familiar one but she had smothered a little smile when she'd thought of the once wild Harry now a consultant and single father.

Who would ever have thought it?

Ready now to tackle the shower, Marnie took down the shower curtain and soaked it with a good measure of bleach then stripped off into her underwear. As she started to scrub the grimy walls she thought about her early student nurse days. She had done the first year of training at Melbourne Central before, for personal reasons, transferring to the Royal to complete her training—it had been at Melbourne Central that their paths had loosely crossed. Loosely because, apart from 'What's his blood pressure doing?' or 'Can you get me his file?' Harry had never so much as spoken directly to her when she had been there, though she had felt the ripple effect when he'd entered the ward or canteen and she had heard an awful lot about him!

As a junior doctor, his wild ways, combined with very good looks, had assured that Harry had never lacked female attention. The mere whisper that Harry would be at a party in the doctors' mess would guarantee that the number of attendees swelled. Marnie had been head over heels with Craig, her first boyfriend, at the time. Living away from home, away from her strict parents and the responsibility of taking care of her younger brothers, Marnie had been too busy embracing her first taste of freedom to give Harry Worthington more than a moment's thought. But, a fair bit older and a whole lot wiser, kneeling back on her heels, Marnie thought about him now.

She remembered that he was tall and very long-limbed. His hair was brown and had always been superbly cut because no matter what the hour, be it nine a.m. and just starting or eight p.m. and just heading for home, it had always fallen into perfect shape. He had surely invented designer stubble and there had often been sniggers in the staff canteen when a nurse had appeared with Harry rash! He had worked hard, partied harder and completely lived up to his decadent reputation—though everyone had loved Harry, from porter to consultant, domestic to senior nursing staff, patient to relative, he somehow had charmed them all!

Not her, though.

Now that she thought about it, now that she sat quietly, they'd had one brief conversation away from work.

'Come on, Marnie, stop moping around…' She could hear her flatmates urging her to go out and, even though she hadn't felt like a party, to keep them from nagging, Marnie had agreed. She had stood there clutching lemonade and watching the good times unfolding as, unbeknown to her flatmates, Marnie's world fell apart. In the end she had decided to just slip away.

'Leaving so soon?'

Harry had caught her as she'd headed for the door and had offered to get her a drink. Marnie had looked into very green eyes and watched them blink as, completely impervious to his charm, without explanation, she'd simply walked off.

Marnie wondered how the charming Harry would be faring these days! He'd be in his late thirties by now—surely all those years of excess would have caught up with him. Marnie stood and turned on the shower, aiming the water on the walls and laughing to herself at the thought of a ruddy-faced Harry, who surely by now had a paunch.

Oh, and a single father to twins.

There'd been no chance then of him charming her and there'd be even less now—she could truly think of nothing worse than a single father.

Marnie was decidedly free and single and liked her men to be the same. ·

Selfish, some might think, not that Marnie cared a jot what others thought.

As evening descended, perhaps the light was just being kind but the place looked far nicer than it had when she had arrived. Though Marnie would never admit the same to Dave when she spoke to him about it on Monday, she actually liked the main bedroom—it had high ceilings and a huge bay window, as well as a fireplace, which would surely be gorgeous for snuggling up in bed with a good book or a man in winter.

Not that she would be here in winter, Marnie reminded herself. She would see this lease out, given she had been foolish enough to sign, but she would be finding herself a new home and Dave certainly wouldn't be her agent of choice.

Marnie made her final trip to the car and pulled out her yoga mat, which would serve as her mattress tonight, a duvet and pillow, and a box of personal effects.

Marnie set out her toiletries in the now sparkling bathroom and had a shower then headed to the main bedroom. There she put out her clothes for the morning and set up her bed for the night. Then she put her photos up on the mantelpiece.

First she put up the family favourite—Marnie and

her parents with her five younger brothers, all together on the day Ronan had graduated.

Ronan, her youngest brother, was unashamedly Marnie's favourite. She had been nearly eleven when he was born and Marnie had had a lot to do with raising him—changing his nappies, getting up to him at night, feeding him before she went to school. It was funny to think of Ronan now at twenty-one—he was a gorgeous geek who loved computers and playing the piano, though not necessarily in that order.

Marnie placed the photo above the fire and took out another. There she was, a fourteen-year-old Marnie with her best friend Siobhan on the day the Johnsons had left Ireland to emigrate to Perth, Australia, and start a new life. Though the two young girls were smiling in the photo, Marnie could see the tears in both their eyes—for Marnie and Siobhan it had been a terribly difficult time. Marnie hadn't wanted to leave her home, her school, her dancing and her friends, especially Siobhan. Still, she had made the best of it and had started to make friends—only then her father's work had dictated that the family again up sticks and move from Perth to Melbourne.

'You'll soon make new friends,' her mother had again insisted.

Yes, Marnie had made new friends but none had come close to Siobhan.

Marnie chose wisely and so when she gave her heart it was for ever and she and Siobhan were still best friends nearly twenty years later. They shared daily emails and video-called often, as well as catching up every couple of years face to face. Marnie smiled as she put out the photo and was still smiling when she pulled out the last one—but maybe it had been a long day, because she felt the sting of tears at the back of her eyes. Marnie cried rarely and she hadn't expected to feel that way today. She was tired, she reasoned, as she gazed on the familiar and much-loved photograph of an eighteen-year-old Marnie holding Declan.

Finally holding Declan.

It was such a bitter-sweet time because until he had been two weeks old Marnie had never got to hold him, though her body had ached to, her breasts leaking as much as her eyes as she'd peered into the incubator and craved the feeling of holding her son in her arms. Until the day of the photo his tiny body had been smothered in tubes and equipment but, when it had been deemed that nothing more could be done for Declan, they had all been taken away. She and Craig had been given a comfortable room away from the hustle and bustle of the neonatal unit and had had a few precious hours alone with him.

Her parents Marnie had allowed in only briefly.

'There will be time for other babies.' No, her mother hadn't been insensitive enough to say it on that day. It had been said when Marnie had first told her she was pregnant—that there would be plenty of time for other babies later down the track had been a large portion of her mother's advice.

No, there would be no other babies.

Declan was her son and he forever had her heart.

Marnie ran her finger over the image and felt not the cold of the glass but the soft warmth of her baby's skin. She looked into his dark blue eyes that were so weary from fighting and, just as she did every night, Marnie said goodnight to him.

Setting the photo down, Marnie set her alarm for six

and then settled down on her yoga mat to get ready for an uncomfortable night, sleeping on the floor.

Not that she minded.

Yes, Marnie had been through far worse.

CHAPTER TWO

'I THINK YOU'VE already met Marnie...' Lillian, the director of nursing, said as she introduced Marnie to Dr Vermont.

'I have.' The elderly doctor shook her hand and Marnie smiled back at him warmly. 'We met at Marnie's first interview. I was thrilled to hear that you had accepted the position,' he added to Marnie. 'Hopefully you can bring some order to the place.'

'I have every intention to.' Marnie smiled again. She had, on sight, liked Dr Vermont. He was old school and liked things done a certain way and had had no qualms in telling her such, which was exactly how Marnie liked to work.

'Harry!' Lillian called, and Marnie turned to the sight of Harry Worthington, fast realising that instead of his wild youth catching up with him, he had left it behind, only to improve. Rather than the scrubs she remembered him wearing, that tall, muscular physique was now dressed in a well-cut charcoal-grey suit. He seemed taller, a touch broader, but there was far from a paunch; if anything, he was slimmer than the Harry of yesteryear. He wasn't quite perfection. It was no longer designer stubble that graced his jaw—Harry needed a good shave! He also needed to put on a tie. He had an

unfinished look to him that ten minutes would soon take
care of. Perhaps, though, the most surprising thing to
see was that the once terribly sexy, laid-back Harry was
now late and clearly rushing with a little boy and girl
hanging off each hand as Lillian made the introductions.

'This is Marnie Johnson, the new nurse unit manager. You didn't manage to come in for her interviews.'

'No, I was on night duty for the first and on a day
off for the other,' Harry explained, 'but Dr Vermont
has said many good things about you.' He let go of his
daughter and shook Marnie's hand, albeit briefly, because the little girl, as soon as she was let loose, started
to wander off.

'Charlotte!' Harry warned, giving a brief eye-roll
to Marnie before retrieving his daughter's hand. 'How
many times do I have to tell you? You're to stay with
me.'

'But I'm hungry.'

'That's because you didn't eat your cornflakes,'
Harry said to his daughter as he returned to the group,
and Marnie watched as Lillian's lips pursed in disap-
proval. Marnie couldn't see that there was an issue—
clearly, Harry had just arrived for work and was taking
his children to day care. It was hardly his fault that there
was a group to meet him.

'You and Marnie might already have met.' Lillian
pushed on with the conversation when really it would be
far easier to make the introductions once Harry didn't
have his children with him. 'Marnie, didn't you train
at Melbourne Central?'

Harry frowned. He looked at Marnie's raven hair and
china-blue eyes and couldn't quite believe they might
have worked alongside each other for three years and
that he didn't recognise her at all.

'No,' Marnie corrected Lillian. 'I only did my first year of training at Melbourne Central. After that I transferred to the Royal.' She turned to Harry. 'I do remember you, though…' Marnie said, and suppressed a smile at the slight flare of concern in his eyes—perhaps Harry might be a little uncomfortable with people who could remember him in his wilder days.

Perhaps, Marnie thought, noticing again, after all these years, his stunning green eyes, it was time for some fun. Dr Vermont was talking to Harry's son and Lillian was briefly distracted by her pager going off and Marnie simply could not resist a tease, even though they had barely ever spoken. 'You remember me, though, don't you?'

'Actually…' Harry let go of Charlotte's hand again as he rather worriedly scratched at the back of his neck. 'Now I think back on it…'

'Surely you remember,' Marnie implored, enjoying herself.

'Charlotte!' Harry called, but Marnie could hear the relief in his voice at a brief chance of escape.

'I'm just about to take Marnie on a tour and introduce her to everyone,' Lillian interrupted the fun. 'Marnie, do you want to go and get your jacket before I show you around?'

'I'm fine.' Marnie shook her head. 'We'll just get on.'

But Lillian had other ideas. 'We actually like the managers to wear their jackets, especially for things like formal introductions—it adds a nice authoritative touch.'

'I don't need a jacket to be authoritative,' Marnie responded, and it was Harry who was suppressing a smile now as he watched her walk off.

Not many people spoke to Lillian like that.

Clearly Marnie was setting the tone.

'I think,' Dr Vermont said as Marnie clipped off with Lillian moving fast to catch up, 'that Marnie Johnson might be just what the doctor ordered—did you see Lillian's face when she said that she didn't need a jacket?'

'I did.' Harry grinned.

'So, do you remember her from Melbourne Central?'

'I don't.' Harry swallowed, paying great attention to Adam and failing to see the twinkle in Dr Vermont's eyes.

'She seems to remember you!'

'I'd better get these two over to day care,' Harry said, again glad of the excuse of the twins to escape. He walked behind Marnie and Lillian on his way to day care, trying and failing not to notice her very petite, trim figure in the navy dress. She had stopped to shake hands with Juan Morales, one of the new consultants who was just finishing up after a night shift. 'And Dr Cooper starts when?' Harry heard Marnie asking as he walked past.

'In four weeks' time, I believe,' Juan answered.

Harry didn't hang around to hear the rest of the conversation. Just wait until Lillian and Marnie found out that he had approved Juan's annual leave, commencing in one week's time! Yes, the place was almost running well with Juan finally on board, but it was all about to go to pot again some time soon.

Harry signed his name alongside Charlotte's and Adam's in the day-care register and tried to focus on today instead of worrying about the weeks ahead.

Since Jill had died, he had learnt that it was the best he could do.

'Are you picking us up?' Adam asked.

'I'll do my best to be here at six,' Harry said. 'But if

it looks as if I won't be able to get away on time, I will ring Evelyn and she'll pick you up.'

Harry could not stand Adam's nod, or that his son was trying not to cry. He knelt down to look Adam in the eye. 'We had a good weekend, didn't we?'

They'd had a brilliant weekend—the first in ages.

With Juan working, both Harry and Dr Vermont had finally had a full, undisturbed weekend without being rung for advice or called in urgently. Dr Vermont had taken his wife away to celebrate their upcoming wedding anniversary, which fell today. He himself had taken his children to the beach on the Saturday and had spent Sunday finally tackling the garden then watching movies in the evening.

Simple pleasures perhaps, but they hadn't shared a weekend so straightforward in ages.

'I just…' Adam started, but he didn't finish and Harry waited. He was worried about Adam's talking, or rather the lack of it. 'It doesn't matter,' Adam said.

Oh, but it did.

Harry looked at Adam's dark, serious eyes, so like his mum's. And, like Jill, Adam never complained about Harry's ridiculous work hours, which only served to make Harry feel worse. 'Hey,' Harry said. 'Tonight we're going to take those bruised bananas and make banana bread.' It was completely off the top of his head. 'So tomorrow you and Charlotte will have something nice waiting for breakfast that you can eat in the car if we're in a hurry.'

'Promise?' Adam checked.

'As much as I can promise,' Harry said, because the very nature of his job meant that nothing could be guaranteed. 'But if we don't get to make it tonight then the bananas will be even blacker tomorrow and the banana bread even sweeter.'

Finally, Adam smiled.

'I hate banana bread!' Charlotte, the louder of the two, had to have her say as Harry gave her a kiss goodbye.

'I know.' Harry smiled. 'But you do like eating the frosting.'

'Can I make the frosting?' Charlotte was more easily cheered, though, unlike Adam and Jill, she did protest loudly whenever Harry was late picking them up or was called into work.

'Yep,' Harry said, and then, because he had to, he qualified again. 'If I get home in time.'

'Try,' Charlotte said.

It was all he seemed to be doing these days.

He hugged them both and then, as good as gold, they headed off to join their little friends to start their very long day.

Something had to give.

Harry headed back towards the department and tried, for now, not to think about the unpalatable decision that he was coming to.

As well as being an emergency consultant, Harry was also a renowned hand surgeon. He was reluctantly considering moving into the private sphere and focusing on his second love—hands. Emergency and single fatherhood, he had fast found out, simply didn't mix.

Harry had decided that he was going to take some annual leave while he made his decision. Once Juan was back from his honeymoon and Dr Cooper had started work and the department was adequately staffed, he could take some proper time off and work out what to do.

He just needed to get through the next few weeks.

Harry headed straight for the changing rooms and took the ten minutes Marnie had noted that he needed. He quickly shaved, combed his hair and added a tie, then walked back into the department, and the first person he saw was Marnie.

'That's better!' Marnie commented, when others perhaps would not have.

'Better?'

'You've shaved, put on a tie...'

'I don't need a tie to be a consultant.' Harry made light reference to her jacket comment to Lillian but still he bristled. She should see how Juan dressed some days, stomping about in Cuban-heeled boots, and, until recently, Juan's black hair had been longer than shoulder length—imagine what she'd have had to say about that! Harry had always prided himself on his appearance and tried to look smart for work, and he really didn't need a lecture today.

Heading to her office, Marnie gave it a good wipe down with alcohol rubs and then, deciding it was too drab, she rang a local florist and asked for flowers to be delivered. Then she asked Cate Nicholls, who had been filling in after Christine had left, to bring her up to date with certain protocols and paperwork.

'Most multi-trauma goes straight to the city, though it depends on transport availability, so we can get a sudden influx,' Cate explained, but Marnie had gone through most of this at her interviews. The paperwork took a while—there were all the patient complaints and staff incident reports to go through.

'They're mainly about waiting times,' Cate commented.

'And cleanliness,' Marnie observed, flicking through

them. 'Is there a protocol for cubicle preparation for the patients?'

'Not one that's written as such,' Cate said.

There soon would be! Still, Marnie moved on to the budget lists and all the stuff that Cate had loathed but which Marnie just loved to tackle.

'I hope everything is up to date,' Cate said. 'If it's not…'

'I'll just ask you,' Marnie answered.

'I won't be around, though,' Cate reminded her. 'I'm going on annual leave next week.'

'Of course, you're getting married…are you going anywhere nice for your honeymoon?'

'We're getting married in Argentina,' Cate answered. 'Juan and I—'

'You're marrying Juan?'

'That's right.'

'The new doctor?' Marnie checked, and Cate nodded.

'How long are you going to be away for?'

'Three weeks.'

Cate was still smiling. Perhaps, as most would be, she was waiting for congratulations—she just didn't know Marnie, whose only interest at work was work. 'Are you saying that Juan's got three weeks off!' Marnie exclaimed. 'But he's only just started.'

By nine a.m. both Lillian and Cate had glimpsed what was to come.

By midday the rest of the staff were starting to.

'Are there four of her?' Kelly, one of the nurses, grumbled as she sat on a stool beside Harry.

'Sorry?' Harry looked up from the notes he was writing. 'Four of who?'

'Marnie.' Kelly sighed. 'It seems that everywhere I go, there she is.'

Harry grinned. Marnie certainly wasn't hiding in the office, as Christine had—she darted in and out and wherever you looked it seemed that she was there.

Harry *had* noticed and, as if to prove Kelly's point, Marnie soon appeared.

'Where are the nursing roster request forms kept?' Marnie asked Kelly.

'In here.' Kelly opened a drawer and pulled out a large diary, which Marnie took.

Then Marnie sat on a stool at a computer, quietly working her way through the rosters before disappearing.

'See!' Kelly said. 'She's everywhere...' She launched into another moan but her voice trailed off as Marnie returned with not just a new diary but instructions.

'From now on, all of the off-duty requests are to be written in the new diary, along with a reason for requesting that date,' Marnie said, as she pinned up a laminated note stating the same. 'If you would prefer to speak to me personally, rather than write your reasons down, that's fine.'

Satisfied the note was up straight, she turned and Harry realised that, though the nursing rosters had nothing at all to do with him, he was watching her. He quickly looked away, telling himself he hadn't just been admiring the rear view of the new nurse manager and the way her dress had lifted just a fraction as she'd pinned up the note.

Surely he'd remember if anything had ever happened between them?

Surely?

'Do you have a moment?' Marnie asked.

'Sure.'

'Not here.'

Harry had guessed this would be coming—Cate had warned him that Marnie had been less than impressed about Juan taking time off. With a slight roll of his eyes he headed to her office and took a seat, leaning back in the chair and stretching out his legs, absolutely refusing to jump through hoops for Marnie, as everyone else seemed to be.

'I was just looking through the doctors' roster and it would seem that we are very short of senior medical staff.'

'We have been,' Harry said. 'But things are steadily improving. We've got Juan now and there's another new consultant—Dr Cooper—starting soon.'

'Which would be great but I've just found out that Juan has been given three weeks' annual leave, starting well before Dr Cooper commences.'

'He's going home to Argentina—you can hardly go there for a long weekend.'

'But that will leave us with just you and Dr Vermont to cover the department.'

'I'm aware of that.' Harry was more than aware—things had only just started improving and now the nightmare was going to begin all over again, not that he was going to reveal the logistical nightmare to Marnie. 'Juan's getting married,' Harry pointed out, assuming that there the discussion would end.

He just didn't know Marnie.

'Could he not have delayed his wedding till Dr Cooper had started?'

'It was a whirlwind romance,' Harry answered with a wry smile.

'Please!' She rolled her eyes. 'There's no such thing and, even if there was, surely true love could at least wait a month.'

'Apparently not!' Harry said. 'Look, Juan is an amazing doctor and believe me when I say such a highly skilled doctor is usually pretty hard to entice to come and work at Bayside Hospital. Once immigration and everything is sorted, Juan's going to be a huge asset to the place but he only agreed to take the role if I accommodated his annual leave request.'

'You *acquire* annual leave,' Marnie said. 'Juan hasn't acquired any, from what I can see.'

Harry tried a different tack. 'The guy broke his neck a while back, he was barely able to walk when he got to Australia. As well as getting married, he really wants to return home and let his family see how well he's doing.'

Oh, but Marnie was having none of it. 'So Juan breaking his neck means you have to bend over backwards and break yours to accommodate his love life?'

Harry was sure then that he hadn't slept with her!

He'd certainly remember—Harry had never met anyone like her in his life! 'You're not a romantic, I take it?' Harry's voice was dry.

'There's not a single romantic bone in my body,' Marnie said. 'But so long as you can assure me that the department will be adequately covered with senior medical staff then it's not my issue.'

'It will be covered.'

'Good.'

Harry stood up and turned to go, but how well they might have known each other was driving him crazy, so he decided to simply bite the bullet and ask, 'What year were you at Melbourne Central?'

'You really don't remember?' Marnie said. 'I was blonde then, if that helps.'

'Blonde?' Harry looked at her very thick black hair. 'That would have taken some peroxide.'

'It did,' Marnie said. 'You still don't remember me, do you?'

She loved his discomfort—loved the small swallow in his neck—and she watched as he drew in a breath while attempting to come up with a suitable answer. Then those green eyes met hers and a smile spread on Harry's lips, lips that had been just a little insolent and teasing in their day, Marnie recalled, and they were becoming that now.

'How could I ever forget you, Marnie?'

The little game Marnie had been playing had suddenly gone too far because it was Marnie, most unusually, who struggled to calm a blush, and she rapidly decided to put an end to it, while still keeping the upper hand. 'It's okay, Harry, I've been teasing you. You don't have to worry—I'm very possibly the only student nurse at Melbourne Central that you didn't sleep with.'

'Glad to hear it,' Harry said, still smiling back at her, except the smile sort of wavered, because maybe that wasn't the right answer to give.

What was the right answer to a statement like that? Harry wondered as he walked off.

He couldn't make Marnie out. She was a strange mix. Forthright yet distant, funny yet stern but, even if he was smiling at the little game she'd played on him, Harry knew as he headed back to the patients that the holiday was over. Not that you could ever call this place a holiday, but there would be no asking Marnie if she could keep an eye out for the twins in the staffroom, even if it was right near her office. There would be no appealing to her feminine side and asking her to grab them from day care, or would she mind if one of the nurses in the obs ward kept an eye on them for an hour.

Harry just knew it.

CHAPTER THREE

YES, MARNIE WAS everywhere.

As Harry sat having his lunch he found out, if he hadn't known already, just how forthright she was—the pint-sized Marnie didn't even try to mince her words when she answered a personal call.

Marnie didn't excuse herself from the staffroom to take the call—instead, she tucked the phone between her neck and chin and squirted salad dressing over her home-made salad. As she thanked Dave for returning her call, she stirred in the dressing.

Oh, her accent was as soft as butter as she spoke but you could almost feel it choking the rather unfortunate Dave's arteries.

'Absolutely, I signed the contract but let me ask you this, Dave—was one month's rent really worth it? I certainly shan't be staying on when my lease is up.' Harry listened as she made it very clear that she wouldn't be using him in the future and hopefully, if the hospital grapevine served her well, neither would anybody else from Bayside. 'So, to be clear,' Marnie concluded, 'you have my notice and I have photos of before and after so I'll be expecting to receive my deposit in full—the place was nothing but a filthy swamp before I set to work.'

'Ripped off?' Kelly asked, and Marnie nodded.

'It's my own fault for signing a lease on a place that I hadn't seen. He only showed me the first half of Beach Road…' She didn't elaborate and she didn't sit around for much longer—after finishing her salad, Marnie stood and left the staffroom.

'I can't make up my mind whether or not I like her,' Kelly grumbled.

'Well, I've made up my mind and I don't.' Abby, another of the nurses, sighed. 'I was given a ten-minute lesson on the correct way to wash my hands, as if I didn't already know. I think that she's got OCD!'

'She's got ADHD,' Kelly grumbled. 'She just never stops.'

'Ladies!' Dr Vermont said, and didn't even look up from his newspaper as he delivered a warning for the nurses to stop gossiping.

Though, a few hours later, he indulged in a little gossip of his own as he put on his jacket to head for home. 'What do you think of Marnie?' Dr Vermont asked Harry.

'I don't know what to think,' Harry admitted. 'She's not exactly here to make friends, is she? Marnie doesn't seem to care who she offends.'

'I like that about her,' Dr Vermont said. 'The trouble with Christine was that she was either your best friend or your worst enemy.' He thought about it for a long moment. 'I know that it's very early days but so far I'm impressed.'

Dr Vermont was more than a colleague to Harry. He was a friend and mentor and Harry admired him greatly. If Dr Vermont liked Marnie, that was high praise indeed and almost as good as a reference.

'Well, so far so good,' Harry conceded. 'But enough about this place—hadn't you better get going?'

'Sorry that I have to dash off.' Dr Vermont didn't elaborate. They both knew that it was his wedding anniversary today and Dr Vermont was kind enough to realise that milestones such as the one he and Marjorie had just reached might cause a twinge of pain for Harry.

'You go and enjoy yourself,' Harry smiled. 'Forty years is quite an achievement.'

'I know that it is,' Dr Vermont agreed. 'We've got all the family coming over tonight...' He paused as Harry took a beautifully wrapped bottle from his desk and handed it to him.

'Well, you'd better hide this from them, then.'

Dr Vermont thanked Harry and after he had gone to celebrate with his wife and family Harry sat for a long moment.

Jill had been dead now for more than a year and a half. Birthdays and two Christmases had passed. Two wedding anniversaries had been and gone as well—and still it hurt. Some days more, some days less, but the pain was always there. Not just for Jill and all that she was missing out on, but for himself and more pointedly for the twins. Harry twisted the ring on his finger—he still couldn't bring himself to take it off. It wasn't just the hurt, there was also guilt—perpetual, constant guilt about whether or not he was doing a good job with the children. Certainly they weren't being brought up as Jill would have wanted. She had wanted to stay home at least until the twins had started school.

Yes, he was doing his best—he was just all too aware that it wasn't quite enough.

Harry headed back out to the department, which was, for once, quiet. The late staff were all trying to pretend to be busy as Marnie sat at the nurses' station and went through the policy manual, and of course she was making notes and had several questions for Harry.

'Sheldon just brought back a puncture wound of the hand for review in the hand clinic tomorrow.' Marnie had been surprised; it was a very small injury that could easily have been followed up by a GP. 'When I questioned him he said it was policy. Now I've checked and it says here that all hand injuries, regardless of how small, are to be brought back the next day for review in the hand clinic.'

'That's right.'

'All?'

'All.' Harry nodded. 'A lot of things get picked up in the hand clinic and for the most part the patients are in and out in less than a minute. It's worth it, though, because something that seemed minor at the time is often picked up. I've found it works better to just bring everyone with a hand injury, no matter how small, back the next day for review.'

'Fair enough.' Marnie turned the page and then glanced up at the clock. 'What time do you finish?'

'Now,' Harry said. 'Day care closes at six.'

'Dr Morales comes on at nine?' Marnie checked.

'That's right. Though you can call me for anything you're concerned about—all of the staff know that.'

'They do,' Marnie said. 'I'll see you tomorrow, then.'

'You shall.' Harry smiled. 'It's nice to meet you, Marnie, and I'm very glad that we never...' He halted. He wished he could take that back and wondered what had possessed him to even go there in the first place.

'New girl's tease.' Marnie smiled. 'I couldn't help myself.'

'I thought it was supposed to be the other way around, that we were supposed to be teasing you.'

'I make my own fun,' Marnie said.

She really was the oddest mix and, if there was any doubt as to that, she proved it when she continued talking. 'I should be offended really that you're so relieved nothing ever happened.' Marnie winked. ''Night, Harry.'

He turned to go but as he did so the alert phone rang and Miriam, one of the late staff, took the call. 'There's a multi-trauma coming in, they've just diverted and are bringing him here,' Miriam said. 'ETA ten minutes. Harry, would you like me to run over and grab the twins for you?'

'That would be great,' Harry said, taking off his jacket but pausing midway as Marnie's soft voice carried the length of the nurses' station and promptly halted everyone.

'Instead of running over to day care, Miriam, shouldn't you be setting up for the multi-trauma?'

Miriam hesitated and when Harry gave her a nod, instead of racing to get the twins, Miriam headed into Resus.

'You'd better get going,' Marnie said to Harry. 'You don't want to get caught up in this.'

No, he didn't want to get caught up but if it was serious he would call for the trauma team to come down and if it wasn't serious Sheldon could deal with it, except Marnie was already speaking into the phone.

'Could you fast-page the trauma team to come to Emergency?' she said, but as she replaced the receiver Harry was waiting for her.

'They might not be needed.'

'Hopefully not,' Marnie said, 'but if they are then surely it's better for the patient to have them waiting here.'

Harry heard the overhead intercom crackle into life to summon the team.

''Night, Harry,' Marnie said again.

For Harry it was the strangest feeling to be leaving the department knowing full well there was an emergency on its way in.

He was always running towards an emergency; instead, this evening, he was walking away.

It just didn't feel right.

And however assured Marnie was, he couldn't help but wonder how she'd deal with a less-than-impressed trauma team if she'd called them at five to six for something minor, just when they were due to go home…

Harry paused as he reached day care, dropped one ball from the many he was juggling as he heard the sound of his colleagues' footsteps racing down the corridor to greet whatever was being brought in.

Harry let out a breath and walked into day care. No, he wasn't the first parent to get there but at least he wasn't the last.

'Daddy! We thought you'd have to help with the emergency!' Charlotte squealed, and flung herself at him. Her brown curls were bobbing and her green eyes, the same as her dad's, were smiling with excitement as she realised it was home time. *And* she remembered the promises made.

'Can I make the frosting?'

'You can.'

Even though the trauma team was arriving, the blasted intercom was summoning the team for the second time as Harry signed the twins out.

As he walked down the corridor, carrying Charlotte and holding Adam's hand, he felt Adam still as the stretcher was raced in. He looked down and saw Adam blinking. 'He'll be okay,' Harry assured him.

But the injured man on the stretcher didn't upset Adam, he'd seen way more than most children had already. No, he was bracing himself for his father to return them to day care, Harry realised, or to pop them around to the staffroom; instead, they headed to the car.

'Who's looking after him?' Adam checked, because normally his father was needed.

'He's going to be fine,' Harry said, wishing for the hundredth time his children didn't know or see so much, but the hospital day-care centre was his only choice if he was going to work here. 'There is a team of specialists waiting for him.'

Harry strapped the twins into their car seats and drove the short distance home as Charlotte filled him in on her day, talking non-stop till they were turning into their street.

'How about your day, Adam?' Harry asked, trying to encourage Adam to speak.

'We did paintings.' Adam looked at his father as if Harry must have briefly lost his mind. 'Charlotte just told you.'

'I know.' Harry smiled. They were just so different. Charlotte liked every gap in the conversation filled with her voice, whereas Adam was only too happy to sit back and listen.

Evelyn came out to help him with the twins as they pulled into the driveway, but as she ushered them in, knowing he wouldn't be able to relax till he knew things were okay at work, Harry told Evelyn he'd join them soon. He stood in the hallway, took out his phone and called Emergency. It was Marnie who answered.

'How's the multi-trauma?' Harry asked.

'All good,' Marnie replied. 'Well, not so good if you're the patient, but it's all under control. He's just heading round for an MRI.'

'I can come back if you need me,' Harry said. 'My babysitter's here.'

'There's really no point,' Marnie said. 'As I said, it's all under control. The team have been fantastic.'

'Shouldn't you be at home?' Harry asked, glancing at his watch. She'd been there since long before nine after all.

'Shouldn't you be?' Marnie asked, and Harry gave a thin smile as he heard the chatter coming from the kitchen.

Marnie had made a very good point.

Happy that the patient was being well looked after, Harry headed into the kitchen and to the delicious scent of dinner. 'Smells good,' Harry said.

'I'm trying something different.' Evelyn smiled at the twins. 'Tonight we're eating Russian!'

'Ooh!' Charlotte was delighted, Adam not so sure, and Harry was simply grinning because Evelyn was so Australian she thought beef stroganoff was exotic.

Having Evelyn look after the children had, absolutely, been the best idea Harry had had.

Actually, it had been Juan's idea that he get an older carer for the children.

Yep, *mea culpa*, Harry had slept with the last nanny and the one before that.

It was exhausting being a widower at times!

Seriously.

Harry didn't want a wife—he'd had Jill. Sex, though, that was another matter entirely. Why did women always have to complicate things by falling in love?

At least Evelyn didn't read a single thing into it when

Harry suggested that instead of dashing off she join them for dinner.

'Are you sure?' Evelyn checked, but she was already pulling out a chair. 'How was work?'

'Good,' Harry said, because, given he was home on time, it must have been a good day. 'We've got a new nurse manager just started,' Harry said. 'She seems very efficient.'

'She's rude,' Charlotte said.

'Rude?' Harry looked at his daughter, who was spooning sour cream onto her dinner, and tried to recall them meeting her. 'How can you say Marnie's rude? You barely even met her.'

'She didn't say hello to us,' Charlotte said.

'It was her first day,' Harry commented. 'I'm sure she had other things to think of.' Though, as Harry wrestled the sour cream from Charlotte, he did dwell on it for just a second. Charlotte was right, well, not the rude part but usually people did comment on the twins, especially when they realised that they were twins. Charlotte, Harry decided, was just far too used to having people drop to their knees and tell her how cute she was.

Dinner was nice and Harry refused Evelyn's offer to stay and do the dishes. 'I can stack a dishwasher!' Harry said, as he saw her to the door.

'If you need me tonight,' Evelyn offered, 'you just have to call.'

'I shan't tonight,' Harry said. 'Juan's on. Things might get a bit busy, though, once he's off on his honeymoon.'

'No problem.'

Evelyn really was fantastic, Harry thought as he saw her out. Evelyn was their next-door-but-one neighbour. She had lost her husband many years ago and desperately missed her daughter, who had moved with her husband and baby to China. Evelyn had actually cried when Harry had taken up Juan's suggestion to get someone older and Harry had asked if she could be there for the twins.

For cash!

Perfect.

Evelyn was saving up to go and visit her family in China and she got to spoil Charlotte and Adam in the interim.

The twins went to day care but on the odd day they were sick, Evelyn was there, and if Harry was on call, Evelyn slept in the nanny's room. She didn't even mind the odd time when Harry had to call her during the night.

It wasn't a complete solution but for now it was working.

Wow!

It was just after seven. Dinner was done and the dishwasher was on.

'Can we make the banana bread?' Adam asked.

'Yep.'

Oh, the bliss of the absence of parental guilt, Harry thought as Adam mashed bananas. In no time there was the lovely scent of banana bread filling the house as he got the twins bathed and ready for bed.

'The frosting!' Charlotte said. 'You promised that I could make the frosting.'

'I know, but the bread had to cool.' Harry looked up the recipe on the Internet and squeezed some orange juice, which Charlotte mashed into cream cheese. By nine p.m. the twins were in bed, there was a slice of banana bread wrapped for Adam's breakfast and a small bowl of frosting for Charlotte. And there was just a glimpse of order to the home for the first time in a very long time.

Harry lay back on the couch and yawned.

They'd made it through another day.

He thought of Marnie stopping Miriam from going to fetch the children, and the strangest thing was he was actually grateful for it. Harry didn't want people rushing to pick up his children and he loathed all the favours that he constantly had to ask.

It was Marnie who had done him a true favour today.

She'd given him an evening at home with the twins.

CHAPTER FOUR

'EXCUSE ME!'

Harry's tongue rolled in his cheek as he heard Marnie's beguilingly soft voice. She walked over to Sheldon, the resident, who was washing his hands at the surgical sink.

Poor Sheldon, he had no idea what was coming.

Harry did. Marnie had delivered Harry exactly the same lecture she was now giving Sheldon.

'You see these long taps, Sheldon?'

'Yes.'

'Well, it might surprise you to hear that they're not designed for helping doctors who happen to have big hands.'

Harry couldn't resist looking up. He could see Sheldon blushing and Marnie smiling as she delivered a very firm lecture but in the sweetest voice. 'And, neither were they designed for busy doctors so that they could just push them back quickly. The designers were far more thoughtful than that—do you know why the taps are so long, Sheldon?'

'Okay, Marnie, I get it,' Sheldon said through gritted teeth.

'But I don't think that you do. You see, they're de-

signed that way so that you can turn them on and off
with your elbows. I'll show you...'

'I already know,' Sheldon said as Marnie demon-
strated how to turn the taps on and off with her own
elbows.

'You know that?' Marnie checked. 'I'm so sorry,
Sheldon, I didn't think you did because when I saw
you just washing your hands...'

Harry shook his head and got back to his notes as
Marnie continued to give Sheldon a lesson on hand-
washing. She was obsessed with cleanliness and hand-
washing was at the top of her list, along with cleaning
the curtains and light switches.

'What,' Marnie had demanded, 'is the point of cleaning your hands and then opening a filthy curtain with
them?'

Oh, and she had a thing about sunlight.

'It's cheaper than bleach,' Marnie had said when she
had called Maintenance down to prise open windows
that had never, in all the time Harry had been there,
been opened. 'Sunlight kills everything.'

In the two weeks that Marnie had been at Bayside
she had turned the *Titanic*.

The place was glistening, the cupboards were well
stocked, and breaks were being taken, though heaven
help you if you left the kitchen without washing and
putting away your coffee cup.

Love her or loathe her, there was no doubt that the
place was well run under Marnie's command and, as
a consultant in the busy emergency department, Harry
should be feeling extremely pleased at that fact.

He was pleased.

It was just...

Marnie did not give an inch. No, Harry didn't want

favours, but a bit of flexibility wouldn't go amiss either. With Juan now in Argentina and Dr Cooper's starting date still a few weeks away, for Dr Vermont and Harry the wheels were again starting to come off. They were relying heavily on locums—some were excellent, others not. But locums were exactly that, they didn't have the investment in the place that the regular staff had. Sheldon, for one, was becoming increasingly exasperated about who the latest boss was and at what point he should call the regular senior staff in.

'Marnie!' Harry heard the surprise in Sheldon's voice and looked up as Sheldon spoke on. 'Did anyone ever tell you that you could be a hand model?'

'I get told it all the time!' Marnie said.

'I'm serious.' Sheldon was turning her hands over and examining them. 'They're amazing.'

'I know they are,' Marnie said. 'Really, I should just take the plunge and get them insured and go off and make my fortune.'

'Harry,' Sheldon called, 'have you seen Marnie's hands?'

'Er, no,' Harry lied. He'd noticed them when Marnie had given him the little hand-washing lecture the other day and Sheldon was right—they were incredible. Her skin was unblemished and pale, with long, slender fingers that tapered into very neat, oval nails. They really were beautiful.

'Show Harry,' Sheldon said.

Marnie duly walked over and held out her hands. Emergency was a mad place at times, so this sort of thing wasn't in the least peculiar. Even Kelly came over to admire Marnie's hands.

'They're lovely,' Harry said.

'Harry's got a bit of a *thing* about hands,' Kelly

teased, but even she was surprised when Marnie took it a stage further.

'Do they turn you on, Harry?' Marnie said. Harry couldn't help but smile back and Kelly gave a slightly shocked laugh. Marnie was a minx—sexy yet cold, flirtatious at times but only when it suited her mood. And… Harry liked her.

Yes, it was another reason Harry wasn't feeling best pleased. Liking Marnie was too inconvenient for words.

'I have an *interest* in hands,' Harry said, and Marnie smirked at his response, 'not a fetish.'

'You *really* should be a hand model,' Kelly said, peering at them and then at her own.

'And who would keep you lot in place?' Marnie asked. 'Though I do know what you mean. Sometimes I look down at them and find myself smiling.'

No one was smiling a little while later when the nursing off-duty was revealed. It was the first one Marnie had done and a group of nurses had fallen on the diary the moment that it had appeared.

Abby, who loathed night duty, found that she was about to do her first stint after two years of having managed to avoid it.

Harry, who should be moving on to the next patient, couldn't help but stretch out his patient notes just so that he could listen as Abby voiced her concerns to Marnie.

Of course, they fell on deaf ears.

'I hate nights too.' Marnie smiled. 'Which is one of the reasons that I went into management, though I'm doing a stint myself soon, just to see how the place runs at night. We can be miserable together.'

Harry didn't look up as Abby slunk off, only for Kelly to take her place. 'Er, Marnie…' Kelly started. 'I wrote in the request notes that I don't do early shifts at the weekends, yet you've put me down for an early shift on Saturday next week and again a fortnight later.'

'I saw that you had requested that, Kelly, but you didn't write down a reason. I really am trying my best to accommodate everyone. Why can't you do an early shift on a Saturday?'

'Well, the thing is…' Kelly attempted, and Harry listened to the discomfort in her voice as she tried to give a suitable reason. 'I like to go out on a Friday night.'

'Of course you do!' Marnie answered calmly. 'We all love to go out and get blethered on a Friday night—heaven knows, we need it after a week in this place—which is why we share around the pleasure of a lie-in on a Saturday. Everyone takes their turn.'

And with that she walked off.

'I want to loathe her,' Kelly said. 'I have every reason to loathe her and yet…'

Harry glanced up. There was Marnie, catching the poor maintenance man before he escaped as she had plenty more jobs for him.

'She's efficient,' Harry said.

'She's cold,' Kelly corrected. 'She's been here for a couple of weeks and, do you know, nobody knows one single thing about her.'

Kelly was right and it was unusual. Emergency was a place that thrived on gossip, yet Marnie just didn't partake. Yes, long before he'd noticed her beautiful hands he had noticed that there was no wedding or engagement ring. Not that that meant anything—after all, he still wore his. He'd also noticed a large bunch of flowers has been delivered on the day that she had arrived. But, as she had taken delivery and inhaled the fragrances of the bouquet, Marnie had offered no explanation as to the sender. She never spoke about last night or what her

plans were for the weekend. All she really spoke about
was work and yet, no matter how he tried to tell himself
it didn't matter, Harry kept finding himself wanting to
know a little bit more.

She was intriguing.

It was as if she looked at the world through a different end of the telescope from everyone else—a case in
point was Juan. All the staff raved about Juan and how
lucky Cate was, how wonderful the wedding would be
and what a great catch he was.

Marnie screwed up her nose.

'He's a fine doctor, but he'd drive me bonkers to live
with,' Marnie said. Everyone was trying really hard not
to like her but sometimes she just lit up the department
with her commentary. Just like the windows she insisted on opening, she made the drab suddenly brighter.

'But he's gorgeous,' Abby said.

'He's a bit too New Age for me and I'd get tired of
him being, oh, so understanding.' Marnie seemed to
think about it for a moment and then shook her head.
'Imagine trying to have a row with that...'

'So you like a good row?' Harry asked.

'Of course,' Marnie said. 'Can you imagine trying
to row with Juan? "No, I don't want my shoulders mas-
saged..."'

Yet as funny and as intriguing as she could be, Marnie was also, as Harry had guessed she would be, completely immutable in certain areas.

'Marnie...' Harry approached her after taking a call.
'Day care just rang and Adam's not feeling too well.
There's still a bit of a backlog and I thought I might just
pop him in the staffroom—'

'Harry,' Marnie interrupted, 'the staffroom really
isn't the place for a child that is not feeling well.'

'I know that but it will only be for an hour. I'm just asking if the nurse in the obs ward could pop her head in now and then.'

'Sorry.' Marnie didn't look remotely sorry as she shook her head. 'She's got post-op patients to keep an eye on. If Adam is unwell, he needs to be at home.'

'You know…' Harry gritted his teeth and stopped the words from coming out as they reached the tip of his tongue.

'Feel free to say it,' Marnie invited.

Instead, he chose a different tack. 'Fine, if no one can keep an eye out then I'll ring my seventy-year-old babysitter and ask her to drive over…'

'Grand.'

Except, when he rang Evelyn, Harry received the worrying news that she had just been to the doctor. The rash that she hadn't told Harry about just happened to be shingles and she wouldn't be able to help out with the children for a few days at least.

'Don't worry about the kids, you just get well, Evelyn,' Harry said. He didn't want to worry Evelyn with the places his mind had suddenly gone to—namely the twins contracting chickenpox. They had been immunised, surely? But, then, Jill had seen to all that. As both a doctor and a parent Harry's mind was racing through several scenarios even as he put down the phone. 'She can't come,' a rather distracted Harry told Marnie.

'Then you'd better get Adam home.'

'You know, you really are inflexible at times,' Harry snapped.

'Oh, but I'm very flexible, Harry,' Marnie responded. 'In fact, if twenty critically ill patients came pouring through that door at this very moment you'd see just how flexible I can be. I know exactly where my staff are and what they are doing, and I can call them at any given time because they are *not* keeping an eye out for a sick child.'

She made a very good point; unfortunately, Harry was in no mood to see it. He was trying to do the best by the department and do his best by his children too. He was worried that an unwell Adam might be in the early stages of chickenpox, which meant, if he was, no doubt any day Charlotte would be too. Marnie just didn't seem to understand.

'You just don't get it,' Harry said, picking up his jacket. 'You're not a mum.'

CHAPTER FIVE

IT HURT.

And it still hurt as Marnie drove home but she did her best to push it aside when there was a knock at the door a little while later and it was her youngest brother, Ronan.

He'd just started work and was frantically saving up to move out from home, but every now and then he came and stayed for a couple of days with Marnie.

'How's the new job?' Ronan asked.

'Frustrating,' Marnie said. 'It would be a great department if there were enough staff and people didn't keep using the place as a drop-in crèche...' She stopped herself from elaborating. 'Don't mind me,' Marnie said, but Harry's words were still smarting and, in no mood to make dinner, she suggested that they eat out. 'My treat,' Marnie said. 'On the condition that you have dinner waiting for me tomorrow when I get home.'

It was nice to get out. Marnie drove along the beach road and into the small town and they soon found a gorgeous pub and sat outside, overlooking the bay, in the late sunlight.

Ronan, who was permanently hungry, dived into a huge steak while Marnie had prawns and a mango salad and enjoyed just sitting back and relaxing in front of the view, as she had promised herself she would of an evening. She wouldn't trade places with anyone. Watching a family on the next table, the mother spooning puréed pumpkin into a hungry baby's mouth as the father tried to amuse an overtired toddler, Marnie was very glad to be able to simply linger over her meal with her brother. She listened as Ronan told her about his work, and then got to, perhaps, the real reason he had asked to visit.

'You know what Mum's like,' Ronan said. 'I'm just warning you that she was upset you didn't come and visit at the weekend, or the last.'

'She surely knows how busy I am with work,' Marnie said. 'And moving! She could've come and helped with the move, like you did—she knows she doesn't need a written invitation to come and see me.'

'I think that she's just upset that you've moved so far.'

'It's not as if I've gone back home to Ireland.' Marnie sighed. 'I'm an hour's drive away.'

'She thinks you're punishing her for us emigrating…' Ronan attempted to make light of it but it was a bit of a dark subject and Marnie had to push out a smile.

'I'll try and get over one evening, but…' Marnie shook her head; maybe she was avoiding her parents a bit at the moment but she just didn't want to discuss it with Ronan. Or rather she simply couldn't discuss it with anyone in her family. *That* time of the year was coming up. The time of year that no one in her family ever spoke about because no one in her family knew what to say.

Declan would soon have been thirteen.

She looked over to the little family at the next table— the toddler was eating ice cream now, the baby falling asleep on its mother's lap, and sometimes, just sometimes, she *would* like to trade places.

Marnie took a long sip of her iced water and couldn't come up with a suitable line as to why she had been avoiding her mother, so she settled for the usual instead. 'I'm just busy, Ronan.'

So too was Harry.

After an evening spent trying to find vaccination certificates, as well as asking his parents if they could have the twins for a couple of days, Harry was in no mood for a very groomed Marnie the next day. She was busily writing on the white board while telling Kelly, who was frantically fishing to find out more about the elusive new manager, that the prawns she had had last night at Peninsular Pub were the best she had tasted.

He doubted Marnie would have been eating alone.

Yes, his response was terse when Marnie had the gall to ask him how Adam was.

'He's at my parents',' Harry said. 'Along with Charlotte.'

'Is she sick as well?'

'Neither is sick. Well, Adam's got a bit of a temperature,' Harry said. 'But my babysitter has shingles and I can hardly send them to day care knowing that any minute now they could break out in spots.'

'Weren't they immunised?' She was so annoyingly practical; she might just as well have been asking if the puppies' shots were up to date.

'You'd have to ask my late wife,' Harry snapped. 'I can't find the records.'

Ooh, they bristled and they snapped their way through the day, though the animosity was put on hold when a worried-looking Kelly came over and had a word with Harry, just as Marnie was finishing checking and ordering the scheduled drugs.

'I've got a seventeen-year-old girl in who's pregnant and bleeding. Sheldon estimates her to be around twenty-four weeks. The thing is, her parents are with her and Emily keeps insisting that she doesn't want them to know that she's pregnant. They keep asking for updates and are getting really angry that I won't let them in to be with her and that the doctor hasn't been in to speak with them. I'm just not sure how to deal with patient confidentially and Sheldon's concerned…'

'I'll come now,' Harry said, but as he made to go so too did Marnie.

'I'll come with you,' Marnie said, then spoke with Kelly. 'I'm happy to deal with her and the family.'

'Please.' Kelly let out a sigh of a relief. 'I don't blame Emily a bit for not wanting to tell her parents. They're not exactly the most approachable pair.'

Emily was very young, very scared but very determined that this baby was wanted. Sheldon had already started an IV and an ultrasound machine was being wheeled in as Harry and Marnie took over. 'Reece was going to come over at the weekend and tell my parents with me,' Emily tearfully explained as Harry gently examined her abdomen. 'Do we have to tell them now?'

'Well, we don't have to tell them,' Marnie answered, 'though I think they might start to guess what the issue is when they see you strapped to a foetal monitor or they see the sign for Maternity when I take you up.' Harry saw the small smile on Emily's lips as Marnie softened things with wry humour. 'Do you not think they have an idea?'

'I'm not sure,' Emily admitted. 'Dad did say that I was putting on weight and I was about to say something but then Mum said it was because I was spending all my time sitting down, studying.' Emily started to cry. 'They're going to be so angry.'

'They're going to be concerned,' Harry said, squirting some jelly on Emily's abdomen.

Marnie bit down on her lip because, as good a doctor as Harry was, until you'd been there you simply didn't understand.

Harry hadn't been there.

Marnie had.

She took Emily's hands. 'We can tell your parents for you.'

'You don't understand…'

'I do,' Marnie said. 'Sometimes news like this is better coming from someone who's not so involved. Once they know about the baby and have calmed down, they can come in and speak with you.'

'They'll never calm down.'

'Let's just see,' Marnie said. 'For now you just worry about staying calm. The last thing we want is you stressing yourself and raising your blood pressure and things.'

'Why am I bleeding?'

'It looks as if your placenta is lying rather low,' Harry said, running the ultrasound probe over Emily's stomach, and Marnie watched Emily's face as she stared unblinking at the screen and saw her baby for the first time. 'The heartbeat is a good rate and strong,' Harry said, pointing to the screen.

'Can you tell if it's a boy or girl?'

'The one time I tried I got it wrong.' Harry smiled. 'I'm going to get the obstetricians down and they'll examine you but for now I'll let your family know what's going on, if that's okay with you?' Emily gave a wary nod and then Harry asked about Reece and got a bit of history before they left to tell her parents. Marnie gave Emily's hand a little squeeze before she left.

George and Lucia really were a rather formidable pair—the air was thick with tension as Marnie and Harry came in and sat down.

'It's ridiculous the length of time that we've been kept waiting,' George said by way of introduction.

'Well, we've been with your daughter,' Harry calmly responded. 'I just wanted to have a chat before you went in.'

'We'd like to see her,' Lucia said, instead of asking what was wrong with her daughter.

'I'd like to speak with you before you do.'

'I really just want to see her,' Lucia insisted. 'If you could just let us know what cubicle she's in.'

They knew, Marnie realised, they simply didn't want to hear it, and thankfully Harry wasted no time getting to the point.

'Emily is pregnant,' Harry said to the two rigid faces. 'We estimate that she's about twenty-four weeks, though when she sees the obstetrician she'll have a more detailed ultrasound to confirm dates.' They all sat in silence for a moment, Harry and Marnie waiting for questions as the parents awaited the doctor's solution. 'This must come as a bit of a shock,' Harry offered.

'She's in her final year at school,' George said, as if that might change things, then he turned to his wife. 'I told you that she shouldn't be seeing him. I knew this would happen.' His fists balled as he gritted his teeth. 'She's got school to think of,' George said, and then turned back to Harry. 'She can't have it.'

'Emily wants to have the baby,' Harry said, 'and, as I've said, she's about twenty-four weeks' gestation and bleeding quite heavily. She's terribly worried for her baby and frankly so am I…'

'Baby!' George simply would not accept it and Marnie was pleased this conversation was taking place well away from Emily. 'How is she supposed to take care of a baby? She's still at school herself and doing very well. She's completely messed up her life.' He started to stand and his wife went to grab his arm.

'George, please.'

'Please what?' George demanded as he started pacing. 'How the hell is she supposed to support it?'

'Sit down,' Harry said. 'The last thing Emily needs now is to be upset.'

'Well, she should have thought of that. Maybe she should think of that…' George started heading for the door but then, realising he didn't know what cubicle Emily was in, he turned to Marnie. 'You'll take me to my daughter now.'

'Emily's not allowed visitors at the moment,' Marnie responded. 'At the moment she needs calm.'

'Don't you tell me what my daughter needs.'

'I really think,' Marnie continued, 'that it might help if you go for a walk before you visit Emily, or go to the canteen, or even just sit here and get used to the idea for a little while.'

'What would you know?' George shouted, and Harry was about to step in, perhaps even get Security, because there was no way he wanted Emily being subjected to her father's anger. But Marnie didn't need his help.

'I know plenty,' Marnie said. 'I can remember every word my parents said when I was eighteen and I told them I was pregnant.' She looked at Lucia. 'My son died when he was two weeks old and, given what had been said, I wouldn't let my mother comfort me. I still can't. I can guarantee that your next conversation with your daughter will be replayed in her mind for the rest of her life.' It was Marnie who stood then. 'She's in cubicle seven but, again, I suggest that before you go in there you take some time and really *think* about the kind of parents you want to be during this difficult time for your daughter.'

Yes, she loathed bringing her private life to work but she'd loathe even more Emily's parents speaking in haste.

Marnie walked into the cubicle, glad that it appeared George wasn't following. Emily was being seen by the obstetrician but she looked over anxiously as Marnie stepped in.

'How are they?' she asked, and Marnie hoped it would soon be the other way around—with her parents asking how Emily and the baby were.

'They're just taking it all in,' she said. 'You just focus on yourself for now.'

Her parents must have been doing some thinking because it was a good half-hour later, when Emily was about to be wheeled up to Maternity, that they came in.

'You could have told me,' were her mother's first words.

'I tried,' Emily said, and now Marnie said nothing as she escorted them up to Maternity and saw Emily settled in. Steroids had been started to mature the baby's lungs in case it needed to be delivered, but for now the bleeding had slowed down and things seemed a whole lot calmer.

'Thanks, Marnie,' Emily said, once Marnie had handed over to the midwife taking over Emily's care and had popped in to say goodbye.

'I'll pop back and see you when I...' Her voice trailed

off as a very pale and clearly terrified young man came into the ward.

'I told you not to come yet,' Emily said tearfully.

'I couldn't just stay at work.'

Marnie watched as, instead of anger, George somehow found it in himself to go over and shake Reece's hand, and as Marnie headed back down to the department she knew that of all the things that had moved her about today, Reece had moved her very much. A young man who, instead of letting Emily deal with it alone, had been brave enough to leave work and come and face the music.

She could still remember the feel of Craig trembling beside her as they'd told her parents. She hadn't wanted him there but had been so proud that he had insisted on it.

Was it any wonder they had broken up even before Declan had been born?

Yet he had still been there for the birth of his son.

She could see Harry chatting to a colleague and Marnie decided she would go to lunch.

She was a touch embarrassed that she'd told her tale in front of him, but then, he wasn't the first colleague that had heard the same. Part of her job, and the reason she loved it, was that you saw people at their most raw and could actually make a difference. It had just felt a little awkward and clearly Harry thought it an issue because a few moments after she'd sat down he knocked at her office door.

'How's she doing?'

'Better,' Marnie said. 'The bleeding has stopped and the parents are a lot calmer. Her young man just arrived and George actually shook his hand.'

That wasn't what Harry was there for.

'I'm sorry for what I said yesterday,' Harry said, and he sat down when Marnie really would have preferred a more fleeting visit.

'It's really not a problem—believe me I've heard that, or similar, many times before.'

'I didn't know,' Harry said, then shook his head. 'Not that that's an excuse. I'll be more careful when I say things like that in the future.'

'Good.' She gave a small smile; he really did look uncomfortable and that had never been her intention. 'Harry, I don't broadcast what happened to me to everyone but, on the other hand, I don't hide it either. I am a mother, I had a son. I felt today that it was appropriate that I tell those parents what had happened to me before they marched into Emily and made exactly the same mistake my parents made…'

'A lot of parents do.'

'Well, hopefully Emily's parents shan't now,' Marnie said. 'I certainly didn't tell them to make you feel uncomfortable.'

'They didn't take it well, then?' Harry asked. 'Your parents?'

'No.' Marnie hesitated. Normally she'd add something sharp here, like, 'Just because you know about it doesn't mean that I want to discuss it.' Except today, right now, she did. Maybe it was because Harry, given he had lost his wife, surely knew grief. Or maybe it was just with Declan's birthday coming up and Ronan hinting that her mother was upset, it had all been brought to the surface.

Then she looked up to his green eyes that were waiting patiently and realised that maybe it was just because it was Harry. 'They're very strict,' Marnie said. 'Or rather they were when we were younger. My mum went crazy when she found out. She said that it would kill my granny and my father...' She gave a tight smile. 'Though not till he'd killed the baby's father.' Marnie closed her eyes at the weary memory of that time. 'All the usual stuff.'

'Like?'

'I'm sure you can guess.' Marnie gave a tight shrug. 'She also made it very clear that she didn't think I should keep my baby. Anyway, a few months later when my son was on the neonatal unit, the person I wanted was my mum but at the same time I didn't want her. We can't discuss it, even now.'

'Have you tried?'

'Nope.' Marnie shook her head. 'And I won't be trying either.' She looked at Harry. 'It couldn't end nicely.' Marnie felt uncomfortable now; the only person she really discussed Declan with was her friend Siobhan and, feeling she'd said more than enough, Marnie changed the subject. 'I'm just very glad that Emily's father didn't march in and vent his spleen. She had a big abruption, and she could start bleeding again any time soon,' Marnie said. 'That baby's far from safe.' She wanted to stop talking about it, she wanted to just end the conversation, to dismiss Harry and get on with her day, except Marnie felt her nose redden and Harry saw a flash of tears in her eyes.

'Marnie...' Harry was struggling for words—he was used to death, both personally and professionally, and had it been anyone else he'd have stood, gone over, but it was Marnie, and he didn't. Not because he didn't want to, more because of how much he did.

'It's fine.' Marnie filled the silence. 'I'm fine. It was all just a bit too close to home.' She blew out a breath. 'It's his birthday coming up.'

'Look, do you want to…?' Harry's voice trailed off as there was a knock at the door.

'Matthew!' Harry noticed that she flushed a little as a rather well-dressed man entered. 'What are you doing here?' Marnie asked.

'I had a client nearby,' Matthew said. 'I thought I might see if you were free for lunch. Oh, and I wanted to tell you in person that I got the tickets.' He handed an envelope to Marnie. 'Opening night, don't ask me how I got them!'

'Oh!' Marnie's anger at having her workspace invaded was temporarily thwarted because, more than anything, she loved the ballet and the opening night had sold out the day the tickets had been released. 'Wow!'

'It might be better if you look after them,' Matthew said, not even bothering to introduce himself to Harry, who had already made up his mind that he didn't like him.

'I'll leave you to it,' Harry said, and walked out.

Harry wasn't sure if he was jealous of Marnie's freedom or just plain jealous—Harry had been very close to suggesting they leave the department and get lunch.

Stupid idea, Harry, he told himself. Those days were long gone—he kept things well away from work.

A moment or so later he looked up from a patient and saw them walking out of the department, Matthew sliding a hand around Marnie's waist.

He didn't like that and neither did Marnie—she wriggled out of Matthew's embrace and it was clear she was cross.

'Are you going to show me where you live?' Matthew asked as she got into his car and he started the engine.

'Sure,' Marnie said, her tongue firmly in her cheek.

'My brother Ronan is over for a couple of days. You can say hi if you like…'

'Maybe not, then.'

Sitting in a bayside café a little while later, Marnie told him that she was far from impressed.

'Why would you drop in on me at work?' Marnie asked.

'I told you—I was in the area and I wanted to give you the tickets for the ballet or I'd end up losing them. I'm going straight from here to the airport.'

Marnie refused to buy it. 'Until recently I lived a stone's throw from your office and I would never have dropped in on you!' She was angry, very angry—part of the loose arrangement they had was that there would be no popping in. She and Matthew went out now and then. They were social and, yes, they slept together, but they did not invade each other's lives and that was the way Marnie wanted it. 'Whatever possessed you?'

'Okay, okay,' Matthew said, deciding against suggesting that she call in sick this afternoon. 'I shan't stop by again.' He watched as Marnie's hand, which had just dipped her bread in oil, paused over the salt. 'I wouldn't want to disturb anything.'

'Excuse me?'

'You and your colleague looked very cosy.'

'We were talking about a patient!' Marnie so did not need this. 'He's got two children…' Marnie shook her head and then reached for her bag. 'I need to get back.'

They drove in silence. Marnie was still cross, not just that Matthew had dropped by at her work but cross with herself for all she had told Harry. Cross too that Matthew had interrupted them.

'The ballet will be great,' Matthew said, as he dropped her off. 'Get you back to civilisation.'

Far from being offended, she actually laughed. Maybe she did need a night of being spoilt, it might stop the constant thoughts about Declan's birthday.

And about Harry.

As she went to get a drink of water from the staff kitchen she was met by a very stony-faced Harry, who was rinsing his mug.

'Nice lunch?'

'Lovely, thanks.'

'Your boyfriend—?'

'Boyfriend?' Marnie rapidly interrupted. 'I'm thirty-one—I'm a bit old for boys.'

'Sorry.' Harry gave a wry grin. She was the most impossible person he had ever met, yet, for reasons of his own, which he didn't really want to examine, he ploughed on. 'Your partner, then?'

'Partner?' Marnie challenged him right there and then. She was sick of men and the different rules that applied to them, and Marnie told him so. Despite never gossiping herself, Marnie was very clued in and had heard all the rumours about Harry. 'Is that what you called your last nanny? Your partner, your girlfriend?' Harry let out a breath as Marnie continued, 'Or did you upgrade her title to your live-in lover?'

'I was just going to say he seemed nice.'

'Well, I'll let you know when I need your opinion.'

Marnie dived into work, refusing to go to her office because that would look like she was hiding. And why would she be hiding? There was nothing to feel embarrassed or awkward about—a friend had merely dropped in to take her to lunch.

It was just that Marnie didn't like her worlds colliding and, as the afternoon progressed, the tension seemed to increase. Near home time she glanced up and briefly caught sight of a very dark-looking Harry walking past, and she knew it wasn't just that Matthew had dropped by that was unsettling her.

It was Harry.

In a nice way, though.

There was a tiny flutter in her chest as she met his eyes and it was still fluttering as she looked away and tried to concentrate on what Kelly was calling out to her.

'Sorry?' She looked at Kelly.

'There's a guy on the phone for you,' Kelly repeated. 'He says it's personal.'

'I'll bet it is,' Harry muttered, but thankfully well out of earshot.

What the hell did Matthew want now? Marnie thought as she made her way over. Only it wasn't Matthew calling her at work and she saw Harry's jaw grit as she said another man's name.

'Ronan, what are you doing, phoning me at work?'

He wanted to take the receiver from her and replace it. He wanted to turn her round and tell her part of the reason for his dark mood.

He couldn't get her out of his mind.

CHAPTER SIX

HARRY REACHED FOR his jacket. It was ten to five and he was in no mood for *another* dose of salt to be rubbed into a very raw wound, and anyway he had to get to his parents to pick up the twins and inspect them for chickenpox.

Fun!

'Are you heading off?' Dr Vermont said, and Harry nodded.

'You're not in tomorrow?' Dr Vermont checked.

'I can't leave them with my parents for too long,' Harry said, and Dr Vermont nodded. He knew Harry's father's health wasn't brilliant and the twins were hard work at the best of times. By the time Harry had signed off on some paperwork, Marnie had gathered her bag and was walking briskly through the department, jangling her car keys.

'You're in a rush, Marnie,' Dr Vermont commented, because Marnie never usually left till well past six. 'Is everything okay?'

'I'll be back,' Marnie said. 'My brother just called and he's cut himself—his finger. I'm just going home to fetch him and bring him in.'

'I'll stay around to see him,' Dr Vermont said, and Marnie gave a grateful smile, though, in truth, it was a bit of a forced one because she desperately wanted Harry to offer to stay back. He was, as she was starting to find out, not just considered the best hand surgeon in the hospital but one of the top in the country.

Harry made no offer; instead, he joined her as she headed out.

She walked to the car park with him. Their footsteps were rapid and the atmosphere between them was tense but it was Harry who broke the strained silence. 'Do you think it's serious?'

'It's deep. I told him to make dinner and he couldn't find my tin-opener so he decided to use a knife…' She was waffling, stupidly feeling guilty for insisting that Ronan cook, but she was evading the real answer, not because she didn't want to tell Harry, more because she didn't want to think what it might mean to Ronan. 'He says it's bad.' Harry could hear the slight panic in her voice as she elaborated, 'I'm worried he might have cut a tendon.'

'You haven't even seen it yet.' Harry was practical.

'He plays the piano.' Marnie glanced at Harry. 'I mean—he plays it really well.' She closed her eyes for a second. If Ronan had indeed injured his tendon it was going to be a tough few months ahead for him, with no guarantee his hand would return to full dexterity.

'If he has injured his tendon, Dr Vermont will refer him to Stuart. He's on tonight and he's a great surgeon.'

She wanted Harry.

They were now at her car and, given how inflexible Marnie had been with his children, she was in absolutely no position to ask him a favour, except it was Ronan. For that reason, and that reason only, Marnie swallowed her pride and went to speak, but the words wouldn't come out. Harry watched as she ran one of those very beautiful hands through her dark hair as again she tried to swallow her pride.

For Ronan, Marnie told herself.

'If it needs doing, is there any chance of you repairing it tomorrow?' There were two spots of colour appearing on her pale cheeks. 'If Dr Vermont orders it to be elevated tonight, you could—'

'I'm not coming in tomorrow.'

'Oh, I thought you were on.'

'No.'

When Harry didn't elaborate, Marnie just nodded and got into her car. She loathed that she'd asked him but, more than that, she loathed that he'd said no.

When she got home, Marnie let herself in and Ronan called out to her. 'I'm in here.'

He was sitting on the floor of Marnie's bathroom with his hand wrapped in a towel and he was holding it up.

'You don't have a bath to sit on,' was the first thing he said, and Marnie managed a smile as, first things first, she washed her hands.

'It was the first thing I noticed about the place too.' Marnie knelt down beside him and gently pulled down his arm.

'Sorry about the towel.'

'Don't worry about it,' Marnie said.

'I made a mess in the kitchen.'

'Ronan, stop.' She unwrapped the towel and Marnie, who was very used to looking at injured fingers, surprised herself by feeling a bit sick when she examined Ronan's cut. Marnie blew out a breath as she saw the white of Ronan's partially severed tendon as he attempted to move his finger.

'Don't try to do anything for now,' Marnie said. 'I'll put a dressing on it and we'll get you to the hospital.'

She went to the kitchen and it was a bit of a mess with Ronan's blood, as he'd said. She reached for a glass and took two long drinks of water then refilled the glass.

It was ridiculous really, Marnie thought. There wasn't a single thing at work that made her feel faint but as soon as it was family, it was a different matter entirely.

She stood, remembering the nurses insisting she wait outside as they stuck another needle in Declan…

Not now!

Marnie tipped the water down the sink, got out her first-aid box and headed back to Ronan. She sorted out the wound, wrapping the injured finger in a saline dressing and bandaging it, then applying a sling, before she got him into the car and headed to the hospital.

'It's bad, isn't it?' Ronan asked, as Marnie concentrated on driving.

'I think you've done your tendon,' she admitted.

'That can be fixed, though, can't it?'

'Of course it can.' She glanced over and smiled but said nothing more just yet. Ronan's tendon could certainly be fixed but it would take a lot of time and patience to get back the function that Ronan had had.

She wished that Harry was on tonight.

The department was quiet and Marnie took Ronan straight through and into a cubicle, where she told him to lie down.

'I don't need to lie down,' he said, then changed his mind. He was tall and geeky and didn't try to hide it, and Marnie loved him for it. 'I do feel a bit sick.'

'I know,' Marnie said, because the phrase 'as white as a sheet' could have been coined just for Ronan—

Marnie was quite sure that had he not lain down when he had he would have passed out.

'Can a have a glass of water?'

'Nothing.' Marnie shook her head. 'You can't have anything till a doctor's seen it. Just wait there and I'll go and get you registered and then…' Her voice trailed off as the curtain opened and Harry walked in.

'Harry!' Marnie couldn't quite believe that he was here—especially since she'd seen him drive off.

Harry couldn't quite believe it either. He'd got five minutes down the road, feeling as guilty as hell for saying no to Marnie's brother, when his phone had rung with the news from his mother that Adam was coming out in spots.

Harry had pulled over and sat with his head in his hands, listening to the sound of the traffic whizzing past.

Of course, if Adam had them, then Charlotte would get them soon.

Something had to give and at that moment it did.

Adam was fine when Harry rang back—he was the centre of attention for once when usually it was Charlotte.

'He's tired, though,' his mum explained. 'I was just going to put him to bed. Why don't you stay here to-night? It would be a shame to wake him.'

Harry hesitated. He had been about to say yes, but at the last moment he asked his aging parents for yet another favour.

For the last time.

Sure, he'd need them in the future, Harry didn't doubt that, but the madness had to stop and so he had ended it.

'Marnie.' He gave her a tight smile and then aimed a much nicer one at Ronan. 'So, I hear that you've cut your finger, cooking.' Harry helped Ronan out of the sling and when he saw the neat dressing he made a wry joke about Ronan's big sister having a fully equipped first-aid box.

'Yeah, well, she might have a well-equipped first-aid box but she doesn't have a tin-opener,' Ronan said, as Harry washed his hands and put on some gloves while Marnie removed the dressing.

'I do have tin-opener,' Marnie scolded. 'Just because Mum keeps hers in the second drawer, you didn't think to look in the third.'

Harry grinned to himself at the good-natured banter between brother and sister and then he came over and carefully examined the wound as well as testing for sensation in Adam's finger. 'You're a pianist, Marnie tells me?'

'I'm a computer programmer,' Ronan said.

'Well, you'd need your fingers working for that...' Harry opened a needle and checked Ronan's sensation more thoroughly as Marnie stood wondering if Harry was thinking he'd been brought in under false pretences.

'He's a very good pianist,' Marnie said. 'I didn't mean to make it sound like he was a maestro.'

'You didn't,' Harry said. He looked at Ronan. 'I'm sure you've realised that this injury is more than just a straightforward cut that can simply be stitched.'

'I pretty much knew straight away,' Ronan said. 'Will I still be able to play?' he asked, and Marnie found she was holding her breath as Harry dealt with the issue that she hadn't been able to talk about during the journey to the hospital. 'I mean, will I still be able to play at the level I was?'

'First I have to do my part,' Harry said, 'then the rest is going to be up to you.' Harry was honest. 'You'll be in a splint afterwards and looking at a lot of hand therapy. It's early days yet. For now we have to repair it and then see where we're at.'

'Harry's an amazing hand surgeon,' Marnie said. 'You couldn't be in better hands.'

'Excuse the pun,' Harry said, and Ronan gave a pale smile, then Harry went through more of what Ronan could expect. He was very calming—even as he discussed the extensive rehabilitation ahead. 'Right, we'll get you around to our minor theatre. The tendon's still partially intact so I'll be able to do it under a block, but first I need to go and get something to eat as it might take a while.'

'Can I have a drink?' Ronan asked.

'Sorry,' Harry said with a brief smile. 'That was cruel of me. No, you can't have anything in case you do end up needing a general anaesthetic.'

'You're doing him tonight?' Marnie checked.

'I told you I was!' There was a slight edge of irritation to Harry's voice when he addressed Marnie, which he quickly fought to check. 'I'm not available tomorrow and the sooner that it's repaired the better.'

'I can assist.'

Harry rolled his eyes. 'Have you looked in the mirror?' Marnie hadn't. 'Even your lips are white. I'll ask Kelly.'

Kelly came in and introduced herself to Ronan and Marnie excused herself as Kelly said she was going to get him into a gown and prepared for Theatre.

'I'll be waiting in my office,' Marnie said, but of course it didn't end there because Kelly was asking about Ronan's next of kin. 'I should ring Mum and tell her.'

'Not tonight.' Ronan shook his head. 'Please, Marnie, can that wait till tomorrow?'

Marnie was only too pleased to agree.

She gave Ronan a brief cuddle and then headed to the kitchen for another glass of water, where she found Harry feeding bread into the toaster.

'Thank you for coming back to do this.'

'It's fine,' Harry said.

'What about the children?'

'Charlotte and Adam are staying the night at my parents'. I'm going to get them tomorrow.'

'I feel awful…'

'Well, don't. You were right not to want Adam hanging around the department—he has got chickenpox.'

'Oh, no,' Marnie said. 'I feel terrible that he doesn't have you tonight.'

The toast popped up and Harry started buttering it but he did turn and speak at the same time. 'Marnie, it's my job—it's what I do. It's what I've been *trying* to do since Jill died. I can't count the times I called Jill and said someone had come in and that I needed to be here…'

'It's appreciated.'

'Good. I am the best hand surgeon in this hospital. I'd want me for this.'

'I'd want you to,' Marnie said, and from nowhere, absolutely from nowhere, a blush spread over her cheeks and, given how pale she had been, there was no chance of hiding it. 'I meant—'

'It's fine.

The strangest thing was, as the colour soared up her cheeks, Harry, who never blushed, thought that he might be as well.

Or was it just terribly warm?

'The thing is—' Marnie started, but Harry interrupted.

'Right, now I would just like ten minutes' peace before I go and do surgery,' Harry said, and, taking his toasted sandwich, he stalked off to his office rather than the staffroom, but there was no peace to be had there either.

There was an inbox that was so full it spilled over the edges and he daren't check his emails because he'd need a week to get them clear.

Harry ate his sandwich then changed into scrubs and headed into the minor theatre where Ronan lay, chatting with Kelly, who was setting up for the operation.

'I was just telling Ronan that he's got his sister's hands.' Kelly smiled.

'I don't remember Marnie's being quite so hairy,' Harry said, as he put in the nerve block that would ensure Ronan couldn't feel anything during surgery. 'Your accent isn't as strong as Marnie's. Though I guess you were much younger when you came to Melbourne.'

'We came to Perth first,' Ronan told him, and it wasn't, Harry noted, just Ronan's hands that were similar to Marnie's—he could talk for Ireland too. 'But Dad got transferred to Melbourne a couple of years later. I don't really remember Perth. I think I remember more about Ireland, though I'm not sure if it's from going back or Mum talking about it. I've been back twice now, though Marnie goes back far more often. She misses it like crazy.'

Harry looked up. 'Didn't she want to emigrate?'

'No,' Roman said. 'Though she didn't want to leave Perth either. She always said the moment she turned eighteen and she had her own passport she'd be straight back to Ireland, but she got into nursing…' Ronan didn't continue.

He didn't have to.

Harry pretty much knew what had happened from there. As he waited for the block to take effect, he spent a moment thinking about Marnie.

Harry's heart seemed to constrict for a moment.

No wonder she was so tough, she'd had to learn how to be.

He checked each finger in turn, making sure that the anaesthetic had taken full effect before starting.

It was a very intricate operation, which required Harry to wear magnifying glasses and to focus extremely hard, but every now and then Kelly would take his glasses off and he would sit up straight for a moment and take a very brief break. Sometimes he found himself listening to Ronan and Kelly talking, mostly about music and computers, but now and then the conversation drifted to Marnie.

'I fight all the time with my sister,' Kelly was saying.

'It's not worth fighting with Marnie,' Ronan said. 'It's her way or the highway.'

Ten years older than Ronan, Marnie had, it would seem, been a second mum more than a sister to him.

Funny that he found out more about Marnie during a sixty-minute operation than he had in all the time he'd worked alongside her.

'You're done,' Harry said, finishing off the splint. 'For tonight you'll stay in and we'll keep it elevated. You'll be given analgesics as it's going to be painful as sensation starts to return and I want to start you on antibiotics. The last thing we want is an infection.'

'Harry will come in and see you tomorrow,' Kelly said, 'and then you'll probably be discharged home.'

'Actually, I'm off tomorrow,' Harry said. 'It will be Dr Vermont and then there will be follow-ups in the hand clinic and a referral to the hand therapist.' He really couldn't tell Kelly and Ronan his news before he'd told Dr Vermont.

And Marnie too.

'Take care,' Harry settled for instead.

He had a drink before heading into Marnie's office, and when he got there she was sitting with her head in her hands, just as he had in the car earlier, as if bracing herself for the news that her brother had died!

'It's a tendon!' Harry said.

'I know.' Marnie looked up and there was a grimace on her face as she tried to force a smile. 'I just came off the phone to my mother—you wouldn't believe me if I told you how difficult that conversation was. She actually rang me and I caved and told her about Ronan's accident.'

'Oh.' Harry was surprised. He'd got the impression they barely spoke. 'I thought you didn't…' Harry halted. It was none of his business.

'We may not talk about certain things,' Marnie said, 'but, as difficult as they can be, I love my parents very much.' Marnie lifted her eyes to the ceiling. 'Ronan's accident is all my fault.'

'Of course it is,' Harry said calmly.

'If she woke up tomorrow and the sky was purple, she'd be on the phone, blaming me.'

'Well, if you'd just kept the tin-opener in the second drawer, all this could have been avoided.' Harry wagged his finger and somehow made her smile, and then she looked away because Harry was usually in a suit. She didn't think she'd seen so much of his skin before, at least, not this close up. His arms were very long but muscular too, and she could see just a smattering of chest hair when Marnie was rather more used to smooth. He looked tired yet there was a certain air of elation to him that Marnie didn't quite understand.

'I've managed to convince her to not visit till tomorrow, it would be after ten before she got here. How did the repair go?'

'Very well,' Harry said. 'Kelly will be bringing him round to the obs ward soon....' His voice trailed off as his pager went and Harry read the message, then asked if he could use her phone.

'Sure.'

'Hi, Mum,' Harry said. 'Yes, sorry about that, it took a bit longer than I thought. Put him on.' Marnie tried to look away as he chatted to Adam but her eyes kept drifting towards him.

To think she'd expected him to have a bit of a paunch by now—he had a very flat stomach and very muscular legs and, as he sat on the edge of her desk as he spoke, Marnie could see the hair on his arms.

He was, as if Marnie didn't already know, very, very beautiful.

Dangerous too.

Dangerous, because Marnie rarely opened up to anyone, yet with Harry she did too easily. Even the brief conversation about her phone call with her mother was far more than she would usually share and Marnie's foot tapped, with tension rather than impatience, as Harry spoke on.

She wanted to get away from him.

She wanted to go home, just so she could give herself a good talking to.

After speaking to Adam, he chatted at length to Charlotte, though he could see Marnie's foot tapping in mid-air out of the corner of his eye, but then she stood and went and stared out of the window as Harry laughed and talked on. 'What do you mean, it's not fair?' He spoke a little while longer and then said goodnight and put down the phone.

'Charlotte's jealous that Adam has got chickenpox,' Harry said to Marnie, who was still looking out of the window. He watched her shoulders move in a small laugh and then wretched guilt at keeping him from his children caught up and Marnie turned her head.

'Say it,' Marnie challenged, her blue eyes glittering.

'Say what?' Harry frowned.

'Go on,' Marnie insisted. 'Say whatever's on your mind.'

Harry gave a wry grin. 'Such as…'

'It's different when it's you or your family,' Marnie offered, turning to face him.

'That's not what's on my mind.'

'Hypocrite, then?' Marnie suggested.

'No…' He was walking towards her.

'Just say it.'

'You're quite sure?' Harry said, and it was at that moment exactly that she realised that Harry had something else on his mind, something very similar to what was on hers as she saw the burn of arousal in his eyes. 'You're quite sure that you want me to say what's on my mind?'

She looked at him properly then, saw the Harry she hadn't seen in a very long time. There was an energy to him that had been missing, an energy that she hadn't seen since a certain night in the doctors' mess when he'd asked why she was leaving so soon—only this time it was potent.

If he'd been on the other side of the desk, she might have had a chance to deny him. Might have been able to rein in common sense and come up with some witty retort that would end things before they were started.

Except he was standing in front of her. She could smell the lust, the want, the need, and it was intoxicating and, quite simply, Marnie couldn't resist. One small nod was all the affirmation needed for Harry to tell his truth.

'I want you.'

His mouth came down and crushed Marnie's. He was so tall he had to, not just stoop but almost lift her to exert the pressure that this kiss demanded.

Marnie was no stranger to lust but she'd never felt it as ferociously or as deliciously as this.

Every snap, every snarl, every flirt, every tease was now being paid back tenfold by the probe of his tongue and the roaming of his hands.

Or was it her hands? One was in his hair, messing it to the way she had first seen it, the other moving down over his arm, but only so she could force a space to get to his back and to the taut buttocks she had admired from behind on far too many occasions.

It was lust uninterrupted, Marnie for once out of control, and she liked it.

'I remember you now...' He was opening the buttons to her navy dress and not for a moment did she think of halting him. Whatever was wrong in the world, this was the antidote and for now, this moment, they celebrated their discovery. 'Harry...' She could feel his arousal pressed into her; one hand was lifting her dress and he moaned into her mouth as he felt her soft thigh. As he slipped his hand higher, it was Marnie who moaned.

'Not here...' Marnie pulled back but her words were contrary to her actions; she was kissing his face, her hands lifting his top just to get to his skin, just to bury her mouth in his salty chest and taste him. 'Not here...'

Marnie moaned again, and Harry almost came as he looked down at her licking her lips. 'Harry.' She was wrestling for control. Hell, she was the nurse unit manager, her mother could have changed her mind and arrived any minute, Kelly could knock at the door...

'I don't get involved with anyone at work.'

'Not a problem.' Harry turned the lock on her door and then picked her up and lifted her over to the desk. 'I just resigned.'

CHAPTER SEVEN

'You what?'

He was back to her mouth but now Marnie understood his earlier elation.

'Harry? You can't.'

'I already have.' He looked down at her breasts, pale in their bra, and he wanted to bury his face in them, to simply forget, but he knew then that the moment was over and, still breathless, still hard, still wanting, he did the right thing and started to do the buttons up.

Yes, it had been about escape, Marnie realised, for a man who wasn't thinking particularly straight, and it was time for her to steer things towards reason.

'Harry…' She was struggling to get her breath back too. His groin was still leaning into hers, her body still tingling and aroused, and it would be so much easier to dive back to his mouth, but instead she offered no resistance as he straightened up. In fact, she shivered a little at the coolness when he was gone.

'I apologise.'

'For what?' Marnie attempted to laugh it off. 'I didn't notice me doing much resisting, but I don't think a quick shag on the office desk is going to solve things.'

He smiled at her directness. 'I don't think anything

is going to solve things,' he admitted. 'Might be nice to give it a try, though.'

Marnie retied her hair and brushed her dress down then unlocked the door. 'As if the person on the other side wouldn't know what was going on!'

Harry wanted to pull her down to his lap, perhaps take it more slowly this time, take her home even—after all, he had the house to himself. He didn't want to think about what he had done—the handing-in-the-notice part, not the Marnie part. He'd love to think more about that! No, it was handing in his notice. His ten-past-five phone call to Admin that he didn't want to examine, but Marnie refused to let it drop.

'You love your job, Harry.'

'I love it when I get to do it,' Harry said.

'So what are you going to do?'

'Go private,' Harry said. 'Hand surgery...'

'Will it be enough?' Marnie asked. 'Harry, you love this place...'

'I love my children more,' Harry said. 'There will still be accident and emergency departments needing a consultant in a few years' time—right now the children need some stability.'

'You can give them that,' Marnie said, horrified to think of the department without him. Harry and Dr Vermont were the lynchpins of the place. Yes, there were new doctors starting but they needed guidance.

'It's not up for discussion,' Harry said. 'The deed is done.'

'How long's your notice?'

'Two weeks,' Harry said, 'but I'm not working it. I'm taking parental leave to look after the children.'

'That's it?' Marnie said, understanding more and

more where the emotion of the night had come from. Harry really was leaving the place.

'That's it,' Harry said. 'There will probably be a leaving do in a couple of weeks, which I'll do my best to get to—' his voice was wry '—providing I can get a babysitter.'

'Harry—'

'Leave it.'

Sex would have been so much easier.

Harry hadn't cried since the night before he'd lost Jill. He hadn't been able to, there had been two bewildered twins to look after and Jill's shocked parents as well as his own—all his grieving had been done on the ICU ward before the machines had been turned off, yet, on this day, he was precariously close to breaking down.

He loved his job—an A and E consultant was all he had ever wanted to be and it was killing him to walk away.

Yet it was impossible to stay.

'Come home with me?' he said, looking at her very full mouth.

She could feel his eyes there, wanted again the weight of his kiss, but not like this…

'Harry, if I come home with you, it will be to talk some sense into you.'

'You can talk sense into me over dinner.'

She was tempted, so tempted, and that was the problem.

She wanted dinner with Harry, and bed, and she wanted to know so much more about him. She looked into eyes that were as come hither as they had been all those years ago, only now it would be so terribly easy to say yes.

Dinner with Harry would be lovely.

Bed even better.

There was just one little problem.

Make that two.

How could she best put it?

'I'm busy tonight, Harry,' Marnie said. 'What about Saturday?'

It hit Harry where she had intended to—right below the belt. Ardour faded as Marnie flexed the freedom muscle she guarded so fiercely. It would take a whole lot more than the occasional night off, babysitter permitting, to lure Marnie.

'Saturday might be a problem.'

Yes, she'd rather thought that it might.

'I'm going to go,' Harry said, but Marnie hadn't finished discussing her favourite subject.

Work.

'Harry, you're rushing into this decision—'

'I'm not rushing into anything,' Harry interrupted. 'If anything, this is long overdue. I'll come in and say goodbye to everyone when the time's right, but now I need to take care of my kids.'

He left her in the office, stunned from the news, from his kiss, from the sudden absence of Harry.

He wanted his last walk through *his* department alone.

''Night, Harry,' Kelly called.

''Night,' Harry called back. 'Thanks for your help with Ronan.'

He nodded to Helen, the locum who was covering for tonight, and, yes, the place was going to struggle, but it would soon move on. Juan would be back and Dr Cooper would start.

He'd just miss it so much.

* * *

Dr Vermont broke the news to the staff the next morning.

'We all know what a struggle it's been for Harry since Jill died. It's not an easy decision to make but for Harry it must have been the right one.'

Marnie felt terrible—she kept beating herself up, wondering if she'd just been a bit more flexible the outcome might have been different. And, on top of all that, over and over she kept remembering the steamy kiss they had shared. Yes, she fancied Harry, but the impact of him close up had shaken her more than she had thought it would. Still, she didn't have much time to dwell on it. As the staff spilled out of the staffroom, all talking about the news of Harry's sudden departure, Marnie walked straight into her parents.

'Mum!' Marnie gave her mother a smile and a kiss.

'What was he doing, using a knife to open a can?' Maureen accused.

'You can't blame Marnie for this.' Ronan laughed and tried to sit up with one hand attached to a pole as Dr Vermont came over to visit the patients in the obs ward.

'Mr Johnson,' Dr Vermont said, and Marnie smothered a smile as her father stepped forward, because Dr Vermont was speaking to Ronan. 'I hear everything went very well last night.' Marnie took down Ronan's hand from the pole and Dr Vermont checked the colour and sensation in the tip of Ronan's heavily splinted finger. He asked Ronan to try and move the finger and Marnie watched with relief as the pink tip lifted just a little.

'You can feel this?' Dr Vermont checked as Ronan closed his eyes.

'Yes.'

Marnie let out a breath and then smiled as Ronan again said he could feel the touch of the needle as Dr Vermont checked the other side.

'It's doing everything it should,' Dr Vermont said. 'I'll see you in two days and then…' He hesitated as he looked at the address on the admission notes. 'Do you do want to be followed up here?' Dr Vermont checked. 'I see that you live quite a distance away.'

'Here would be great,' Ronan said. 'I can catch up with Marnie when I have an appointment.'

'It's the only way you'll get to see her,' Maureen Johnson muttered, and Marnie chose not to respond to her mother's barb and stayed silent as Dr Vermont spoke to Kelly. 'Could you schedule in some hand appointments for Mr Johnson?' he asked, and then turned to Ronan. 'If we book the next couple in, at least you'll know what you're doing.'

He gave a few more instructions and then moved on to the next bed.

'You can get dressed,' Marnie said to her brother a little while later when Kelly had come off the phone.

'I'll give him a hand,' Kelly said, as she pulled the curtains around the bed. 'I've made the appointments. We'll see you the day after tomorrow and then again on the twenty-third. Is that okay?'

Ronan looked up at his sister, but thankfully the curtain swished past and Marnie had a second to collect herself before she answered for him.

'The twenty-third's fine,' Marnie said, and deliberately didn't look at her mum as the one date they all dreaded was, for the first time in a very long time, mentioned.

Trust the Irish to not make a fuss when it mattered!

CHAPTER EIGHT

'THIS TOO WILL pass,' Dr Vermont said. 'It's my favourite saying and one I've used often over the years working in this place.'

It was two in the morning and Marnie was on her first night shift at Bayside. It had been difficult logistically without Harry as they struggled to cover the department but, more than logistics, he was sorely missed by everyone, including Marnie.

Especially Marnie.

She was missing him on a whole different level, though—the flirting, the teasing, just the fun of having someone as shamelessly male as Harry around.

Not that she told that to Dr Vermont, of course. They were going through the doctors' roster for the next couple of weeks and trying to cover the gaps as they ate Marnie's chicken and mango salad that she had brought in from home.

'I've been through staff shortages, work to rule, the whole lot,' Dr Vermont continued. 'And, though it feels like it will never end, invariably it does. It will all get sorted, and I'll say it again—this is not your fault.'

Dr Vermont was lovely and extremely practical when Marnie had confessed what was on her mind.

'Even if you had let Charlotte, or was it Adam, lie on the sofa, this still would have happened.'

'I was trying to make things easier for him,' Marnie admitted. 'I know I looked like I was being mean when I told him to go home a couple of times but I was trying to show him that he wasn't completely indispensable...'

Dr Vermont laughed. 'Well, you did!'

'I know.' Marnie ran a worried hand over her forehead. 'I was trying to prove to him that we could call the trauma team or the medics, that it didn't have to all fall to him,' Marnie explained. 'I just wish that I'd handled things a little differently. I wish—'

'Marnie,' Dr Vermont interrupted, 'Harry has been struggling to find balance between work and home since Jill died. I honestly don't know how he's managed to do this job for so long without a partner. Marjorie, my wife, managed to have a career and raise our family, but we had a lot of support too. Harry's sister and parents all live a couple of hours away.'

Dr Vermont thought for a moment. 'I could not have done this job and raised a family without Marjorie. Even when the place is fully covered you can still expect to be called in. I can't tell you how many nights I've been on take and yet I've still rung Harry to come in to give an opinion, or there's been a multiple trauma and another pair of hands has been needed. Marjorie was more than used to it—long before coffee machines were around she made sure there was a flask of coffee by my bed so that I could have a drink as I drove in.' He smiled at the memory and so did Marnie. 'What I'm trying to explain...'

His voice trailed off and Marnie looked up from her salad, waiting for him to continue. 'Dr Vermont?' Marnie stood. For a bizarre, still hopeful, second, she hoped

that he might have fallen asleep in mid-sentence, but
even as she called his name again, Marnie knew what
was happening. As she dropped her salad and raced
around her desk, he took a couple of laboured breaths
and she watched as Dr Vermont's skin tinged to grey
and he let out an ominous gurgle.

'Dr Vermont!' Marnie shouted, as she tried to locate
a carotid pulse. Her mind was in twenty places—she
held onto his shoulder as he toppled forward and Marnie knew she couldn't get to the phone or door without
him falling to the floor.

'Can I have some help?' Marnie shouted, trying to
break his fall and kick the chair away at the same time,
but no one was answering. 'Can someone…?' She laid
Dr Vermont on the floor and raced to open the door,
shouting loudly for help as she grabbed the phone from
her desk.

Summon help, the nursing part of her brain told her,
yet she wanted to start compressions. Marnie put out a
crash call, explaining to the startled switchboard operator that she had to be specific. 'Code red, Emergency
Department, in the nurse unit manager's office.' She
was shouting, Marnie realised, when usually she was
calm. 'Make sure you say that.'

She started compressions as the intercom crackled
into life. But, alerted by her shouting, Clive, the night
porter, came running.

'Oh, no…' he moaned, but he knew, without Marnie
telling him, exactly what to do.

'I'll get help.'

'Get the crash trolley as well,' Marnie called, as she
carried on with the compressions.

There was nothing emergency staff dreaded more

than family or friends being brought in, but to have a colleague suddenly collapse at work was truly awful.

The staff came running and in no time Marnie's office looked more like the resuscitation room. Eric, the on-call cardiologist, arrived first. His shocked expression as he saw Dr Vermont lying on the floor, his shirt open, his glasses off, was one Marnie would never forget.

Abby was trying not to cry as she charged the defibrillator and Marnie could see the resident's hand shaking as he delivered yet another shock.

'Nothing.'

'We need to get him to Resuscitation,' the cardiologist said. He was breathless from running but helped to lift Dr Vermont onto the trolley that Clive had brought in. They sped Dr Vermont through the department and the resuscitation continued en route—Marnie kneeling on the trolley to continue the compressions as Abby pushed oxygen in with an Ambu bag.

The night supervisor came, as she often did when an emergency page had been put out, but she too had run just a little harder when she had heard the strange alert.

'It's Dr Vermont,' Marnie said, stepping down as Eric took over the compressions, frantically trying to pump the medications through Dr Vermont's system in the hope the next shock would have some effect.

It didn't.

'We need to let his wife know,' the night supervisor said as the team grimly worked on.

Marnie's hands were shaking as she went through the contact sheets, dreading the thought of calling Mrs Vermont in the middle of the night to tell her that her husband was critically ill.

'Get Harry to call her,' Eric shouted over. 'Has he been told what's going on?'

'Harry no longer works here,' Marnie said, and Eric shot her a wide-eyed look.

'I can guarantee Harry would want to be the one to tell her,' Eric said.

'Even if he's on leave, Harry needs to be informed,' the night supervisor said. 'Right now the emergency department doesn't have a consultant.'

Harry didn't deliberately not pick up the first time the phone rang. He was putting anti-itch cream on a miserable Adam, who had woken at one a.m. and couldn't get back to sleep.

'So much for a mild dose,' Harry said to his son. Apparently you could get a mild dose after a child had been immunised. Harry had found all the immunisation records and had spent half an hour looking at Jill's handwriting—she had recorded every milestone, every little detail of their little lives and, yes, bang on the suggested dates, Charlotte and Adam had received their immunisations.

Adam getting chickenpox was just another thing that had gone wrong on top of another thing that had gone wrong, Harry was thinking when the phone rang.

Would they not just let him leave? Harry sighed, letting it ring out, but then, worried it might be his parents, he tucked Adam in and went and checked the machine.

'Harry, it's Marnie, could you call me back at work please?' He could hear the strain in her voice. 'I'm sorry to call you but it is an emergency.'

What the hell was he supposed to do from here? Harry thought, picking up the phone when it rang again.

'Harry, it's Marnie.'

'Marnie, I've got a child who's sick—'

'Harry, please,' Marnie broke in. 'I have some very difficult news to tell you.' Harry heard she was struggling and the line went very quiet for a moment before he spoke.

'Go on.'

'Dr Vermont collapsed a short while ago,' Marnie said, and she heard his sharp intake of breath as she spoke on. 'He's in full cardiac arrest.'

'Oh, no.'

'We're doing everything we can but I have to tell you, Harry…' She glanced over, they were still going but more and more it was looking hopeless. 'It doesn't look good at all.'

'Is Marjorie there?'

'It's only just happened,' Marnie said. 'I was just away to inform her when Eric said that you'd want to know and perhaps be the one to tell her.'

Harry sat on the edge of his bed and he remembered the kindness the Vermonts had shown him; he remembered all they had done for him when Jill's accident had happened, and, yes, it was right that he be the one to tell Marjorie.

'I've got the twins…' He didn't want to wake them up and drag them out; he didn't want that for them but sometimes, no matter how inconvenient, certain things just had to be done. There was no choice—the doctor in charge of the department was critically ill, no doubt the staff were distraught and, given Dr Vermont had given more than thirty years of his life to the place, certainly his wife deserved to hear it from him. 'I'll ring her now and then I'll pick her up,' Harry said. 'Marnie, I'll have to bring the twins in.'

There was no argument this time.

And no little barbs either.

It was all too sad.

'Adam's infectious, probably Charlotte is too,' Harry said.

'So were half the patients that came through tonight,' Marnie said. 'The observation ward is empty, I'll make up two beds and close it off for further admissions.' Her voice was back to practical and it helped because Harry felt as though the whole pack of cards was falling again, just as he'd almost rebuilt it.

'Do you need Marjorie's number?' Marnie asked.

Of course, he already had it.

Harry rang off and he'd have loved to gather his thoughts for a moment but instead he dressed and then woke the twins and put them into their dressing gowns.

'I'm sorry, guys,' he said as he carried them down the stairs and out into the night, 'but Dr Vermont is very sick and we need to go and get Marjorie so that she can be with him.'

Only when they were strapped in and already nearly back to sleep did Harry stand in the driveway and call Marjorie.

He told her what was happening as best he could, and of course he knew Marjorie well, knew she would be dressing as they spoke and about to get into her car and fly through the night to be beside the man she had been married to for forty years.

'I'm on my way now, Marjorie,' Harry said. 'I'll be there in a few minutes.'

He was—Marjorie was out on the street and she was trying not to cry as she climbed in

'You shouldn't have brought the children out,' Marjorie told him. 'I could have got there myself.'

Except her knees were bobbing up and down as she

tried to sit still, the adrenaline coursing through her as the enormity of what was happening started to take hold. 'Is he….?' She couldn't even say it. 'I'd rather know now.'

'They were working on him when I last spoke to the hospital,' Harry said.

Harry didn't know if it was a good sign or bad when he saw Abby and Marnie waiting for them in the ambulance area.

'There's half the hospital in with Dr Vermont,' Marnie said as Harry came around and briefly pulled her aside. 'Abby said that twins would know her.'

'How is he?'

'We're just waiting for Marjorie,' Marnie said, taking a sleepy Charlotte as Abby carried Adam, freeing Harry to help Marjorie into the department.

Harry knew from her voice and words that they were just keeping things going till Marjorie arrived.

'Hello.' Marnie felt the sleepy weight of Charlotte stir in her arms as she lowered her onto a bed. 'Daddy's just in with a patient; he said to make sure you had a comfy bed. I'm Marnie.'

'I know,' Charlotte said, and turned over and went back to sleep.

Adam was a bit tearful and asked where his dad was. 'I'm here, Adam.' Harry came in at that moment. 'You can go back to sleep.'

'How's Dr Vermont?'

'He's not well at all,' Harry said, 'but Marjorie's with him so that's good. You just turn over and go to sleep and I'll let you know more in the morning.'

Marnie felt a swallow in her throat at the disruption to their little lives. Saw how, with barely a murmur of protest, Adam did as he was told and rolled over.

'What's happening round there?' Marnie asked once they had moved away from the sleeping twins.

'Marjorie told them to stop.' Harry's voice wavered and Marnie watched as he struggled to keep it together. After all, less than half an hour ago he'd been putting cream on Adam's spots.

He went over to Abby, who was sitting at the desk, crying quietly, and put a hand on her shoulder, but he spoke to Marnie. 'I think you might want to put the ambulances on diversion—a lot of the staff are going to be really upset.'

'Sure.' Marnie nodded. 'I've arranged for a couple of nurses to come down from the wards to help out.'

'Good. Are you okay?' Harry asked.

'I'll be fine,' Marnie said, though she could feel tears stinging at the back of her nose, but, really, it wasn't her place to be upset. She'd only known Dr Vermont a short while and, more importantly than that, she was the manager. Like Harry, tonight really wasn't about her—it was about doing their best for Dr Vermont and his family and the colleagues who would miss him so much.

'Who found him?' Harry asked. 'Eric said that he collapsed in his office.'

'We were in my office,' Marnie corrected. 'We were having supper and talking...' She pressed her fingers into her eyes for a brief moment and then recovered. 'He just stopped talking in mid-sentence.'

'You might need to speak to Marjorie,' Harry said, as he headed back out there. 'She might want to hear what happened from you.'

Marnie nodded. 'Harry!' She called him back. 'I don't know his first name.'

'Gregory,' Harry said. 'Gregory Vermont.'

* * *

Marjorie was as lovely as Dr Vermont had been and, though devastated, she was very stoic too.

'He spoke very highly of you,' Marjorie said when she'd been in to see her husband and was sitting down in his office, which was filled not just with his many certificates but with photos of his family too. 'He said you were going to bring a bit of order to the place…' She swallowed. 'Harry said that you were with him when it happened?'

'We were in my office,' Marnie said. 'We were having our supper break and talking about…' She glanced at Harry, who filled in for her.

'The Harry problem?'

'The staff issues,' Marnie said. 'He was actually talking about you. How you'd managed to have a career but how he couldn't have been an emergency doctor without all your support.' There was a flash of tears in Marnie's eyes as she recalled the conversation, such a simple one at the time but it was so much more meaningful now. Marjorie gave a grateful smile as Marnie recalled Dr Vermont's final moments, gave her the comfort of knowing he had been speaking about his wife and a marriage that had so clearly worked.

'He was telling me how you used to keep a flask of coffee by the bedside. Then he just stopped speaking, Marjorie,' Marnie said. 'There was no pain, no discomfort, I promise you that. For a moment I honestly thought that he'd fallen asleep…'

She heard a sniff and looked over. It was Harry. He'd been holding Marjorie's hand but now it was more that she was holding his.

'He thought the world of you,' Marjorie said to Harry, and Marnie watched as Harry nodded.

She felt as if she was glimpsing something incredibly private as, just for a moment, Harry gave in to his grief and screwed up his face, trying and failing not to weep.

'When you came to do your residency, he said what a great emergency doctor you'd make,' Marjorie said, and Harry nodded again but pulled himself together, when perhaps he didn't have to. Dr Vermont and Marjorie were, Marnie was fast realising, so much more than a colleague and his wife to Harry. They clearly went back years.

Marjorie went to sit with her husband again and to speak with her family, who were starting to arrive.

It was a wretched night and looked no better by morning. Marnie had placed the department on by-pass so that no ambulances were bringing patients in, though the walking wounded still trickled in. There were a couple of ward nurses helping out and one of the surgeons had come down to assist too. The nursing staff had known Dr Vermont for a lot longer than she had and needed each other more than they needed her, so Marnie took herself around to the observation ward and sat with the twins. She went through the doctors' rosters and tried to work out how the department could possibly work without even one senior doctor.

'Are you okay?' Harry came in a little later to check on the twins. He didn't want to wake them again and also wanted to be there to tell the day staff the sad news himself when they started to arrive.

'Of course.' Marnie nodded. 'You?'

'I just can't take it in,' Harry admitted, sitting down at the desk beside her and talking in a low voice so as not to disturb the twins. Harry picked up the doctors' roster. It was already a mess—a mass of red crossings-out and locums and gaps in the schedule, and that had been before Dr Vermont had so suddenly died.

'So much for leaving,' Harry said.

'What are you going to do?'

'I don't know,' Harry admitted. 'I've just about used up every last favour. I'll have to do something, though. I simply can't imagine this place without him. He and Marjorie were so good to me when Jill had her accident…' He hesitated, not sure if Marnie was interested in hearing his thoughts or if she was just being polite.

'Go on,' Marnie offered, but Harry looked over at the sleeping twins and shook his head. 'Not here.'

They moved to the small kitchenette where they could talk and still keep an eye on the children.

'Jill was on ICU for two weeks after the accident.' Harry paused for a moment, which he so rarely did—he simply didn't have the time or the reserves to examine the past, but the emotion of losing such a close friend and colleague forced a moment of reflection. 'Jill had massive head injuries.'

'How?'

'A car accident. The only saving grace was that she didn't have the twins with her at the time. I knew as soon as I saw her that things were never going to be the same again and so did Dr Vermont. Even if she had lived, her injuries were so severe that things would never have been the same,' Harry explained. 'Dr Vermont told me that the time Jill was on ICU was my time. I can't really explain it, but we both knew at some level how difficult things would be, whether she lived or died. Cathy, my sister, had the twins and brought them in now and then to see their mum.

'Dr Vermont took care of the department. Marjorie brought dinner in for me every night and clothes, and just did so many things for me that I didn't even notice. I was so focused on the time I had left with Jill. I think I did all my grieving in ICU. I have bad days of course, but, really, when she died it wasn't about Jill, or Jill and I any more, or me, it was about the twins and work and just surviving.' He looked at Marnie, suddenly aware that his words might be hurting her for reasons of her own. 'Was it the same for you?'

'No,' Marnie admitted. 'The whole time Declan was in ICU I was convincing myself that he'd live and making plans for taking him home. Right till the last day I thought that he'd make it.' Marnie shook her head—she just didn't want to go there.

As the day staff arrived and the news was broken there were tears on the floor and more tears in the staffroom. Marnie worked her way through the contact sheets, ringing the staff who were not on duty today, or not due in till later, to let them know what had happened.

It was a department in mourning but, of course, the patients continued to arrive.

'I've come to get the twins.' It was Harry's sister, Marnie could tell. Her face was strained and yet she gave Harry a hug when he came over.

'I'm sorry, Harry. I know he meant the world to you.'

'Thanks.'

'The thing is...'

Harry halted her.

'I know you can't keep doing this,' Harry said for her. 'If you can just help me out till the funeral.'

It was close to eleven by the time Marnie got home and she had to be back there at eight for her night shift.

Despite the warmth of the house, Marnie was shivering as she climbed into bed and recalled her last conversation with Dr Vermont.

This too will pass.

Yes, Marnie thought, her body tired but her mind just too busy for sleeping.

When?

CHAPTER NINE

THERE WEREN'T JUST cracks appearing, there were gaping holes in the roster and a couple of nights Marnie was close to putting the department on bypass again. Harry's sister had taken the children for the rest of the week and he was covering the department as best he could but, of course, he couldn't work twenty-four hours a day. He told Admim that he would work till the funeral on Thursday but, after that, it was up to them to find a replacement.

Sheldon was looking boot-faced when he came on duty on the morning of the funeral to work alongside yet another locum and one he didn't particularly like.

'Harry's hardly going to miss the funeral,' Marnie pointed out. 'But cover's been arranged for the weekend. Helen Cummings is covering the night shifts and she's really good. I worked with her a lot at the Royal...'

'What about next week?' Sheldon said, but Marnie had no answer.

'Who's in charge this morning?' Lillian asked.

Marnie explained what had been arranged. 'Miriam's working till ten then going to the funeral. I'm going to have a couple of hours' sleep in the on-call room and then we're running a skeleton staff till two p.m. and the place will be on bypass.'

Marnie watched Lillian's lips disappear. Putting the department on bypass cost the hospital a lot in fines, but Marnie almost dared Lillian to question the decision on the day of Dr Vermont's funeral. It was going to be huge—several surgical lists had been rescheduled so that colleagues could pay their respects, a huge entourage would be leaving from the hospital, then there would be drinks and refreshments for those who wanted them after the official wake. Whoever had said no one was indispensable had never met Dr Vermont.

'We're all trying our best,' Marnie said. 'I called Dr Cooper but he can't start any sooner as he's working his notice till the last day. I think I might have to call Juan…'

'He's on his honeymoon.' Even the hard-nosed Lillian was reluctant to go that far, or perhaps she knew Juan too well. He was one of the rare few who had worked to get balance in his life and knew his priorities. Terminating his honeymoon wouldn't be an option. 'I doubt he's going to fly back from Argentina,' Lillian said, but Marnie just shrugged.

'Well, he is a consultant, perhaps he'd want to know that the place is collapsing.'

'Rather you than me,' Lillian said.

Marnie checked the local time in Argentina on the computer and, seeing it was early evening, decided to give it a try, but even the switchboard operator was reluctant to give her an outside line.

'Yes, it's a mobile I'm trying to call!' Marnie rolled her eyes at Miriam, who had just come on. 'Well, I don't know his landline number in Argentina, he could be anywhere. I just want to be put through to his mobile…' She was halted from continuing as the receiver was taken from her hand. Marnie turned to the delicious

sight of Harry in a black suit and tie and, though it was
expertly knotted, it was just a tiny bit off centre and his
collar needed arranging, but thankfully she managed to
resist, focusing instead on the gorgeous waft of cologne.

'Our mistake,' Harry said to the switchboard operator. He hung up the phone and then looked down at
Marnie. 'You'd really do it, wouldn't you?'

'Watch me!' Marnie said, trying to get at the phone,
but Harry blocked her.

'You cannot call a man on his honeymoon to fly
back to work.' Harry hadn't done a lot of smiling this
week and he was trying not to now as he looked down
in disbelief at Marnie. 'We're trying to prevent the next
consultant dropping dead from a heart attack, Marnie.'

'Well, I'd want to know.'

'Really?' Harry checked. 'Lying by the pool on your
honeymoon, next to the man of your dreams, you'd
really want a phone call telling you to get back here.'

'Ha,' Marnie said. 'I hate sunbathing and there'll be
no ring on this finger…' She held up that perfect finger in an almost inappropriate gesture. 'Anyway, Harry,
you've no right to be stopping me. Soon this place won't
be your problem any more.'

'Well, for this morning it still is and you are not
ringing Juan.'

'Fine,' Marnie said, and turned to Miriam. 'I'm going
to the doctors' on-call room to have a sleep. Wake me
when you want to start getting ready for the funeral.'
She looked back to Harry. 'Good luck today. Are you
speaking?'

'I am.' Harry grimaced. 'I'm just going to go and get
my car washed and then—'

'You should have washed it on your way home last
night.'

'I was tired.'

'Bet you wish you'd done it last night this morning!'

'No,' Harry lied. 'Actually, I'm going round to my office now to read through the speech and then go and sort out the car...'

'Keep it short.'

'Sorry?' She was telling him how to speak at a funeral!

'Short's better,' Marnie said.

'This from a woman who never stops talking? So you're an expert in funerals now, are you?'

'Actually, now you mention it...' She gave him a smile but then it turned to a more sympathetic one. 'I hope it goes as well as it can.'

'Thanks.'

'Harry.' She looked up at him, those blue eyes blazing, her lips worrying. 'I'm sorry, I just can't stop myself. It is a funeral you're going to after all...' Two very cold but terribly beautiful hands were at his neck, fixing his collar and tie.

'I can dress myself.'

'I know,' Marnie said, 'but you were right, Kelly.' She briefly glanced at Kelly, whose cheeks turned to ruby as she found out first hand that Marnie knew exactly what was being said about her. 'I think I do have a touch of OCD and I just cannot let you go without fixing your collar, Harry.' Oh, it was perfect now, collar down, knot in the centre. 'After all, you're representing the department!'

It wasn't intimate in the least, Harry told himself, and that was confirmed two minutes later when he saw her in the corridor, dusting down Eric's shoulders with a lint brush she just happened to keep in her office.

No, it wasn't intimate, but why could he still feel her fingers on his neck?

Why, when he saw from his office Marnie disappearing into the on-call room, did he sit there, wondering if she'd undress for bed?

Oh, help, Harry thought as she came out shoeless in stockinged feet with her hair down and returned a moment later with a pair of scrubs in her hand to change from that navy dress into pyjamas.

No, the little finger gesture hadn't been inappropriate—what was inappropriate was his thoughts on the morning of Dr Vermont's funeral.

He got up and closed the door, so as not to think of her.

It didn't work.

She'd drive you crazy, Harry told himself.

And as for bed, Harry attempted to alleviate the ache in his groin with the thought of Marnie moaning that she'd just changed the sheets, or maybe putting little towels down in case he dared to so much as spill a drop.

'Filthy business!' He could almost hear her saying it and, yes, that thought almost worked, except he remembered only too well their kiss and two minutes later Harry gave up focusing on the speech and headed out to get the car washed.

Anything for the distraction.

Marnie, his mind had decided, would be deliciously filthy.

'Marnie!'

Marnie peeled her eyes open as she heard Miriam's voice at the door. 'Marnie.'

'I'm up,' Marnie called, and on autopilot headed to

the sink and brushed her teeth. There was *nothing* worse than a two-hour sleep after a night shift.

Well, there was a whole lot worse, Marnie told herself as she washed her face, but the point she was making to herself was that getting up from a short sleep, when you really needed a long one, was one of the reasons she had always loathed nights.

Marnie stood shivering in scrubs and a cardigan in the kitchen, pouring herself a very strong coffee as Harry breezed in with a load of glasses that were on loan to the department. He did a double-take when he saw the usually very groomed Marnie a good inch shorter without her low heels and as pale as the milk she was pouring into her coffee.

'I know.' She rolled her eyes. 'It should be me they're burying today.'

She dealt with death and all the horrible stuff with a black, wry humour that would offend some, but never him. Somehow, on not quite Harry's worst day, but it was certainly there in the rankings, she made him smile.

It felt strange as everyone started to leave. The department was on bypass and quiet, but all morning it had been a hub of activity, a meeting centre. Abby's tears had already started as everyone filed out to get into the cars and Harry put his arm around Abby and then patted his pockets.

'Here,' Marnie said, handing him a box of tissues from the bench, and then they were gone.

The department was eerily quiet. The locum was calm and efficient with the few patients they had but there was an immense sadness that simply wouldn't abate. Every time Marnie looked at the clock or paused a moment she thought about that last conversation with Dr Vermont or wondered how Marjorie was faring.

Harry too.

For that morning, at least, the focus wasn't on rosters or filling in shifts, it was on the huge loss—the tremendous gap that a wonderful man had left.

Staff started to arrive early in the afternoon and the staffroom filled with hospital personnel—those who had been to the funeral and those who hadn't been able to get away for it.

'How was it?' Marnie asked Harry. He seemed beyond exhausted, but had that grim-faced look of just pushing through.

'Awful.' Harry wasn't stopping. 'I just came in to drop some supplies off. Marjorie asked me to take some of the food from the wake for everyone here. I told her it had all been catered but she wanted to contribute to it too. Can you help me get some stuff out of the car?'

'Sure.'

'Where are the twins today?' Marnie asked, as they walked out into the sunshine on what would normally feel a glorious day.

'At Cathy's till this evening.' There were mountains of food, tray after tray of sandwiches and boxes of drinks, and they ended up loading one of the gurneys and covering it with a sheet before pushing it through the department and round to the staffroom.

'So, this is your last day?' Marnie asked.

'It has to be,' Harry said, as they unloaded the food and set up. 'Cathy's had to take this week off work.' He didn't want to think about it now—for the most part, they had Friday and the weekend covered.

'You go home, Marnie.' Miriam, back from the funeral, her eyes red rimmed, took over unloading the boxes. 'You must be exhausted. I hope you're not driving.'

'No.' Marnie shook her head. 'I'm taking a taxi.'

'I'll drive you,' Harry said.

'Shouldn't you stay for a bit...?' Marnie started, and then stopped. After all, it was the story of Harry's life at the moment and the reason he had no option but to quit his job.

'They're talking about building an extension in his name,' Harry said. As they walked to his car, Marnie was shivering again. 'The Vermont Wing.'

'That would be nice.'

'Well, there won't be a Worthington Wing.'

'Just as well,' Marnie said as they climbed into his car. 'Try getting your lips around that after a night shift.'

Harry actually laughed. 'Beach Road?' he said, because he remembered everything she had ever told him.

'The dodgy end.' Marnie smiled.

'I can't believe he won't get to retire,' Harry said as they drove out of the hospital. His phone was bleeping away but he just ignored it. 'Though he'd have hated retirement—even Marjorie said as much—he loved that place.'

'You do too.'

Emotional blackmail wasn't going to work on Harry. He never took his eyes off the road. 'I love my kids. I need to put them first. Charlotte's becoming more precocious by the minute, Adam...' He liked it that she didn't push things, just waited as he voiced a potential problem that he hadn't discussed with anyone. 'I think he's got a speech delay.' His knuckles were white on the wheel. 'I've been thinking it for months and I haven't even had time to do a thing about it.'

'Looks like I'll be ringing Juan to come back from his honeymoon, then.'

'You really aren't romantic?'

'Not at all,' Marnie said. 'Men always have to complicate things.' She watched as Harry's tense mouth curved into a smile—his problem was the same, but with women, of course. 'They say they want an independent woman,' Marnie continued. 'They insist they do but then they get all misty-eyed and start to ask strange things like could I possibly iron a shirt? Or they think that just because you had sex last night it means you're going to be overtaken by this sudden urge to cook for them…'

Harry laughed, really laughed, for the first time since he'd taken the call about Dr Vermont. It wasn't the safest conversation to be having right now. He turned and glanced at her. There was a smile on her lips as she looked out of the window, a smile that told him she knew she was flirting. His phone bleeped again. Harry went to get it, but seeing cyclists up ahead knew better than to risk it, but he was worried that it might be work. 'Can you get it out my pocket?'

She most certainly could.

Harry was used to making strange requests such as that one, used to concentrating on stitching, or something similar, as someone found his phone and held it for him to speak into. He could feel her bony fingers against his chest as her hand slipped inside his jacket and Marnie could feel the heat from his skin through his shirt.

'Mind on the road, Harry,' Marnie said, and he smiled. The air was almost crackling between them. 'You've a text from Cathy.'

'Which means Charlotte,' Harry translated. 'At least it isn't work.'

'What you need,' Marnie said, 'is a wife.'

'I've got one,' Harry said, and in a gesture that certainly wasn't insolent—in fact, for Marnie it was the nicest thing he could have done—Harry held up his ring finger.

'I know,' Marnie said, because she did know. She had a son. It didn't go away because time had passed.

He pulled up at her house and opened up the message.

'So that's that, then,' Harry said as he read it.

'Sorry?'

'I wasn't going to say anything but I was hoping that I might be able to juggle things next week—the incubation period is just about up and there was this tiny window of possibility that the twins could go back to day care on Monday…' He gave a wry laugh as he read out the text. 'Charlotte has spots—don't worry, right now she's delighted.'

'Poor Atlas,' Marnie said as she watched the load he was carrying drop just a touch heavier on his shoulders. She looked at his profile and knew she'd miss him.

A lot.

'Do you need to get back?'

'I'll call her,' Harry said. 'And see how she is.' Except his phone battery was almost flat. 'Can I use yours?'

'Sure.' She went to go in her bag to get it but changed her mind. 'Use the landline.'

'Marnie…' Harry started, and then changed his mind. 'Sure, a coffee would be great.' It was a long drive to his sister's after all.

But Marnie was over playing games.

'Harry, you *know* we're going to sleep together. So we can make this all awkward and have a coffee that neither of us wants and then a quick fumble at the door…' She loved it when he smiled.

'Won't it complicate things?'

'There's nothing complicated about sex.' Marnie smiled. 'And we don't work together any more.'

'I think—'

But she halted him. 'You've done enough thinking for the day.'

She was possibly the perfect woman for Harry right now, he decided as he tasted her moist, full lips.

And there was nothing nicer than the warmth of his kiss when you were freezing, Marnie told herself as his arms slid around hers. And could there be anyone better than Harry to get your second wind with? Because suddenly Marnie wasn't remotely tired.

'Come on,' Marnie said. 'Let's get you to bed!

But first he called Charlotte and congratulated her on her spots.

'I'll stop and get some more supplies before I come and get you,' Harry said. 'Yep. Don't worry, I won't get there till dinner.' Marnie was taking off her cardigan as Cathy must have come on the phone. 'She's worried I'm going to pick her up before she gets to eat your pizza.' He looked at Marnie as he talked on about how today had gone well. Well, as well as funeral could go. 'Thanks for this week,' Harry said. 'No, Cathy, I get it. I know you can't take another week off…' He hesitated. 'No.' Harry's response was firm. 'Mum and Dad are okay for the odd night, but it's not fair to ask for a week.'

They just stared for a very long moment and there was something lovely about no longer working together, something really nice about being two people who were quite comfortable keeping their sex lives separate from the rest of their lives.

They both knew the other's rules.

They'd both wanted the other on sight.

'Come here,' Harry said, and it took just two words. Marnie stepped into his space and Harry looked down, lingering a moment safe in the knowledge there was no need for holding back now.

'You drove me crazy this morning.'

'I know.'

'You always do.'

'I know.' Marnie smiled.

She felt his mouth on hers, felt her tongue slide in and, yes, it was nice not to think.

Marnie, though she would never admit it to herself let alone Harry, was taken slightly aback by her own reaction to his mouth. She'd missed it, had been thinking about their kiss far more than she perhaps ought, and now he was back, his mouth sinking into hers, its demand building. She opened her eyes and saw Harry's were closed and it was an incredible turn-on to see him simply indulge. So lovely to feel his hands stop fighting their need for contact and roam free, down her waist, then to her bottom, and despite his height they were an incredible fit, Marnie thought, so incredible that it would be terribly easy to forget about bed.

Harry lifted her top, slid it over her head and moaned as his hands felt the bare skin he had craved. His fingers unhooked her bra and his mouth was enough to make her sink to her knees with Harry joining her.

'Harry…' She pulled back and he opened his eyes, waited for the inevitable excuses and the reasons that this was a terrible idea, but he still didn't know Marnie.

'I need to have a shower,' Marnie said, and he laughed for the second time in a very short space of time and, no, he didn't mind the delay in proceedings, especially with what she said next. 'I'd like to be clean before we get dirty.'

Marnie headed into her bedroom and picked up the alarm. 'What time do you need to leave?' she asked.

'Six.'

'I'll set it for five, then.' She was almost clinical in her approach yet for Harry it was sexy. He liked independence; heaven knew, there were so many people dependent on him. He liked the rarity of Marnie and her utter ease, combined with the delicious trepidation that he felt as she headed for the shower.

He heard the taps turn on as he closed the curtains of her bay window and undressed. It was an adult reprieve that had been building and with someone who fascinated him more and more. Someone with whom he could be himself, or rather he could go back to the man he had once been.

Naked, he walked into the bathroom and pulled back the curtain, stood watching her washing her hair, and she opened her eyes and smiled.

'You didn't come empty-handed, I hope.'

'No.'

'Come in, then.'

He picked up the soap and put the little silver wrapper in the holder, and there was nothing to stop them now.

'I hate showers,' Marnie said, looking down as his large hands lathered the soap and then slid over her breasts. 'Or maybe I don't.' He was as slow and as deliciously thorough as she had thought he would be. Marnie watched as he soaped her breasts, her nipples stretching and puckering, and then she took the soap from him, lathered her hands and then dropped it.

It was Harry who paused, stared down as her hands stroked the length of him, over and over. He stood, staring as if in some delicious hypnotic trance that they'd be jolted out of any second. Marnie knew it too, she felt the swell and the lift of the balls she cupped in her hand and she was so turned on watching Harry that she wouldn't have cared if his hand hadn't halted her.

He was struggling to hold back, and he kissed her till he was back from the edge. The shiver that went through her had nothing to with exhaustion or cold as Harry lowered his head to her breast.

Her breasts had been on his mind for so long, that long glimpse of them nestled in her lacy bra had been dancing in his mind's eyes since the kiss in her office. The taste of her wet, warm flesh in his mouth was more than worth the wait.

Marnie watched his tongue taking its time, building her urgency, and before she even begged she watched as her nipple disappeared into to the soft vacuum of his mouth. She felt his hand slide up her thigh and she just about folded over, holding onto his head for support.

Maybe she did like showers after all, she thought as Harry tended to the other breast for a while, ensuring she was flushed and dizzy from his generous tastings before his mouth moved down.

'Harry…'

He ignored her, knelt down and parted her legs. He retrieved the soap and washed her intimately, teasing out her clitoris till it was as erect as he'd left her nipples and then burying his face in her sex as his fingers slid deep inside.

Marnie usually took for ever to come but not this afternoon. She was pressing Harry's head in, watching him feast, buckling her legs to him, then accidentally blasting them with cold water as she grabbed a tap for support as she gave in to his mouth.

Harry loved the icy blast to his shoulders as he felt her heat in his mouth; he loved hearing the very controlled Marnie losing it to his tongue then shivering in his arms.

'More hot I think...' Harry said.

It was steamy, it was lovely and Harry had but a few minutes' patience left in him. He stood and watched as she tore the wrapper and both looked down as she gave him a little stroke and a tease.

'Sometimes I look down and just smile,' Marnie said at the sight of her hands tenderly wrapping her present as she slid the condom down.

'We'll slip,' Marnie warned as he picked her up, and she slid down on his length and Harry did his best to hold her, hot and slippery in his hands; but there was just a little too much energy between them, the sex they wanted a touch too vigorous to assure safety. 'We're going to end up in Emergency,' Marnie warned as he tried to get back to her breasts and she wrapped her legs tighter around him.

'They might have to send the flying squad out to us,' Harry said, giving up on the pleasure of her wet breast. She put her arms around his neck and still they kissed, but it was terribly difficult in her tiny shower and Harry wanted to see more of her.

He turned the taps off and carried her to the bed, letting her back till her shoulders rested and Marnie looked up to the stunning sight of him, dripping wet and devouring her with his eyes.

Her ankles were wrapped around his hips and he had one hand under her buttocks, the other stroking her as he thrust into her, but she pushed his hand away and gave full invitation.

She'd thought Harry sexy but she knew now just how sexy he was. Felt the grip of his hands on her hips and the delicious sight of him for once concentrating on himself. It was bliss to be moved by him, to be taken. The slap of wet skin and the feel of Harry unleashed deep inside, so potent even the soles of Marnie's feet seemed to contract as she started to writhe beneath him, not that Harry let her go anywhere.

He held her hips so tight as he shot into her that Marnie fought to arch, the suppression forcing the channels of energy back to where Harry delivered his final thrusts deep inside her. It tipped Marnie into the deepest orgasm of her life—her thighs shaking, her bottom lifting, grateful for the hands that held her firm as she rode the deep waves that coursed through her.

And Harry watched her collapse.

He could hardly breathe, he could see the flush on her cheeks and breasts and the tension in her throat as she spasmed around him. He watched and felt as slowly it all dissipated, yet the sight was almost enough for him to go again.

Yet almost better than the sex for Harry was afterwards. He kept waiting for the comedown, and so did Marnie, but right now it was just a matter of sleeping.

For the first time in what felt like for ever the world was a worry-free zone.

CHAPTER TEN

'PRESS SNOOZE,' MARNIE said.

'It's on your side.'

It was very hard, trying to reach the alarm with Harry spooned into her and his strong arm holding her tight.

Marnie pressed snooze and felt his erection nudging, pulled a little packet from the drawer and, really, she'd have loved not to bother. And Harry would have loved not to bother either.

They were too sensible for that.

It did break the moment, though, a moment that neither usually minded breaking, but Harry soon got back behind her. 'Where were we?' he asked, nuzzling the back of her neck. The alarm going off the second time didn't actually ruin things as she reached over and turned it off. It felt natural for Harry to pull her back to his warm body and slide himself in.

Marnie loved half waking to Harry. She loved this slow, lazy sex where she barely had to move, and she loved his breath in her ear.

'I remember you now,' Harry said. 'I offered to buy you a drink.'

'No,' Marnie corrected, as he rocked deep inside her. 'The drinks were free that night.'

'I offered to get you a drink...'

'No,' Marnie corrected again, but she couldn't really think straight. She was trying to turn her head to meet his mouth, trying to stop her own orgasm because she didn't want it over just yet, or maybe she did because conversation was forgotten now as both surrendered to the bliss and then lay there for a few moments afterwards. Harry stroked her stomach; Marnie felt him soften and gradually slip away.

She didn't want him to leave.

Harry didn't particularly want to go home either. On a wretched, black day he'd glimpsed peace and it would be so incredibly easy to just drop all balls completely and close his eyes and sleep.

But he never would.

'I'd better go soon.'

She turned to him and decided that, yes, he'd better because she was so comfortable, so warm, so *enjoying* being with him; it would be too easy to kiss him, or for them to both close their eyes and convince themselves they could wake up if they had just five minutes' more sleep.

'Go on.' She disentangled herself and for Harry it was incredibly hard to haul himself out of bed.

'When the twins are better...'

'Harry...' She shook her head, didn't really want to spell out to him that a single father of two wasn't quite the date she had in mind.

He picked up his shirt and held it up. 'You couldn't give this a quick iron, could you?'

'Don't even joke.'

As he did up his shirt, Harry caught sight of a blonde Marnie holding her son and, yes, he hadn't been lying, he did remember her now.

'I asked why you were leaving,' Harry said. 'You didn't answer.'

'Yes, well, you wouldn't have liked it if I had,' Marnie said. 'I'd just found out I was pregnant.'

'What went wrong?' He wondered if he'd asked too much. There were so many no-go areas with Marnie—it would seem from her previous response that dinner and a bottle of wine was a no-no, yet, Harry realised as she started to answer him, she was prepared now to talk a little about her son.

'Premature,' Marnie said. 'Poor little thing didn't stand a chance—I had a placenta the size of an AA battery…' It was a dark joke and Harry didn't smile; he just picked up the photo and looked at them both as Marnie spoke on. 'So not only was he premature, he was also small for dates. Then he got an HAI and was just too small to fight it.'

No wonder she was obsessive about hand-washing and curtains being changed, Harry thought—a hospital-acquired infection explained a lot of things but it was as if she'd read his thoughts.

'I was always a clean-freak.' Marnie smiled. 'Even before Declan got so ill but, yes, I go a bit overboard at work.'

'I don't blame you.'

'You'd better go,' Marnie said. It felt strange to watch him holding her picture. It felt strange to be discussing that time with anyone other than Siobhan, who, even on the other side of the world, still nursed her through the yearly hell of birthdays and anniversaries and all the things you really needed a cuddle for, but a computer screen or telephone call had to suffice.

Harry didn't want to go, not just because he wanted to climb back into bed and forget the world for a moment. It was more that there was so much to Marnie that he'd like to know, so much about today he was having trouble letting go of.

So many things that he didn't want to end, and so he tried again.

'Do you want to go out at the weekend?'

'I'd imagine you'd have trouble getting a babysitter for twins with chickenpox.'

'I guess…' He felt strange walking off, as if he'd been using her, when for Harry it had been anything but. 'Have you had chickenpox?'

'I have.'

'Maybe you could come over. I could cook.'

'Harry, don't spoil it.' She was incredibly direct.

She made no excuses, Harry noticed as he dressed, and he should be glad of it. Glad for a woman who knew what she wanted—and a single dad to twins wasn't high on her list.

She was just moving to the top of his.

Marnie was lying in bed, watching him as he did up his tie but then, as he came over and sat down to kiss her goodbye, she suddenly found a solution.

This too will pass.

She could almost hear Dr Vermont say the words.

'Thank God we don't work together…' Harry gave a rueful smile as she reached for his tie and, as Marnie so loved to do, straightened it.

'About that,' Marnie said.

'About what?'

'Do you have a bath?'

'Yes.'

'How about I move in for a week?'

Harry grinned. 'This from a woman who doesn't even want to come out with me for dinner.'

'I'm not talking about dating or romance,' Marnie said. 'I'm talking about me moving in and, between us, taking care of the children. Harry, you're in the eye of the storm at the moment but in a week's time you'll have your lady back to help with the children, Juan will be working... If by then you still want to take yourself off and become hand surgeon of the year...' She made a little joke and then stopped because actually she was completely serious. 'My moving in for a week would give you a pause.'

'Why would you do that?'

'Because, I don't want the department that I've just started running to fall apart.'

'I can't drag you from your home.'

'It's hardly a home,' Marnie said. 'I've only been here five minutes!'

She simply didn't get attached to anything, Harry realised, but it would be so very easy to get attached to her, and he wasn't just thinking about himself when he spoke.

'It would be too confusing for the children,' he said, because, for all his faults, he had managed to keeps his flings well away from them, and Marnie in his bed for a week... He shook his head but then realised that for Marnie this *was* strictly business.

She really could separate the two.

'I'm not going to be sleeping with you, Harry, especially if there's a chance we are going to continue working together. There'll be no confusion.' Marnie smiled. 'I only want you professionally, Harry. It will be a working arrangement.'

'I can't ask you to take time off work to look after my kids.'

'Who said anything about that? I have the weekend

off already, a day off in lieu of nights on Monday, and I'll take a management day on Tuesday and sort out those bloody rosters once and for all from home.'

His mind was turning faster. It was maybe, possibly doable.

'I could do a couple of nights on the days you're working. If I can sit down with Helen and work out some shifts…'

'We can work it,' Marnie said. 'It's just one week. I need a doctor for my department, Harry. I have no intention of failing.'

He looked at Marnie, sitting on the bed, the tiniest yet strongest woman he had ever met, and the most determined too. 'I doubt you could.'

CHAPTER ELEVEN

'I FEEL LIKE Mary Poppins,' Marnie said as Harry opened his front door.

'Oh, you're no Mary Poppins.' Harry grinned, taking her case. He was looking more rumpled than usual and that clean-shaven look of yesterday was fading. 'Come in. Charlotte's just starting to realise that chickenpox isn't so much fun after all.'

No, Marnie was no Mary Poppins. Mary was a good girl who didn't notice things like Harry's bum as she followed him through to the lounge, but, then, she'd never seen Harry in just a T-shirt and jeans and barefoot too. Oh, she'd seen him in a suit, in scrubs and stark naked, but there was something very attractive about him in a T-shirt because it showed off his very flat stomach and in jeans his legs just looked longer.

No, she was no Mary Poppins, but Marnie was still a good girl because she didn't give that bottom a pinch as they walked and she kept her thoughts well to herself too—butter wouldn't have melted in her mouth as she gave his children a smile.

'This is Marnie,' Harry introduced her. 'You both met her at the hospital.'

Adam looked up and smiled and said hello, but Charlotte's eyes narrowed. 'A nurse isn't a nanny.'

'I'm not a nanny,' Marnie said. 'I'm here to help look after you so that Daddy can work.'

'Have you looked after children before?'

'Charlotte,' Harry warned.

'It's fine,' Marnie said. 'I don't mind being interviewed—I'd want to know who was looking after me too.' She turned to Charlotte. 'I've looked after plenty of children and I have lots of nieces and nephews and many younger brothers, so I've have a bit more of a head start than most.'

Harry showed her around—it was a lovely old home, though the stairs creaked terribly as Harry lifted her case upstairs.

'It's a beautiful home.'

'It's needs a demolition ball,' Harry said. 'It looks nice but everything needs fixing, apart from this...'

He opened a door and Marnie almost whimpered at the sight of a beautiful bathroom—it was completely white except for a few dots of dark tiles on the floor. 'It's the one thing that has been renovated,' Harry said. 'I think they gave up after that. I can't wait to see the back of it.'

Marnie was surprised. Surely this home would be filled with memories and the last thing he would want was to let it go, but he must have read her confusion.

'Oh, no...' Harry shook his head. 'We'd just sold our house and were looking for somewhere when Jill died... It was hell—the buyers had sold too and there was no getting out of it. I didn't want the upheaval for the children.'

'Poor things.' It just poured out of her mouth. 'I hated moving, more than anything, I hated leaving Ireland and then when we had to leave Perth...' Marnie stopped. She didn't really like talking about herself but she was just trying to say that she understood how hard it must have been for the children to move so close to losing their mum.

'It wasn't exactly great timing,' Harry said when Marnie went quiet, 'but there was no real choice, so I rented this. Your friend Dave put me onto it.'

'Ah, Dave!' Marnie gave a bitter smile.

'It was supposed to be for six months...' He turned round and there was Charlotte, standing at the top of the stairs watching them.

'I'm itchy,' she said.

'I'll just show Marnie her room and then I'll come and put some cream on.'

They walked down the hall and he opened a door and put Marnie's case inside. 'I hope this is okay.'

'It's lovely.' It was, a large room with an iron bed dressed in white linen and lovely wooden furnishings that mismatched perfectly.

Charlotte, who had followed them, stood in the doorway and watched as Harry showed Marnie how the dodgy windows worked. 'Do you want to come in and help me put some things away?' Marnie offered.

'We're not allowed in the nanny's room,' Charlotte said, and huffed off.

'Fair enough,' Marnie said.

'She's normally much more friendly.'

'She's normally not covered in spots,' Marnie pointed out, as Harry, a touch awkward now, headed for the door. 'Do you want to go through our diaries?' Marnie suggested. 'Get it out of the way?'

'Sure.'

'I'll just unpack and I'll be down.'

Marnie unpacked her case—it only took a moment. She put her clothes in the wardrobe and hung her dressing gown up on the door and sorted out her toiletries. She put Declan's photo in the drawer of the bedside table. She didn't want questions if the children came peeking, but she couldn't bear to leave him at home, then she headed downstairs.

It was a working arrangement.

They sat at a large table and drank tea as they tried to sort out the upcoming week. 'I phoned Helen and I've got the shifts she can do, as well as Lazlo, he's on now and I'm going in tomorrow.'

'Who's Lazlo?'

'He used to work there and said that he can come in for a couple of shifts…'

Marnie looked at the schedule and saw Harry pencilled in for a shift on Friday night.

'I'm out that night,' Marnie said, and didn't elaborate, but Harry's jaw did tighten just a fraction as he recalled that she was going to the ballet.

With Matthew.

'Not a problem.' Harry cleared his throat before continuing. 'Okay, if I can get Helen to cover that night I can, if it's okay with you, be on call for the rest of the weekend and then Juan's back.'

It *was* a working arrangement.

She made that very clear.

When Harry opened a bottle of wine once the kids had gone to bed, Marnie politely declined.

'I'm going to have that bath.'

'Sure.'

She was a strange person, Harry thought—Marnie didn't even come down and say goodnight. But, ages later, when he headed for bed himself, he could hear her chatting away in her room and it took a moment for it to click that she was on the computer.

'You're living with him?' Siobhan checked, and Marnie was very glad for her headphones. 'You've slept with him and you've moved in but there's nothing going on?'

'You're making this more complicated than it is,' Marnie said.

'What does Matthew have to say about it?'

'I don't discuss things like that with Matthew,' Marnie said, but she did worry for a moment. 'Matthew and I...' She looked at Siobhan, who'd been married for nine years now and just loved hearing about friends with benefits and her best friend's rather glamorous life. 'I don't know,' Marnie admitted.

'What would Harry have to say about Matthew?'

'Nothing!' Marnie said. 'Because he's not going to find out.'

Except Harry had been there when Matthew had invited her to the ballet.

Marnie's conscience was pricking as she turned off the computer and tried to get to sleep.

She and Harry had been a one-off, an indulgence, safe in the knowledge they wouldn't be working together again.

See what happens when you take your eye off the ball, Marnie scolded herself.

It certainly wouldn't be happening again.

No, there was no hint of anything. The next morning she was up and dressed and even had lipstick on as Harry held up the kettle and asked if she wanted tea.

'Leave the tea bag in this time,' Marnie said.

'You're sure you don't mind doing this?' Harry checked. 'Charlotte's been up half the night crying. It's hardly a great day off for you.'

'Harry, I'm just relieved to know that the place is being looked after. It's been nothing but a headache trying to get the department covered.' She turned as Adam came down. 'Good morning.'

'Morning, Marnie.'

She was *lovely* to Adam. She chatted away and found out that he'd like cornflakes and juice and yet, Harry couldn't put his finger on it, she still held back. Then Charlotte appeared.

'Do you want babies?' Charlotte asked as Marnie sorted out her breakfast.

'Charlotte,' Harry scolded.

'It's fine.' Marnie smiled. 'No, Charlotte, I don't want babies.'

'Why?'

'Because…' Marnie filled a bowl with cornflakes as she spoke '…I like my work, I like my holidays, I like lots of things. And,' Marnie added, 'as I told you, I had lots of younger brothers. I've changed more nappies than most!'

'Don't scratch,' Harry warned, as Charlotte started to.

'I keep forgetting.'

'I'll paint your nails red later,' Marnie said. 'That will remind you.'

After Harry had gone, she did paint Charlotte's nails red and then she went about opening the windows and stripping the beds between putting on anti-itch cream at various times throughout the day.

'Do you like our house?' Charlotte asked as she showed her the cupboard at the top of the stairs where the fresh sheets were kept.

'I think it's lovely,' Marnie said, as she pulled out some sheets. 'Right! Which ones are yours, Adam?'

'The blue ones, silly,' said Charlotte. 'Mine are pink.'

* * *

Harry could not have done it without her.

The children could not have been better looked after and a wary Charlotte had quickly warmed to Marnie's chatter and rather offbeat humour. Despite refusing to iron a thing for Harry, Marnie hauled out the ironing board on the Tuesday evening and made a major dint in the piles of children's bedding and clothing.

'Do you ever stop?' Charlotte asked. She was helping Marnie to fold things as a distraction from scratching.

'Not till the work's done,' Marnie said.

Only Harry noticed that Charlotte's smile wavered.

CHAPTER TWELVE

'YOU'VE DONE WELL during an extremely difficult time.'

She was sitting in a management meeting. Lillian had blinked a bit at the budget report, and there had been a couple of explosions. The maintenance hours had trebled and there had been fines for the department for twice being on bypass. That had been nothing to do with lack of beds or waiting times, though—in fact, waiting times were down as Marnie was very clued up about the wards hiding beds and had threatened a few times to go up and make a bed herself unless the patient was accepted soon.

Patient complaints were down too.

Marnie put out fires as they happened rather than letting them simmer and, overall, she was pretty pleased as she made her way back down to the department.

No one knew she was staying at Harry's. Certainly no one could know that the reason she hadn't arrived until ten past nine this Thursday was because of the patient Harry had been stuck with. There had been a couple of raised brows as she'd rushed in because she was so rarely late.

But, apart from that, things had ticked along.

Marnie was enjoying her time with the twins—she liked children. She had been adored by her brothers as they'd grown up and was now a favourite aunty. Yes, she liked children, she just didn't want any of her own.

She'd had her baby and wasn't going to put herself through it ever again—she admired those that did.

Making her way back from the meeting, Marnie walked into the pre-natal ward and couldn't help peeking in.

'Hello!' She knocked on the open door and smiled as Emily looked up from the book she was writing in.

'Marnie!'

'Am I disturbing you?'

'Not at all.' Emily smiled. 'I'm on bed rest till the baby is born. I've never been more up to date with my homework.'

Marnie looked at the huge pile of books by her bed. 'You've got no excuse not to get a good grade,' Marnie said. 'How have your parents been?'

'They've been marvellous!' Emily said. 'I can't believe how good they've been, even though I do I think Dad's disappointed.'

'Maybe he's just worried,' Marnie offered.

'I guess,' Emily said, 'but we've spoken about what we're going to do and they're looking at doing up the granny flat so that Reece and I can live in that.'

'Wow.' Marnie smiled.

'Reece has got another job while I'm on bed rest...'

'You're going to get there,' Marnie said. 'It sounds like you're both using this time to put your heads down and get a future happening.'

'We will.' Emily nodded. 'I wanted to nurse before all this happened but now I'm thinking of teaching.'

'You'll get school holidays off!' Marnie smiled. 'And that's something to think about because, by the time you're qualified, you'll almost have a school-aged child.'

She looked at a very mature seventeen-year-old. 'What a great teacher you'd be,' Marnie said, 'having already earned your qualifications in the school of life.'

'Thanks, Marnie.'

'I shall come and see you again, if you like.'

'I'd love it.'

That night she told Harry about visiting Emily as they ate dinner before Harry went to work.

Charlotte and Adam had already eaten and were making a lot of noise upstairs as cabin fever started to seriously hit.

'I stopped in on Emily today. She's doing really well.' Marnie smiled. 'She's got her head down studying, hoping to be a teacher, and Reece is working an extra job.'

'They still have to be teenagers, though,' Harry said, mashing butter into his potato.

'She won't have time for being a teenager once the baby comes along. It's good that she's getting ahead.' Marnie stopped. Even she could hear that she sounded like her own mother and she tried to soften it. 'It's going to be hard for her but Emily will get there.'

'Did you work right through your pregnancy?'

'I went on bed rest when it was clear my placenta was failing,' Marnie said. 'But I'd have been straight back to my studies even if Declan...' She really didn't like talking about it. There was an uncomfortable silence and after a moment Harry filled it.

'What were your friends like?' Harry asked.

'Siobhan was great,' Marnie said. 'She's my best friend in Ireland, but can you believe she came all this way for the funeral? She'd saved up enough to go travelling for a year and she spent half of it getting here to help console me.'

'What about the girls you trained with?'

'Scathing.' Marnie pulled a face. 'Well, they weren't really friends, we'd all started just a few months back, and I think they thought I was mad to be going through with it.'

'And after you lost him?'

'It was awkward,' Marnie admitted. 'They were busy being teenagers and I guess I wasn't my sunniest. I took my nursing very seriously…'

Oh, he could just imagine that she had!

'That's why I transferred to the Royal. I just didn't want to be around anyone who knew what had happened so I gave myself a fresh start. Of course, I was always an old head on young shoulders even before…' She looked up at him. 'I did know what was involved having a baby—I was nearly eleven when mum had Ronan. I got up to him at night. It might have been an accident but I did know what I was taking on.'

Harry took the plates to the sink. He could see her sitting there, staring, and he thought about a teenage Marnie, let loose for the first time. Those first few months of freedom and, oh, what a price…

'Marnie. Why don't—?'

'I'm going to get the children ready for bed.' She just halted him. Marnie didn't want pensive conversations that changed nothing. 'You're off tomorrow?' Marnie checked their plans before she headed off.

'Yep, but I'm on all weekend.' He felt as guilty as hell, not that Marnie seemed to mind.

'That's fine. What time do you have to be in Saturday morning?'

'Eight.'

'I'll make sure I'm back early, then.'

'Early?'

'Saturday morning,' Marnie said. 'I told you I'm out Friday.'

'Of course…' Harry shook his head. 'I forgot.'

He hadn't forgotten, not for a moment, he'd just kind of hoped things might have changed.

But, then, why would they?

Marnie wasn't giving her heart away to anyone.

CHAPTER THIRTEEN

'I'VE BOOKED THE Langham.'

Marnie was trying to get Charlotte to brush her teeth when Matthew called.

Marnie loved The Langham—it was a beautiful hotel on the river and possibly her favourite place on earth, but not even the prospect of The Langham could soothe a rather awkward conversation.

'Who's that?' Matthew asked, as a very demanding Charlotte called out for Marnie.

'I'm just watching a friend's children for a couple of days.' She didn't give him a moment to question it. 'I'll try to get there for six.'

'Who were you speaking to?' Charlotte asked, when Marnie hung up.

'A friend,' Marnie said. 'And you should be paying more attention to your teeth than my phone calls—you didn't do the back ones.'

'I hate brushing my teeth.'

'I'd noticed!' Marnie said. 'You'll end up like Adam.' Marnie smiled at Charlotte's brother. 'All your teeth will fall out. Show me...' she said, and Adam took his finger and wobbled a tooth that was barely hanging. Marnie felt a curl in her stomach as he pushed it too far.

'Stop now!' Marnie said, but Adam just laughed and wiggled it harder.

They were fun but exhausting and, as Marnie cleaned up the bathroom, she told herself there'd be fluffy towels and champagne waiting tomorrow.

It just didn't cheer her as much as it usually would.

Marnie was in bed early, knowing the chances of a full night's sleep were remote, and that was confirmed at two a.m.

'Daddy!' Marnie heard Charlotte's first cry and got up and headed to go to her, then turned and put a dressing gown on over her pyjamas.

'It's Marnie, Charlotte,' Marnie said, as she opened the door. 'Daddy's at work, remember—I'm looking after you tonight.'

'I itch.'

'I know,' Marnie said. 'It's that horrible chickenpox but they'll be gone soon. Shall I put on some lotion?'

Charlotte nodded.

'Would you like a drink?'

Charlotte nodded at that suggestion too.

'Why don't you go off to the loo,' Marnie said, 'and I'll be back with a drink and some nice cold cream?'

Marnie was very used to patients waking at two a.m. and more often than not it was the need to go to the toilet that had woken them. So she turned on the lights for Charlotte and then headed down the stairs, made her a drink and found the cream.

Charlotte was back in bed by the time Marnie got back up there and, despite the hour, Charlotte was her usual talkative self as Marnie dabbed on the cream.

'What's a code blue?'

'Why do you ask that?'

'Code red is for a fire and all the doors close,' Charlotte said, and Marnie's hand paused as she realised that the children must hear the overhead intercom alerts in the crèche. Well, of course they would, Marnie reasoned. If there was a fire or the crèche needed to be evacuated, then they needed to hear the alerts too, but it didn't sit right with Marnie that the twins heard them.

'So,' Charlotte pushed. 'What's a code blue?'

'It's when certain doctors are needed.'

'Like the trauma team?'

'Yes,' Marnie said. 'Right, you're done.' As Charlotte lay down Marnie tucked the sheet in around her and went to turn out the light. ''Night, Charlotte. You just call if you need anything.'

'Can you read me a story?'

'I'll tell you a story,' Marnie said, because the light was already off and Charlotte didn't need any more stimulation. Marnie sat on the edge of the bed and told her the same stories she had told Ronan when he had been little. About the fairies that lived at the bottom of the garden and all the good work that they did.

'In your garden?' Charlotte asked.

'In my garden back home in Ireland.'

'But what happens when you move?' Charlotte asked, and Marnie had been about to say they stayed to help the next lot of children who lived there but she could hear the anxiety in Charlotte's voice. She remembered that they'd already moved at a very difficult time and would perhaps soon be moving again.

'The fairies move with you,' Marnie explained, and in the darkness she could see Charlotte's eyes shining, waiting for her to go on. 'They fly along with the removal truck.'

'So the fairies from our old house are here?'

'Of course they are,' Marnie said. 'We'll take a little treat down for them at the weekend.'

Charlotte seemed to like that idea and it was she who said goodnight this time, but as Marnie went to go Charlotte halted her.

'Did your fairies move with you?'

'Of course,' Marnie said, but if she'd been making things up before, now she really was lying. All the lovely imaginings of her childhood were still there in Ireland, all the games and the fun and the innocence were still there in her old home and garden.

'Maybe not all of them, though.' Charlotte yawned. 'Fairies are very small and Australia is a long way to fly.'

She really did need to get out more, Marnie told herself as she climbed into bed, because all this talk of fairies and flying and her fairies being left behind had Marnie suddenly on the edge of crying.

It had been an emotional time, she told herself. The department was struggling not just with the doctor shortage but with the aching gap Dr Vermont himself had left behind.

But it wasn't just that.

She'd never expected she might get attached to Charlotte and Adam—Marnie's heart lived on ice—yet getting up to them at night, hearing their chatter, the things they said that made her laugh… Marnie could almost hear the drip of her heart thawing and it wasn't just that she didn't want it to, or that it terrified her, there was also an appalling sense of guilt because she was a mother of one and in a few days' time it would be Declan's birthday.

Not here!

Marnie lay in bed and refused to give in to tears—

she was here to look after children. What if Charlotte called or Adam woke up?

She needed tomorrow, Marnie told herself as she lay there, trying to picture the ballet while frantically trying not to picture afterwards.

She wanted a night at The Langham with Harry.

Or just a night with Harry would do.

'Marnie!' She was almost asleep when she heard her name called.

'I'm coming,' Marnie said once she had ungritted her teeth, grateful for the three a.m. reminder of why she didn't want a single father!

She needed a night away to get back to herself and normality, instead of crying over fairies and made-up stories.

Harry let himself in the following morning a little earlier than usual. The place had been quiet and he'd slept most of the night in the on-call room.

He was greeted by the sight of Marnie's small case and a slightly flustered Marnie who, as usual, was fully dressed and had her hair tied back and make-up on.

'I was just taking that out to my car.'

She'd hoped to do so before Harry got home or the children were up. She'd hoped to completely avoid any discussion about tonight.

She was looking after his children, Marnie told herself as she took out the small case. Certainly she was entitled to a night off.

Harry was trying to tell himself the same. 'How were the twins?' he asked, as she came back in.

'I never heard a peep from Adam, and Charlotte just got up a couple times because she was itchy.' She hesitated a moment, it was none of her business after all.

'She was asking what a code blue was and things. Did you know they hear all the intercoms?'

'I know,' Harry said. 'They have to be on.'

'Even so…'

'Marnie, I'd love them to be somewhere local but I struggle to get across the corridor to pick them up as it is.'

'Of course.' She changed the subject. The child-care arrangements really had nothing to do with her after all. She just loathed the hospital being so much a part of their young worlds.

Except it wasn't her place to loathe it.

'You'll be tired, watching them all day,' Marnie said.

'I got a few hours' sleep last night,' Harry said. 'Anyway, I'm not working tonight.'

'No.'

'About tonight…' Harry turned to fill the kettle, trying to work out what to say. He'd hoped for a busy night so he wouldn't have had time to dwell on it. What had happened to the wild Harry of old, or even the not-so-wild Harry of late who would have loved a woman who didn't want to get serious…?

He loved this woman.

No.

He tore his head from that thought, told himself that he was just a bit infatuated, that was all. Intrigued perhaps. Or maybe it was just his ego because the one woman who didn't want him…

The one woman.

'I think the kettle's full,' Marnie said, as water gushed into the sink.

'Daddy!' Charlotte was delighted to see him. 'Morning, Marnie.'

'Morning, Charlotte.'

'Can we take the treat to the fairies today.'

'I'm off to work,' Marnie said.

'When you get home, then?'

'I'm away tonight,' Marnie said, but again didn't elaborate. 'I'd better get going.'

It wasn't even eight o'clock.

'See you, Marnie…' Charlotte was hanging by the door as Marnie put her jacket on, and Marnie gave Charlotte a lovely smile and a wave as she headed out the door, but it was clear to Harry that Charlotte wanted a kiss.

Yes, they all wanted more from Marnie.

She'd be gone on Monday, he told himself.

It would be a relief, because it was killing him to have her here yet not.

In bed at night.

But not his.

CHAPTER FOURTEEN

THE DAY WENT far faster for Marnie than it did for Harry.

While he was trying not to pace at home and trying not give any leeway to the mounting disquiet that churned every time he thought of her out on her date tonight, Marnie never got a moment to think till she was flying through the door to her home just before five.

She'd left work early for once and, incredibly organised, her overnight bag was already packed. Even as she undressed, Marnie had flicked on her heated rollers and turned on the taps.

Okay, she conceded as she pulled on a shower cap and hopped under the water, showers were good for some things—at least she didn't have to wait for a bath to fill.

And showers were good for other things too, Marnie thought dreamily, recalling Harry, his hands soaping her body.

Marnie didn't really do feelings and as for loyalty, she wasn't deep enough into anyone to demand such a thing—but her moral compass was spinning in circles as, turned on for Harry, she turned off the taps and did her best to get ready...

For Matthew.

Her hair she piled into rollers.

Her make-up she had down pat and she was soon painted and sitting on the edge of the bed, pulling on gorgeous underwear and stockings and then arranging her cleavage into a very lacy bra. She took out her dress and laid it out on the bed—it was a gorgeous deep navy in the softest velvet and had cost a small fortune.

Yes, all the things she could afford because she didn't have children, and it wasn't just the financial benefits Marnie was taking into account as she quickly dressed—there was time to stop and get her nails done, time to linger in the make-up department, splurge on the ballet and a night at The Langham without having to worry about babysitters.

She wanted this life, Marnie insisted to herself. But her hands were shaking and she tipped on far too much perfume.

She'd been desperate to go when she'd heard the ballet was on—especially as it was Declan's birthday next week. She'd known she'd want a night staring in the dark and just seeing beauty, and then sex for sex's sake at a beautiful five-star hotel with her friend with benefits. Matthew didn't even know about Declan—he'd made a brief comment when he'd seen the silvery lines on her stomach and she'd mumbled something about being a fat teenager.

Marnie pulled out her rollers and sorted her hair, smiled at her reflection because she looked like some high-class tart standing fully made up in her underwear.

She'd be pushing it to get to the hotel, so she dressed quickly, doing up the zipper and then putting on her shoes before transferring all she'd need from her handbag into her evening bag.

'Tickets might help,' she told herself, and unzipped the flap in her bag, and then Marnie stilled.

'Oh, no!'

She'd put them in her computer bag. Marnie remembered now but it didn't stop her from tipping out her handbag in the futile hope that they'd suddenly appear—that she wouldn't have to stop by at Harry's to get them.

It's tickets! Marnie told herself.

She was simply making a big deal of it.

If she rang and warned Harry that she was on her way, then she might not even have to see him; she could just let herself in, fly up the stairs and fly out.

It really was no big deal, Marnie told herself as she dialled Harry's number.

'Harry!' Marnie cringed at her own voice, it came out too jolly and bright. 'I just need to stop by and grab something…'

'Something?' The last thing he needed was to see her on her way out. What if that bloody Matthew was driving her? No, he didn't like the idea of Matthew sitting in the car outside, but how could he put it delicately? 'I think it might be a bit confusing for the children.'

'Confusing?' Marnie checked—was this man serious? 'Did your previous nannies not go out?'

'Of course they did. I meant—'

'So the children won't be confused,' Marnie said, snapping off the phone.

It was the adults who were confused.

Harry was making dinner when he heard her key in the door and her breezy call, and he just called out hi and carried on chopping.

'Marnie…' Adam shouted. 'Look.'

Adam, who never asked for attention, was asking for it now. She could see him standing in the living room, holding his lips open like a horse.

'Adam's tooth came out,' Charlotte informed Marnie. 'He was eating popcorn.'

Marnie walked down the hallway and looked at Adam's gap and said all the right things as Harry stood in the open kitchen, chopping away. He felt like the most boring person in the world. He should be wearing a cardigan and slippers, Harry thought to himself. He was doing his best not to look up as Charlotte chatted.

'So the fairies will come tonight…' She stopped talking long enough to take in Marnie in her very lovely velvet dress and very, very high-heeled shoes. 'Marnie! You look…' Charlotte turned round to her dad. 'Doesn't she look beautiful, Daddy?'

Harry had no choice but to look.

In a very dark navy—or was it black?—velvet dress, she had stockings on and high heels and her hair was curly and worn down, her cleavage was gleaming white and her lips were painted red. Harry took a moment to find his voice.

'Very nice.'

'Where are you going?' Adam asked.

'Just out.'

'Where?' Adam persisted.

'Adam!' Harry warned, and then he let Marnie know he knew *exactly* what was going on. 'Marnie's going to the ballet, aren't you, Marnie?'

'I want to go to the ballet,' Charlotte said. 'I'm going to start ballet, aren't I? Soon, Daddy—you said, didn't you?'

He could barely get them home for dinner on time, Harry thought—try adding in dance lessons too. Only it wasn't Charlotte's excitement and chatter that had him chopping and chopping, it wasn't that Marnie was going out and he was at home, and it wasn't her freedom. It was none of those things.

It was jealousy.

It was possessiveness that was filling his throat from the stomach up. A black jealousy that was as sickly and sweet and as potent as the perfume she had put on for *him*, Harry thought, shooting her a look that made Marnie turn and run.

As Marnie raced up the stairs to retrieve the tickets, Harry's possession seemed to chase her.

She stood in her bedroom, trying to get her breath for a moment—she didn't deserve that look!

She was looking after his kids, for God's sake, she wasn't his wife.

For Harry, the alarming thing was that it felt like it.

It felt, as he stood there pulverising the vegetables, as it might have felt if Jill had stood there dressed to the nines and wafting perfume. *I'm just going out to the ballet and for a shag afterwards, darling. Don't wait up!*

He was as angry and as defensive and as pissed off as he would have been had it been Jill clipping down the stairs. That meant something he didn't want it to mean, that it couldn't mean, because Marnie didn't want kids and family, she'd made that perfectly clear.

It was business to her.

It was supposed to be business to him—he was more than used to the nanny racing out the door on a Friday night, or their boyfriends dropping in.

He and Marnie had slept together *once*.

It was no big deal to him.

Usually.

'See you,' she called from the hall, and he heard the door open.

'See you,' he tried to call out, but the wrong words

came out. 'Could I have a word before you go?' Harry said. He nearly added, 'Young lady.'

He felt like her father as he strode down the hall.

He felt *nothing* like her father as he caught her arm and turned her round. 'Call me old-fashioned,' Harry said, 'but I'll tell you this much…I don't like this, Marnie.'

'Harry, I'm only here to help with—'

'I don't care,' Harry interrupted. 'I don't care if it's too much too soon, I don't care if you don't want to hear it, but…' He tried to stop himself, she was thirty-one, he could hardly tell her she'd be better be back here at a reasonable time, that if she slept with him…

His eyes did the talking and so did hers. Marnie was not a woman who liked to be told.

'I don't know where we're going, but there are certain things that you can't come back from,' Harry said. 'And this is one of them.'

'Oh, but it's all right for you.'

'No,' Harry said. 'You have every right to be as angry and as pissed off as I am right now if I…'

Marnie wrenched her arm from his and clipped out to the car.

Bloody men!

Sleep with them once and the next thing you know you're ironing for them, watching their kids. He'd be asking what was for dinner next!

Harry let out a few harsh breaths as he stood in the hall after she'd gone.

'Daddy?' called Charlotte.

He ignored it.

'Daddy!'

He tried to ignore it a second time.

'Daddy, what have you done to the potatoes?'

Harry walked back into the kitchen, saw the mountain of minced potatoes he'd produced and gave a wry grin as he came up with a suitable answer. 'They cook faster if they're small.'

Even Charlotte didn't seem convinced.

'Marnie looked pretty, didn't she?' Charlotte simply didn't let up. 'Is she going out with her boyfriend?'

'Charlotte.' It was Adam who fired Charlotte a warning. Perhaps it took another guy to get it, Harry thought.

What the hell was wrong with him—issuing warnings like that?

A few weeks ago, Marnie would have been the perfect woman—no strings, no commitment. Marnie had been everything he'd wanted in a woman.

He just didn't want that any more.

Marnie wasn't faring so well either.

The traffic was hell as she approached the city—there was a match on at the MCG and Marnie could cheerfully have turned round and headed for home, except she had the tickets.

She was angry with Harry for making such a big deal of things, but it felt like a big deal—she didn't want to see Matthew.

She didn't even want to see Harry.

Right now, Marnie wanted a night at home to curl up alone and try and sort out her feelings.

'Where are you?' Matthew rang and she told him she was running late and that rather than going to the hotel first she would meet him at the Arts Centre.

It was busy and there really wasn't much of a chance to talk. Marnie bought a programme and they ordered a drink and one for the interval, and then Matthew tried to make her smile. 'We could always skip the ballet and head straight to the hotel.'

And she took a breath and just said it. 'I think I might skip the hotel.'

'Marnie?'

'I need to be back by seven.' He just looked at her, nonplussed. 'I told you, I'm looking after a friend's children.'

'Who's the friend?'

'Just someone from work.'

'That was quick,' Matthew said, and Marnie sucked on her lemon. It was far sweeter than the conversation. She knew he was referring to how Marnie didn't exactly jump into friendships. 'I assume it's the doctor you were holed up in your office with.'

'Matthew, we agreed that we don't have to run every detail of our lives—'

'No, *you* decided that, you're the one who decides how much to give,' Matthew said, and Marnie could feel the people beside them briefly turn and then halt their conversations so they could listen to hers.

Matthew looked at her. 'The doctor wants a wife… Well, God help him, then,' Matthew said, 'and God help…' He halted then but Marnie knew what he'd been about to say and she challenged him.

'Meaning?'

'I never pictured you as a stepmother.'

'Oh, for the love of God.' Marnie rolled her eyes. 'I'm looking after his kids for a week.'

'Would you move in for a week to help look after mine?'

It wasn't really the time to point out that he didn't have any—even if the question was hypothetical, Marnie knew then the answer.

There'd be no Mary Poppins stopping at Matthew's door.

Even if she hadn't recognised it at the time, she had moved in because it was Harry.

When she said nothing, Matthew drained his drink. 'You're the coldest person I know, Marnie. The good doctor just hasn't worked it out yet.'

He left her standing there and Marnie wasn't about to follow.

She sipped on her drink as the bell went and people went through. She could just go home, Marnie realised, and have the evening alone she'd so desperately craved.

Shouldn't it hurt more? Marnie thought.

But it wasn't Matthew leaving that was hurting her now.

She wanted superficial. She wanted, for want of a word, relationships where it didn't feel as if you might die if the other person were to leave.

Yes, she wanted to go home, yet more than that she needed escape.

Marnie sat watching the ballet with an empty seat beside her, but not even the dancers held her mind for more than a moment. She wanted something she had never wanted before. It wasn't just Harry and giving things a go that scared her so—it was pink tights and Charlotte and the serious eyes of Adam and his wobbly tooth that had made her stomach curl, and her stomach only curled for family. Marnie was petrified—if she did try to make things work with Harry, she had to love them.

What if it didn't work?

She wouldn't lose one, she'd lose three, and Marnie truly didn't know if she could stand to lose like that again.

It was a wretched night, a long, lonely drive home,

and she was too upset to go to Harry's—she simply
didn't want him to see her as confused and raw as this.

She'd feel better in the morning, Marnie assured herself as she let herself into her own home and set her
alarm.

But she didn't.

'Hi.'

Harry couldn't even look at her as she let herself
in at six a.m. 'I was just up with Charlotte, she should
sleep for a couple more hours.' He was putting the medicine back in the cabinet and wearing only hipsters. He
hadn't expected her back just yet, but more worrying
than that was the effort needed to keep his voice normal, to somehow try and pretend that he hadn't said
what he had last night.

Clearly, given the hour, it hadn't mattered a jot. She
must have spent the night with him.

'I got a programme for Charlotte.'

'She'll love it.' Harry glanced up. There were the
smudges of last night's make-up under her eyes and her
hair was still curly, and his skin was alive and screaming for her, though his head denied that fact.

'About last night…' Marnie attempted. Usually she
could talk, usually she found it easy to say what was on
her mind, but in this she was utterly confused.

'I don't want to talk about last night,' Harry said. He
was doing everything he could not to think about it.

'Matthew said—'

'Oh, so you're going to stand there quoting him now!'

She didn't want to quote Matthew, she was trying
to tell him how scared she was, to warn Harry that he
might be making the most terrible mistake. Marnie truly
didn't know if she was capable of love. 'He said…the
doctor wants a wife, and if that's the case—'

'Believe me,' Harry swiftly broke in, 'if I was on the lookout for the perfect wife...' He stopped himself. Last night's anger hadn't been dimmed by sleep—Harry had barely had any. A night spent watching the clock, a night knowing she was out and with *him*, despite the fact that he'd told her they could never come back from that!

Yes, Harry was having trouble keeping this pleasant.

'Harry, please...' Marnie walked towards him. She had never wanted the feeling of somebody else's arms around her more. She had never wanted to halt a row more, and words were failing her this morning, so she attempted a more basic form of communication—one that had always worked till now. 'I don't want to argue.'

He could smell the remnants of last night's perfume as her hand moved to his chest. His mind put it more bluntly than he chose to voice, but as her mouth moved towards his, as much as he wanted that kiss, he really didn't know where she'd been.

'It's a bit much, Marnie.' He pushed her off. 'You know, I never thought I'd say this, but I think I'm over meaningless sex.'

She went to kiss him but he moved his cheek and then he put his blunt thoughts into words

'I don't know where you've been.'

It was no surprise that she slapped him.

CHAPTER FIFTEEN

MARNIE STRIPPED OFF and pulled on her pyjamas and lay there bristling with anger, wishing Harry would just go to work, but she could hear him downstairs on the phone and then the anger faded as realisation hit.

She hadn't told him.

In all her attempts to tell him how she was feeling, she hadn't told him the one thing that he'd needed to know.

She hadn't been with Matthew.

Marnie was half expecting it when she heard the creaking stairs and then heard him walking towards her room and a soft knock before he came in.

She wished he would just leave it, yet she was glad that he didn't.

'I'm sorry.'

He handed her a mug of tea.

And he'd left the bag in!

'You should be at work.'

'I rang Helen and said I'd be in late.'

'Why?'

'To apologise. I was jealous,' Harry admitted. 'It was jealousy speaking. Just pure and simple jealousy.'

'We'd had the tickets since before—'

'I know.'

'Nothing happened. Last night.'

'Marnie, you don't have to explain yourself to me—the thing is, you don't owe me anything. It's me who owes you. And the department,' Harry added. 'The lines got blurred. Well, they did for me and I loathe what I just said.'

'Matthew and I had words as soon as we got there,' Marnie said. 'I didn't even want to go but I had the tickets. He didn't even stay for the ballet…' Marnie gave him a small smile. 'Where's Juan when you need him?'

'Sorry?'

'Instead of rowing, I could have been having a shoulder massage,' Marnie said. 'He'd be far more understanding.'

'I'm not Juan,' Harry said, and he smiled at her.

'I'm glad.'

'Though I reckon even Juan's understanding might have been pushed to the limits last night.' He looked at Marnie all rumpled in bed and that was the trouble, he liked what he saw. As naturally as breathing, Marnie moved her legs as she took a drink of her tea and Harry sat down.

'I'm confused, Harry.' She was nothing but honest as she put her mug down. 'You're the last thing I want but also the only thing I want.'

'And I feel the same about you.' He gave a half-smile and she swallowed.

'I have to love your kids?'

'Marnie…' he looked at her '…no one is asking you to suddenly love anyone.' He didn't know how best to explain it. 'You're just so closed off…' He put his hand up to her cheek and his thumb smudged a bit of last night's eyeliner away. 'You've got me rearranging you now.' He was so gentle as he told her the bit that was hurting. 'You're wonderful with them, absolutely lovely…' Then he said it, because he could—they both managed to speak their truths. 'You're just as lovely as you'd be with any patient.' He watched the wetness of a single tear fall and slither beneath the pad of his thumb. 'I just wish you'd open up a bit.'

'I don't know how.'

'I know.'

'The deal was I just looked after them,' Marnie said. 'You were the one who didn't want them getting confused.'

'Yep,' Harry agreed, 'but that deal ends on Monday.' He watched her swallow. 'If you're ever here after that, you won't be sleeping in this room. You're not a fling, Marnie, that I'm going to hide from them.'

'I'll be your girlfriend?' Marnie tried to tease, waited for him to say, as she once had to him, that he was a bit old for that, but Harry wasn't joking now.

'Yes,' Harry said, and she saw his eyes drift briefly to his ring and he addressed it. 'We've both got things that we need to sort.'

And just when Harry thought she was considering the possibility of them being together, he felt her pull back, simply retract, and he *had* to reach her.

'We've slept together once, Harry.'

'Twice.'

'Well, technically twice…' Marnie started, but his mouth was on hers and he mumbled the word into hers.

'Twice.'

He kissed first her mouth and then her face. Marnie felt the scratch of his chin on her cheek and it was sublime. He moved to her neck and lifted her hair and nuzzled at the sensitive skin as he lifted her top.

'The children…' Marnie said, as he pulled her top over her head.

'They're asleep,' Harry said, 'and they'd never come in.'

'You've made sure of that!' Marnie said, trying to keep things light, but Harry refused to be drawn. He didn't want to joke; instead, interspersed with soft, deep kisses to her stomach, he was peeling her pyjamas down her hips and then sorting out the little clothing he wore. Then he joined her, face to face, both naked.

Not for the first time.

It just felt like it as he kissed her.

Slowly, deeply, he lingered, on her mouth, her neck, her breasts, as his hand crept lower, and she moaned as his fingers stroked her. She wanted him inside her, yet she was holding him as he stroked her, forgetting to kiss, forgetting everything except the bliss of his fingers and the feel of him in her hands.

'Please,' Marnie said, guiding him to her entrance and then remembering. 'We need—'

'Not yet.'

He stroked first with his fingers and then teased her with what she wanted. Harry's hand closed around hers, both stroking him till Marnie could only marvel at his control because she was coming, just from watching him and feeling the wet velvet strokes, but even as she came he was pressing her onto her back.

'Harry.' Marnie wanted her breath back, wanted to collect her thoughts, which seemed to be dancing in the air around the bed. She felt a flail of panic as she realised she was being made love to—and Marnie didn't do that. She wanted to halt him, to stop him, to remind him how casual they were, except right here, right now, they were not. Her legs parted to him and her eyes opened to him and he waited.

He waited till she could wait no more.

'I'm on the Pill.'

It was the second time in her life she'd got carried away, but this time it wasn't a mistake.

She heard the delicious moan of relief and want as Harry moved in but his eyes didn't close.

It wasn't the absence of a condom that rendered this unprotected sex—her heart was bare and stripped and the tears she had held back last night were there in her eyes, and there was anger too for somehow he exposed her.

'Crazy about you, Marnie.' He looked at her as he said it, and she pressed her lips tighter and swallowed back the words she wanted to say, for she *was* crazy about Harry.

It was sex, Marnie told herself—so why were her eyes closing and why was her mouth demanding his? Why was she now pinned beneath him, wrapped around him? She wanted to pierce the silent morning with a scream, but on the periphery she knew they were trying to be quiet. She could hear them building, could feel Harry's back sliding beneath her fingers, and then the moment of perfect acceleration as he drove her to the edge and joined her falling.

Marnie lay there afterwards, breathing in his scent, feeling his chin in her shoulder, and she should be jumping up as she had once, gripped with panic and guilt, but beauty laced with fear silenced her for a couple of moments.

'You're not being fair on Helen.'

'I know.' He rolled off her and smiled.

'Love me and leave me,' Marnie joked, but it was a

very dangerous joke and, perhaps wisely, Harry didn't answer.

She'd be out the dodgy windows if he did.

Instead, he gave her a small kiss and climbed out of bed and, of course, there were the practicalities to discuss.

'I'll be back by eight on Monday.'

'Are they going to day care?'

'Not sure,' Harry said. 'I'll give Evelyn a call over the weekend and let you know.'

'You'll call the twins?'

'Of course,' Harry said. 'They call me all the time when I'm on take.'

She'd never worked a weekend with him.

It was a little awkward as he went to go.

'Harry?'

He turned.

'Did you remember to be a fairy last night?'

'Amazingly—yes,' Harry said. 'A very grumpy fairy.'

He wasn't grumpy now.

Marnie lay in the bath after Harry had gone to work and thought about his words earlier about the way she was with the twins.

He hadn't offended her—Harry had spoken the truth.

Yes, this last week she had looked after the twins and had a nice time with them, looked after their itches and given them their medicine. Harry was right, she gave as much of herself to them as she would to a patient.

It was all she ever gave to anyone.

How, though?

How do you open up when you don't know how?

Marnie got out of the bath and, wrapped in her dressing gown, she headed to the bedroom to dress and put on her make-up.

Her uniform, Marnie realised.

Every morning she presented herself as neatly as she would for work.

This morning, though, the very meticulous Marnie pulled back on the pyjamas Harry had so firmly discarded, combed her hair and, instead of blasting it with the hairdryer, tied it back damp.

The children were still asleep so Marnie made herself a large mug of tea and some toast and, instead of unloading the dishwasher, went and sat down and tried to relax, though it wasn't long till she heard footsteps.

'Oh!' Charlotte blinked in surprise at the sight of Marnie in pyjamas, drinking tea and looking through her ballet programme.

'I got this for you,' Marnie said.

'For me?'

'Come and have a look,' Marnie said, and Charlotte climbed onto the sofa beside her and Marnie showed her the programme and they oohed and ahhed at the costumes until Adam appeared. He showed Marnie the money the fairy had left him and then turned on the TV to watch some cartoons.

'I'd give anything to have been a ballerina,' Marnie said, getting back to the programme, looking at the gorgeous costumes she had barely taken in last night.

'You could change jobs,' Charlotte suggested.

Marnie laughed at Charlotte's simplicity. 'I think I've left it a bit late.'

'Were you good at ballet?' Charlotte asked.

'I've never done it,' Marnie said. 'I did Irish dancing.'

'What's that?'

'Irish dancing,' Marnie said, as Charlotte sat there nonplussed, and then Marnie did something she never did, or hadn't in what felt like for ever. 'I'll show you.'

The sound of Charlotte laughing and Adam joining in too made Marnie dance faster.

'Stop.' Charlotte was standing on the couch, both crying and laughing; Adam was curled up, laughing too.

'I haven't got to the really fast bit yet.'

It was *their* day.

They made a tiny miniature feast for the fairies and had their own picnic in the living room—Marnie opened the French doors and let the sun stream in as they sat on a blanket and pretended they were in a field.

Harry rang that evening to say goodnight but Marnie made sure she was busy upstairs, blushing a bit at the memory of the morning, still feeling a little as if she was playing house.

'Can we put more food out for the fairies tomorrow?' Charlotte said, but Marnie shook her head.

'They'll be too fat to fly if we keep feeding them. Now, you get some sleep.' She gave Charlotte a smile and headed out of her room and then into Adam's.

''Night, Marnie.'

'Would you like a story?' Marnie said because, unlike Charlotte, Adam never really asked for anything, and she smiled when he nodded.

It was a slightly different version of the one she had told Charlotte, and her nieces and nephews and brothers, but it was lovely to see Adam smiling and asking questions, though not as many as Charlotte had.

'Are we going back to day care on Monday?'

'I think so.' Marnie smiled but it faded after she had turned out the light and closed the door and realised this could well be her second-last night at the house.

Charlotte had the same question the next day after lunch. As she seemed a little bit tired and tearful, Marnie had suggested she have a little sleep, but it had been met by scorn.

'I don't need a sleep.' She looked at Marnie and made a quick amendment. 'Though I still don't feel well,' she added hurriedly. 'When do we go back to day care?'

'I'm not sure,' Marnie admitted. 'I think Daddy was going to call Evelyn over the weekend.'

'I'm going to ring him,' Charlotte said, but was upset a few minutes later when she came back into the lounge. 'Daddy can't come to the phone.'

'He's just busy,' Marnie said, because she'd just been watching the news. There had been an emergency in the city and now a pile-up more locally. 'He'll call you back as soon as he can.'

Even though there was nothing she could do to help, Marnie still called Emergency and spoke with Kelly.

'We're a bit snowed under,' Kelly said. 'But we're coping. Thankfully it happened just after the late staff came on, so there were plenty of us.'

Yes, there were plenty of nurses but as Harry examined a potential spinal injury, he wished there were a few more consultants.

An eighteen-year-old who had got his driving licence on Friday had taken a friend out and met up another newly licensed friend.

And his friend!

Harry had seen it and heard it and dealt with it more times than he should be able to remember.

Yet he remembered each one.

The trauma team had taken the first driver straight to Theatre and Harry was dealing with the passenger, who, though conscious, was displaying worrying signs. 'Squeeze my hands,' Harry said, and the patient did so. 'Okay, try and lift your left leg…'

'I can't.'

'Okay. Can you wiggle your toes for me?'

'Harry!' He could hear Kelly calling him from behind the curtain. 'Harry, now, please!'

He needed two of him.

'You paged the second on trauma?' Harry checked with Miriam, who nodded. 'Fast-page them again,' Harry said, and quickly gave Sheldon some instructions.

'Harry!' Kelly was calling him again as he stepped in. 'He's not responding...'

'Carl!' Harry pinched the young man's ear; he had been talking just a few minutes ago when Harry had been called for the spinal injury. When pinching his ear failed to elicit a response Harry tried a sternal rub. 'Carl!' Harry ran his pen over the young man's nail bed and watched as he extended to pain.

'Start some mannitol,' Harry said, prescribing an IV solution to reduce intracranial pressure. 'Let's him round for an MRI.'

'Are you going with him?' Kelly checked, and just as Harry was coming to an impossible decision, just as he heard the roar of the storm become louder, a deep accented voice brought calm.

'Can I help?'

'Juan!'

'I heard on the radio that there had been a big accident. I thought you and Dr Vermont might need a hand.'

There wasn't time for conversation, let alone to break the terrible news. 'I've got a query spinal in the next curtain who I'm very concerned about...'

'I've got it.'

For Harry there was almost a feeling of dizziness—it was such a relief to know that Juan was back, that there was another consultant to share the load, to know that he didn't have to think about the young man in the next bed—he was getting the best of care from Juan. Harry could focus now on Carl.

The afternoon passed in a blur of MRIs and transfers, but later, as Juan returned from Theatre, where his patient had been taken for halo traction, he caught Harry as he came off the phone.

'So, is he playing golf?'

'Sorry?'

'Dr Vermont.' Juan rolled his eyes because Dr Vermont did love his golf at weekends, or rather had.

'Juan…' There was no one critical now, it was time to tell him properly before he heard it in passing. He asked Juan if he could have a word in his office and once there Harry closed the door. 'Dr Vermont passed away.' He saw the shock on his colleague's face. Even though Juan was fairly new to the department, it was still a terrible shock. 'He was doing a night shift and suffered a massive myocardial infarction.'

'Who was on?'

'Sheldon,' Harry said. 'And Eric was the cardiologist. They did everything they could, of course. He was having supper with Marnie in her office and just…' Harry shook his head and gave a weary shrug.

'Poor Marnie.'

'Yep,' Harry said. 'She got help, she did everything right, but there was nothing to be done.'

Juan was stunned. He asked about Marjorie. 'They were having their fortieth wedding anniversary.'

'They had it,' Harry said. 'It was after that.'

'So how have you managed?' Juan asked.

'Barely,' Harry said. 'Juan, there's something else I ought to tell you—I handed my notice in a few days before Dr Vermont died. The twins have both had chickenpox, something had to give. Oh....' he gave a wry laugh '...and my babysitter got shingles.'

'So you're leaving?'

'I don't know,' Harry admitted. 'Now that you're back, hopefully things will be better, but I need to put the children more to the front than the back of the queue. Speaking of which...' he grimaced when he saw the time '...I was supposed to call Charlotte.'

'Go home,' Juan said.

'You're not due back till tomorrow..'

'What did you just say about putting your priorities in order?' Juan checked. 'Go and spend the evening with your children.'

Harry smiled. It was so good to have Juan back. 'How was the wedding?'

'Amazing. I will tell you about it properly later. Right now I am going to call Cate and let her know I am here for the night.'

'Thanks.'

'Who's been helping with the children?' Juan asked.

'They've been here there and everywhere,' Harry said, which was in part the truth. It had only been since Marnie had stepped in that things had been so stable, but certainly Marnie didn't want anyone knowing she had temporarily moved in.

Temporarily.

Marnie was starting to sort out her case, and was just putting Declan's photo in when there was a knock at the front door and she opened it to a lady who introduced herself as Evelyn. 'Harry rang me last night and told me the twins had been sick.'

'I'm Marnie,' she said. 'A colleague of Harry's. I've been watching the twins over the weekend while he's been working.' It was easier than saying she'd been here for a week.

'Evelyn!' Charlotte came charging down the stairs.

'Charlotte! I've missed you so much!' Evelyn was so effusive and loving and the children ran to her. 'I was so upset to hear you'd got chickenpox.' As she hugged the twins Evelyn looked over to Marnie. 'If I'd known I was infectious, I'd have stayed well away.'

'They're fine,' Marnie said.

'Poor Harry, how on earth did he manage?'

'It's been a bit of a juggle but he got there.'

'Well, I can help now.' Evelyn was clearly at home here. While she chatted to Charlotte, who was filling her in on every detail of her spots, Evelyn was filling the kettle.

Charlotte was so thrilled to see her that when Marnie's phone rang, Charlotte barely looked over as Marnie excused herself and headed upstairs. She was feeling horribly rattled and suddenly entirely replaceable.

'Hi, Mum.' Marnie did her best to sound cheerful, not that Maureen appreciated the effort.

'I know you're busy, Marnie, but it's been more than a month since you visited.'

'I know, Mum.'

'Well, on Thursday Ronan has his hand appointment. I was thinking, your father and I could bring him and then, when you've finished work, we could go out for dinner.'

Was she serious? Thursday was Declan's birthday.

'Ronan said you liked the prawns at the pub—'

'Mum.'

'And your dad loves a nice steak.'

'Mum!' Marnie picked up Declan's photo from the case—did her mother really think she wanted to be sitting eating prawns and talking about the bloody weather? 'I've got plans that day.'

'I know you do, Marnie, but, I think it would be nice if we could all be together.'

'I told you, I'm busy.'

She turned off the phone and stared at Declan.

Her son.

Did her mum really think they could get through the night of his birthday not talking about him?

Avoiding his memory and the terrible hurt.

Guilt filled Marnie as she looked at a photo that had been placed in a drawer while she'd played houses, looking after someone else's children, telling fairy tales that, yes, she'd once told Declan, even if he'd been far too young to understand them.

A part of her knew her guilt was misplaced, but this was her hardest time. She wanted it to be the week after next when she was over the hurdle of Declan's birthday.

But a fortnight from then it would be the anniversary of his death.

It never entered her head she could share her pain.

Oh, God, tears were filling her eyes but, as she was fast finding out, there was no such thing as suitable quiet time with a house of four-year-olds. She could hear Charlotte racing up the stairs, calling her name.

'Marnie!'

'I'll be there in a minute.'

'Daddy's home!'

Marnie headed downstairs to find Charlotte telling Harry about their weekend as Evelyn looked on happily.

'The fairies came and ate the food we left them...'

'Wow!' Harry said, but she could see it was all a bit forced. Still, he made plans for tomorrow with Evelyn and once she was gone and Charlotte was upstairs, Harry let out a sigh of relief.

'How was it?' Marnie asked.

'Grim,' Harry admitted. 'Juan's there now. I can't tell you how good it felt to hand the lot over to him.' He glanced at the television that was on in the background, the news regaling them with details of the accident. 'Who'd have teenagers?' Harry said, and looked over at Adam as Marnie busied herself wiping the bench down, terrified she might break down, because right now she'd give anything to have one. 'I've got it all to come,' Harry said.

'We'll be good.' Adam smiled.

'That's what they all say!'

'Can you read me a story?' Charlotte was walking in with a book. 'Mummy, can you—?'

'Marnie!' She snapped a little more than she'd intended. 'It's Marnie,' she said again, and Charlotte's cheeks went very pink and she turned and ran off.

'Adam,' Harry said, 'go and help Charlotte choose a story and I'll be in.' As Adam walked off he turned to her. 'It was a simple mistake,' Harry said. 'She's four.'

'I know,' Marnie said. 'I just…' She couldn't explain it properly, the little reference to teenagers, hearing Charlotte call her Mummy—it hurt and it hurt and it hurt and she wanted the hurt to stop. 'I'm not going to have her call me Mummy and get all confused.'

'Sure.'

'Harry, I think I ought to go,' Marnie said, and Harry stood silent. 'I've got so much to do at home…'

She was back to being the babysitter and there was nothing Harry could do.

'Stay for dinner?'

'I'd rather not. I'm ready for home.' She gave him a tight smile. 'I'll go and speak to the children.'

She was terribly nice to them.

Harry stood at the door as she said goodbye to Charlotte and told her she was sorry for snapping.

'Some things make me sad.'

'Like what?'

'Like—' Marnie was as honest as she could be with a four-year-old '—I don't have children.'

'You said you didn't want babies.'

'Well, most of the time I feel like that,' Marnie said. 'Just not all the time.'

Harry hadn't seen her with the children over the weekend. He watched as she was very kind and very honest with the twins...but, yes, she held back. 'I'm going to go back to my house now,' Marnie said. 'Dr Juan starts tomorrow, your spots are all gone...'

'Will we see you again?'

'Of course!' Marnie said. 'I'm sure you'll be dropping in to the department.'

It wasn't what they wanted, though.

They got their first and last kiss from Marnie.

Just a brief one.

She didn't want them, Harry realised.

Which meant she didn't want him.

'Thank you.' Harry helped her take her stuff out to the car.

'It's been great,' Marnie said, and then she sent their relationship straight back to where it had started. 'Not that we'll be telling anyone at work about it.'

'Of course.'

'If I had an umbrella I'd put it up!'

He couldn't even smile at her pale joke.

'Next week,' Harry said, 'once Juan's back, I'd like to take you out to dinner to properly say thank you.'

'There's no need for that.'

No, she could not have made it clearer.

'I really am grateful,' Harry said, remembering the reason Marnie had been there.

The only reason.

Work.

'We got through it,' he said.

'We did!' Marnie smiled. 'Two consultants and another soon starting! We'll be back on track in no time.'

CHAPTER SIXTEEN

IT REALLY WAS business as usual.

At work at least.

The house had been as cold as a morgue after she'd gone.

It was strange, because there were always nannies and aunts and people coming and going, but without Marnie it felt like some sinkhole had opened up and plunged them back into darkness.

'I love Marnie…' Charlotte was crying.

'Charlotte!' He'd been about to tell her she was too dramatic, but she did love her, Harry realised, and Adam did too, because Harry could hear him crying in his bedroom. 'Marnie adores you.'

'Then why isn't she here?'

It was one question he couldn't answer.

He wanted to remind the twins she'd only been there for a few days, yet by the end of a week without Marnie—near midnight on the Sunday night—Harry had done what he'd thought he'd never be ready to do and taken his ring off.

He loved Jill so much but it felt wrong to be wearing it when he was mourning someone else.

All he knew now was that being in bed with Marnie was amazing, but more than that, when she laughed,

when she smiled, or when her honesty was so breath-
taking your biscuit snapped in mid-dunk, Harry wanted
more.

But Marnie didn't want intimacy.

Marnie didn't want them.

You had to admire her really.

Harry sat at work, late afternoon on the Wednes-
day, trying to write, trying not to turn to the sound of
her voice.

'Did you forget how to use surgical taps when you
were on your honeymoon?' Like a hawk swooping, she
was off her stool and straight onto Juan. 'I'll remind you
how to use them, Juan.'

'Marnie, I'm not about to see a patient…'

'It's about good habits,' Marnie said. 'Which means
if you use the surgical sink then you're to use it as such
and turn it off with your elbows.' She was demonstrating again and Juan was grinning.

'Show me again, Marnie,' Juan said.

Harry could stand it no longer and anyway he had
somewhere he needed to be. In an attempt to cheer Charlotte he'd rung up about ballet lessons and she had her
first one at five. 'Got to go,' Harry said.

'Before you do I need you to witness my signature.'
Juan had an interview with Immigration the next day
about getting permanent residence in Australia. 'For
the immigration forms…'

'No problem,' Harry said. 'I need to get Charlotte
changed here anyway. I'll just go and get them and, if
you can have everything ready, I'll sign them on my
way out.'

Marnie didn't hide in her office, neither did she disappear, but she was glad she was with a patient as she

heard Charlotte's excited chatter from behind a curtain a little later.

'I want to show Marnie.'

'She's busy,' Harry said. 'Come on.'

'But I want her to see—'

'We'll be late,' Harry said.

She waited just a moment before walking out, relieved that they'd gone, but then Harry dashed back.

'You've pocketed my pen,' Harry said to Juan, who was always borrowing things and forgetting to give them back. 'I was just—'

'Marnie!' Charlotte was running behind him. 'Look!'

She had on pink ballet tights and a pink headband and she looked so gorgeous and excited that Marnie wanted to drop to her knees. She wanted to tuck in her curls under the headband and to tie her cardigan properly, because Harry's attempt at a bow was already unravelling, but she just stood and smiled as Charlotte spoke. 'I've got my first ballet lesson.'

'Good toes, naughty toes,' Marnie said. 'Have a wonderful time.'

She said everything right, Harry thought, and she smiled as she did, but it was like watching the security screen shoot up at the bank, he thought as Marnie stepped forward then halted.

'Come on, Charlotte,' Harry said. 'You don't want to be late.'

Marnie stood watching as Harry took his children's hands and walked off, and he didn't look back—his priority was his children.

No matter the cost.

She felt Juan watching her and turned quickly, taking out an alcohol wipe to clean down the bench. 'That'll be you before you know it,' Marnie said, trying to make conversation, embarrassed to have been caught watching Harry and the twins. 'Dashing off to take your little ones to their activities.'

'I hope so,' Juan said, and got back to his work. Marnie just stood there cleaning, hating how easy and honest his answer had been—that Juan could admit his hopes for the future, that he wasn't whipping out an alcohol wipe and cleaning something that didn't even need to be cleaned.

'Marnie—' Juan started, perhaps sensing her sudden distress.

'Don't!' Marnie snapped, and walked briskly to her office. She didn't want Juan waving his fairy dust on her and giving her one of his, oh, so meaningful talks.

Oh, she couldn't deal with this today.

Or tomorrow.

Especially tomorrow.

CHAPTER SEVENTEEN

'Hi, Juan!' Charlotte was still practising her dance moves when Juan arrived unexpectedly. She was sitting on the floor and doing good toes, naughty toes.

'Marnie said that's what we'd do!' she said to Harry, and Juan saw his colleague's jaw tense and knew that he was right.

'Sorry to drop in,' Juan said. 'I messed up the form.'

'It looked fine to me.'

'I had to do it again.'

Harry wasn't in the mood for conversation, though Juan was chatting about work—Helen was covering tonight and considering a permanent position. He witnessed Juan's signature again but tensed when he still hung around. 'I'd invite you for dinner but it's nuggets and tinned spaghetti…' As he served up dinner, Harry turned briefly to Juan. 'Don't you have a new wife to get home to? You're barely back from your honeymoon.'

'At least we had one. I hear Marnie was going to ring and try to haul me back.'

Her name was everywhere.

'Yes, well, it worked out without her having to.'

'She wouldn't have had much luck, anyway.' Juan shrugged. 'I turned off my phone.'

'Wouldn't that be nice?' Harry said, taking the children's dinner over and calling them to the table.

'How did you manage?' Juan, oh, so casually asked.

'Marnie looked after us,' Charlotte said, as Harry poured the twins drinks.

Harry's smile was wry as he ruffled Charlotte's hair.

'I'll see you out,' Harry said. He needed to be on his own with his children right now.

'Harry,' Juan said. Since his return he'd been worried about Harry. Juan had thought it was grief and from the look of his friend it was, yet it wasn't just Dr Vermont he was grieving for. 'If you want to talk—'

'I don't,' Harry broke in, though he'd love to open up to someone who had been out there a bit more recently, to discuss how the hell this friends-with-benefits thing worked, or just the hell of loving someone who didn't want love.

Yes, he loved her.

And because he loved her, he knew Marnie would loathe it to be discussed. She would hate Juan, and therefore Cate, knowing what had briefly gone on between them.

So he said nothing—he just wished Juan good luck with Immigration tomorrow.

'I should be back by midday.'

'No problem,' Harry said.

He was glad that everyone wasn't rushing to get to the department, that finally there was some calm to the place.

Just not to his heart.

'What time's hand clinic?' Kelly asked.

'Three,' Harry answered.

'I'm going to go and set up while it's quiet.'

Harry said nothing. He was past multi-tasking—just filling out a doctor's letter was taking all his concentration. Marnie was holed up in her office and Harry would love to do the same, except Juan wasn't back yet from Immigration.

'I'm here to see Marnie Johnson.' Harry glanced up as Kelly asked a man in a suit if she could help him.

Perhaps it was one of her brothers, Harry attempted, but he didn't have an Irish accent.

It had nothing to do with him, Harry told himself and carried on writing as Kelly buzzed Marnie and she came through to the department.

'Craig.' He heard Marnie's voice and deliberately didn't look up. 'I said to text when you were here and I'd meet you outside. Kelly, I'm going to be away from the department for my lunch break.'

Now, as she walked away, Harry did look up.

There was a wedding ring on Craig's finger. Harry could see it as he put his arm around Marnie's shoulders, but unlike with Matthew she didn't wriggle away.

Instead, Harry watched as her hand moved up to catch his.

Did she have to rub his face in it? Harry thought.

Was she so cold she could nip off to lunch with a married man and not care who knew?

Even him?

Yes.

It got worse as he took his lunch break.

'Guess who got picked up by a man and has now rung in with a sudden migraine?' Kelly smirked as she plonked herself down and opened her sandwich.

'Oh, but she'd have something to say if we did it,' Abby bristled.

But there was no Dr Vermont to say 'Ladies,' so Harry had to sit through it.

It was a relief to go back to work.

For ten minutes.

'Ronan.' Harry forced a smile as yet another reminder of Marnie came through. 'How are you?'

'Nervous,' Ronan admitted, as Harry carefully took the splint off and examined his finger for sensation.

'I couldn't be happier with it,' Harry said. 'It's going to take time to get back full range and function...'

'I know.'

'But for now everything looks better than I'd expected. Keep the splint on and I'll see you again in two weeks, but you can start now with the hand therapist.' He couldn't not mention her. 'Marnie is—'

'Oh, no, don't disturb her,' Ronan interrupted and shook his head and Harry frowned because it sounded as if Ronan was avoiding her.

'I was just about to say I'd let her know you were here, but she's actually off sick.'

'Okay.' Ronan stood and, although he was usually articulate and friendly, he didn't express concern or say that he knew; instead, he was suddenly awkward and Harry watched as Ronan shrugged and blushed and then shook Harry's hand.

Harry knew.

He knew then what day it was today—the day the Johnsons always avoided each other, the day that no one could discuss.

'Don't bring the next one in.' Harry halted Kelly and buzzed through to the main section. 'Is Juan back yet?'

'He's just getting something to eat before he starts,' Miriam answered, but Harry had other ideas.

He found him in the kitchen.

'Juan, can you take over hand clinic? I need to go.'

'Now?'

'Now.'

He just walked away from hand clinic, from Emergency, from all of it, without a backward glance and went to his car.

He drove to her street. If there was a car outside then he'd just keep going and come back later, but he guessed that there wouldn't be—Harry knew she would get through it and then want to be alone.

She didn't have to be.

That much he knew.

'Marnie...' He knocked and she didn't answer, so he knocked again. 'I'm not going till you open the door.'

'Make yourself comfortable on the doorstep,' came the smart answer.

'I know that it's Declan's birthday.'

There was no movement for a moment but then the door opened. Marnie looked as if she did have a migraine. Her already pale face was a chalky white and her eyes were glittering more with pain than tears.

'I don't talk about it.'

'But you can.'

He took her in his arms.

'I don't know how to,' she admitted, because it was easier to sob into a phone to Siobhan and then end the call when it got too hard.

'We'll work it out.'

'I've just been to the cemetery,' Marnie explained. 'I couldn't face coming back to work. Craig, that's his father, well, we don't go every year, sometimes he's away with work, but this year we went together. His wife's pregnant with their third...' She looked up at Harry.

'I am pleased for him and there's nothing like that between us, it's just...'

'Hard?'

'Not all the time,' Marnie admitted, 'but this birthday has been a bad one. He'd have been a teenager today.'

'I'm so sorry.' He still held her in his arms.

'I'd have a thirteen-year-old and be dealing with acne and rebellion and dirty bedrooms.' She leant on him. 'I want him to be thirteen.'

'I know.'

Harry did know. He knew about impossible wishes and guilt, because if his wish for Jill had come true, then he wouldn't be here with Marnie.

But he wanted to be here.

Especially now that she let him be.

She cried and she cried and he held her and then she cried for other things.

'I'm sorry I snapped at Charlotte.'

'Forget it.'

'I can't.'

'She loves you. Adam loves you.' He looked at her. 'I love you.'

'I'm so scared,' Marnie said. 'I'm so scared to fall in love and to love and—'

'You don't have a choice,' Harry said. 'In case you hadn't noticed, love doesn't let you choose. If it did, you'd be an amazing cook, a stay-at-home kind of woman...'

'You'd be bored.'

'I know.' Harry smiled. 'And you wouldn't have chosen a single father.'

'How do you know that?'

'You told me,' Harry said. 'Several times.'

'I didn't choose a single father,' Marnie said. 'I

chose you and your children...' She thought of Adam so guarded and Charlotte so dazzling. 'They chose me.'

And on a day when she ached for her own son, there was room too for his, because a while later she found herself talking about another child who had wormed his way to her heart. 'Adam doesn't have a speech problem,' Marnie said, as she drank yet another mug of tea that Harry had made her. 'He's got the same problem that Ronan had—an older sister who says everything for him.'

'Perhaps.'

'No perhaps about it,' Marnie said, and just as she was almost smiling, Harry changed her world.

'Come home.'

'Not like this.' Marnie crumpled, terrified at the final hurdle. 'I can't go there all sad.' She used his trump card. 'It will confuse them.'

'Do you think they've never been sad?' Harry asked.

'Of course they have.'

'So let us take care of you today.'

Marnie didn't know how to have her heart taken care of, Harry realised. She was an expert in every department but that one.

He packed her overnight bag and led her to his car, and in no time they were back at Harry's.

'You can't tell them about Declan...'

'Come on.' Harry took her hand and led her up the path and he saw their little worried faces as Marnie came in and it was clear that she had been crying.

'Hi.' Marnie stood there shy and awkward as Harry had a word to Evelyn, who made herself scarce.

'I'll be over in the morning,' Evelyn called.

'Thanks, Evelyn,' Harry said, and then led Marnie to the lounge.

'Okay.' He looked at the twins. 'You know how you feel sad about Mum sometimes?'

Charlotte nodded.

'How I feel sad sometimes?' Harry checked. 'Well, that's how Marnie feels today. I'm going to go and run her a bath and then make something to eat, so for now can you guys look after her?'

He left them to it.

'Sorry I was mean, Charlotte,' Marnie said.

'That's okay,' Charlotte said.

'You can call me whatever you want,' Marnie said. 'Well, so long as you remember Miss Manners.' She smiled and so too did Charlotte, but then Marnie stopped smiling and she wanted to turn and run because tears were threatening, but instead of running she sat down.

There was one good thing about grief, they knew what to do. Adam climbed on her knee and hugged her and she hugged him back and buried her face in his hair and just held him.

'Sorry,' Marnie said as she started to cry.

'Don't be sorry,' Charlotte said, and cuddled her too, and the twins were like little grown-ups and babies at the same time; they had been through so much and therefore could give so much.

Harry came in a little while later to find his three favourite people all cuddled in on the couch.

'Your bath's ready.' He took her hand and led her up the stairs and told the twins to wait there. Harry was so careful not to flaunt anything in front of the children but as natural as breathing he led Marnie up to the bathroom. There were bubbles and towels and not a hint of anything but love in the room as he helped her out of her clothes and into the warm bath and then left her.

'Is she okay?' Adam checked.

'She will be,' Harry said, and they headed to the kitchen to sort out something for Marnie to eat.

'Did her husband die?' Adam asked, as they loaded a tray.

'No,' Harry said.

'Her baby died,' Charlotte whispered. She was far too wise. 'I saw the photo…'

'Yes,' Harry said. 'Marnie's baby died a long time ago but it still hurts. Today would have been Declan's birthday.'

'We could make him a cake.'

'Charlotte!' Harry warned, and then almost dropped the kettle when he heard Marnie's voice and realised that she must have heard that little gem. 'She didn't mean—'

'It's fine.' Marnie smiled and gave a very worried-looking Charlotte a hug. 'It's a lovely thought but right now I'm so tired.'

'Go to bed,' Harry said. 'We'll bring this up.'

They headed upstairs together and Marnie went to turn left for her old bedroom, because surely it was too soon to do otherwise?

But it wasn't too soon. It was now.

'This way,' Harry said, and she stepped into her new bedroom. And was there any nicer way to be installed in your new bed than to have a very excited Charlotte pulling back the cover and Adam waiting with a tray? It was normal, it was natural, and it was the nicest way it could have happened.

'Okay,' Harry said, sending the twins away and pulling the curtains and putting on the bedside lamp. 'Have something to eat and a rest.' He looked at her glittering eyes and it was a relief to sit down on the bed and to take one beautiful hand in his and hold it as he perhaps said the entirely wrong thing.

'Why don't you ring your mum?' He held on tight to her hand as she pulled away. 'You need your mum.'

And her mum needed her too.

'My battery's flat.'

'There's a phone by the bed.'

An hour or so later Harry had got the children to bed when he heard the click of the phone, and then he heard the tears and the murmurs of conversation as Maureen got her wish.

'If I could take back one day in my life...' Maureen said. 'I know you can never forgive me.'

Marnie closed her eyes but not in anger.

'I do, though,' Marnie said. 'I know you were just angry.'

'I'd have loved him, though, Marnie. I was so cross but I'd bought a little coat for him and I was looking at cots. I was brought up in a world where the worst thing was your daughter getting pregnant, but it wasn't the worse thing, it was losing Declan and losing you...'

'I'm here, Mum.'

'I'm proud of you, Marnie. I know I didn't act as if I was then. Have you been to the cemetery?'

'With Craig,' Marnie said.

Yes, Marnie had chosen well.

She had a son.

He had a father—that foolish mistake wasn't so foolish all these years on.

That Declan was buried in Australia had been the only thing that had kept her here at times, but now, finally, she knew the reason she was here. Finally she felt at home.

'Let me come over. I don't want you to be on your own.' Gushing in, high on maternal waves, Maureen wanted to be with her child, but when Marnie said no, this time it wasn't because she was avoiding her.

'I'm with someone, Mum.'

'Craig?'

'No.' She looked around the bedroom, a room she'd never so much as kissed Harry in, but she could feel the love.

'His name's Harry and he's got twins.'

'Twins!'

'Their names and Charlotte and Adam,' Marnie said. 'You'll get to meet them soon. Harry's a consultant where I work.'

Maureen sat silent for a moment as Marnie opened the doors to all the separate compartments of her life and finally let her mother in.

'It sounds as if the two of you are serious.'

She wasn't serious, though.

Marnie was happy.

As he crept in the room later, trying not to disturb her, Marnie watched as he undressed, and then Harry saw the glitter of her eyes in the darkness. 'You're awake!'

'Very.'

Oh, it was lovely to feel him climb into bed and lie there beside her, and Harry lay wondering what to say to her.

Or if they might…

No, not tonight, Harry told himself.

'Are you just going to lie there?' Marnie asked, and Harry found himself laughing. 'I told my mother we were serious,' Marnie warned him, 'so you'll have to marry me now.'

'Done.'

'On one condition.' They turned to face each other. 'We're keeping this house.'

'Marnie,' Harry warned, 'we'll be buried under renovations.'

'I don't care.'

'Can we talk about this another time?' Harry said, because their legs were twining around each other's.

'I like to know what's happening,' Marnie said. 'I like things organised.'

And he knew then he had her for ever.

'Yes, Marnie, we'll keep the house.' Harry smiled as he kissed her.

Marnie had found her home.

EPILOGUE

'I SWEAR THAT she is.'

Kelly took off her shoes and stretched her feet. 'Her dress is too tight and she never takes that jacket off.'

Harry just smiled to himself and carried on watching the television.

'Her boobs are bigger,' Kelly went on. '*And* she's being nice. I've got the next four Saturdays off.'

'Marnie doesn't do nice,' Abby grumbled, because Marnie had just given her a long talking to about being consistently late, which, of course, Marnie never was.

Not once.

'She's so cold that if she is pregnant she'll lay her eggs in a river—'

'Hey!' Juan said, because Juan liked Marnie and the way she ran the place.

Harry just smiled.

Juan had an inkling but the rest of them had no clue, and that was the way Marnie had wanted it. She was determined to prove, before everyone found out, that they could work together and argue and clash at times, and Harry certainly got no favours.

At work.

Marnie was twenty weeks pregnant, and everything was going perfectly. The children were besotted with her and called her Marmie—a mixture of Mummy and Marnie—and it was their own in-joke. Marnie had found a day-care centre near their home rather than in the hospital. It was one Evelyn could walk to if Harry or Marnie couldn't get there, but that happened rarely. Marnie took her management days at home and the occasional sick day too, and somehow they had a routine and the children were absolutely thriving

Charlotte was doing ballet; Adam was desperate to be an older brother. They had put in an offer on the house, even though it needed a demolition ball. Marnie had listed every single thing that needed repairing and read off the list to a very weary Dave, several times, until finally their offer was accepted.

Marnie came in and opened her salad and stirred in the dressing, just as she always did.

She was still slim, but even with her jacket on it was getting more obvious with each passing day and she really needed to speak to Cate about filling in for her when she went on maternity leave.

'I'm sure you've all heard the rumours,' Marnie said, and Kelly gave a triumphant eye-raise. 'And they're correct. I'm getting married next Saturday.'

'Marnie!' Juan came over and Marnie stood as he gave her a kiss to congratulate her, and so too did his wife, Cate.

'Oh!' Cate looked at the engagement ring on Marnie's finger. 'That's beautiful.'

'I know,' Marnie said. 'I'm just wearing it to show you. I'll be taking it off at the end of lunch break.'

Cate suppressed a smile. Marnie *loathed* anything other than the simplest of jewellery, lest there be a germ beneath it.

Marnie looked down at her beautiful hand and even

more beautiful ring, and it made her so happy that she couldn't help smiling.

'And, yes…' her cheeks were a bit pink as she told her colleagues what they probably already knew '…I'm expecting.'

'I'm thrilled for you, Marnie,' Juan said.

'I'm thrilled for myself,' Marnie said. 'Now, it's just a small wedding, well, as small as it can be with my massive family, but you're all very welcome to come—all very informal but there'll be a good party after.'

'I didn't know you were seeing anyone,' Abby fished.

'I don't bring my personal life to work,' Marnie said.

'Will you be changing your name?' Kelly asked.

'No.' Marnie shook her head. 'It would be too confusing.'

'Confusing?'

'Marnie Worthington,' she said. 'I think having the consultant and the manager with the same surname…'

'You mean…?' They all looked at Harry, who smiled back at them, and although they never usually showed affection at work, in this instance, he reached out and pulled his soon-to-be wife onto his knee.

'I'm very disappointed in all of you,' Harry said. 'I can't believe that you didn't work it out sooner.'

Harry watched as Abby's cheeks went purple as she remembered her little reptilian comment earlier, but he just smiled back at her.

Harry couldn't stop smiling.

He loved it that no one could quite work out Marnie, not even he at times.

But he'd spend the rest of his life trying.

'Harry?' Juan went over, his smile never wider, and,

because it was Juan, he wrapped Harry and Marnie in a hug. 'This is wonderful, unexpected, amazing…'

'I know,' Harry said. 'Like Marnie.'

* * * * *

BREAKING THE PLAYBOY'S RULES

EMILY FORBES

For my Mum, Barbara, and my mother-in-law, Tess, both of whom dreamt of working on outback stations- it's not too late!

And for Michelle, an English ex-pat, who came to Australia on a working visa, fell in love and now lives on a cattle station on the Cooper Creek in outback Queensland with Jon and their four boys, including my godson, Keegan.

CHAPTER ONE

Emma!
When are you coming to visit? You know I'm seri-
ous—I'm actually taking time to sit down and write!!!

Use some of your inheritance and get your butt
on a plane. You can hang in Sydney with the olds
until you get over your jet lag and then fly out to me.
You'll love it out here—remember when we were
teenagers and you loved everything Australian? Do
you remember watching that television series about
the flying doctors? (How could you forget—you took
all the videos back to England with you☺!) Well, this
is where the real ones are! Come on, you HAVE to
come and visit.

I promise you, the minute you see the Outback
and I introduce you to some real Aussie men you'll
forget all your worries. It'll give you a chance to get
some distance and perspective and get what's-his-
name OUT OF YOUR SYSTEM!!!!

Don't think about it, Em, just do it!
See you soon,
Love, Soph xx

SOPHIE's letter read exactly the way she talked and lived.
Her words, like her speech, were peppered with exclama-

tion marks. Everything she did she did quickly and with passion. She never seemed to stop and her enthusiasm had been the prompt that had got Emma on this plane. Without Sophie's cajoling Emma knew she'd still be sitting in England, feeling depressed and wondering if she could really make this trip on her own. Without Sophie's insistence she might not have booked her ticket. But now she was almost there.

Emma folded the letter and slid it back into its envelope, taking care not to tear the paper. She'd read it every day for the past month and it was beginning to show signs of wear but even though she knew the words verbatim she couldn't bring herself to put it away permanently.

Sophie's letter wasn't the reason she'd packed her bags and said farewell to her stepmother and half-sisters in order to fly halfway around the world but it had been the catalyst. Emma needed the letter. It was her anchor. It kept her tethered to reality. It helped to make this whole adventure seem real—even when she could scarcely believe she had actually made it Down Under.

Thinking back to the events that had led her here was upsetting so she focussed again on the landscape beneath her as she tried to think of happier, more positive things. But as she looked out the window at this strange land she felt a trace of unease. She'd had a few moments of trepidation over the past month, although not as many as most people seemed to expect her to have, but looking at the vast, dry, red land beneath the plane's wings she questioned the wisdom of leaving the familiarity of England to fly to the middle of nowhere.

But you were miserable in England, she reminded herself.

Yes, but you might still be miserable here.

At this point she wasn't sure which was preferable—

being miserable in familiar surroundings or being miserable in a strange, new world. She hoped Sophie was right and a change of scenery would keep her too occupied to notice she was miserable. Sophie had promised her that it was hard to be depressed in a place where the sun was almost always shining, and because Emma had long wanted to come back to Australia she chose to believe her. And now she was here. Almost.

As Emma felt the plane start to descend she slipped the envelope between the pages of the novel she was reading and stowed it in her handbag. She took a deep breath. It was too late to turn back now. She let her breath out with a long sigh.

'Are you okay?'

It took Emma a moment to realise the girl in the seat beside her was talking to her. And another moment to realise she was asking because she'd sighed out loud.

She turned to face her. They hadn't spoken to each other during the flight; they'd smiled a greeting when they'd first sat down but then Emma had pulled her book from her bag and started reading. She didn't like striking up conversations with fellow travellers as there was always the danger that they'd talk non-stop for the entire trip and Emma then found it difficult to politely excuse herself from the contact. But looking at her now she wondered if she'd seemed rude. The girl was about the same age as her, in her mid-twenties, and she did look genuinely concerned.

'Yes, I'm fine, thanks,' she replied. 'Just thinking.'

'You're English?'

Emma nodded.

'Are you here on holiday or for work?'

Emma wasn't really sure how to describe her visit. She wanted to make herself believe it was a holiday, although it felt more like an escape. She knew she was running away from her old life, just temporarily, but she didn't want to admit that out loud. Not to a stranger, not even to herself. 'I'm visiting family,' she said. That was the truth, even if it wasn't the whole truth.

'Are you staying long?'

'I'm not sure yet,' she replied. She hadn't planned any further ahead than getting to Broken Hill. Her life tended to move in cycles and she'd found, on more than one occasion, that things seemed to happen without her input. Sometimes she was happy with the way events unfolded, sometimes not, but she had always had a sense that there were some things she couldn't control so sometimes she didn't bother trying. More often than not, too, her plans, when she did make them, went awry so she avoided making them whenever she could. Right now her only goal was to get to Broken Hill. Once she was there there'd be time enough to work out what she was going to do next.

Emma was certain the girl beside her was going to continue the conversation but she was too caught up in her own thoughts to find the energy to chat to a complete stranger. She turned back to look out of the window as the noise of the plane's engines changed. She searched for signs of life beneath the wings in the red dirt.

Where was the town? The pilot was obviously planning to land somewhere but as far as she could tell only miles and miles of nothing lay beyond the windows. When she'd visited Australia before she'd never travelled away from the coast and the landscape beyond the plane window looked so alien.

The country wasn't completely flat. She could see undulations in the earth, but from this height she only got a sense of their size from the shadows they cast onto the red dirt. There wasn't a speck of green to be seen—even the trees and bushes looked faded and grey. They'd long since left the ocean and the mountains west of Sydney behind and the world she was entering now looked untamed and hostile.

The land was vast and barren and it looked as though it could swallow people. It was no stretch of the imagination to think of people disappearing out here in the back of beyond, never to be seen again. Was she going to survive this?

A sudden wave of homesickness swept through her and the feeling took her by surprise. Although she'd been born and bred in England she'd always longed to really experience the Australian way of life. After all, she was half-Australian, and this was her chance to really immerse herself in the culture, her chance to experience life here as an adult as opposed to the self-absorbed teenager she'd been when she'd last visited.

As a teenager she'd existed on a diet of Australian television, everything from suburban settings to beachside settings to the Outback, but now it seemed that fantasising about the Australian Outback was one thing; actually experiencing it might be something else entirely.

She hoped this trip would give her a chance to heal, a chance to recover from what had been a terrible twelve months and a chance to work out what made her happy, but looking at this foreign landscape she was beginning to think that she might not find the answers here at all. It might take all her strength just to survive. She hoped coming here wasn't going to turn out to be a mistake.

The plane continued to drop lower in the sky and Emma felt the undercarriage of the plane open as the pilot prepared to lower the wheels, but a minute later the plane was levelling out and she heard the flaps close again. She looked out of the window at the red dirt and the green-ish-grey, almost leafless trees and stunted bushes. They weren't getting any closer.

The plane's undercarriage opened a second time, before closing again just as rapidly. Emma frowned and watched as the plane began to circle. As the plane turned she could see the airport buildings below them. At least she knew now that there was civilisation out here. That was comforting. But the next words she heard, however, were not.

'Ladies and gentlemen...' The pilot's voice came through the plane's audio system. 'Due to an unforeseen technical problem with the landing gear, I would like to inform you that we will be carrying out an emergency landing.' He paused momentarily and there was complete silence in the plane as every passenger waited to hear what he had to say next.

'However, there is no need to be alarmed. Please remain in your seats with your seat belts tightly fastened. Your cabin crew will pass through the cabin, demonstrating the brace position and landing procedures.'

His tone suggested this was more of an inconvenience than a problem but Emma did wonder how he intended to land the plane. She could only assume he'd been trained for this sort of thing. In her experience pilots were trained for all sorts of emergencies but the pilots she knew flew for the air force, and she had no idea what experience pilots in Outback Australia had. Surely they'd have to return to Sydney? But even as she waited for the pilot to make that announcement she realised it was ridiculous.

Returning to Sydney wouldn't miraculously resolve the problem. The landing gear would still be stuck. It couldn't be fixed in mid-air. So what was he going to do? They couldn't fly around indefinitely. At some stage they'd run out of fuel and then they'd drop out of the sky.

As her fellow passengers also put two and two together

she could feel fear building up around her. Like a living breathing presence in the air it moved from one person to the next, wrapping its icy tentacles around each and every one of them, binding them together in a potential tragedy.

Everyone was silent. Were they thinking about crashing or were they too terrified to utter a sound? Whatever the reason for the silence it was there and it was complete and there was nothing to distract anyone from the pilot's next words.

'This is going to make landing difficult but not impossible. The airport has a dirt landing strip, which we can use in this situation, but I ask you all to assume the crash position as directed by our cabin crew.'

His last sentence succeeded in breaking the silence. There was yelling, there were tears and there was screaming. It seemed as though everyone had found their voices at once and the cabin reverberated with noise. Emma's heart leapt in her chest and she felt it seem to lodge at the base of her throat. Nausea filled the empty space in her ribcage where moments before her heart had been.

In the commotion the crew moved calmly through the cabin. They opened the window shades and instructed the passengers to put their heads into their laps or brace themselves on the seat in front of them. Surely they couldn't be as calm as they sounded?

But gradually, as the plane continued to circle, the cabin crew managed to quieten the passengers and the noise was reduced to a less frightening level.

Emma put her head in her lap. She knew the plane was circling in order to give the emergency crews on the ground time to get into position. She could picture the fire engines and ambulances racing to the edge of the runway and she wondered whose services would be required most.

This was crazy, she thought as she hugged her knees.

She'd flown halfway around the world searching for peace but she hadn't expected it to come in the form of mortality. This was why she should never make plans. They always went wrong. She was going to die at twenty-seven years of age. Just like her mother had.

No. Thinking like that wasn't helpful. She had to believe that the pilot was as confident as he sounded. She took a deep breath and crossed her fingers as the overhead lights were switched off and the cabin was plunged into semi-darkness. The afternoon light bouncing off the desert and coming through the windows was only just bright enough to take the edge off the gloom.

Emma closed her eyes and waited for the moment that everyone talked about. She wasn't waiting for her life to flash before her eyes but for the moment of regret for things she hadn't yet done. But it wasn't things left undone that sprang to mind. It was things she'd lost. Her mother had died when Emma had been a toddler and she barely remembered her, but her father had died recently and Emma felt his loss keenly. She and her father had shared a close bond. For many years it had been just the two of them, and she wished more than anything that he was still part of her life.

She'd tried to fill the void left by her father's death with other relationships but her choice of Jeremy, her last boyfriend, had been disastrous costing her both a place to live and her job.

That was something else she missed, she realised. Her job as a nurse, which she loved. But maybe it was time to put that behind her. Jeremy had said and done some cruel things that had made her question her nursing skills but she shouldn't let him dictate her path. Not any more. She wasn't about to ask for her old job back, she knew she'd never want to work with Jeremy again, but that didn't prevent her from nursing altogether. There were plenty of other hospitals that would love to have her.

Her career was something worth living for and she promised herself that if she survived this landing she would set about returning to nursing.

She had just started running through a mental list of which hospitals she should apply to when her head bounced and her chin slammed against her knees, jarring her teeth as the plane hit the ground and slid on its belly. The collision with the earth took her by surprise as she hadn't realised they were that close.

She could hear the screech of metal as the fuselage complained about being thrown at the ground and she waited for the sound of metal tearing as the plane was ripped apart, waited for the smell of fuel, the roaring heat of flames.

Around her people were screaming, including the girl beside her. Emma opened her eyes. The girl was cradling her left arm and her hand was twisted and lying at an unnatural angle relative to her forearm. She couldn't have been in the brace position properly and she must have slammed into the back of the seat in front of her on impact and fractured her wrist. The break looked painful and, considering their circumstances, there was every chance she'd go into shock. But what could Emma do?

She could feel the plane sliding sideways before it came to a halt. She looked along the aisle. Some of the overhead lockers had sprung open with the impact and contents had fallen out, but incredibly the plane appeared to be in one piece. There were no explosions, no gaping holes, no fires. People were crying but she couldn't see any movement, not from either the crew or the passengers. There was no one to assist them, not yet. What could she do?

Over the sound of crying passengers Emma could hear

the sirens of the emergency vehicles. She looked out the window but the view was completely obscured by a curtain of red dust that billowed around them. The red haze swirled as the emergency vehicles raced through it and the cloud pulsed as the emergency lights bounced off the dust particles. Help was on the way but she couldn't tell how long it would be before they'd be reached.

The girl had stopped screaming but was still cradling her left arm protectively and sobbing. Emma touched the girl lightly on the shoulder, needing to get her attention. 'I think you've broken your wrist,' she said, stating the obvious. 'I'm a nurse. Do you want me to help you?'

The girl looked at Emma. Her face was pale, completely drained of colour, and her eyes were wide. 'I'm a nurse too,' she said, 'but I can't think of what to do.'

Emma understood exactly what the girl meant. Administering treatment to others was vastly different from working out how to self-treat. And even though Emma wasn't used to giving treatment in quite this situation—state-of-the-art emergency departments were more her scene—she knew that any assistance she could give would be beneficial.

She dragged her handbag from under her seat. She knew she probably wasn't supposed to remove it but she needed to do something while they waited. Rummaging through it, she found a packet of painkillers but left them alone. The paramedics would want to be in charge of that.

She dug deeper into her bag and found a large cotton scarf that she carried in case the air-conditioning on the plane was too cold. She gave a wry smile as she pulled it out. Efficient air-conditioning was the least of their problems.

However, she could use the scarf to stabilise the girl's arm because somehow they still had to get out of the plane.

Emma assumed they'd have to exit through the emergency doors, which would mean sliding down the inflatable chutes. That wasn't going to be good. But if she could make the girl more comfortable it might help.

'Would you like me to support your arm with this?' Emma asked, showing her the scarf.

She received a nod and she quickly fashioned a sling, holding the arm close against the girl's body. By the time she'd finished, the cabin crew had got the emergency exits open and were moving through the aircraft, organising the evacuation process. Any injured passengers and those travelling with young children were directed to evacuate first.

A flight attendant stopped by the girl's side. Emma wasn't sure if she'd noticed the sling or just the girl's pallor. She addressed them both. 'Are you travelling together?'

'No,' Emma answered. 'But she's broken her wrist and she needs medical attention.'

'Are you injured?' the flight attendant asked Emma, and when Emma shook her head she continued with another question. 'Can you get off the plane with her? We prefer not to evacuate injured passengers alone and we're all needed up here.'

Emma nodded. She unclipped her seat belt and slung her bag across her chest. She stood up behind the girl and they joined the queue of passengers waiting to be evacuated. Emma slid her sandals from her feet and took the girl's flip-flops and held both pairs of shoes in one hand.

The flight attendant instructed the girl to evacuate first, with Emma following. She paused at the top of the slide as the heat took her breath away. It was oppressive, dry and intense, a bit like standing in front of a furnace. The air burnt her lungs as she breathed it but while it was dusty she couldn't smell fuel or fire. The heat wasn't coming from flames but rising from the red desert sand.

Aware of others queuing behind her, she hurriedly sat at the top of the chute and slid to the ground. She got to her feet on shaky legs and went to the girl with the broken wrist, who was looking dazed and bewildered. She led her away from the chute, away from the streams of people pouring out of the crippled plane, and sat her down.

'Sit here, I'll go and look for help,' she told her as she helped her to the ground. She dropped their shoes beside her and left her sitting in the shade of the plane as she set off in search of the ambulances.

By now there were people everywhere, passengers, airline crew, airport staff and emergency workers, and the chaotic surroundings were exacerbated by the dusty conditions, which made it difficult to see who was who.

A shape materialised out of the red haze in front of her and transformed into a tall, long-legged man with a strong, muscular frame. A rather attractive, rugged man in uniform. For a moment she thought her mind was playing tricks on her, that perhaps she *had* bumped her head. But then he spoke to her.

'Are you all right? Have you been separated from someone?'

He was real. His voice was deep, undoubtedly Australian, but his tone was relaxed and somewhat calming against the noisy background.

Emma shook her head.

'Are you injured?'

Emma shook her head again. She felt perfectly fine. Possibly a bit disoriented but physically okay.

He was staring at her. So she stared back.

CHAPTER TWO

SHE had to look up to see him properly. He was tall, at a guess she'd say five inches taller than her, which would make him about six feet three. His eyes were a clear blue, quite striking against his tanned skin, and his hair was thick and dark with a slight curl. His shoulders were broad and he was solidly built but it appeared to be all muscle. He looked like he could muster sheep or cattle, or whatever it was they farmed out here, all day, and still have energy to spare.

She almost sighed with pleasure. Her first glimpse of an Outback man and he was just what she'd imagined, just what her hours of watching Australian television dramas had led her to hope for. He was gorgeous in a ruggedly handsome way.

While she was busy drooling over his gorgeousness she realised he was still staring at her, waiting for her to answer. He probably thought she was in shock.

'I'm fine,' she replied.

'You've got blood on your lip,' he said.

Despite the noise and disorder surrounding them, Emma didn't need to strain to hear his words. His deep voice carried easily across the small distance that separated them. He was holding a small first-aid backpack and he took some tissues from it and held them out to her.

Emma licked her lip and tasted blood, warm and salty, on her tongue. She must have bitten it when the plane had belly-flopped onto the landing strip. As she took the tissue and pressed it to her lip she was surprised to find that her hand was shaking. Adrenalin was coursing through her system but she hadn't had time to notice until now.

'You've missed a bit,' he said when Emma took the tissue from her lip. He delved into the backpack again and retrieved a bottle of water. He poured a little on the tissues. 'May I?' he asked.

His clear blue eyes were fixed on hers, drawing her in, relaxing her. The chaos, the noise and the crowd of people around them seemed to disappear into the red dust, leaving the two of them alone on the airstrip. The experience was slightly hypnotic and Emma found herself nodding automatically in reaction to his calming blue gaze.

But when he reached out and cupped her chin with his hand her response was definitely not calm and relaxed, it was something completely different altogether. Her skin tingled under his touch as his fingertips grazed her lip, leaving a trail of heat behind as he wiped the blood from her face.

She couldn't speak, she couldn't move, she could barely breathe. Her breaths were shallow but it was the best she could manage, and she could feel her heart pulsing in her chest. She told herself it wasn't him, it was the adrenalin that had heightened her senses. What other possible reason could there be? She didn't have this kind of reaction to perfect strangers. No one did. Did they?

She needed to sit down and catch her breath. She needed to get some perspective. She just needed a moment to collect herself and then everything would be back to normal. She couldn't afford to get spellbound by tall, dark and handsome men. By any men. Not right now.

'Do you want someone to look at that?' he asked.

His question confused her. He was wearing a blue short-sleeved shirt with epaulettes on the shoulders and on his breast pocket was a logo she recognised, a pair of wings, the symbol of the flying doctors service. Why would he get someone else to look at her lip?

'What do you mean?' she asked, aware that her voice was shaky and thin. She sounded as out of breath as she felt.

'Did you want me to get one of the medics to check it for you?' he asked.

Emma glanced at the logo on his shirt pocket again before she looked up at him. 'Aren't you a doctor?'

He shook his head. 'I'm a pilot.'

'Oh.'

A pilot. His answer threw her off course for a moment. She hadn't expected that.

'I'll be okay,' she said. She was a nurse with a bloody lip, she was sure she didn't need to take up anybody's time for that. And then she remembered what she'd been doing before she'd been distracted by the appearance of a handsome pilot in her path. 'But there's a girl back here with a broken wrist, I was looking for a paramedic.'

'Can you take me to her?'

She nodded. 'It's this way.'

She retraced her steps and he fell into step beside her. She watched the ground to make sure she didn't tread on anything dangerous. She couldn't believe she hadn't thought to put her sandals back on her feet, but it also kept her attention focussed on the job at hand. She'd never realised she could be so easily distracted.

Within moments they were back in the shadow of the plane and the handsome stranger picked up his pace and ran the remaining few steps.

'Lisa! What happened?'

'Harry!'

Emma heard the happiness in the girl's voice even as she registered that her name was Lisa. Lisa and Harry. Lisa knew Harry. Harry knew Lisa. They knew each other.

Good, Emma told herself. This handsome stranger was nothing to her. It was just the adrenalin that had caused such an unexpected physical reaction, just the adrenalin that had left her short of breath and made her skin tingle. She could ignore the little flutter of excitement in her belly, the little increase in her heart rate. Even if she'd been in the market for a man, and she wasn't, it looked like this one was well and truly off limits.

'I got caught in the wrong position. I wasn't braced properly,' Lisa replied. 'It was stupid of me.'

'Let's get you to an ambulance,' Harry was saying, and before Emma could blink he'd crouched down and scooped Lisa into his arms. He stood up again, lifting her as if she weighed no more than a three-year-old.

'Thank you for your help.' He was holding Lisa in his arms but he was talking to her. Emma was surprised—she hadn't expected him to remember she was there. 'Do you think you can follow the others to the terminal?' he asked as he inclined his head to his left.

Emma wondered if she shouldn't offer to help other passengers. Surely any help would be gratefully received but as she looked around, now that the dust had settled, she could see paramedics attending to those who needed them and there was a line of uninjured passengers making their way across the dirt towards a small building. Things looked to be under control.

She nodded. She was fine. She could walk. She just needed to put her shoes back on. Her sandals were still lying on the ground and as she bent to retrieve them she caught sight of her filthy clothes. In the few minutes that she'd been out of the plane she'd become covered in a layer of red dust. She slid her dusty feet into her sandals and glanced back up at the man standing before her. His clothes were immaculate, clean and crisp and she wondered how he had managed to stay so pristine.

'Yes, I can,' she answered as she deliberately straightened her shoulders. She was okay. She could manage. 'I'm fine. Go, get Lisa to the ambulance. I'm fine,' she repeated, aware that she didn't need to monopolise any more of his time.

Emma turned and walked away so that he was free to leave. She followed the crowd towards the terminal and left the gorgeous stranger behind in the red dust, making herself look straight ahead even though she wanted to turn around for another glimpse. No doubt he was already whisking Lisa off to the paramedics and would have no time to give her another thought. She wondered if she'd wake up tomorrow and think this was all a dream. Or if she'd run into him again.

As she entered the little terminal building she couldn't resist a final glance over her shoulder but he was nowhere to be seen, already absorbed into the throng that remained gathered around the stricken aircraft.

Inside the terminal a representative from the airline was issuing instructions, handing out paperwork and getting details on whether passengers wanted to wait for their luggage or have it delivered. Emma was swept up in a sea of red tape and it was many minutes before she had a chance to wonder where Sophie was.

She searched the area for a familiar face but she couldn't spot her cousin anywhere. She frowned. With all the drama of the crash landing she would have thought Sophie would be front and centre, waiting to welcome her. Was she in the right place? Was there more than one back of beyond in Outback Australia? God, imagine if she'd crash-landed in the wrong town!

She pulled her mobile phone out of her handbag and switched it on. She was almost certain she was in the right place. There was bound to be a reason Soph wasn't here. Perhaps she'd left a message.

Sure enough, her phone beeped as soon as it came to life.

So sorry, Em, clinic running late, will be there by six. S xx

Emma shrugged her slim shoulders and sat down to wait. There was nothing else for her to do. She watched the other travellers coming and going, their numbers dwindling as the terminal building emptied out. Everyone else seemed to have someone to meet them or somewhere to go. The ambulances had long since departed and Emma wondered how Lisa was and what had happened to the pilot.

She watched as the fire engines drove away from the scene, leaving the plane stranded in the middle of nowhere. She knew how it felt. She wondered how the plane would be moved and assumed it would be towed somewhere, somehow. It was sitting abandoned. Had the luggage been retrieved? What had happened to her bag?

She frowned and started searching for a baggage carousel even as she realised she hadn't seen one. She should go and fetch her bag. She stood up. She would need to make some enquiries.

The first person she saw was the ruggedly handsome pilot. Harry, Lisa had called him. He was walking towards her. He walked quickly, his long strides eating up the distance between them, and she expected him to continue on past her as he looked as though he was walking with a purpose, but he came to stop in front of her.

'Are you still here? Is someone meeting you?' He assessed her with his blue gaze as his eyebrows came together in a frown.

Emma looked up at him. He towered over her, but his size wasn't intimidating, in fact she found it oddly reassuring. He gave off a sense that he was a man who could be relied on, a man who would get things done. Maybe it was just the uniform, she'd always seen uniforms as a symbol of order and control, but she sensed that with this man it was more about his personality and less about his attire.

'Yes, but they're running late,' she replied. 'I'm just going to look for my bags while I wait. Do you know where the baggage carousel is?'

'First time in Broken Hill?' he asked.

He was smiling and by the expression in his bright blue eyes she could tell he wanted to laugh. At her. She couldn't imagine what there was to laugh about but whatever it was that amused him he at least had the good grace not to laugh out loud.

'Yes, why?'

Harry watched as Emma straightened her slim shoulders and lifted her chin and he knew she was just daring him to make fun of her. He wasn't about to take the mickey out of her, not when she'd just had a less than stellar welcome to the Hill, but he always found it amusing to see how first-timers coped with Broken Hill. Listening to her English accent, he imagined that in her case it would be a vastly different experience from anything she'd had before. He wondered what she was doing here, this English girl in the middle of the Outback. She didn't look like the average backpacker and she appeared to be travelling alone. What could possibly have brought her here? Who was she waiting for?

'There is no carousel,' he explained. 'Your luggage will be outside on the trolley. It's this way.' He could have directed her to the trolley, it wasn't difficult to find if you knew where to look, but he wasn't in a hurry and he'd never been able to resist a damsel in distress, especially not a pretty one.

He'd seen her again the moment he'd entered the terminal and he'd kept one eye on her even as he'd helped get other passengers sorted. Technically, sorting out the chaos from the crash landing wasn't his job but in a town like Broken Hill, where everyone knew everybody else, or at least that's what it felt like, many hands made light work. Particularly in situations like this, when things had gone haywire, it was the country way to pitch in and do your bit. But he'd made sure he'd done his bit while keeping an eye on the tall, willowy brunette.

The terminal was almost empty now. Most of the passengers had been taken care of and only a few remained. She was one of them.

He'd half turned away from her, towards the exit and the baggage trolley, waiting for her to follow him, but she wasn't moving. She was standing still and frowning. A little crease had appeared between her green eyes and she was fiddling with the end of her ponytail.

A moment later she appeared to come to a decision. She flicked her hair back over her shoulder and he watched as she stowed her mobile phone in her handbag. Her wrists were brown and slender, her fingers slim with short, polished nails, and her movements as she slung her bag over her shoulder were fluid and graceful. Even though her white cotton dress and silver sandals were covered in red dust, she still managed to look elegant.

Her outfit alone was enough to convince Harry she wasn't a local. Not too many people were brave enough to wear all white in the country's red centre.

But it wasn't her outfit that had told him she wasn't from around here. Neither was it her English accent. Even before she'd spoken one word or asked the question about her luggage Harry had known she wasn't from the Hill. He knew he'd never seen her before. He would have remembered.

'Did you want to come with me to the trolley?' he asked, eager to prolong the encounter. His offer was rewarded with a smile that made him catch his breath. Her green eyes sparkled but it was the twin dimples that appeared on each side of her mouth that made him do a double take. At first glance there was no denying she was an attractive woman but when she smiled she was spectacular.

She reminded him of the wildflowers that suddenly appeared after the desert rains—stunningly beautiful and completely unexpected—and he wondered if, like the native flowers, she would appear fragile yet turn out to be resilient.

'Thank you,' she said without protest. She didn't tell him she'd be able to find the luggage trolley on her own; she didn't tell him she didn't need his help.

She simply fell into step beside him and made him feel good about himself for helping. He watched the reaction of the remaining passengers as they walked through the terminal. He was used to being with beautiful women but it seemed as though every person in the building was looking at them and he didn't flatter himself that he was the one who'd captured their attention. It was most definitely the willowy brunette they were watching.

He felt like the schoolboy who'd caught the attention of the prom queen. He knew that was ridiculous and fanciful

but that made no difference—it was how she made him
feel and the sensation was unexpected but not unpleasant.

The half-laden luggage trolley sat just outside the terminal doors.

Emma reached up to grab a large duffel bag from the
top of the pile.

'Here, let me get that for you,' he offered. 'It looks
heavy.'

She could have managed to lift her bag and find the
trolley, she'd just needed to know where it was. But she
didn't tell him she could manage because she found him
fascinating and she was more than happy to let him help
her. So she stepped back to let him past her.

As he retrieved her bag from the trolley his biceps
bulged, straining against the fabric of his shirt. She'd
bet her last pound that his muscles came from physical
work, not from lifting weights in a gym. He looked vi-
brant, healthy and solid, totally male. He seemed a far more
masculine version of the men she was used to in England.

Maybe it was the tougher environment out here, maybe
it was the sun, the fresh air or the physical activity, but,
whatever it was, someone had definitely got something
right when they'd made him.

'You're staying in town for a while?' he asked as he
hefted her bag and slung it over his shoulder.

He was grinning and once again she had the feeling that
he was doing his best not to laugh at her. She knew her bag
was heavy, even though he made it look light.

When she'd packed she hadn't really known what she'd
need and as usual she knew she would have brought far too
many pairs of shoes. She'd already noticed that everyone
in the airport wore no-nonsense sturdy shoes or flip-flops
and she hadn't seen one pair of sparkly shoes on anyone
over the age of thirteen.

She knew her bag was bulging at the seams and she knew she might not need the three pairs of strappy stilettos she'd packed, or even the two pairs of ballet flats, but surely she didn't have to sacrifice her fashion sense completely just because she was in the middle of nowhere?

'I'm not sure,' she replied. Her plans hadn't evolved at all past getting on the plane and arriving in town.

'What brings you here?' He was frowning as he carried her bag into the terminal.

'I'm visiting my cousin.'

'Is that who's running late?'

She nodded in reply.

'How late?' he asked.

Emma checked her watch and felt his eyes follow her movement. 'About an hour. She sent me a message, something about the clinic running late.'

'The clinic?' he queried. 'What does she do, this cousin of yours?'

'Do you always ask this many questions?' she countered, wondering if it was the country manner to be this direct or just his manner.

'Yep,' he answered, with a smile that made his blue eyes sparkle.

'Sophie's a physio at the hospital,' she told him, realising she'd tell him just about anything he wanted to know provided he was smiling at her.

'You're not talking about Sophie Stewart, are you?'

'Yes, do you know her?'

He was nodding.

Just exactly how small was this town? Emma wondered. First he'd known Lisa and now Sophie. But it was good news for her as it meant she was in the right place after all.

'She's out on a clinic run with the flying doctors,' he

said. 'There's a storm out over Innamincka that's delayed their return.'

Emma remembered Sophie mentioning something about the allied health hospital staff sometimes working with the flying doctor service. Her eyes flicked to the logo on his shirt pocket, the wings of the flying doctors. Soph got to work with this man? No wonder she'd said she planned to stay in Broken Hill for a while.

'I'm a pilot with the flying doctors,' he said when he saw the direction of her gaze. 'I'm Harry Connor…' he extended his hand '…and it's a pleasure to meet you, Sophie's cousin.'

'Emma. My name is Emma Matheson,' she replied, as she reached for his hand.

And there it was again. That same tingle that made her catch her breath. The feeling that he was taking all her oxygen and causing her light-headedness. Only this time she couldn't blame adrenalin. That had had plenty of time to settle while she'd been sitting waiting.

'So, Emma Matheson, what do you plan to do now?' he said as he released her hand.

She wasn't big on plans but fortunately Harry hadn't finished. He continued speaking and gave her some options. 'Did you want to hang around here? Or you could wait at the flying doctor base or I could drop you off at Sophie's place.'

'I don't have a key.'

He laughed. Out loud this time and it was such a pleasant sound, deep and full and it resonated through her. It was so genuine she couldn't find it irritating, even though she knew it was at her expense. 'I doubt the house is locked and if it is I know where the key is hidden.'

Did he and Sophie have history? And what about Lisa? He read her mind. 'Don't look at me like that. It's all perfectly innocent. And I promise I'm completely trust-worthy.'

She doubted very much that he was innocent but she wanted to believe she could trust him. Jeremy's behaviour had shaken her faith in men but she had a good association with men in uniforms. Besides, she'd seen how he treated Lisa and he knew Sophie. She wanted to think he was a man who could be trusted, and with a laugh like that, one that reached right into his bright blue eyes, how could he be anything but nice?

'Now, where can I take you?' he asked, obviously deciding she'd had enough time to make up her mind.

'If it's not too much trouble, I'd love to go to Sophie's. I need a shower and a change of clothes.'

'Done.'

'But aren't you supposed to be working?'

'Nope. My shift's over. I came across to the airport when I heard the distress call. I have clearance to be on the airport apron and I thought I might be needed. Turns out I am.' He grinned and Emma's insides skittered. She wasn't about to complain about his presence. It did feel as though he'd been sent to help her.

'Come with me,' he invited. 'Send Sophie a text and let her know I'll drop you at her place—that way you know I'll have to get you there safely,' he added as Emma still hesitated.

'That's not…' Emma was about to protest and say it wasn't that she didn't trust him but she knew that was exactly the issue. And Harry knew it too. She nodded—it was a good suggestion. She pulled her phone out and sent Sophie a message even as she decided to consider this one of those times when things were going to unfold without her input. A pilot, in uniform, who'd already helped her

and Lisa. If she was going to learn to put her faith in people
again, this was as good a place as any to start.

Harry waited for her to put her phone away before he
headed for the exit. Emma had to hurry to keep up with
his long strides as he walked through the terminal. Not
even the weight of her bag, which he still had slung over
his shoulder like a beach towel, slowed him down. Not
that his strength should have surprised her considering
how easily he'd lifted Lisa earlier.

Harry loaded her bag into the boot of a large four-wheel
drive and held the passenger door open for her. As they
left the airport he pointed out the sights as he drove across
town.

Normally Emma would have debated whether what he
was showing her qualified as 'sights' as in her opinion the
best thing she could see was Harry and she was more than
happy to keep him in her view. But she didn't want to appear rude so she tried to look interested as he showed her
another sight—a huge pile of dirt in the centre of town.

According to him, this was the old mine and the reason
for Broken Hill's existence. The town had been founded
on the back of a mining boom when lead, zinc and silver
had been found in the area, but Emma found it hard to get
excited about a heap of dirt, although she did agree that it
made a useful landmark.

Emma tried to remember what Sophie had told her
about the town as Harry negotiated the streets. She knew
it was first and foremost a mining town but there was also
a thriving artists' community and it was a popular location for movie-making. Looking around, Emma couldn't
imagine why but apparently the surrounding country was
quite spectacular. Sophie had told her there wasn't enough
in the town itself to keep her occupied for the three months
she planned to stay, which was why she'd spent the first

month in Sydney with the rest of Sophie's family. Soph had popped back for a weekend, which had given them time to catch up, but Emma was looking forward to spending more time with her cousin. Sophie was always like a breath of fresh air and Emma needed that.

Sophie's house was on one side of the mine and the airport was on the other, but even so it took less than twenty minutes to arrive at the house. It was a large, old, single-level, double-fronted stone building with a wide veranda and iron roof, and Emma remembered that Sophie shared the house. It was much too big for one person.

'Sophie shares with a girl called Grace, is that right?' Emma asked, as she followed Harry along the driveway. She'd expected him to try the front door but instead he was walking down the side of the house and entering through the back. Just as he'd predicted, the door was unlocked.

'Yes, she's a flying doctor,' Harry replied, as he led Emma through a casual living room and up the hall. 'She was on the clinic run today with Sophie. This is their spare room,' he said, as he opened a bedroom door and deposited her bag. 'If you're okay, I might call past the hospital and check on Lisa. Will you be all right here on your own?'

Lucky Lisa. Emma nodded. 'I'll be fine. I'll have a shower and a cup of tea. Thanks for the lift.'

'No worries.' Harry's responses were as easygoing as he appeared to be, and Emma was sorry to see him go. She was suddenly aware of how big and empty and quiet the house was now that she was alone so she headed for the bathroom and the comfort of a hot shower, wanting to keep busy until Sophie got home.

She had showered and changed into shorts and a strappy tank top and was sitting at the kitchen table with a pot of tea in front of her when Sophie exploded in through the back door. There was no other way to describe it, Soph only ever seemed to have one pace and that was full steam ahead.

'You made it! I can't believe you're actually here,' she squealed. 'I heard about the plane trip. Thank God it didn't crash.'

Emma didn't know what else you'd call it when a plane dropped from the sky and slid along a runway on its belly instead of its wheels, but she agreed it could have been worse, much worse, so she wasn't about to argue.

'I'm so sorry I was late. Are you really okay?' Sophie looked her up and down.

'I'm fine.'

'You've got a bit of a fat lip.'

Emma touched her lip self-consciously. It was tender but it was hardly a catastrophe. She started to stand but Sophie had enveloped her in a hug before she could get out of her seat. 'I'm fine, really. All in one piece and delivered safe and sound to your door.'

'I can't believe you've met Harry already. How did he know who you were?'

'He didn't at first. He was on the landing strip when we were all evacuated from the plane. He sort of appeared from nowhere through the dust—'

'Did you collapse into his arms and make him carry you to the terminal?'

Emma shot her cousin a withering glare. 'No.'

'Pity,' Sophie said with an exaggerated sigh. 'That would have been so romantic.'

Emma ignored that comment. She happened to agree with Sophie but it would have sounded ridiculous to say so. 'He had his arms full already.'

'With what?' Sophie asked.

'With a nurse called Lisa,' Emma said, keen to see Sophie's reaction to that bit of news.

'A short, curvaceous, blonde?'

Emma nodded, unsurprised that Sophie knew her. She was fast realising that anonymity was hard to find in this town.

'What happened to her?'

'She broke her wrist. Harry carried her off to the ambulance. He asked if I was okay and sent me to the terminal by myself.' Emma left out the part about the tingles and the light-headedness as in her opinion it was far better to play down the events of the afternoon. 'But when I was waiting for you, and the terminal was just about empty, he came and helped me again.'

'I still think it would have been better if he'd swept *you* off your feet instead of Lisa but never mind—isn't he fabulous?'

Gorgeous, Emma thought, but she wasn't going to say that until she had more information. She knew from experience that things were not always as they seemed. 'He seems nice.'

'Nice! He's better than that. If I wasn't madly in love with Mark, I'd chase after him.'

'He's single?' That surprised her. In her experience men who looked like that weren't often single. 'What about Lisa?'

'They're just friends. Harry's single but he's never single for long. He has a bit of a reputation as a ladies' man. Luckily for him, Broken Hill is a very transient place, which means lots of the women with broken hearts are just passing through and don't stay around to cause him grief. It seems to suit Harry. I'm sure his motto is "plenty more fish in the sea". I bet he'd be happy to help you get over Jeremy.'

'I don't need help. Distance is all I need. I think I'm done with dating for a while.'

'We'll see.' Sophie laughed.

'What's that supposed to mean?'

'I've never known you to be without a boyfriend for more than a few months and it's been, what? Four months now?'

'Five.' Not that she was counting. But Sophie was right. She was never single for long and didn't actually like being on her own. She'd spent too much time on her own as a child and because of her nomadic upbringing she'd never really had a chance to form close female friendships that stood the test of time so boyfriends had filled that gap. But Emma did intend to take a break from dating.

She needed time to find out who she was and what she wanted, without any complications. 'I'm not looking for a boyfriend.'

'That's okay,' Sophie said, refusing to be put off. 'I doubt Harry's looking for a girlfriend but if you have an itch that needs scratching, he'd probably be happy to help you out.'

'I'll keep that in mind,' Emma replied, even though she knew she had no intention of getting romantically involved with anyone for a long time, no matter how gorgeous they were.

Not even if his touch had sent her hormones into overdrive?

Surely that was only because it had been so long since she'd had sex. Five months was a very long time so was it any wonder her hormones were a little crazy? But before Sophie could make any more helpful suggestions, their discussion was interrupted by the arrival of Sophie's housemate.

Grace was a petite woman, short and fine boned with jet-black hair cut in a bob. She was almost the perfect opposite of tall, blonde, Nordic-looking Sophie, and seeing them standing side by side as Sophie introduced her made Emma smile.

Grace's arrival was closely followed by Harry's reappearance and as he let himself in through the back door and despite her vows of celibacy, Emma found herself wishing she'd changed into a slightly more attractive outfit. She had an enormous bag stuffed with pretty clothes and she'd gone for comfort over style. But at least her hair was freshly washed and blow-dried and she was no longer covered in red dust.

Not that Harry even seemed to notice, he was too busy regaling Grace with his version of the drama of the plane crash while Sophie played hostess. Somehow Harry managed to make the plane crash sound almost exciting and if Emma hadn't been intimately acquainted with the events of the day she would certainly now feel as though she'd lived through it. He was an entertaining storyteller and Emma imagined that anyone listening to his version would be sorry they hadn't seen it for themselves, Harry made it sound as though it had been something not to be missed.

Grace asked Emma a few questions and Emma added her comments as best she could, but she was no match for Harry's engaging style and she preferred listening to him while they waited for delivery of the take-away pizza Sophie had ordered.

'Lisa's broken wrist is a complication we don't need at the moment,' Harry said as he munched his fourth piece of pizza. Emma wasn't surprised that a man of his size had a hearty appetite.

'Why is that?' Sophie asked.

'She's supposed to be taking a locum position with the flying doctor service while Kerri is on maternity leave. She was due to start next week but she'll be out of action now.'

'Why don't you do it, Em?' Sophie said. 'Emma's a nurse,' she added for Harry and Grace's benefit.

'A hospital nurse,' Emma clarified.

'You're trained in emergency work, though,' Sophie added.

'Are you?' Grace asked, and when Emma nodded her face lit up. 'Do you think you'd be interested?'

'What, in working with the flying doctor service?'

'Yes,' Grace replied.

'I'm here on a tourist visa. I'm not allowed to work,' Emma said, thinking that surely Grace's comment was just one of those off-the-cuff remarks people made without any real intent behind it.

'I think you can do volunteer work,' Grace said.

Emma shrugged. 'I'm not sure I'm qualified to work with the flying doctors.'

'If you've got emergency training, you'll be fine.'

'Yes, but I'm trained to work in a hospital, not out in a field in the middle of nowhere,' she protested. She didn't know the first thing about nursing outside a hospital environment and she hadn't even done that for four months. Grace must be mad to think it was something she could do.

'Technically it won't be a field.' Sophie laughed. 'Out here we call them paddocks and the chances are you'll just be in the dirt in the middle of nowhere, but it's a once-in-a-lifetime experience. You couldn't get enough of that flying doctors show when we were teenagers; imagine getting to do the real thing.'

'I'm sure it's hardly the same.' She had loved that television series but to hear Sophie say it, in front of people who actually did it for a living, made her sound like a crazy groupie.

But Sophie wasn't going to give up. 'Are you kidding? It's brilliant! I reckon you'd love it.'

Harry caught Emma's eye. He was grinning at her and suddenly the proposition seemed quite appealing. Maybe it would be fun.

'You don't need to decide today. You've probably had enough to deal with,' he said, coming to her rescue once again. 'But why don't you come out to the base and have a look around? You can't judge the job on an ancient television drama.'

'That's true,' Grace added. 'We work harder and we're not all as good looking.'

'Don't scare her off, Grace,' Harry said, laughing, and Emma relaxed. That was a sound she could get used to.

'At least go and have a look, Em,' Sophie encouraged her. 'It's not like you've got any other plans. You said you thought you'd stay for a while.'

Emma nodded. Soph was right, she wasn't in a hurry to go home. There wasn't anything to hurry back for. Her family was there, what was left of it, but they'd still be there whenever she returned. She'd left her job and she didn't have another one waiting. She definitely wasn't planning on going back to her old job, there were too many people there who knew her business. She was here for two more months and she didn't intend to go back to London before that, which meant she really did need to come up with another option. And hadn't she promised herself that if she survived the crash landing she'd look at returning to nursing?

'You might as well have something to keep you busy.' Sophie's words echoed Emma's thoughts.

'It could be the perfect solution,' Grace added. 'Why don't I get Irene to check out the volunteer situation? I'm sure there's a loophole there somewhere.'

'And in the meantime you could drive out to the base tomorrow to have a look. You'll show her around, won't you, Harry?' Sophie sounded innocent enough but Emma recognised the gleam in her eye.

She chose to pretend not to notice. It seemed as if her life was being organised for her, at least for the next few weeks, but as she had no firm plans of her own there was nothing to argue about.

'I'll think about it,' she said. After all, what harm could there be in just looking?

CHAPTER THREE

BUT she didn't think about it any further until the next morning. She slept well, despite the events of the previous day, and when she woke the sun was already high in the cloudless, blue sky.

Sophie had left a note saying she'd walked to the hospital for her eight o'clock start but she'd left her car keys so Emma could drive out to the flying doctor base.

Did she really want to do that?

It couldn't hurt to go and have a look, could it? It would be interesting to see the base and it didn't mean she had to apply for a job. She wasn't sure what she wanted to do. But when did she ever know? When had she ever had a plan? She'd tried a couple of times but her plans had a habit of going distinctly pear-shaped. Perhaps she was better off sticking to her usual style, which was pretty random.

She had a shower, made herself some toast, did the dishes, watered some of Sophie's plants that looked rather thirsty and when she ran out of things to do she switched on Sophie's computer, logged in to her emails and printed off a copy of her CV, which she'd stored online. Telling herself it didn't hurt to take it with her just in case, it didn't mean she wanted the job, she picked up the car keys and the map Sophie had left for her and headed out the door.

The drive across town—coming from London she

couldn't bring herself to think of Broken Hill as a city—along the almost deserted, dusty streets took the same amount of time as yesterday—not quite twenty minutes. Which was not enough time to work out what she intended to do once she got to the flying doctor base. She sat in Sophie's car for another ten minutes until she realised she couldn't remain there for the rest of the morning.

Viewed from the car park, the flying doctors building was modern and much larger than she'd expected. She walked through a pleasant grassed courtyard, pushed open the door and stepped into the cool, dark foyer. A sign in front of her directed her to head left for the museum or right for the shop and tours.

She hesitated, thinking the museum might be worth a look, but she knew that was just further procrastination. Harry had offered to show her around and if she could have him as her tour guide around the real-life base she didn't need to look at the museum. She hoped he would be there and not off flying the plane somewhere. There was only one way to find out.

Emma stepped to the right and introduced herself to the lady behind the counter.

'Harry told us to expect you. Can you wait here for just a second and I'll fetch Irene,' the woman said, before she disappeared through a swing door that was set into the wall behind her, leaving Emma staring after her.

The woman returned within a minute, followed by a short, round woman who was speaking to Emma before she'd even come through the door.

'Emma, hello, I'm Irene, the base manager. It's good to meet you.' She reached out and grabbed Emma's hand as she was talking and shook it vigorously. 'Why don't you come through to my office and we can talk about the job? I can't believe our luck that you're here and able to work.'

Emma tried to protest as she trailed behind Irene down a short flight of stairs and along a corridor. 'I'm not sure that I can work,' she said. She also wasn't sure if she wanted to.

'You can work on a volunteer basis,' Irene told her. 'Grace was right about that. So if you're interested in a volunteer position, I'm sure we can work something out. Besides, if you're in town for a while you'll soon realise there's not a lot to keep you occupied. You'll soon get bored so you might as well work. Think of it as good experience.'

Emma could tell that Irene wasn't a person who could easily be dissuaded once her mind was made up. This town seemed to be full of strong-willed people. She'd need to try a different tack or she knew she'd find herself signed up before the day was over.

'I might not have the qualifications you're after. I've never worked outside a hospital before.'

But Irene was not going to be put off. 'Neither have most of our nurses when they first come to us. I was told you've got Emergency experience, is that right?'

Emma nodded as Irene led her into an office and closed the door. The office had one glass wall that overlooked a larger, open-plan office that appeared to be a communications centre. The walls were covered with whiteboards, charts and maps and there were several staff members at work within the room.

'If you have emergency experience, I'm sure we'll want you,' Irene said as she indicated to Emma to take a seat. 'Did you bring your CV?'

Emma was in shock. She had her CV in her bag but she hadn't really expected to hand it over. She'd expected to have a relaxed tour of the facility with Harry! Nevertheless, she dug her CV out of her bag and handed it to Irene.

'We're desperate for nurses,' Irene explained. 'We're already down one. Mary's gone to Adelaide to look after her mum who's undergoing chemo, and with Kerri about to go on maternity leave and Lisa with her broken arm, we're going to be short two nurses. One we can cover, two is impossible. I've looked into the volunteering situation and that's perfectly acceptable with the board so as long as your references and qualifications are okay. If that all pans out, you can consider the locum position yours.'

Emma didn't know whether she should be flattered or terrified. She had no idea what she was getting herself into.

Irene leant back in her chair. 'Now, I suppose I should let you ask me some questions. What do you want to know?'

Anything and everything, Emma thought. She had no idea how the flying doctor service actually worked or what they did other than what she'd seen on television, and from what Harry had told her last night it sounded as though the show might have been more fiction than fact.

Before she could work out which question to begin with she heard the sound of a door opening behind her and a familiar voice broke the silence.

'Emma! I heard you were here. How are you? Have you recovered from yesterday?'

Harry.

Emma turned at the sound of his voice. It was just as deep and soothing as she remembered. It reverberated through her and despite the fact that Irene was sitting a few inches away Harry's voice made her feel as if she was the only person he could see.

'Yes, thanks, I'm good. A bit shell-shocked but that has nothing to do with yesterday.'

Harry laughed. 'Irene has that effect on people. Has she convinced you to join us yet? She doesn't like to take no for an answer.'

'I got that impression,' she replied.

Luckily Irene didn't seem to take offence at being discussed like this. 'Harry, do you think you could give Emma the grand tour?' she asked. 'Use your persuasive charms on her to sell the position?'

'That's why I'm here,' Harry answered.

'Good,' Irene replied, and turned back to Emma. 'You could go out on a clinic run tomorrow if you like. Why don't you let me know what you think when you've finished with Harry?' Irene stood and ushered Emma and Harry out the door.

Emma followed Harry through the communications centre and out into another long, narrow corridor. His broad shoulders almost touched the walls on each side, making the corridor seem narrower than it probably was. Harry was the sort of man who needed to be outdoors, Emma thought. She could imagine him on horseback, galloping across the red dirt in jeans and one of those wide-brimmed bushman's hats. She could just imagine how easy it would be to be swept away by the romance of the scene and ride off into the sunset on the back of Harry's horse. She shook her head; her imagination was starting to sound like Sophie.

Still, his ruggedness was better suited to the open air, she thought as she tried to picture him in the cockpit of a small plane. She wondered how he'd look there. Probably just as gorgeous but maybe a bit trapped. It was hard to imagine his energy and size contained in a small space.

'Are you sure you're okay?'

Harry had stopped by a door at the end of the corridor, no doubt wondering why she hadn't said anything.

Emma nodded as she quickly thought of an appropriate response. 'Irene's a bit of a whirlwind, isn't she? I had no idea what she was talking about half the time. And what was that clinic run she mentioned? I don't even know what that is.'

'Clinic runs are flights we do out to the rural towns. Our staff run clinics in the outpatient health centres there,' Harry explained. 'It's really the main part of our work. It's not all emergency retrievals that we do but, because that sounds more exciting, it's what everyone tends to associate with the flying doctors. Every day there are flights out to regional centres so that people living in the more remote areas have access to health care. Some of the trips are for a couple of days and there's always a nurse, usually a doctor and often a dentist or physio or maybe a specialist from the city like an ENT. That was what Sophie was doing yesterday. You should come. It'll be fun.'

'You're going?'

'I am tomorrow. It's my job, remember? Flying planes,' he teased.

She remembered. It was just that she still couldn't imagine how he would fit into the cockpit.

'You like the clinic runs?' she asked.

'To be perfectly honest, I prefer the emergency flights. They're a bit more challenging from my point of view, landing on narrow roads, dodging sheep and cattle, flying into unlit landing strips and through thunderstorms.'

'I'm not sure you're selling the job to me. One botched landing is enough for me for this trip.'

Harry laughed and Emma wanted to close her eyes and soak up the sound and save it for later. 'Don't worry, we're pretty good at what we do. All of us pilots have years of experience.'

'Where are you going tomorrow? Is there a proper landing strip?'

Harry nodded. Beside the door a large map had been

attached to the wall. The map was liberally studded with coloured pins. He pointed to a pin. 'To White Cliffs.'

'Would I be working?' She wasn't sure that she wanted to be thrown in at the deep end and it seemed like that would be the case if she took this job. She didn't know if she was ready for the challenge just yet. She'd come to Australia for a break, a chance to take stock of her life. Diving into this job might not be the best way of sorting herself out. She'd vowed to return to nursing but it didn't have to happen tomorrow.

'I'm sure you could help out if you wanted to. It's Kerri's last day before she starts maternity leave so I imagine you'd really just be a spare pair of hands.'

The distance on the map between Broken Hill and White Cliffs was only a few centimetres. It didn't look far and Emma wondered why they needed to fly. 'How far is it?'

'About three hundred kilometres. It takes a little over half an hour to fly but nearly three hours to drive.'

'It doesn't look that far.'

Harry ran his fingers around a black line that was drawn on the map. 'This is the area we cover—it's the size of France.'

'You're kidding.' Emma was amazed. She knew Australia was a vast continent but she really hadn't grasped the concept. 'All that way in those little planes?'

'Have you been in a small plane before?' Harry was looking at her carefully. 'And I mean really small.'

Emma nodded. 'I grew up around planes. My father was a doctor in the air force.'

Harry visibly relaxed. 'The planes might be a bit different from what you're used to but I'm sure they have one thing in common, which is state-of-the-art technology. Do you want to see inside one?'

'Sure.'

Harry punched some numbers into a numeric keypad and pushed open the door. Emma followed him through into the hangar. It was an impressive structure. Immaculately clean and organised and enormous, its size completely dwarfed the little plane that sat on the polished concrete floor. Emma followed Harry across the floor. The plane had looked small from the doorway but she had assumed it was just because the hangar was so large, but up close it was just as tiny.

Harry climbed in first. He was wearing dark blue overalls, a flightsuit similar to what RAF pilots wore, and as he ducked his head to get through the doorway the overalls tightened across his buttocks, treating her to a very pleasant picture. Harry turned just inside the door and stretched out his hand to help her up the steps. There was only one way to find out if the plane really was as small as it looked. Emma reached up and clasped his hand. It was warm and strong and huge and her hand disappeared inside his palm.

She let him help her into the plane and she almost ended up in his arms before he swivelled out of her way. There wasn't much room to manoeuvre and she was still close enough to notice his scent. He smelt of sunshine, of fresh air and the outdoors. He smelt the way clean clothes smelt when you brought the washing inside on a summer's day. He smelt perfect and Emma wished she could bottle his scent and save it to take back to England. It would be just the thing to bring a smile to her face on a cold, grey winter's afternoon.

While she was daydreaming about bottling sunshine Harry had let go of her hand and turned to sit on one of the seats. He swivelled it round so that it faced the back of the plane, and her. She was almost five feet ten inches tall and there wasn't enough head room inside the plane for her to stand upright, let alone Harry, so she sat down opposite him. Her knees brushed against his as she sat and even through the fabric she was aware of his body heat.

Something about him stirred her senses. She was acutely aware of him. Her hormones were definitely reacting to his pheromones and she was aware of a spark of attraction—not that she would act on it, at least not here. She didn't think it was just her teenage dreams running away with her imagination but regardless she needed to focus. She gathered her thoughts and turned her attention to Harry's words and what he was telling her about the plane.

It was compact and very well organised. All the familiar medical equipment was there, carefully stowed or secured in place. Running along one side of the plane was a stretcher attached to a hydraulic arm and a row of single seats, positioned one behind the other, ran down the length of the plane on the opposite side of the extremely narrow aisle. There wasn't an inch of wasted space in this mini emergency room.

She closed her eyes as she tried to imagine what it would be like to work in this environment. It was difficult to envisage but it was probably exactly what she needed to get her back into nursing. It was so far removed from anything she was familiar with that there would be no danger of triggering memories of working in London. It was perfect.

'Are you all right?' Harry's voice broke her concentration. 'You don't suffer from claustrophobia, do you?'

Emma opened her eyes and found herself looking directly into Harry's blue gaze. He was leaning forward, mere inches from her, and he had a worried look on his face. 'God no.' She laughed. 'Can you imagine?'

She forced herself to look around the plane as if she was taking stock of the confined space but in reality she had to force herself to look away from Harry. It had been only yesterday that she'd told Sophie she was finished with dating but sitting this close to Harry, looking into his blue eyes, breathing in his scent, she knew her body had other ideas. She needed to get her raging hormones under control before they got her into trouble.

'So, what do you think?' he asked. 'Can you see your-self working in here?'

'Actually, I can,' she replied. It would be a challenging job, there was no doubt about that, but she had a feeling a challenge was just what she needed.

'Excellent. Irene'll be stoked.'

'Stoked?'

'Pleased,' he clarified.

And what about you? Emma wanted to know. *Will you be 'stoked' too?* But even if she'd been brave enough to ask, the moment was lost as an alarm sounded.

'What is that for?' she asked.

'It means we've been called out on a flight. I'll have to go,' he said as he stood up, well, not stood exactly, rather unfolded himself as much as possible, leaving Emma to wonder again how he managed to fit into the cockpit. There must be more space up the front than she pictured. He was leaning over her, no doubt waiting for her to move so he could get out. She hustled out of her seat and down the steps, where she was surprised to find Irene waiting for her.

'I'll take you back to the offices, Emma,' Irene said. 'You can't be out here unaccompanied.'

'You should come with us tomorrow,' Harry suggested. 'Get Irene to organise it and I'll see you in the morning.'

There was no time to argue, there was no time to do

anything except watch as Harry was collected by two other people who Emma assumed were the duty doctor and the flight nurse and raced out of the hangar.

Emma frowned and glanced at the plane that sat on the concrete beside her, the one she'd just climbed out of. 'Where are they going?' she asked Irene.

'This is the standby plane. There's a plane out on the apron, ready to go. It takes too long to get the plane out of the hangar, there's no time for that in an emergency. As soon as the plane has been unloaded and restocked it's put back on the apron ready for the next job.'

As Irene finished speaking Emma could hear a mechanical whine as the twin turbo propellers started up and then she saw the plane taxiing past the hangar doors.

'Why don't we go and finish this process? If you're keen to go out with the team tomorrow, I'll need to get some paperwork completed.'

A big part of Emma wanted to be on that plane right now. She loved the adrenalin buzz she got from working in an emergency department and she could just imagine how that was probably magnified a hundred times if the emergency was in an unfamiliar or foreign setting. Every job the flying doctor went to would be different. No two jobs the same. How incredible would that be?

She wanted to work here, she realised. The drama, challenges and variety appealed to her sense of adventure. She missed nursing and she had a feeling the flying doctor service might suit her very well.

She watched as the plane, piloted by Harry, soared off the runway and flew off into the clear blue sky. Tomorrow, she resolved, she'd be on that plane.

Harry almost had a visual on White Cliffs now. The flight had been uneventful, the weather perfect for flying, and

Emma had kept a running commentary going as she'd peered through the aircraft window at the ground below. She hadn't shown any sign of nerves as they'd prepared to take off that morning and judging from the excited tone in her voice she was feeling quite comfortable, despite the fact that the last time she'd been in a relatively small plane things hadn't gone so well. Harry hoped he could manage to execute a smoother landing for her today.

He could hear every word of her commentary over his headset and he didn't need to see her in the back of the plane to be able to picture her face. She was laughing at the sight of a flock of emus racing across the plains and in his mind's eye he could see her matching dimples flashing in her cheeks. Her long brown hair had been secured in a plait and it would be hanging down her back as she pressed her face to the glass.

'What about kangaroos, Harry? When will I see them?'

'Dawn and dusk is the time to spot 'roos,' he told her. 'They don't come out in the heat of the day, they'll be resting under the trees.'

'What are those white hills? Are they ants' nests? They're huge.'

Through the cockpit window Harry could see the hills Emma was referring to. They weren't ants' nests. 'They're the mullock heaps,' he explained. 'White Cliffs is a mining town and the piles of white are the soil that's been excavated and brought up from below by the miners. You should be able to see lots of holes in the ground now, which are the mine shafts.'

The red dirt was dotted with myriad white mounds of white shale, which always reminded Harry of mini-volcanoes. He could picture Emma's green eyes sparkling as she searched the ground for the landmarks he was telling her to watch out for.

'I can. They're perfect little circles, hundreds of them. It looks like we're flying over the moon.'

She was right, there was something rather alien and lunar about the landscape. 'They reckon there are over fifty thousand mine shafts around here, so watch where you walk.'

'Old mines aren't sealed off?' Emma asked.

'Not usually.'

'What do they mine here?'

'Opals,' Harry said as he guided the plane down to the airport runway in a near perfect landing.

'Opals! My birthstone is opal,' Emma said as Harry brought the plane to a stop.

'Really? Well we might have to see if we can show you some.'

'Today?'

'Maybe,' he replied as they began to load gear into the back of a four-wheel-drive vehicle that had come out to meet them. 'Shall I see if I can borrow a car at lunchtime so I can take you for a quick tour of the town? It's an interesting place.'

'I'd like that,' she said as she climbed into the back seat of the four-wheel drive with Grace, leaving the roomier front seat for Kerri and her swollen, pregnant stomach.

Harry waved them off and Emma waved back as Grace began to fill her in on the day's schedule.

'What happens now?' Emma asked.

'The clinic is held in the community health centre. There will be a flexible booking system. We tend to see the more urgent cases first—we need to get them seen to just in case we get called out on an emergency.'

'What happens to the people who don't get seen?'

'There are local nurses who take care of basic health care like ante- and postnatal care, immunisations, health screenings and the like so they can manage anything that's not too complicated. If necessary, people can access more comprehensive services in Wilcannia. We only visit White Cliffs three times a month but we're in Wilcannia four times a week and there are inpatient facilities there too. It's only about a hundred kilometres away.'

That was a long way in an emergency, Emma thought, but she didn't have time to dwell on it. She was well occupied once they got under way with everything from ultrasounds on expectant mothers to applying a cast to a teenager who'd broken his arm the week before. He'd had a backslab applied in Wilcannia but now that the swelling had subsided he needed something more restrictive.

Emma could scarcely believe she was actually working as a nurse again. She'd been in Broken Hill for less than thirty-six hours and complete strangers had convinced her to get back to work. A week ago she wouldn't have thought it was possible that not only would she return to nursing but that she would be enjoying it. She hadn't realised how much she'd missed it. And even though this wasn't quite the fast-paced emergency work she used to, it felt like a step in the right direction.

She smiled to herself as she finished off the boy's cast and washed her hands. She'd thought she would have plenty of time to recover from the trials of the past twelve months while she was here, she'd thought time would go slowly in the back of beyond, but it seemed she'd been mistaken. But being busy might just be the best thing to happen to her. Being busy might be the answer to putting herself back together again and feeling like the person she used to be.

Next on her list was a fifty-year-old miner who presented with a deep gash on his left forearm. In Emma's opinion it should have been sutured two days earlier when the accident had happened but her patient hadn't seen the urgency. He'd simply bandaged it up himself and continued working.

'I only called in here because I had to come into town for supplies,' he told her as she cleaned and rebandaged the wound. Perhaps that's what happened when medical care wasn't easy to come by, she thought. People just got on with things. She taped the end of the bandage and was about to give him a precautionary anti-tetanus injection when she heard Harry's voice.

She didn't find it surprising that his deep drawl was recognisable to her after only a couple of days. Already she felt as though she'd been in the Outback much longer. While her surroundings were still unfamiliar, she didn't feel out of place. She was as comfortable here in the middle of nowhere as she'd ever been in England.

She could hear Harry's voice getting closer and as she pulled off her gloves and gave the miner his last-minute instructions Harry and Grace appeared by her side.

'It's a bit early for lunch, isn't it?' she asked.

'We have an emergency,' Grace said.

CHAPTER FOUR

'AN EMERGENCY?' Emma repeated.

Grace nodded. 'A farmer has come off his motorbike and it sounds like he has a compound femoral fracture. We're the closest available team. We need to get out to him.'

'Did you want me to continue on here while you head off?' Emma assumed that's what Grace would want but she was shaking her head.

'No. It's a bit more complicated than that. Can you come with us? We'll explain on the way.'

'Okay.' Emma quickly threw her gloves and the other rubbish into the bin and headed for the door. Harry fell into step beside her while Grace stopped to talk to Kerri.

'So what's the complication?' Emma asked Harry.

'The airstrip on the station is dirt and because of recent floods the strip is still too wet to land on.'

'So are we driving?'

'No. The station is only about a hundred kilometres east of here as the crow flies but it's a good two-hour drive. It doesn't sound as if the patient has got that amount of time. We have to fly.'

Emma wasn't following the conversation. 'But—'

'We've got a chopper coming in from another station to pick us up and fly us out there.'

Grace caught back up to them. 'Okay, let's get going.' She'd collected a couple of medical kits and Emma and Harry helped load these into the car. Emma expected them to wait for Kerri and she was surprised to find Harry driving away without the other nurse.

'What about Kerri?' she asked.

'Kerri won't have room to manoeuvre in the chopper. It's not designed for heavily pregnant women,' Harry said as he drove the car back to the airport.

'And we won't have any lifting equipment to load the patient into the chopper either, which would be a risk for Kerri,' Grace elaborated. 'She'll stay with the clinic until we know what the situation is. We'll either chopper the patient out to Wilcannia or if he needs to go to Adelaide we'll transfer him to the plane here. Either way, we'll come back for Kerri and depending what the time is we'll make a decision on the clinic then. That's why I want you to come. I need your help.'

There wasn't time to protest, and Emma had no intention of refusing to go anyway. She was about to experience authentic flying doctor work. She was starting to think she could get used to this job. For someone who tried to avoid making plans, unforeseen changes to her schedule weren't a problem and she thought the variety would suit her very well.

When they reached the airport Emma saw a chopper sitting on the dirt beside the flying doctor plane, its blades spinning slowly.

'Grace, if you and Emma can grab what we need I'll work out the flight plan with Neil. Give me a yell if you need a hand.'

'Harry's not flying the chopper, is he?' Emma asked Grace.

'No, he's coming as the navigator.'

Everything was happening very quickly and Emma had no option but to follow Grace's lead and help out where she could. Grace quickly selected supplies and then Emma helped her to load the stretcher into the helicopter. It was a tight squeeze once the stretcher was laid across the floor and Emma had to sit with her legs crossed and her feet on the seat. Grace was straight onto the radio to communicate with the injured farmer's wife so by the time they landed at the station they would have an idea of what they would be dealing with.

Chris had been out checking his sheep but because of the recent rains and floods east of Broken Hill and White Cliffs, the grass was high and his vision had been obscured. He'd collided with a sheep and been thrown over the handlebars of his motorbike. He'd apparently tried to stand up, only to see bone sticking through the fabric of his trousers. He had been out of radio contact as the radio had been taken into Broken Hill for repairs yet somehow he'd managed to get back on his quad bike and travel, very slowly, the seven kilometres back to the house, where he was now in the care of his wife, Ros.

'Is he bleeding a lot?' Grace asked.

'No. I've put a tourniquet around his thigh but he's in a lot of pain.'

Emma didn't doubt that and she noticed Grace gave a wry smile in response to Ros's comment.

Grace kept chatting to Ros and Chris as the chopper made its way east. There was nothing for Emma to do except listen and look at the view, through the windows. It changed as they travelled away from White Cliffs. They crossed a river, swollen after recent rains, and the surrounding land was marked by secondary flood channels and interspersed with green grass. The country was beautiful and not at all what she'd imagined the Australian Outback to look like. In contrast to the greyish-green colour of the flora around Broken Hill, the land out here looked lush and most definitely green. But as unexpected as it was, it couldn't keep her attention.

She could see Harry in profile, where he sat beside the chopper pilot, and her focus kept drifting away from the windows and to Harry. She could see where his hair curled slightly above his ears. He had very nice earlobes, but it was his jaw that caught her attention. Strong, square and masculine, it suited him.

'We're almost with you.' Grace's comment through the headset brought Emma's attention back to the matter at hand. She needed to focus, needed to put Harry to the back of her mind.

Within minutes they were on the ground. Emma and Grace grabbed an emergency pack each and ducked low to avoid the chopper's blades as they ran to the house.

The house was elevated on short stilts that lifted it a few feet above the ground. Chris was lying in the mud at the foot of the stairs, his quad bike inches away, his wife kneeling beside him, clutching his hand. It was clear Chris hadn't been able to make it any further. He must have collapsed when he reached the house and fallen off his bike and that's where he'd stayed.

Emma had been worried about working away from a hospital environment but when she saw Chris lying in the dirt, injured and in pain, she realised the location didn't matter. It was secondary to the drama. All that mattered was attending to Chris and getting him stable enough to move. All that mattered was saving a life.

He was pale and sweaty, his eyes were glazed. His shirt was streaked with vomit and his trousers were torn and bloodstained. His right leg lay at an unnatural angle with his femur fractured in two. He wasn't in good shape.

They might not be in an emergency department or a sterile operating suite but Emma knew what she had to do. Her job.

'I'll do his obs,' she said as she unzipped an emergency pack and pulled out a sphygmomanometer and the oximeter, leaving Grace to start her assessment.

'Pain out of ten?' Grace asked.

'Ten,' Chris answered. His voice was barely audible over the noise of the helicopter, and the effort it took him to get that one word out was obvious.

'BP eighty on fifty. Pulse one-forty. Oxygen ninety-eight per cent.' Emma relayed her readings as she reached for a bag of saline and began to prepare a drip.

Harry appeared beside her and reached for the saline bag. 'Let me hold that for you,' he said.

'Are you sure?'

'I won't faint at the sight of a bit of blood, if that's what you're worried about,' he replied with a smile. 'We're bred tougher than that out here. Think of me as an extra pair of hands. You'll find I can be pretty useful.'

Emma finished inserting the canula and got the drip flowing then passed the bag to Harry. He held it above Chris, and Emma could tell he'd done the same thing many times before.

'Can you draw up twenty milligrams of morphine too? I think it's best if we sedate him before we try to move,' Grace said, when she saw what Emma was doing. 'Then we'll splint his leg and get him in the chopper. He needs to go to Adelaide.'

Emma drew up the morphine and, out of habit, held it out for Grace to check before she administered it through the drip. She was aware of Harry standing behind her, waiting patiently for them to finish attending to Chris. She could feel the air around them crackling with electricity and her skin was tingling. But she still had work to do. She had to block Harry from her mind; she had to ignore her crazy reaction to his presence.

Grace had cut through the leg of Chris's trousers and the extent of the damage he'd done was plain for everyone to see. Emma couldn't resist glancing at Harry, seeking his reaction. She was surprised to find him smiling at her.

'I told you there's no need to worry about me. I've broken my fair share of bones and had more stitches than I care to remember.'

He certainly looked fine. More than fine, she thought as she turned back to help Grace. She poured an antiseptic wash over the wound before padding the fracture site and fixing an inflatable splint around Chris's leg. Harry had brought the stretcher across earlier and had left it on a tarpaulin that he'd spread over the muddy ground. As she and Grace prepared to roll Chris onto the stretcher, Harry handed the drip to Chris's wife and squatted down beside Emma. His forearm brushed against hers as he knelt in the mud and Emma's pulse beat a little faster.

'What are you doing?' she asked.

'I'll help you roll him. Grace can slide the stretcher under and then we're good to go.'

Harry was calm and matter-of-fact and his relaxed demeanour was reassuring. On the count of three they rolled Chris towards them on his left side as Grace positioned the stretcher before they rolled him smoothly back.

She and Harry lifted Chris and loaded him into the chopper while Grace carried the drip. Harry was right. Having an extra pair of hands made all the difference out in the middle of nowhere. He was able to lift, carry or hold whatever they needed and his size and strength made everything look easy. As Emma and Grace settled Chris into the chopper ready for the flight Harry packed up the medical kits and stowed them on board.

Emma was impressed at how well co-ordinated the team was. She even felt like she'd contributed to a successful retrieval. She didn't feel like the new kid on the block. She felt good. Getting back into nursing felt like the right thing to be doing.

Every minute on the short flight was spent trying to keep Chris alive. Emma was aware of Harry in her peripheral vision but she had no time on the return journey to watch him.

Kerri was waiting for them at the little airport in White Cliffs and as quickly and smoothly as possible the team transferred Chris to the plane for the flight to Adelaide.

'That was a baptism by fire,' Harry said to her as she buckled herself into the co-pilot's seat. Grace and Kerri would monitor Chris on this flight and Emma was relieved to hand over her responsibilities. Not because she liked the alternative option, which was sitting up the front with Harry, well, not only because of that, but because she was exhausted.

The cockpit was as small as she'd imagined. Harry kept reaching in front of her as he fiddled with controls and prepared for take-off, and each time he leaned across her she breathed in deeply, inhaling his scent. He smelt wonderful. Emma suspected she did not. The uniform she was wearing was filthy, covered in blood and splattered with mud while, once again, Harry was pristine and immaculate. How was it that she was the one who always ended up looking a mess?

'How are you feeling?' he asked.

'Worn out,' she replied. 'But happy. It was a good outcome.' She yawned and stretched, encouraging air into her lungs and blood to her brain in an effort to keep herself awake. 'How does everyone manage to keep up the pace?' she asked as Harry pulled back on the controls and the plane left the runway.

'I think the adrenalin keeps everyone going. There's no time to think about how tired you are until after the patient has been taken care of and in this case it'll be hours before we get down to Adelaide and back again.'

'We'll be back today?'

'Yep.'

'That's a long day for you, having to fly us back again.'

'I'm used to it.'

'Do you love it?'

'What?'

'Your job.'

'I love flying,' he replied honestly. He did love flying but if he was going to be honest he'd admit that he found the clinic runs monotonous. There was too much time spent sitting around in his opinion and not enough time flying. He preferred the excitement and variety required when he had to fly the team to emergencies.

His ideal job would be running Connor's Corner, the family cattle station, but that was his brother's domain and Emma didn't need to hear his feelings on that topic. He didn't want to talk about his life.

'You did a terrific job with Chris,' he told her. 'You and Grace worked well together.'

Emma turned towards him and smiled broadly. Her green eyes were shining and her dimples flashed in her cheeks, and Harry made a mental note to compliment her more often.

'I'm sorry you didn't get to see anything of the town, though,' he added.

She shrugged. 'No matter. I'm glad I got to go out for the emergency. It gave me a taste of real flying doctor medicine and I preferred it to the clinic session, it's actually more similar to the work I'm used to. I think I prefer the challenge of an emergency.'

Harry knew the feeling. Emma's sentiments echoed his. There was nothing quite like challenging yourself, pushing your own boundaries and seeing how good you could be.

'Perhaps I can bring you back to White Cliffs on the weekend. What do you think? Do you have plans?'

'No, I don't, I'm not big on plans. But I'm not sure if Sophie's made any arrangements. Can we wait and see?'

'Of course.' He was disappointed that she hadn't leapt at his invitation but what should he expect? He needed to remember that she had an aversion to making plans. At least he hoped that was her reason. He'd rethink his approach and try again. 'It's no problem.'

Harry had refuelled and prepared the plane for the return trip from Adelaide to Broken Hill and was waiting for the team to finish their patient handover when he saw Grace striding towards him.

She stopped one pace from him. 'You're not wasting any time.'

'What are you talking about?'

'Inviting Emma out to White Cliffs.'

Harry didn't need to ask how she knew. His conversation with Emma had been conducted through the headsets of the plane so Grace would have heard every word.

'Do you think it's wise?' she asked.

'What?'

'I know she's just your type but she's Sophie's cousin.'

'My type?' Harry was intrigued. He didn't realise he had a 'type'. 'What exactly is my type?'

'Attractive brunettes with long legs. But, most importantly, they're always transient.'

'What do you mean by that?'

'I've known you, what? Three years? And you've only ever dated girls who are here for a specific, and by that I mean short, stay. No one local. No one who might like to stick around and make your life difficult.'

'Is that what you think?'

'Yes. You're not going to tell me I'm wrong, are you?' Grace asked. 'But just be careful. After Emma's performance today I'm hoping we can persuade her to consider volunteering to cover for Kerri until Lisa is back in action. I don't want you jeopardising that. It can be dangerous playing so close to home.'

Harry had to admit Grace had a point but he was willing to risk her wrath, just this once. In his opinion it was always a good day when an attractive woman arrived in town and he wasn't going to pass up the chance to spend time with Emma if she was willing.

Her long legs, sparkling green eyes and flashing dimples were a combination he found hard to resist and if she had no objections to accompanying him back to White Cliffs he wasn't about to let Grace talk him out of it. 'I'm just offering to show her the sights. It's all perfectly innocent.'

Grace laughed. 'I've seen you in action, Harry Connor, and innocent does not describe you. You have a way of getting what you want and making the women think it was all their idea.'

Harry grinned. 'If they come willingly, I'm not about to argue. Emma might like a bit of old-fashioned country hospitality.'

Grace laughed. 'Is that what you're calling it these days?'

'Yes, as a matter of fact.'

Grace was shaking her head at him but he could see

more laughter bubbling up behind her dark eyes. 'When are you going to settle down, Harry? You can't play around for ever.'

'Don't try and ruin my fun. There's no point even thinking about settling down until I find somewhere to settle,' he told her.

He had to pretend all he wanted was to have fun. If Grace or anyone knew how much he longed to settle down he'd never hear the end of it, but he'd meant what he'd told Grace. First he needed somewhere to settle, then he'd worry about finding someone to settle with. He had a picture of his ideal partner in his mind but until he had something to offer he was in no hurry to go and find her. Until he had something to offer he intended to have as much fun as possible. And if Emma was up for it, he was happy to include her in his merriment.

Harry was at Emma's door early on Saturday morning. Not early enough to be considered rude but early enough to make sure she wouldn't have gone elsewhere. He waited for what seemed like ages for the door to be answered. Just as he was starting to wonder if he was too late, Emma greeted him with her megawatt smile and flashing dimples. A feeling of delightful anticipation swept over him.

'Harry! What are you doing here?'

She looked fresh and lovely and had obviously just climbed out of bed. She was wearing pyjamas and her eyes were luminous and green. Harry imagined that was exactly how she'd look after she'd just been thoroughly satisfied and it was all he could do to stop himself from taking her in his arms right then and there and kissing her soundly. In just a few days she'd captured his attention completely.

'Have you ever slept underground?' he asked her.

'Have I what?'

'Ever slept underground? It's an amazing experience, so quiet and peaceful, almost as good as sleeping miles from anywhere under the stars. I'm here to see if you'd like to come back to White Cliffs with me for the weekend. There's an underground motel there, I've reserved two rooms—you said you don't like making plans, so I was hoping this invitation might be spontaneous enough for you.'

'It's not about being spontaneous. It's just that whenever I make plans something seems to go wrong,' she replied. She looked over his shoulder at the people walking in the street. She stepped back, out of the doorway. 'You'd better come in.'

He followed her down the passage into the open-plan kitchen at the rear of the house.

'How do you know I don't have other plans?' she asked.

Harry laughed. 'There aren't too many secrets in this town.'

'Oh, I'd been hoping for anonymity.'

'That will only be a temporary status,' he told her. He smiled and admitted a little guiltily, 'To be honest, Sophie told me she's rostered on at the hospital this weekend and she asked me to keep you company, and I figured, seeing as you don't like to make plans, that I'd take a chance and be spontaneous. So what do you think? Would you like to come with me?'

She stood still, silent, considering. He couldn't believe how nervous he was. How badly he was hoping to hear her say yes.

'What are we going to do there?'

Was that a 'yes'?

'A friend of mine is just about to open a tourist mine. I thought we could go fossicking to see if we can find your birthstone.'

She smiled at him again and his heart pounded in his chest. 'What do I need to pack?'

A definite 'yes'! 'Nothing fancy but you'll need something warm for the evening.'

'Okay, give me five minutes.'

When she returned she'd changed out of her pyjamas and into very short shorts and a sleeveless top. Just as he'd suspected, she had magnificent legs, long and toned and tanned. She was wearing canvas sneakers and in one hand she held a broad-brimmed sunhat and in the other she carried a small bag. It was a tenth of the size of the duffel bag he'd carried for her on the day they'd met.

'Is that all?' he teased.

He was rewarded with another smile and he decided her could get used to seeing her dimples.

'I didn't think I'd need four pairs of shoes for one night away,' she told him.

He took her bag from her and loaded it into the boot of his four-wheel drive while Emma left a note for Sophie. She knew Soph wouldn't mind—in fact, she was pretty sure Soph would have insisted she accept Harry's invitation.

But Sophie wasn't there and Emma told herself that was why she was going to White Cliffs because it was preferable to spending the weekend alone while Sophie worked. She wanted to see as much of the country as possible and the fact that Harry was offering to be her tour guide was a bonus.

She couldn't deny she was attracted to him but she was certain she could keep her hormones under control for two days. Besides, he'd given no indication that the invitation was anything but friendly. She could do friendly.

'Who is this mate of yours with the opal mine?' Emma asked once they were on the road, heading out of town.

She was intrigued with the idea of meeting someone who mined opals but more intrigued with the prospect of meeting one of Harry's friends.

'Tony and I were at boarding school together. He was always coming up with ways to make money—it started with him selling our boarding-house lunches to the day students and at the moment it's him excavating an opal mine for tourists. He's originally from rural South Australia but he caught the opal-mining bug one holiday when he came to stay with my family.'

'Your family is from White Cliffs?'

'Apart from the Aborigines no one in Australia is really from anywhere local, particularly in the case of mining towns. Every family still talks about where they came from originally. In my case it was Ireland. My great-grandfather ended up in White Cliffs and made his fortune with opals. He then bought land north of here and started a cattle station. That's where I grew up but we spent some time here as kids just fossicking.'

'Who's on the station now?'

'My parents still live there but my brother runs it.'

'Is it far from here?'

'Not really, about seven hundred kilometres or nine hours on dirt roads, as long as there's no flooding.'

Emma laughed. 'That's not far?'

'Not out here it's not.'

Harry was pleased she'd agreed to spend the weekend with him. He was keen for her to see something of his place for he was part of this country just as it was part of him. He knew he wanted everyone to feel empathy and awe and wonder for what he believed was the most amazing place on earth and he loved getting the chance to show people the beauty of this sometimes harsh and unforgiving land. Emma, he suspected, would appreciate the majesty of the Outback.

It was still very much a wild frontier and it suited people like Emma, people who didn't like to make plans, people who Harry thought would benefit from being away from regimented city life. He also had a feeling she was searching for answers and there was every chance she'd find them here.

The scenery was unchanging for mile after mile and Emma was beginning to lose track of how long they'd been travelling when she finally saw the road signs welcoming them to White Cliffs. But Harry ignored the signs pointing to the town centre and instead turned off onto a side road marked 'Tourist Trail'.

'Tony's expecting us about now so we'll call at his place first and then go on to the motel,' he told her as he negotiated the dirt road.

Emma assumed he was following the green tourist trail signs, although it was quite possible that he knew where he was going, but how anyone could tell one turn from another out here was anyone's guess.

The road wound around several mullock heaps and Emma held her breath, hoping there wasn't an unmarked mine shaft in their path that was large enough to cause a problem. From the air it had been easy to spot the myriad mine shafts but from this perspective it was much harder and quite disconcerting. But Harry's posture was relaxed. He seemed to know what he was doing and Emma trusted him.

Eventually Harry slowed and pulled to a stop beside an old winch. The buckets hanging from the chain had long since rusted but a new sign had been fixed to the metal frame: 'White Cliffs Tourist Mine—experience the underground life of an opal miner.'

'This is it,' Harry said as he climbed out of the four-wheel drive.

Emma stepped out of the car and looked around. There was nothing that distinguished this spot from a dozen others around them, save for the sign.

'Where do we go?' she asked.

'Down there,' Harry said, as he pointed behind the sign to a long slope that disappeared around a corner. The slope was wide enough to take a vehicle and down one side of it a flight of wide steps had been cut into the red dirt.

Emma followed Harry to the steps but she mistimed the first step and slipped off the edge of it onto the second step. She caught her breath in surprise.

'Are you all right? Harry asked, as he reached for her hand, steadying her. 'We probably should have got you some sturdier shoes.'

'I'm fine,' she replied, but Harry slowed his pace and held onto her hand anyway as they descended into the cutting. Emma didn't protest. Harry's touch sent little flutters of excitement racing through her and she didn't want it to stop.

As they rounded a corner at the bottom of the cutting, the steps ended at a flattened area about twice the size of a double garage. The walls of red dirt towered above them and Emma figured they were about fifteen metres below surface level in what looked like a small quarry. She could see a doorway cut into the side of the quarry, which had been reinforced with thick wooden beams, and the door itself was ajar. A sign above the door repeated the information she'd read on the sign by the car.

'This all looks very civilised,' she said to Harry. The

steps and doorway were not what she'd expected. 'I had visions of having to climb down one of those skinny shafts.'

Harry laughed and Emma wanted to close her eyes and let the sound wash over her.

'Tony didn't want to make it too difficult for people to get to him so access has been simplified. He dug out this area so that small tour buses can drive right to the door and he's going to make a car park at the top that will be able to take the caravans and camper trailers favoured by the grey nomads.'

'Who are grey nomads?'

'That's the nickname for the people who spend their retirement driving around the country, seeing Australia. Once you're inside the mine the experience becomes a bit more authentic, you'll see.'

'Harry, good to see you, mate.' A solidly built man, who was slightly taller than her, came out of the mine to greet them. His salt-and-pepper hair was cut short and his jaw was covered with grey stubble. He was dressed in light brown cotton drill pants and matching shirt and on his feet were thick-soled workboots, probably just the type of thing she should be wearing, Emma thought.

'Tony!' Harry greeted his friend with a hug.

Finding out that Harry was a hugging type pleased Emma but it didn't surprise her. He seemed to be a warm, happy, genuine man, just the type who would hug his mates, but again very different from most of the men Emma knew and totally different from her ex. It made her feel good to spend time with someone like Harry.

Sophie was right. It was hard to be miserable out here but it wasn't because of the weather. It was because of Harry.

'Emma, this is Tony. Tony, Emma.' Harry interrupted her rambling thoughts.

'Welcome, welcome,' Tony said, and kissed her on both cheeks, European style, catching her slightly off guard.

'Hello, Tony, very nice to meet you,' she said, thinking that Tony's kisses didn't send a tingle through her like the touch of Harry's hand did.

'Emma, Emma, you're just what I need, a real tourist.'

Emma wondered why everyone seemed so surprised to hear her English accent. Harry had just finished telling her how everyone here had come from somewhere else and Tony himself looked as though he had European heritage, Italian or possibly Greek. Surely they were used to visitors, wasn't that why Tony was working on this project?

'Come in,' he said. 'You're perfect for my market research. I'm almost ready to open to the public so I want your honest opinion on everything you see today.'

Tony led them through the doorway and the red cliff face opened into a large room that he had styled as a visitors' centre. Newspaper articles and pictures depicting the history of White Cliffs were displayed on the walls, along with aerial photographs and maps plus descriptions of the different types of opal found throughout Australia and what was found in the White Cliffs area. Despite being underground, the room was well lit and a flat-screen television was mounted on one wall. Emma could hear the distant hum of a generator in the background.

'This looks fantastic, Tony.'

He was bouncing around like an excited schoolboy. 'My friends who run the cafés and art galleries and souvenir shops have been saying for years that all the tourists ask if there's a mine they can visit. There's been nothing so I decided to build one. I'm going to show a video of how opal is mined today and then through this archway people can travel back in time to see what the working conditions were like fifty years ago.'

'Can we see it? Is it ready?'

'It's almost ready. If you'd like to see it, I can show you.'

He picked up two bright yellow hard hats from a shelving unit behind a counter and passed them to Emma and Harry. 'You'll need to wear these,' he said as he put his own on his head. 'Occupational health and safety requirements.'

Through the archway was a passage, high enough for even Harry to stand upright in. Lights were strung along one wall and behind panes of Perspex set into the wall Emma could see seams of opal.

'This spot isn't rich in deposits,' Tony said, 'but I've displayed some of what I've found so people can see what it looks like in the rock. A bit further along there's an area where people can have a go at digging for opal.'

'And what if they get lucky?' Emma asked.

'It'd be unlikely.' Tony grinned. 'The geologists reckon this area is pretty well mined and I think most tourists wouldn't recognise unpolished opal if it fell into their laps.'

Emma put her hands on her hips in mock indignation and turned to Harry. 'Harry Connor, you got me here under false pretences! You said we'd be fossicking for my birthstone.'

'In that case, anything the two of you can dig up is yours, Emma. It wouldn't do for Harry to look bad,' Tony told her as they continued walking.

Emma could see why Harry and Tony had remained such firm friends, they both had the same smooth, swift charm about them. Above their heads a mine shaft stretched to the surface, the blue sky just visible at the top. A ladder ran the height of the shaft, reaching for the sky, and past the mine shaft the passage widened again into a large circular cavern. Replica lanterns hung from the walls and their light flickered convincingly. Small picks hung on chains from the walls. 'This marks the point where we go backwards in time,' Tony said.

Past the cavern the passage continued but it was half the height of before.

'What's down there?' Emma pointed towards the low-ceilinged tunnel.

'That's going to be a display tunnel showing working conditions of the early opal miners. Because everything they dug was by hand, they only dug large spaces if they were chasing an opal seam, otherwise it was a waste of energy. Most likely they would have been working on their knees.'

The lights flickered again and briefly went out, plunging them into darkness. Emma instinctively pressed closer to Harry, taking comfort in his warmth and size. She felt him move his arm and she was certain he was about to wrap it around her but then the lights shone again and his arm stayed by his side.

'I'd better go and check the generator,' Tony said. 'You're welcome to stay here and have a go with the picks. Harry will show you what to do.'

Emma looked at Harry. Who wouldn't want to hide away in a dimly lit room with him?

Harry ran his hand lightly over the surface of the wall. His fingers were long and slender and appeared to caress the rock. He traced his fingers over a line that ran across the wall a few feet from the floor.

'You need to look for lines in the rock. Opal tends to form on a fault line. You can quite easily chip away at the soft sandstone and you'll hear if you hit anything harder. Try here.'

Harry passed her a pick that was attached to the wall on a long chain. Emma chipped at the sandstone and the pick left gouge marks in the stone as though she'd run across it with a fork. The air underground was cool after the warmth of the sun at the surface and she shivered as her body temperature dropped.

'Are you cold?'

'A little.'

Harry rubbed her bare arms. The friction from his hands warmed her skin and heat flooded through her body. She felt it flow through her like a living thing, running through her belly and groin.

'Shall I go and fetch you another top from the car?' Harry asked.

Emma would have preferred him to stay and warm her with his hands but she didn't say that. How could she? *Friends. They were going to be friends*, she reminded herself. 'I'll be okay,' she said.

'It's no trouble. Will you be all right on your own for a few minutes? I'll be quick.'

She nodded. 'As long as the lights don't go out,' she said, and she smiled.

'I'll be right back.'

Harry was watching her closely and for a moment Emma thought he was going to lean in towards her. Was he going to kiss her? No, he just gave her arms another quick rub and disappeared along the passage, leaving her trying to prolong the sensation of the touch of his hands and wondering what she would have done if he had kissed her. She didn't think she would have resisted too vehemently. Actually, she doubted she would have resisted at all.

She moved further into the cavern, following the fault line that Harry had pointed out to her, and in the distance she heard a rumble that sounded like thunder. She was touching the wall and felt it vibrate under her hand in time with the noise. Dirt fell from the ceiling and little stones landed on her helmet, knocking it askew and making her jump.

As she reached up to adjust her hard hat she heard another rumble and this time she felt it through the floor of the cavern. The lights flickered again but although they stayed on, Emma felt nervous. She should have gone with Harry. She didn't like being alone at the best of times and she realised she liked it even less when she was underground. Surrounded by flickering lights and in complete silence, she felt very alone.

More debris fell from the roof and landed on the floor in front of her. She backed away, not wanting the dirt to fall on her safety helmet. She made a decision. She'd head out and meet Harry back at the entrance.

She was just about to make her way across the cavern when another rumble shook the mine and she watched in horror as one wall collapsed, trapping her on the wrong side of the mine exit. The exit was in front of her, on the other side of a pile of dirt.

Harry was on the other side of the pile of dirt.

She was totally alone.

The lights flickered again. Trapped underground.

By now she'd figured that there was blasting occurring somewhere on the opal fields and that was causing the damage, but what would happen if there was a fourth blast? What would happen if the ceiling came down on top of her?

She couldn't go forwards but behind her there was only the low-ceilinged tunnel and she had no idea if she'd be any safer in there. It would only take a small amount of falling debris to fill that tunnel.

She stood frozen to the spot. She couldn't go forwards and she didn't want to go backwards. Backwards would take her further into the mine and further away from Harry. He would come for her, wouldn't he?

But what if they were trapped too? She had no way of knowing where they were or if they were okay.

'Harry?' she tried calling, but her voice sounded muffled and pathetic as it was absorbed into the pile of dirt. She doubted it could be heard on the other side.

As she tried to fight back the first wave of panic, the lights flickered again.

Her heart was racing. She concentrated on breathing, counting her breaths, in, one, two, three, and out, one, two, three, while she thought about her options.

The lights flickered once more, plunging her into darkness. She waited—breathed in, breathed out—but the lights didn't come back on. It was pitch black, deadly silent and she was alone.

'Harry!'

She called out again, not expecting an answer, but any noise was preferable to the deafening silence that surrounded her in what felt like her solitary tomb.

CHAPTER FIVE

'EMMA?' Harry yelled. 'Emma, can you hear me?'

He had his hands on the pile of dirt that blocked their path as he waited for a reply. He was holding his breath, not daring to breathe in case the noise of his breathing prevented him from hearing Emma's voice. But there was nothing. Nothing but silence.

'She's on the other side of this?' Tony asked.

'She has to be,' he told Tony. She wasn't on their side and the alternative was that she was under the dirt and Harry wasn't prepared to contemplate that. He should never have left her alone.

He and Tony were standing under the old mine shaft with the cavern, or what remained of it, in front of them and a tiny portion of cloudless blue sky above. If only the collapse had occurred on this side of the shaft, Harry thought, Emma would have been able to climb out.

'There's another shaft,' Tony said. 'It's covered over but it leads down into the low tunnel on the far side of the cavern. We may be able to get to her that way.'

'Let's go.' Harry didn't hesitate and he refused to think Emma wouldn't be getting out.

Tony put his hand on Harry's forearm, holding him back. 'I think we should call the SAR team. They'll have the right equipment.'

'You can call them but I want you to show me where
the mine shaft is. We can get it opened while we wait for
the SAR team.' Harry knew that protocol probably meant
that the White Cliffs Search and Rescue team should be
involved, but if there was a way of getting down to Emma
he had no intention of waiting, although he was prepared to
go through the motions. He almost dragged Tony back to
the entrance, demanding that he take him to the old shaft.

It was pitch black. And silent. There was not a sound. And
it was as still as it was silent. There was no breeze.

*Why would there be a breeze fifteen metres under the
ground?* she asked herself.

How long would the air last?

Hopefully as long as it took for someone to come for
her, she thought. She refused to think that Harry wouldn't
come.

She reached out one hand, wanting to feel the solid
wall of the tunnel. She'd told Harry she didn't suffer from
claustrophobia but that had been before she'd been buried
alive. Feeling the wall gave her some comfort, some perspective, and grounded her. Perhaps she wasn't suffering
from claustrophobia. If it was claustrophobia then surely
feeling the wall behind her would reinforce the idea that
she was trapped, but she found the solid wall comforting.
Perhaps it was simply disorientation.

She laughed and the noise sounded harsh in the silence.
There was nothing simple about this situation.

Maybe she was afraid of the dark or of being buried
alive? Who wouldn't be afraid of being buried alive? Surely
that was quite a rational, sane fear? She wondered what
those phobias were called but she forced herself not to
go down that path. She needed to be thinking positive
thoughts, not naming fears.

There was no sound and no movement but at least that meant the blasting had stopped. That was a positive thing.

Gradually her eyes adjusted to the darkness and her gaze was drawn to her left, down the low-ceilinged tunnel. She could see tiny slivers of light in the distance.

She was drawn to the light like a moth to a flame. She needed that light.

She felt her way along the wall of the mine, reluctant to step away into the darkness, and followed the wall around until she reached the tunnel opening. It wasn't high enough to stand up in and she had to get on her hands and knees and crawl along. The dirt floor was rough against her skin and she could feel the little stones pressing into the soft skin of her palms and knees, but the light kept drawing her forwards.

For a long time the light didn't seem to get any closer and she wondered whether her eyes were playing tricks on her. But she pushed on. There was nothing else to do.

By the time she reached the light her knees were grazed and she was certain her palms were bleeding, but she'd made it. She found she was under another old shaft but when she looked up the opening was covered. There was no patch of blue sky at the top of this shaft, just tiny holes in a covering, emitting pinpricks of light. She stood up and searched the walls of the shaft for a ladder but could see nothing. She stood in the middle of the shaft and ran her hands around the wall just in case, but there was nothing but dirt. Light was coming in but there was still no way out. It wasn't an escape.

She was about to retrace her steps but when she looked at the darkness behind her she decided that the meagre bit of light coming down this boarded-up shaft was preferable to the pitch blackness that waited for her at the other end of the tunnel. It wasn't an escape route but at least there was air and some light. She sat cross-legged on the floor, her back to the wall, and waited for Harry.

Harry burst from the mine, still half dragging Tony with him, only letting him go once they were out in the fresh air. Tony pulled his mobile phone from his pocket and called the SAR team as they hurried up the steps to climb out of the cutting and emerge at ground level. Tony finished the call and stopped beside his utility vehicle.

He took a crowbar, an axe and two pairs of leather gloves from the tray of the ute and passed the crowbar and one pair of gloves to Harry. He paused for a moment as if to get his bearings.

'It's this way,' he said, before he headed north-east across the dirt road.

It was late afternoon and the sun was well on its way to the horizon but the heat of the day was still strong enough to be uncomfortable. They skirted mullock heaps and scrubby vegetation, keeping a vigilant eye out for any unmarked abandoned shafts. As the sunlight bounced off the hot, dry earth and the air shimmered around them Harry could taste the dust in the air. Their footsteps startled a flock of grey and yellow cockatiels that were feeding on the ground and they took to the skies in a flap of wings, screeching noisily.

Tony stopped beside a huge tyre that must have come from an excavator or bulldozer. Fixed across the tyre was an old wooden pallet topped with sheets of corrugated iron. The iron had rusted through in places, leaving dozens of small holes in the sheets.

Something passed across the top of the shaft, creating a shadow. Emma was vaguely aware of something blocking the light but before she could look up it had passed. Had she imagined it?

But there it was again and this time it was accompanied by a loud noise. Emma feared it was another blast and her initial reaction was to look for cover. But there was no-where to hide. Then she realised the noise wasn't vibrating through the earth but instead it was echoing down the shaft. The noise was coming from above her.

'Hello, is someone up there? Can you hear me?'

'Emma?'

His voice was distorted as it bounced off the walls of the shaft but she knew it was Harry. No one else would know her name but it wasn't that, it was the fact that hearing her name on his lips made her heart somersault in her chest.

'Harry!'

He was coming for her.

'Are you hurt?'

'No. I'm fine. I'm just stuck. I can't get out.'

He was here. She hadn't doubted he would come for her.

'We'll have you out in a minute. We just need to get this cover off.'

Harry's words were drowned out by another bout of banging before the cover was levered off, the shaft was flooded with light and his head appeared above her. Even though she couldn't make out his features, just knowing he was there was all she needed.

'You're really okay?' he asked.

'Yes.' The word came out as a half laugh, half sob but it was pure relief that she felt.

'Okay, give me a second to work this out,' he said, and his head disappeared from the opening. She could hear him talking to Tony. 'There's a ladder running down the wall,' he said, and she knew he would choose to climb down to her.

Now that there was more light, she could see a rusty ladder but it stopped halfway down the shaft. A good six metres from the floor. He might be able to drop down to her but then they'd both be stuck. It wasn't going to help her. Or Harry.

'Harry, wait! The ladder doesn't reach the bottom,' she called.

'Don't worry, Em, we'll work something out,' Harry called down to her, even as Tony was arguing the point. Their voices drifted down the mine shaft.

'We should wait for Search and Rescue.'

'Why? You heard her, she's not injured, it's just a simple evacuation. We just need a way of getting down there. We can have her out before SAR even get here. What else have you got in your ute? Rope? Anything I can use as a harness?'

'There's rope and a winch on the front.'

'Can you bring it over?' Harry asked. 'I'll wait here, I'm not leaving Emma again.'

Despite her predicament Harry's words sent a warm glow through her. Harry was waiting. He wasn't going to leave her.

Emma heard the sound of the engine as Tony brought the ute closer. She could hear them working out how to fashion a rope harness for Harry and she could hear Tony trying once more to convince Harry to wait for the search and rescue team and then Harry insisting again that he could do this. Harry won the argument and Tony agreed to winch him down to her.

His face appeared at the top of the shaft again.

'Okay, Em, we're good to go. Can you slide out of the way into the tunnel a bit? I'm going to come down feet first so I won't have a good line of sight and I don't want to land on you.'

She scooted backwards into the tunnel and craned her neck so she could see what was going on. Her heart was in her throat as she watched him enter the shaft feet first. What if something happened to him?

Somehow, despite the makeshift harness, Tony managed to lower him steadily and smoothly. The moment his feet touched the bottom she leapt into his arms. The knotted harness rope and the winch cable dug into her stomach but she didn't care. Never in her life had she been so pleased to see someone.

Her knees were shaky and she clung to him, letting him support her. She'd managed to get off the ground and into his arms but she knew that she was now incapable of holding herself up. Adrenalin coursed through her system. She looked up into his bright blue eyes and her heart skipped a beat.

She saw his blue eyes darken before he tipped her hard hat back and claimed her lips with his mouth, kissing her swiftly and soundly.

His lips were soft but they weren't gentle. The kiss was hungry, intense and passionate. Emma had no time to think and Harry wasn't asking for permission. He wasn't asking for anything. He was demanding a response. And Emma gave him one.

She kissed him back, unreservedly. Her hormones took control, blood rushed to her abdomen, flooding her groin, and her legs turned to jelly. She knew she would have collapsed to the ground if she hadn't been in his embrace.

Eventually Harry broke away, letting her breathe, but he didn't let her go. She was shaking, panting. She wanted more. But it looked like she was going to have to wait.

'I knew you'd come for me,' she said, surprised to find she could talk and construct a coherent sentence.

'If something had happened to you, I would never have forgiven myself,' Harry replied.

'I seem to be developing a penchant for trouble.' She

smiled up at him, able to relax now she was no longer alone.

'This is a new thing for you?'

Emma nodded. 'Yes, bad luck I'm used to, trouble is something different altogether.'

'It's a good thing I'm here, then.' He looked down at her and grinned, and Emma could not disagree. There wasn't anyone else she'd rather have beside her right now.

Tony poked his head over the edge of the shaft. 'Everything all right down there?'

'Couldn't be better,' Harry answered, but his attention remained focussed on her. His bright blue gaze was fixed on her face and he was still grinning broadly.

'Shall I bring you up or do you have other plans?' Tony asked.

Emma could quite happily have stayed where she was. After being so desperate to get out of the mine, now she had to admit she was pretty comfortable.

Harry laughed. 'Let me get Emma sorted.'

She liked the sound of that.

Harry took a length of rope that was hanging from the harness and Emma saw that he had fashioned a second harness for her. He helped her to step into it and secured it around her hips. The bare skin at the tops of her thighs, where her short shorts ended, burned under his touch and her knees nearly buckled as desire flared in her groin. His kiss had her hormones working overtime. His hands were at her waist now, luckily for her as he was able to keep her upright, but the sensation of being held against him made her breathless. She could hear herself panting as she tried to breathe normally.

'Are you okay?'

She nodded. She couldn't speak.

'You're not nervous, are you? I'm going to get Tony to

take you up first and I'll be right behind you,' Harry said as he unclipped the winch from his harness and attached it to hers.

It wasn't fear that was making her breathless, it was desire. Until now she hadn't even thought about how she would physically get out of the shaft.

'You ready?'

She didn't want to go up alone. Not because she was afraid but because she didn't want to leave the sanctuary of Harry's arms. But she had no choice. She nodded and Harry called up to Tony to start winding.

As she was pulled away from Harry she hoped she hadn't had her only chance to be in his embrace. A few hours ago she'd been telling herself she and Harry could be friends, that she could control her hormones. But now she had a terrible feeling that her hormones had just hijacked her brain and she knew she'd do just about anything to convince him to satisfy the desire he'd ignited in her.

A few days ago she wouldn't have thought she'd be considering taking someone into her bed. Jeremy's behaviour had damaged not only her self-confidence but also her trust. But if she couldn't trust Harry, a man who'd just rescued her from the bowels of the earth, a man who she just happened to find extremely attractive, a man who had made her smile again, a man who had made her forget how miserable she'd been, then she doubted she'd ever be able to trust again.

Not all men were like Jeremy. She knew that. And she doubted she had enough self-control to resist the pull of attraction, to resist the flare of desire, not now that the spark had been well and truly lit. Being in Harry's embrace had reminded her that she was a woman and he was very much a man, and she was determined to see if she could get herself back in his arms.

She knew his reputation but that was of no concern, she wasn't talking about a big commitment, she wasn't thinking about anything other than a holiday fling, scratching an itch. If nearly being buried alive had taught her anything, it was that life was short. She wanted to celebrate life. She wanted to prolong this feeling of happiness. She wanted Harry and if she got the chance, she would have him. There was no place for self-control, not today.

Emma was luxuriating in a deep, hot, bubble bath at the underground motel as she examined her wounds. She had a few grazes on her hands and knees from crawling along the passage but other than that she was relatively unscathed and, she had to admit, extremely lucky.

By the time Harry had driven her back to the motel the word had spread and Denny, the motel proprietor, greeted them as if they were returning from battle. Emma's initial reaction to finding out that the entire town seemed to know of her flirtation with disaster, and of Harry's rescue, had been one of annoyance. She hated being the topic of gossip, hated having people know her business.

However, her irritation had rapidly subsided when she'd found out that her little drama had afforded her the luxury of her own bathroom. She'd been amazed to learn that the guest bedrooms didn't have private bathrooms because of the difficulty with plumbing and waste disposal in underground dwellings, and when Denny had insisted on giving her the only room with an en suite bathroom, she'd been happy to accept. That her room had an interconnecting door to Harry's was an added bonus.

She sank deeper into the bath and closed her eyes as she daydreamed about being in Harry's arms and tried to work out how she was going to get herself back there. She was planning on celebrating being alive the best way she could think of—with Harry. She just had to work out a way of getting him to agree.

'Emma? Is everything all right?'

Excellent, she thought as she heard Harry's voice at their interconnecting door. His timing was perfect.

'Denny sent me with some hors d'oeuvres and a glass of wine for you,' he called out. 'She thought it might help you relax.'

Emma appreciated the gesture but she had another form of relaxation in mind, although she wouldn't say no to a glass of wine. 'I'm still in the bath. Do you want to bring it in to me?'

'Are you decent?'

She didn't care if she wasn't but she put his mind at ease for now. She hoped there'd be time to get indecent with him later. 'I'm covered with bubbles.'

She saw the doorhandle turn and then Harry backed into the room. His denim-clad backside presented a very pleasant view. He turned round and Emma could see he had his hands full. He had two glasses and a bottle of wine in one hand and he carried a platter laden with nibbles in the other. His hair was damp, he was barefooted and his jeans and T-shirt were clean. He'd obviously had time for a shower, which was a pity as she'd vaguely entertained the idea of inviting him to share her bath. He carefully set the platter down beside the bath and once he had a hand free he poured two glasses of wine and handed one to her.

'Thank you,' she said.

'Thank Denny, it was her idea,' he replied.

'Tell me,' she said, as she helped herself to a handful of cashew nuts from the platter, 'how is it that everyone knew what had happened almost before we did?' She guessed Harry wouldn't plan on hanging around chatting while she was in the bathroom but she wanted to strike up a conversation to delay him leaving. She had another idea and needed some time to implement it.

Harry leant against the hand basin. If he felt uncomfortable chatting while she lay naked in a bath full of bubbles, he kept it well hidden. He looked happy enough to be there.

'A lot of people have their UHF radios on constantly, it keeps people connected and helps them feel less isolated out here in the middle of nowhere.'

She sipped her wine and asked, 'Don't people mind that everyone knows their business?'

Harry shook his head. 'No. I think it gives people a sense of community and a lot of them can remember the days when the only communication was through the radio, and whether you were contacting the flying doctor or doing School of the Air or chatting to a friend, everyone could listen in. People got used to having no secrets, or to choosing their words very wisely.' He grinned.

'And, quite often, it can mean the difference between life and death. If someone's in difficulty out here, the more people who know about it the more likely the problem is to get solved. It's a good thing.'

Emma hated the thought of everyone knowing her business and it was strange to think that having people so involved in each other's lives could be a good thing.

'Why does it bother you so much?' Harry asked. 'No one knows you.'

'They do now!'

'They know about you,' he said. 'That's different. You could still walk down the street and not be recognised. They won't be gossiping about you.'

Had he realised that was what was bothering her?

'It's not all about me, is that what you're saying?' she asked.

'It's not *only* about you. The mine collapse will be the

talk of the town and the airwaves for the next day or two until something else happens and then someone else will have centre stage. Is anything else bothering you?'

'Nothing that I want to talk about. In fact,' she said as she finished her wine, 'I don't want to talk at all.' She put her wine glass down and picked up the towel that was folded at the foot of the bath. If she wanted to get herself back in Harry's arms, it was now or never.

She shook the towel out and stood up, letting the towel shield her from view. She wanted to tempt him but she also wanted to test the water. If he looked horrified she would be able to back out gracefully with her pride almost intact. But she hoped he'd be tempted.

She wrapped the towel around her body and stepped out of the bath, tucking one end of the towel inside the other to keep it in place. She had Harry firmly in her sights and she was pleased to see he hadn't moved. His blue eyes were locked on her as she walked towards him and she could see his pulse flickering in his throat as he swallowed. He licked his lips as she crossed the floor.

Harry felt as though his eyes were about to pop out of his head as Emma stepped out of the bath. The towel barely covered her torso and her long brown legs glistened with water. His mouth was dry as he watched her wrap the towel around her body and tuck one end inside the other just above the swell of her breasts. All afternoon, ever since she'd been pressed against him in the mine shaft and he'd given in to temptation and kissed her, he'd been thinking about how it would feel to have her in his arms again. Having her in his arms if they were both naked would be even better.

He swallowed. His heart was racing and he felt quite light-headed—too much blood was rushing to other parts of his body and his eyes weren't the only parts of him that were popping. He could feel himself growing harder as he tried to work out what Emma was doing.

He licked his lips as she took three steps and crossed the room, stopping inches from where he stood with his back pressed against the vanity. He could see bubbles still clinging to her slim, brown shoulders and her skin was damp and shiny with moisture. She had piled her hair on top of her head but wisps had escaped and were curling around her face with the humidity of the bathroom. He could smell her now, she smelt of apples.

Her green eyes were luminous and bright and he thought again of how she would look after sex. He'd bet his last dollar she'd have the same expression in her eyes and he was determined to find out if he was right.

He stood silently, watching, taking in the vision of a semi-naked Emma. He could remember how her body had felt as she'd clung to him, long and lean and sexy as hell, and he wanted to rip that towel away from her and claim her body with his.

She was watching him watching her. She said nothing but when she smiled and her twin dimples flashed in her cheeks he couldn't resist any longer. If she was going to stand so close to him, barely dressed, she couldn't blame him for what happened next.

He hadn't wanted to let her go this afternoon and he wasn't going to let her go now.

He grabbed a fistful of fluffy white towel and dragged her to him. It was only a matter of inches before he could bend his head and claim her mouth with his.

Her lips were soft and forgiving under his. He teased them apart with his tongue and she opened her mouth willingly. She tasted of wine. Her mouth was warm and moist and he felt her arms wind around his neck.

His hands moved lower, cupping her buttocks, which were round and firm under the towel. She moaned and thrust her hips towards him and he could feel her pelvis collide with his erection. Now it was his turn to moan.

She pulled his shirt out from his jeans and slid her hands up his back. They were warm against his skin.

'What do you want, Emma?'

He had a fair idea of where this was headed but he had to hear her say the words. He had to know she wanted it as much as he did. She'd had a traumatic day and he didn't want to take advantage of her but he did want to take her. To claim her. To have her. And if she didn't object he would have her right here, right now, on the cool tiles of the bathroom floor.

Emma stepped back and let her towel drop to the floor. 'I want you to make love to me.'

Harry watched, mesmerised, as the towel fell to the floor. Automatically his eyes followed the movement as gravity took hold, and his gaze was now focussed on the towel where it lay in a pool of white around Emma's ankles. His eyes travelled upwards, up the length of her bare legs, long and tanned, to her slim hips, to the dark triangle of hair at the junction of her thighs.

He couldn't speak. A severe lack of blood to his brain had robbed him of the power of speech. But he could admire. So he did.

Emma was naked and she was gorgeous.

His gaze travelled higher, over her flat stomach and her round belly button to her small breasts and erect nipples. She was perfect.

He could see her pulse beating at the base of her throat. Her lips were parted, her mouth pink and soft, her eyes gleaming. She was dazzling.

Harry swallowed. There was only so much temptation

he could stand. He forgot about not being able to speak. He only had one thought. *Get her into bed before she comes to her senses.*

With one step he closed the gap that had opened between them and, without warning, scooped her into his arms. Her skin was warm from the bath and so soft. Inches of her bare flesh pressed against him as he held her. He could feel his erection growing larger with every passing second.

Emma wrapped her arms around his neck as he carried her to the bedroom. One, two, three, four steps across the room until he reached the bed where he gently laid her down.

He ran his fingers up her thigh, cupping the curve of her bottom. Emma closed her eyes and arched her hips, pushing herself closer to him. He bent his head and kissed her. She opened her mouth, joining them together. Harry ran his hand over her hip and across her stomach, his fingers grazing her breasts. He watched as her nipple peaked under his touch and she moaned softly and reached for him, but he wasn't done yet.

Her eyes were still closed as he pulled the clip from her hair and let it tumble around her shoulders. He pushed her hair back, exposing her breasts. He flicked his tongue over one breast, sucking it into his mouth. He supported himself on one elbow while he used his other hand in tandem with his mouth, teasing her nipples until both were taut with desire. He slid his knee between her thighs, parting them as he straddled her. His right hand stayed cupped over her left breast as he moved his mouth lower to kiss her stomach.

Her hands were on the hem of his T-shirt and he could feel her tugging at it.

'Patience, Em. Relax and enjoy,' he said, and his voice

was muffled against the soft skin of her hip bone. He took his hand from her breast and ran it up the smooth skin of the inside of her thigh. She moaned and thrust her hips towards him as her knees dropped further apart.

Harry put his head between her thighs. He put his hands under her bottom and lifted her to his mouth, supporting her there as his tongue darted inside her. She was slick and sweet and she moaned as he explored her with his tongue.

Emma thrust her hips towards him again, urging him deeper. She had one hand on the top of his head, holding him in place, not that he had plans to go anywhere. He slid his fingers inside her. She was wet and hot, her sex swollen with desire. His fingers worked in tandem with his tongue, making her pant, making her beg for more.

'Harry, please. I want you naked. I want you inside me.'

CHAPTER SIX

But he wasn't ready to stop. Not yet.

He knew she was close to climaxing and he wanted to bring her to orgasm like this. He wanted to taste it, to feel it.

He ignored her request as he continued to work his magic with his tongue, licking and sucking. He continued until Emma had forgotten her request, until she had forgotten everything except her own satisfaction.

'Yes, yes, oh, Harry, don't stop.'

He had no intention of stopping.

He heard her sharp little intake of breath and then she began to shudder.

'Yes. Oh, Harry.'

She buried her fingers in his hair and clamped her thighs around his shoulders as she came, shuddering and gasping, before she collapsed, relaxed and spent.

'God, you're good at that,' she said, and he could hear the smile and contentment in her voice.

'Thank you.' He lay alongside her, his hand resting on her stomach as she cuddled into him.

'Now, will you get naked?' she asked.

He turned his head to look at her. 'What did you have in mind?'

'It's your turn. And I want to feel you inside me.'

His blue eyes had changed colour. They were a dark navy now, the brightness overcome with lust and desire.

She slid one hand under his T-shirt and slipped her fingers under the waistband of his jeans. She could see he wanted to give in. 'Please?' she begged.

'Seeing as you asked so nicely,' he replied with a grin as he flicked open the button of his jeans.

This time Emma took charge. She undressed him. His boxer shorts came off with his jeans and his erection sprang free. Emma spread her legs and straddled him, trapping him between her thighs. She cupped his testes and then encircled his shaft with her hand. It was thick and hard and warm and pulsed with a life of its own as she ran her hand up its length.

Harry gasped and his body shook with lust.

'In the pocket of my jeans,' he panted, 'I have protection.'

Harry's jeans were lying on the bed beside them. Emma found a condom in the front pocket and tore open the packet. It was good to know he'd had the same plan as her, she thought as she rolled the sheath down over him.

She was sitting across his thighs and Harry's eyes darkened as she brought herself forward and raised herself up onto her knees before lowering herself onto him. Harry closed his eyes and sighed as she took his length inside her.

She lifted herself up again, and down, as Harry held onto her hips and started to time her thrusts, matching their rhythms together. Slowly at first and then gradually faster. And faster. Emma tried to stay in charge but she found it impossible to control her body. All she could think of was how good this felt and that she wanted more. And more.

'Yes. Yes.'

'Harder.'

'Oh, God, yes, that's it.'

She had no idea who was saying what, all she knew was she didn't want it to stop.

'Now. Yes. Keep going. Don't stop.'

Just when she didn't think she could stand it any longer she felt Harry shudder and she could feel his release as he came inside her. She held her breath as she let herself go and her body shook with pleasure as his orgasm was joined by hers. Their timing couldn't have been better.

They lay together looking up at the ceiling, breathing heavily as they recovered.

'So, you're not worried about people knowing your business now?' Harry asked with a gentle teasing expression in his blue eyes and a wide grin on his handsome face.

'I'm pretty sure no one is going to hear anything through these walls,' she told him. The limewashed earth walls were at least a half a metre thick and naturally sound-proofed, although she knew she hadn't given it a moment's thought while she'd been caught up in the throes of ecstasy. 'I don't think any sound can get in or out of here, it's as quiet as a graveyard.'

'It wasn't a minute 'ago'. He laughed.

'I was enjoying myself,' she countered.

'I'm glad to hear it.'

A skylight was set into the ceiling, high above the bed. The sun had long since gone down and through the skylight Emma could see a sky full of stars. They were so bright, brighter than any she'd seen before, and they looked close enough to touch. She reached one hand towards the ceiling.

'It's so beautiful,' she said.

Harry turned his head and whispered in her ear. 'I couldn't agree more.'

Emma blushed, knowing he wasn't talking about the stars. He was doing wonders for her self-confidence.

He kissed her on the mouth and then sat up on the edge

of the bed. 'Why don't we get dressed? There's something I think you'd like to see.'

He stood and ducked into the bathroom, emerging with the bottle of wine and the glasses. They dressed quickly and Harry gathered two blankets and some spare pillows from the wardrobe before leading her outside. The motel was dug into the side of a hill and Harry headed for a path that led to the top. They skirted around dozens of skylights that protruded from the hill and led to the motel rooms below.

Harry stopped at the crest of the hill and spread one of the blankets on the ground. He wrapped Emma in the other blanket and pulled her down, nestling her between his thighs. The evening was chilly now, the desert ground unable to hold the heat once the sun had set, and Emma leaned back against Harry, seeking his body heat to keep her warm.

He poured them both a glass of wine and touched his glass to hers. 'Here's to new experiences.'

'Some of them I enjoyed more than others.' She laughed.

She sipped her wine, tipping her head back to look up at the sky above. It looked as though someone had thrown millions of diamonds across black silk. There was no moon so there was nothing to compete with the brightness of the stars. 'It looks like every inch of the sky has a star. I've never seen that before.'

'That's because it's a new moon tonight and there're hardly any town lights so there's no competition. The stars get their chance to shine.'

Harry was right. It was a very dark night and because most of the houses in White Cliffs were underground there were very few electric lights to be seen.

'Look over there,' he said. 'Can you see those two big,

bright stars? They're the pointer stars, Alpha and Beta Centauri.'

'What are they pointing at?' she asked.

'The Southern Cross. See those four stars?' He stretched his arm over her shoulder and Emma's gaze followed his fingers. 'Two on the long axis, two on the cross? When I see the Southern Cross, that's how I know I'm home. But I want to know what home is like for you in darkest Peru.'

'I'm not from darkest Peru.' She smiled. 'I'm from Holland Park.'

'That's in London, right?'

She nodded. It was strange to think that Harry had no concept of her life in England, strange to think she'd known him only a few days. Home already seemed like a lifetime ago. 'What do you want to know?'

'Anything you want to tell me. Do you like your job? What do you do on your days off? Have you got brothers and sisters? A dog? A cat? A boyfriend?' he asked as he topped up her glass.

'Do you think I would have made love to you if I had a boyfriend?'

'I hope not but I really have no idea.'

'No boyfriend,' Emma reassured him. 'As the Queen would say, I've had an "annus horribilis". I currently have no boyfriend, no pets, no job and no place to live.'

'That does sound pretty bad. What happened?'

'I was living with my boyfriend, my ex-boyfriend now, but I had to move my things out in a bit of a hurry when he got another girl pregnant.'

'I imagine that was awkward.'

'I guess that's one way to describe it. So I put my stuff into storage and moved back to Holland Park, into my family home, but when I go back I'll have to decide where I'm going to live.'

'What about your job?'

'I quit. Jeremy and I worked together so I decided it would be better, that *I* would be better, if I quit. So I did.'

'You worked together?'

Emma nodded. 'He's a doctor and quite a popular one too. I was quite used to people chasing after Jeremy but this one particular doctor, she was amazing to watch. She really went after him. There are always relationships happening between hospital staff, some are casual, some more serious, some exclusive, some not, but I figured, seeing as we were living together, we were in an exclusive relationship.

'I thought Jeremy was refusing Maxine's advances, because that's what he told me, but it turns out that he wasn't and now she's pregnant.'

Emma was surprised to find that the whole saga wasn't nearly as painful any more. She wasn't sure whether it was having a chance to get some distance that had changed her perspective, or whether it was Harry, or whether it was simply the fact that she'd just had mind-blowing sex and nothing could take the gloss off that right now, but something had definitely dulled the pain.

'And it's his?'

She sipped her wine and shrugged. 'He doesn't seem to think otherwise and I don't care if it is or isn't. That he thinks it could be was enough of a reason to never have anything more to do with him. They're together for now. Whether they'll stay together once the baby is born remains to be seen, but I couldn't stay working at the same hospital as the two of them. I hated knowing that everyone was gossiping and I certainly couldn't stay living with him. So I moved my stuff out and Sophie convinced me to come for a visit. So here I am.'

'How long are you staying?'

'My visa is for three months but I'm not sure if I'll stay for all that time.'

'You haven't got a return ticket booked?'

'I have, but I can change the date if I want.'

'So no firm plans, you can be spontaneous?'

'Flexible,' she corrected. 'Things work out better for me when I keep my options open. Every time I make plans something happens that throws a spanner in the works.'

'Like what?'

'Well, I guess I never really had a chance to make plans until I was a teenager. Dad was a doctor in the air force so we were always moving. I learnt not to make plans, not to get too attached to people or places, not to look too far into the future because I never knew when we'd be on the move again.

'When I finished school I had my heart set on a gap year in Australia so because I didn't know what I wanted to do for the rest of my life I took a job in a pub to make some money to buy my ticket. I kept thinking I'd earn just a little bit more and then I'd go. That was my most ambitious, if somewhat vague plan.

'But just when I'd booked my ticket the London underground bombings happened. My stepmother was in the city that day and she was right in the thick of it. She was one of the lucky ones. She survived but she had a fractured skull and burns and she was in hospital in an induced coma. I couldn't leave then. I had to help Dad with my sisters, who were still very young. But by the time my stepmother had recovered, I at least had a career path chosen. I enrolled in nurses' college. But the next time I tried to come out here my father was diagnosed with cancer.'

'Oh, Em, that sounds horrible.' Harry wrapped his arms around her and Emma drew comfort from his embrace. It was nice to feel that someone was listening, that someone understood. 'But none of those things happened because of anything you did.'

'I realise that but it's just that any time I plan something to look forward to, something goes wrong. If I don't plan things, I don't get disappointed.'

'But you made it here this time. That must have taken some planning.'

'I have Sophie to thank for that.'

'And it must have taken a little bit of planning to move in with your boyfriend.'

'Yes, and look at what a mistake that turned out to be. Although if I hadn't been so desperate to move out of the Holland Park house, I probably would have realised Jeremy wasn't the right choice for me and not have moved in with him at all.'

'Why were you desperate?'

'Dad wasn't doing so well. He was going downhill but he wanted to be at home, not in a hospital, so I moved back to Holland Park to help my stepmother nurse him, but when he died I couldn't bear to stay there. It was too much for me. Jeremy wanted me to move in with him and because I was desperate for a change of scenery and some company other than grieving family members, I said yes. I didn't really stop to think it through.'

In hindsight Emma knew that her hatred of being lonely had been the driving force behind the move. She hadn't wanted to stay in the house where her father had died and she hadn't wanted to be alone so she'd moved in with Jeremy in haste—and had repented at leisure.

'He said we'd get to spend more time together but because of our shifts we didn't see a lot more of each other. Jeremy is the type of person who craves attention and when he wasn't getting enough from me, he took the next thing that was on offer.'

'So your father died, you moved in with your boyfriend and instead of him being there to help you through a tough time he had an affair?'

'Not immediately. As far as I know, it didn't all happen at once but, yeah, he wasn't the best boyfriend.'

It was easy to talk to Harry while they were sitting in the dark. She didn't have to see him scrutinising her face. Out here in the darkness it almost seemed as though she was talking about somebody else's life.

'He wasn't sleeping with her in your bed, was he?'

'Not as far as I know.' Emma laughed. 'From what I heard, she was telling everyone about how they spent hours together in the on-call room. I didn't know which was worse, having everyone knowing that my boyfriend was sleeping around or having it happen right under everyone's noses. I couldn't stand the idea of going to work and seeing them every day so I quit and licked my wounds until Sophie convinced me to come for a visit.'

'This has all happened in the past year?'

'Pretty much. Dad died just over a year ago. I quit my job and moved out of Jeremy's five months ago.'

'What have you been doing for the past five months?'

'Nothing really. I did a little bit of agency nursing but my heart wasn't really in it. I think it was all a bit much to deal with, Dad dying and then the drama of Jeremy. Sophie recognised that I needed a break before I did and she kept insisting that I visit until I finally gave in and agreed to spend some of my inheritance on a trip out here. I think she was right.'

'Will three months be long enough to put you back together?'

'I hope so. I spent a month in Sydney when I first arrived, I've only got two months left.'

'And then what?'

Emma shrugged. 'I'll go home and look for another job. At least I know now that I want to keep nursing, although I definitely won't be going anywhere near that hospital again, certainly not while Jeremy's fiancée is still working there with her swollen, pregnant belly.'

'They're getting married?'

'Yes. I guess at least he's doing the right thing by her. Hoping he stays faithful is her problem now. Although perhaps he will. He seems to think that a doctor is a better partner for him. Do you know he actually told me that he was moving up, that nurses were okay as girlfriends but he'd never planned on settling down with one. He wanted a doctor. As far as I'm concerned, they're welcome to each other.'

'So you're not planning on moving in with any other boyfriends in the future?'

'I don't know what I'm going to do tomorrow, let alone next year or the year after. Do you have your life all planned out? Do you know what tomorrow is going to bring?'

'Hopefully tomorrow will start with the two of us in bed together.'

'My question wasn't meant to be taken literally.' She laughed.

Harry squeezed her shoulders. 'I know, but I think this is where you and I differ. I am a planner, always have been.'

'Since you were little?'

'Yes.'

Emma couldn't understand how people could be born that way. She wondered if she would have been different if her childhood had been more settled and secure. She wondered what Harry's childhood had been like. 'I suppose that's a good thing as you're a pilot. Was that something you always wanted to do?'

'It's always been something that interested me but the reason I work as a pilot is because I can't do what I really want yet.'

'And what is that?'

'Run cattle.'

Emma frowned. 'What does that mean?'

'I wanted to run our family cattle station but from when I was very young I knew that my older brother was going to get first option and unless he didn't want it, I wouldn't get a chance.'

'Is it just the two of you?'

Harry nodded.

'And he's on the station?'

'Yep.'

'But you said you can't do what you want *yet*. What's going to change?'

'I'm going to buy my own place. I just have to save enough money.'

'It sounds expensive.'

'It is. But I have a plan.'

'Of course you do,' she said with a smile. Sometimes she thought she was the only person in the entire world who *didn't* have a plan. 'Can you tell me what it is? Or is it a secret?'

'There are no secrets out here, remember? I have a deal with my next-door neighbour. When he's ready to sell his property, I have first right of refusal.'

'You're going to live on the property next door to your brother?'

'Don't sound so concerned, we won't get in each other's way. Next door is a day's drive away.'

'Oh.' She knew she still had no real concept of the size

and scale of this country. 'So how long do you have to wait to get a place of your own?'

'I'm not in a great hurry. The longer I have before Sam wants to sell out and retire, the more chance I have of saving the money. I'm a long way off still but I'll get there eventually.'

He sounded very confident and Emma envied him his goals and self-belief and conviction.

'I can't imagine settling anywhere permanently. I think that's a legacy of my nomadic air force upbringing.'

'And I can't imagine settling anywhere else,' Harry replied, as Emma's stomach rumbled noisily, interrupting the silence of the desert night.

'Are you hungry? Shall we go in for dinner?' he asked.

'No,' she said as she shook her head. 'This all feels so surreal, being out here under the stars with no one around. I don't want to see anyone else. I don't what to share tonight with anyone but you. I'd prefer it if you took me back to bed.'

'Again?'

She nodded. 'I've been in Broken Hill for four days and I could have died twice. I want to make the most of tonight.'

'I guess you haven't had the best introduction to the Outback,' he conceded.

'You can help to make up for that,' she suggested with a smile.

Harry didn't need much convincing to skip dinner in favour of going back to bed and Emma had absolutely no regrets about the decision. She spent the night getting intimately acquainted with Harry's body and his numerous scars. He'd been telling the truth when he'd said he'd broken more than his fair share of bones and had had more stitches than he could remember.

'What's this scar from?' she asked, as she kissed a thin white line that ran above his right eyebrow.

'My head got in the way of Lucas's golf club.'

'Lucas is your brother?'

Harry nodded as Emma's fingers followed a scar under his chin. 'And this one?'

'Lucas and I were racing our motorbikes. We were going much too fast and I couldn't avoid a rock. My front tyre hit the rock and I flew over the handlebars and landed on my chin and split it open.'

'Do all your scars have something to do with Lucas?'

'No,' he grinned. 'Only half. But everything was a competition between us. Who could get to the gate first on our motorbikes, who could kill the biggest snake, who could swim the furthest across the river underwater, who could kiss the most girls.'

'Didn't you ever get tired of competing with each other?'

Harry shook his head. 'It's the way we were. Still are to a degree, although our lives are quite different at the moment. Lucas is a responsible husband and father to two kids with another on the way. It's his turn to referee the contests between his own boys now. But it was mostly friendly rivalry. You said you have a sister—didn't you compete?'

'I have two sisters, half-sisters, really, and they're much younger than me. My mum died when I was two so for years it was just me and my dad. When he remarried I had competition for the first time and I have to admit I didn't really like it.'

'How do you get on with your stepmother?'

'Good now. But I was pretty horrible initially. I was fourteen when they got married and I didn't want to share my father with anyone. When my half-sister was born I was acting up so much that Dad sent me out to Australia to stay with Sophie's family for six months. That's when I got hooked on all things Australian, but I also missed my dad and the baby so when I got home again I was a model child with dreams of a gap year. I'd grown out of my rebellious teenage phase and Dad and I did things that he couldn't do with my half-sisters so I still had time with him by myself. The next time I really had any competition was as Jeremy's girlfriend and I didn't like that either.'

'I like the challenge of a good competition. Sometimes I succeed, sometimes I don't, but it's all good.'

Emma ran her fingers over a scar that bisected Harry's left shoulder. 'Was this one from a successful challenge?'

'That one hurt,' Harry admitted. 'I came off second best in a battle between me, my motorbike and a fence post.' He held up his left hand. There was a scar running through the palm of his hand. 'I had a bone pinned in my hand at the same time and I have a pin in my tibia courtesy of my horse falling on my leg and fracturing it.'

It was amazing that there was anything left of him, Emma thought as she continued her inspection, but there was more than enough to keep her satisfied well into the next morning.

CHAPTER SEVEN

THE past two weeks had flown by in a blur of activity. Sophie and her friends were a very social bunch and there always seemed to be a barbeque, a game of tennis or birthday drinks to go to, and while everyone was more than happy to include Emma in their plans she often felt as though she was living someone else's life. As if this life was on loan to her. Which she supposed in a way it was.

She'd agreed to continue working with the flying doctor service as a volunteer and she was loving that—at least that felt like it was her thing. And it didn't hurt that it meant she was able to spend a lot of time with Harry. He was easy company and a fantastic lover and many mornings Emma was surprised to find she had the strength to get out of bed. She had never had so many orgasms in her life.

And this weekend she was getting to spend time with Harry, just the two of them, alone for the next thirty-six hours. Or almost alone.

Harry had flown her to Innamincka, seven hundred kilometres north-west of Broken Hill. It was an Outback town so small Emma almost wondered why it even existed, but this weekend the population was expected to swell to a few thousand as locals and tourists flocked to town for the annual gymkhana.

Harry and Lucas were competing in an equestrian event

so she and Harry wouldn't be alone the whole time, not once his brother arrived, but Emma didn't care. She would enjoy every minute she got with Harry and being here, away from the social hub of Broken Hill, made Emma feel as though she was at least taking part in an activity that was hers, not just one she'd borrowed from Sophie.

Innamincka's official population was just over one hundred people but Emma was already getting used to flying in and out of tiny settlements and was no longer surprised when a town consisted of a couple of streets, a pub, a petrol station and a handful of houses. What did surprise her was that this tiny town had its own racecourse. She and Harry were sitting in the temporary grandstand at the racecourse, watching the children's competitions, the first of the gymkhana events, while they waited for Lucas to arrive with the horse truck. Harry was checking his watch every few minutes, obviously getting antsy about Lucas's whereabouts.

'How long until your event?' she asked.

'It's not for a couple of hours.'

'I'm sure Lucas will be here soon,' she told him. 'I'm just going to go and freshen up.'

She leant across to give Harry a kiss. She only planned to be gone a few minutes but she enjoyed kissing him so much she wanted to do it as often as possible. She left the grandstand and merged with the crowd. It was still growing and there was a line of four-wheel-drive vehicles towing camper trailers all trying to secure a good position in the campground on the banks of Cooper Creek.

She could hear music blaring from car stereos competing with the loudspeaker as various activities were announced. There were dogs barking, horses whinnying, planes and helicopters flying overhead and motorbikes dodging pedestrians.

Emma ducked and weaved her way through the crowd, dodging kids who were clutching large sticks of pink fairy floss. She could smell onions frying on barbeques and the smell made her stomach rumble. It was dusty and noisy and chaotic and Emma soaked up the atmosphere as she tried to commit the sights and sounds and smells to memory. This would probably be the only Outback gymkhana she'd ever attend and she wanted to remember it all.

On her way back from the toilets Emma detoured past one of the horse yards and a set of temporary stables. She was keen to get a look at the quality of the Outback horses.

In the distance she spotted Harry leading a horse out of a horse truck and down a ramp. His brother must have arrived while she'd been freshening up. She changed direction and headed for Harry. He was bending over, checking the horse's legs, and Emma couldn't resist giving his bottom a pat as she walked up to him.

Harry turned his head and straightened up as Emma slid her hand into the back pocket of his jeans and squeezed.

Only it wasn't Harry. This man was a little bit shorter, a little bit heavier and quite a bit surprised. But he'd walked like Harry and even now Emma could see similarities in their posture and their faces. But it wasn't Harry, not unless he was wearing contact lenses, as this man had brown eyes, not bright blue. But they looked so similar and Emma was confused for a little longer until her brain finally kicked into gear and she realised that this man must be Harry's brother.

She blushed and removed her hand from the inside of his pocket. 'Sorry, I guess you're Lucas,' she said.

'And you must be Emma,' the man said with a smile, and the similarity between him and Harry was even more apparent then.

Emma nodded and apologised again.

'Don't worry, it happens all the time.' He shrugged. 'Twins have to get used to it.'

Emma frowned, Harry hadn't told her they were twins but there was no doubting that Lucas was telling the truth. So he was the older brother who had inherited the running of the cattle station. Was it significant that Harry hadn't told her they were twins?

'Do you know where he is?' Lucas asked, interrupting her rambling thoughts, and when Emma nodded he added, 'Would you mind getting him? I could use a hand with the horses.'

'Sure. We'll be right back,' she said, and walked away.

Harry had moved out of the grandstand and was now leaning on the railing that ran around the racecourse, chatting to a group of men. He saw her approaching and waved to her to catch her attention.

'Lucas is here,' she told him. 'He's unloading the horses and said to tell you he could use a hand.'

Harry excused himself from the group and retraced Emma's footsteps. He didn't seem to think it strange that she'd bumped into Lucas and he obviously assumed, correctly, that she'd come across him somewhere between the grandstand and the toilet blocks. He took off in that direction without waiting for further information.

'You didn't tell me you were twins,' she said as she followed in his wake.

'Didn't I?'

'No.'

'Does it matter?'

'Not to me,' she replied, but she wanted to add that it obviously made a huge difference to Harry. His only brother, his older brother, was his twin—what a difference a few minutes could have made to Harry's life.

He could have had what he wanted, the cattle station.

He could be living his dream right now if it weren't for bad timing. But she kept quiet. It wasn't her business. But she was curious to see what their relationship was like. Were they close or did this dream of Harry's create friction between them? Did Lucas even know about Harry's dream?

She didn't have to wait long for some of her questions to be answered. Harry and Lucas greeted each other with big men's hugs as she stood on the sidelines, observing.

'Where're Jess and the boys?'

'Jess's still suffering pretty badly from morning sickness. She preferred to stay home.'

'You should have brought Will and Jack with you, given Jess a break.'

'Mum and Dad will lend a hand and I don't think Jess trusted me to supervise the boys. I brought Darren instead. He's going to ride in the barrel race. He's just taken Duke for a walk, you know how fidgety he gets after being in the truck. Do you ride, Emma?' Lucas asked as he handed the reins of a pretty grey horse to Harry.

'I can ride,' she answered.

'Harry didn't tell me. I could have brought a horse for you for the weekend.'

'No, no, it's fine. I haven't ridden for a while.'

Harry was looking at her quizzically and Emma knew he'd be wondering why she hadn't told him she could ride. She'd known they were spending the weekend at an equestrian event so of course he'd be thinking it was odd she hadn't mentioned her riding capabilities.

'Can I brush one of the horses down for you?' she asked, trying to divert attention from her omission. She and Harry obviously both played their cards close to their chests.

Lucas disappeared into the truck—it was massive and Emma wondered what else they had stowed in there—and Harry passed her the reins of the grey horse. 'You can take

Lady Jane,' he said as he picked up the brushes and went over to the other horse, a beautiful, glossy black stallion, the one she'd seen Lucas lead out of the truck.

'Why didn't you tell me you ride?' Harry asked as he started to brush his horse down.

'I don't ride any more.'

'Why not?'

'Riding was something I used to do with my dad. It was one of the activities that was just for us. One of the times I didn't have to share him with anybody. I haven't ridden a horse since he died.'

Emma kept her head down. If she focussed on brushing Lady Jane she was able to talk about her father but she knew if she looked at Harry she'd find it a lot more difficult. Brushing the horse was a familiar activity, one she found soothing. The smell of horses, the warmth of the mare's flank under her hand, the sound of the soft puff of air from her nostrils as she breathed relaxed her. She'd missed the horses. She missed her dad.

Harry didn't know how to comfort her. It was clear she was thinking about her father. She was avoiding eye contact with him, focussing on the horse. He hadn't suffered through anything remotely like losing a parent and she'd lost both. He didn't think he had the right words to offer. As he racked his brain, searching for some words of comfort, any words at all, Lucas reappeared from the depths of the horse truck and interrupted his thoughts.

'Do you want to walk the horses or are you going to get a spot to watch the barrel race?' he asked.

Harry glanced at Emma.

'If it's all right, I'd like to watch some events,' she replied.

'Of course it's all right. I'll take care of the horses,' Lucas said as he shooed them off.

Harry wasn't about to argue. He took Emma's hand and walked with her back to the grandstand. Heading up into the seats, he saw someone he was keen to introduce her to. He ducked into the row of seats beside a solidly built man, several years older than him, with close-cropped grey hair.

'Emma,' he said as they sat down, 'I'd like you to meet Sam Cooper.'

'From Cooper Creek Station?' Emma asked.

'Nice to meet you, Emma,' Sam said, as he shook her hand. 'My reputation precedes me, I see.'

'Only by a few days,' Harry told him. 'How have you been?'

'Can't complain. I've got a bit of indigestion from too many onions with my snag today, but other than that I'm good, real good.'

'Where's your better half?'

'Jo is selling Devonshire teas over at the Country Women's Association tent. She loves the chance to have a good gossip, you know how women are.'

Emma listened to the two men exchanging news as she thought about what Harry had told her about Sam. She knew he was the one whom Harry intended to buy out. Harry's heart was set on owning Cooper Creek Station, Sam's home, one day.

The trouble was Sam didn't look a day over sixty and appeared to be fighting fit. It might be years before he was ready to sell his property. Emma had been so certain that Harry, with his well-laid plans, would achieve his dream but now, having met Sam, she wondered if it was going to be more difficult than Harry anticipated.

The first race was about to begin and the competitors were announced over the loudspeaker. Set out in front of the stockmen were rows of barrels, spaced at regular intervals, each with a flag protruding from the top. There were sixteen riders waiting for the start of the race. Their horses were pacing in the dirt, eager to be given their heads. Sam and Harry turned their attention to the riders assembled in front of the grandstand and Harry explained the event to Emma.

'This is a flag and barrel relay. There are four teams of four riders. The first rider from each team has to collect the flags and bring them back to the second rider, who rides out and puts the flags back. The third and fourth riders repeat the moves. The team that finishes first wins.

'Can you see the first rider in the group closest to us? That's Darren, Lucas's head stockman, on his horse Duke. Jonno is the second rider in that same team, he's one of Sam's station hands.'

The starting pistol fired and Darren on Duke shot away to a good start. Darren headed for the furthest flag and pulled it from its holder as he turned for home, gathering the other three flags on his way back. He passed the flags to Jonno, who urged his horse on as he replaced the flags. One of the other teams was not far behind and they rounded the furthest barrel almost simultaneously. The whole scene looked quite chaotic to Emma, with horses and riders passing within a few inches of each other at breakneck speeds.

She held her breath as one of the horses skidded around a barrel. The horse managed to regain its balance and she thought the rider was going to stay on its back but the next thing she saw was the rider being flung to the ground right in the path of an approaching horse.

'Oh, my God.'

Emma heard the collective intake of breath from the crowd and clutched Harry's arm as the rider attempted to jump his horse over the fallen man. For a moment Emma thought he'd succeeded but then she saw one of the horse's back hooves come down, right on the man's head. And he wasn't wearing a helmet.

The crowd was mute, stunned into silence. But the silence only lasted a few seconds and in the time it took for the rider to wheel his horse round and dismount, other spectators had leapt to their feet and raced to be of assistance.

Harry was one of the first out of his seat. He jumped off the grandstand, landing safely a few feet below where they'd been sitting, and vaulted over the railings that ran around the track.

Emma was close behind him but by the time she'd got out of the grandstand and into the arena Harry had already grabbed the reins of the riderless horse and was directing the other competitors to clear the area, keep people back and call a doctor.

Emma knew that Grace was the doctor on duty. They were already here, standing by in case of emergency. Apparently there weren't too many gymkhanas or rodeos that didn't need the services of the flying doctors in some way, shape or form and now Emma understood why. What she didn't understand was why the competitors weren't wearing riding hats.

A couple of competitors were crouched beside the injured man as she approached. 'Don't move him!' she cried. They probably knew not to move him but it was better to be safe than sorry.

She knelt in the soft sand. She licked her fingers to wet them and held them under the man's nose. She could feel small exhalations. There was a depression in his skull and his eyes were closed but he was breathing. She looked over her shoulder, searching for Grace. Where was she?

Emma wasn't used to being the first medic on the scene neither was she used to trying to assist someone without any medical equipment on hand. She didn't like the feeling of helplessness that she was experiencing. She checked over her shoulder again. Harry had cleared all the horses from the arena and was on his way to her but there was still no sign of Grace. Why was she taking so long?

'What's his name?' she asked the two men who were still kneeling beside her.

'Russ.'

She held Russ's hand and started talking to him. His eyes were still closed and he didn't respond. She had no idea if he was aware of her but she needed to talk to him. She needed to do something. Anything.

In her peripheral vision she could see Harry moving towards her but then change direction. He crossed the arena. Her gaze followed him as she kept talking to Russ. Harry was going to meet Grace. Finally she was here.

In reality Emma knew it had probably only been a minute or two since the accident, it just felt like for ever.

Grace was carrying a medical kit in one hand and had a second slung over one shoulder. Jill, one of the nurses, was with her, carrying a stretcher and a third medical bag. They were trying to jog but the equipment was heavy and awkward. Harry took one bag from each of the women, lightening their loads.

Grace knelt beside Emma as Emma told her what she knew so far.

'Right pupil fixed and dilated.' Grace took over patient care and Emma was happy to hand over responsibility. Russ had a fractured skull with intracranial bleeding. It wasn't surprising but it wasn't a good situation.

Harry crouched beside her. 'What do we need to do for Mick?' he asked.

'Who's Mick?'

Harry nodded towards a stockman, who was sitting in

the dirt. 'The guy whose horse stepped on Russ. Can you take a look at him?'

Emma nodded and stood, leaving Grace and Jill to do what they could with Russ.

Mick had had a severe fright but he wasn't injured. By the time Emma got to him his vital signs were all within normal range. 'Give him a sip of brandy and get a couple of the guys to help him away from the area. It's better if he can't see Russ being treated,' she said to Harry.

Within moments Harry had organised for that to happen and Emma was able to return to see if Grace needed any assistance. She had inserted an IV line and had a cervical collar around Russ's neck and was assembling the Jordan frame around him, mindful of possible spinal injuries. Together Harry, Grace and Emma picked up the stretcher while Jill held the drip. There were plenty of offers to help but Grace wanted people who knew what they were doing.

But there was only so much they could control. The airstrip was a few minutes' drive away and Emma wondered how they were supposed to get Russ to the plane. She thought maybe they would have to carry him all the way and she knew that would be a struggle but the alternative was completely unexpected. One of the railings in the track fence had been removed and someone had backed their ute up. They loaded Russ on the stretcher into the tray of the ute and climbed in beside him for a slow, cautious drive to the airstrip.

Emma found this method of transport difficult to comprehend but it seemed to work and they managed to get Russ loaded safely into the plane for evacuation to Adelaide. She and Harry hitched a ride back to the racecourse in the ute. She squashed herself into the front seat for the return trip between the driver and Harry.

'How're you doing?' Harry asked. He had his hand on

her knee and squeezed her thigh gently. There was no room for anything more demonstrative in the close confines of the cab.

'I'm okay now but it was a bit overwhelming,' she admitted. She was looking forward to having a few quiet moments to process what had just happened but her ideas were quickly shelved when they got back to the race track.

Sam was waiting for them as they climbed out of the ute.

'The organising committee has brought the campdrafting forward,' Sam told them. 'It's the next event.'

Emma knew this was the event that Harry had entered. She frowned. 'You're not still planning on competing?' Emma asked.

'Of course I am,' he replied.

Emma couldn't believe what she was hearing. 'After everything that just happened?'

'They're not going to cancel the entire weekend. People have put too much time and effort into organising this. Accidents happen. Things go on,' Harry explained.

'But Grace and the plane have gone. What if there's another accident?' she argued.

'Relax, Em. They'll cancel the high-risks events while the flying doc is out of the picture but campdrafting is one of the safest.'

'But—'

'Sam, could you do me a favour?' Harry cut her off. 'Can you keep Emma company while I ride, explain to her how safe it is?'

'It would be my pleasure,' Sam replied.

'Go with Sam, Em, I'll be fine.' He kissed her swiftly on the lips and added, 'I'll be back before you know it.' And then he was gone, giving her no time to protest.

She was furious. She couldn't believe he was still riding. If she'd had something to throw at him she would have, maybe that would have knocked some sense into him. But it was too late. He'd disappeared and she had no option but to follow Sam back to the grandstand. What if something happened to Harry too?

CHAPTER EIGHT

EMMA's heart was pounding as she climbed the grandstand steps. The thought of Harry being injured made her feel nauseous. She knew she'd have to watch him. It was the only way to keep her nerves under control. She tried to concentrate as Sam talked her through the event but that took some effort.

As far as she could gather, each competitor rode separately. Their performance was judged and scored out of one hundred points, with the highest scoring competitor winning. Each rider had to separate a beast from the mob of cattle and parade it in front of the judges, before driving it through a pair of gates and out of the camp. Once outside the 'camp' they needed to manoeuvre the beast around a course and then through another two narrowly spaced pegs that marked a second gate.

Her hands were shaking with nerves as the event got under way and she sat on them in an effort to stop them from twitching.

'I've never heard of campdrafting until today,' Emma admitted as the first rider completed the course without incident.

'That'd be because it's an Aussie invention,' Sam told her. 'Watch Harry to see how it's done properly. He's bloody good at it.'

Harry was waiting for the starting signal and seeing him sitting in the saddle made Emma forget her nerves. She'd always had a vision in her head of how he would look on horseback and she wasn't disappointed. He looked comfortable and confident when he was behind the controls of a plane but on horseback he looked sublime.

He urged his horse forward. He was effortless, relaxed and seemed perfectly suited to this environment. Emma appreciated the relationship between the horse and rider. She could see how the horse responded to Harry's direction and how hard it worked to separate the steer from the mob and then kept on working, cutting back and forth, to keep the steer from getting back to the mob.

She forgot that Harry wasn't wearing a helmet. She forgot that it was still a dangerous exercise because Harry made it look easy. Okay, she was probably a little biased but she was pretty impressed. Sam was right—Harry was good.

He'd driven the steer through the first set of gates and was coaxing it around the course before heading for the final gate. She could imagine him doing this for a living and she wondered how long he'd be happy to wait until he got his cattle station. Why didn't he work with Lucas? she wondered. Was there enough work for both of them? Why was it that only one could stay on the station? Harry belonged in the bush.

His thighs flexed and strained as he guided his horse and she had plenty of opportunity to admire the way his jeans moulded to his backside as he rose out of the saddle. She could close her eyes and picture how those same thighs had felt between her legs, how his powerful glutes had driven him inside her. Watching him on horseback was almost as good as foreplay. He was sensational and she could feel herself becoming aroused. She wondered what his plans were for the rest of the afternoon. She wondered if she could convince him to sneak off somewhere so she could make love to him.

He lifted his hat to salute the crowd as he finished and she let herself believe he was looking directly at her. She pulled her hands from underneath her thighs so she could applaud him along with everyone else in the stands. He was magnificent. And, for now, he was all hers.

Harry tried to keep focussed on the task at hand but his attention kept wandering to the stands, where he could see Emma sitting, watching him. He wasn't used to being distracted but even at this distance he could feel her gaze on him and he could easily pick her out in the crowd. She was wearing an emerald-green T-shirt that made her eyes pop and a felt cattleman's hat that he'd given her. She'd plaited her hair into two plaits and they fell over her shoulders and made her look like a teenager. Each time he turned his horse in front of the stands his eyes drifted to her, he couldn't help it, but somehow he managed to keep the steer from returning to the mob and get it through the last gate.

He lifted his hat to her in salute as he finished. She was cheering and smiling. He could see her dimples flashing in her cheeks from where he was as she clapped his performance, and even though he knew his effort wasn't enough to give him victory today he knew he'd be going home with a better prize tonight.

He'd known he wouldn't win but even finding out later that he'd come second to Lucas didn't bother him—he had Emma to console him and it was his turn to watch her now.

The gymkhana had finished for the day with no further mishaps and everyone was at the pub for a barbeque. Harry was at the bar, ordering drinks, and Emma was sitting with Sam and his wife Jo. She was leaning forward, talking to Jo, and she had one knee bent and had tucked her foot into her lap. He couldn't work out how she could be comfortable sitting like that, especially when she was wearing jeans and elastic-sided leather riding boots that she'd borrowed from Sophie. Her suppleness amazed him and he felt himself growing hard just thinking about the possibilities of Emma and her flexibility.

'How about that beer you owe me?'

His carnal thoughts were rudely interrupted by his brother's arrival.

'What beer?'

'The one I get for kicking your butt in campdrafting.'

Harry laughed. He had no issue with Lucas beating him. All their lives they'd been involved in friendly competition and they'd both won their fair share of contests. Lucas had been the better rider today and Harry knew that, even without the added distraction of Emma, Lucas probably would have won as he spent far more time in the saddle than Harry did these days. 'Fair enough,' he said. He held up one finger to the barman and pointed to Lucas, asking for another beer to be added to his round. 'But don't get too cocky, you only just got over the line. You'd better watch out next time.'

'Whaddaya mean?'

'You only beat me by six points. If I get some time to practise I'll kick *your* butt next time round.'

'Not if you bring Emma.'

'What?'

'I'm surprised you even finished the course. You spent more time watching her than you did watching the cattle.'

'Can't blame a man for that,' Harry said as he paid for the drinks. 'Emma's a lot more attractive.'

'Can't argue with you there,' Lucas agreed, taking a

long pull at his beer. 'Is she planning on staying around for a while? You gonna bring her out to the station?'

Harry shrugged. 'Dunno. She's only visiting for a few months so unless she gets rostered on for the station run out to you, I can't see us getting there otherwise.'

'She seems to be fitting in all right for a tourist. Maybe she'll want to stay.'

Would she? In Harry's mind Emma was only there because Australia had seemed like a good place to escape to. He didn't kid himself that she was planning on staying. This whole trip was really just a small portion of her life, a small section of the bigger picture, and he was just one little piece of the puzzle that Emma was still trying to piece together at the moment. He knew she had no firm plans for the future and that would include no firm plans to stay in Australia, but the idea that she could decide to do just that held quite an attraction. It certainly wouldn't be a bad idea. He'd heard worse.

He saw her look up and catch him watching her. She smiled at him, her dimples creasing her cheeks. What was he doing standing here talking to his brother when Emma was sitting across the room?

'Come on,' he said, picking up the drinks.

Lucas laughed, knowing exactly where Harry's mind was. 'Am I boring you?'

'Yes,' Harry retorted. 'And I have plans for tonight that don't include chewing the fat with my brother.'

But there were plenty of other people around who were also capable of thwarting his plans. He handed Emma her drink and was rewarded with her megawatt smile and flashing dimples, but before he could slide into the seat beside her Tony arrived at the table.

'Harry, I thought that was you, mate.'

Emma had been watching Harry as he waited at the bar.

He was a man of many faces—the immaculate, organised pilot, the attentive, skilful lover, the good mate—and today she was seeing yet another side to him, that of the younger brother. She couldn't decide which one she preferred.

That was a lie—the skilful lover was definitely her favourite—but there was so much more to him and she was amazed at how all his personas suited him equally well. The pilot's uniform suited his meticulous nature but he looked just as comfortable in the Outback uniform of jeans, riding boots, shirt and cattleman's hat. That suited his physical presence and ruggedness and emphasised his masculinity.

There was no denying his masculinity. Or the fact that he was a complete package. He was a man's man but he held plenty of appeal for women too. He seemed to be everybody's friend. Everyone seemed to know him and wanted to have a few words with him. People seemed to feel a similar way about Lucas too, she'd noticed.

There was something special about the Connor boys, she thought as she watched them crossing the room, but there was only one Harry. And as each new layer of his personality was revealed to her she felt herself falling a little more under his spell.

He handed her a beer and as she smiled at him in thanks she felt a hand on her shoulder. She was so engrossed in her thoughts about Harry that this unexpected touch from behind startled her.

'Emma, I'm glad to see you're still in one piece.'

She turned her head and recognised Harry's friend from the almost ill-fated trip to the White Cliffs tourist mine. 'Hello, Tony.'

'You remember me.' He sounded pleased.

'I won't forget anything about that day in a hurry,' she told him. Out of the corner of one eye she could see Harry break into a smile and she knew he was thinking about that night, just as she was. She could feel herself blushing and forced herself to continue a conversation with Tony.

She knew if she looked at Harry her feelings would be written all over her face for everyone to see and she wasn't ready for her feelings to be on public display. She'd learnt the hard way about keeping some parts of her life private.

'What's happened at the mine? Are you going to be able to open it?'

'Yes, luckily,' Tony replied, just as Sam and Jo excused themselves from the table. Tony sat himself down in the chair Sam vacated and spoke to Emma. 'It turns out the miners who were blasting that day didn't have permits. Geologists had pegged that area as unstable so they couldn't get a blasting licence but they blasted anyway. Turns out it wasn't my excavating skills that were the problem. I'm going to add some more supporting beams just to be safe but I hope to have it open properly next month. I still can't believe our luck that it wasn't worse.'

'I'm starting to think that luck has a big hand to play out here,' Emma said. 'It's a bit like living on a roulette wheel.'

'Speaking of luck, I have an update on Russ.' Sam was back at the table and everyone fell silent at his announcement as they waited for further information. 'He's in Theatre but doctors are pretty confident he'll pull through. We're passing the hat around for a collection to help him through his recovery.'

Sam passed a large tin around the table that looked as though it had been pinched from the kitchen. As the tin did the rounds and people dropped money into it Sam pulled a large handkerchief from his pocket and mopped sweat from his brow. It was warm but not hot in the pub. The overhead fans were keeping the air circulating and Emma wondered why Sam would be feeling the heat now when he'd seemed comfortable during the heat of the afternoon.

'Are you okay, Sam?'

'Just my indigestion playing up again. It's a nuisance, that's all, especially as I deliberately avoided having onions on my burger tonight.'

It sounded to Emma as though Sam was having difficulty breathing. His breaths were shallow, making his words clipped. 'Why don't you sit down next to me for a minute?' she said. 'Catch your breath.' She put her hand on his wrist, as if to encourage him to sit, but she took the opportunity to check his pulse. His skin was clammy and his pulse felt rapid. 'Where exactly are you feeling the indigestion pain?'

'Here, at the bottom of my sternum,' he said as he rubbed his chest.

'Do you have any history of heart problems?'

'No, why?'

'I think this may be angina, not indigestion,' she told him. 'Harry, is there likely to be a flying doctor medical chest in town?' Emma knew that Grace and the plane weren't back from Adelaide yet but she also knew that the flying doctor service supplied and maintained medical chests for emergency use to the Outback towns and stations. There should be one in Innamincka somewhere.

'The pub has one.'

'Can I access it?'

He nodded. 'I'll get it for you.'

'Any other health problems?' she asked Sam as Harry went in search of the chest.

Sam shook his head. 'I'm fit as a fiddle.'

'No liver problems, kidneys okay? Are you on any other medication? Any allergies?'

'Never been sick a day in my life. Other than broken bones and a dodgy appendix, of course.'

Emma raised one eyebrow. 'Of course.'

Tony offered to keep passing the tin around in Sam's place, leaving Emma to concentrate on Sam and Sam to concentrate on his symptoms. Harry came back with the chest—a heavy, bulky, contraption that looked about as old as the town—and he also had Sam's wife, Jo, in tow.

Harry unlocked the chest and proceeded to calm Jo down as Emma searched the chest for the GTN spray. She found it quickly and administered it to Sam. The spray resolved Sam's symptoms and his 'indigestion' settled within about ten minutes.

'It's not indigestion,' Emma said. 'It's your heart.'

'Is he having a heart attack?' Jo asked.

Emma shook her head. 'No, it's angina but Sam will need to see his doctor for a check-up as soon as possible,' Emma replied.

'Don't forget Sam lives on a cattle station hundreds of miles from any medical support,' Harry reminded her. 'The next doctor he sees will be Grace when she gets back here.'

It was amazing that people survived out here at all in this remote corner of the world, Emma thought. If it wasn't for luck and the flying doctor, she doubted anyone would! 'Well, you need to have some tests done,' she said to Sam and Jo.

'Can't I just get some of that spray?' Sam asked. 'That's done the trick.'

'You need to find out what's causing the angina. Some things are more serious than others. In the city I'd be booking you in for a cardiac work-up.' She turned back to Harry. 'What happens out here? Where can we refer Sam to?'

'A cardiologist visits Broken Hill once a month. Grace can refer Sam to that clinic, otherwise he'll have to wait until the cardiologist does a clinic run and the closest one would be at Thargomindah.'

'And how often is that?'

'That's run by the Queensland division of the flying doctor service but if it's anything like the specialist clinics in our region, probably once every six months.'

Emma raised both eyebrows. What she considered basic health care was certainly hard to come by out here.

'If I find out when and where the next clinic is, can you get to it?' she asked Sam.

'I'll make sure we do,' Jo replied. 'But what do we do now?'

'Are you staying in town tonight?'

'Yes. We're in our camper trailer.'

Emma paused for a minute as she tried to work out what the best course of action would be. 'What time is Grace expected back?'

'They're on their way now,' Harry said. 'ETA in the next half-hour.'

'There are a couple of sprays in the chest. Can I give one to Jo?' she asked, and when Harry nodded she handed Jo a spray and issued instructions. 'Take this with you. Sam can have it as often as needed. If he gets chest pain during the night, give it to him again and then wait five minutes. He can have more after five minutes if his symptoms haven't eased but if there's no change after three doses you'll need to get the flying doctor. Is that clear?'

Emma waited for Jo to nod before she turned back to Sam.

'How are you feeling now?'

'As good as gold.'

'No dizziness, no headache?'

He shook his head. 'Not a thing.'

'Okay, I guess you're good to go. Off to bed is the best thing for you but no strenuous activities.'

'The idea never entered my mind,' Sam replied.

'It entered my mind,' Harry whispered in Emma's ear as Sam and Jo thanked her and headed for the door. 'Are you ready to make a move?'

'Shall we walk back to the campsite with Sam and Jo?'

'We're not going to the campsite. Lucas, have you got my keys?'

Lucas tossed Harry a set of keys, which he caught in one hand.

'What are they for?' Emma asks.

'My motorbike.'

'Your motorbike?' Was there anything Harry couldn't do? He could ride horses, muster cattle, fly planes, drink beer, satisfy women *and* ride motorbikes. No wonder men wanted to be him and women wanted to be with him. 'Where are we going?'

'To a friend's property, somewhere a bit more intimate than a campsite we'd be sharing with five hundred others,' he said as he picked up their packs and they said their farewells.

Emma knew that as they left the pub she'd be getting plenty of envious glances from the women but she much preferred this to the looks of pity she'd got in England after the disastrous relationship with Jeremy.

Harry stopped beside a large dusty bike and strapped their packs and a canvas swag onto the back of the seat.

'How did Lucas get your bike here?'

'In the horse truck. There was plenty of room for a few horses, a bike and a couple of camp beds. That's where Lucas and Darren will bunk down for the night.'

'You're a self-sufficient lot, aren't you?'

'Out of necessity,' Harry said, handing her a helmet.

'But you've seen how we'll all pitch in when needed. We need to work together if we're going to survive.'

Emma knew what he meant and she could see the attraction of this rural community. While the location might be isolated, the people certainly weren't.

She swapped her hat for the helmet, pulling it onto her head and fastening the chin strap as Harry stowed their hats on the bike. She climbed up behind him and wrapped her arms around his waist as they rode out of town.

His back was warm and solid against her chest, her groin was pressed up against his pelvis and the motorbike vibrated between her thighs. She'd never ridden a motorbike before and she was finding the whole experience rather erotic.

The full moon bathed the dirt road in yellow light. The sand here was much whiter than the land around Broken Hill and in Emma's eyes it looked as though they were travelling along a beach. Eventually she felt the bike slowing and Harry turned off the road and bumped over a cattle grid as he rode onto his friend's property. He negotiated a few dips and turns for several minutes before stopping under a stand of trees and switching off the engine. The ground dropped away in front of them.

Emma jumped off the bike, not at all surprised to find her legs were a little unsteady, and walked to the edge of the little dip. She found herself looking down onto a small billabong. The water was moving with a slight rise and fall and the moonlight was dancing on the rippling surface. She wondered where the current was coming from.

'Fancy going skinny-dipping?' Harry asked.

'Are we the only ones here?'

Harry laughed as he pulled his shirt over his head, not bothering to undo the buttons, and threw it onto the bike.

'The nearest person would be fifty kilometres away; I don't think they'll happen to come past at this time of night.'

'So it's just you and me and miles and miles of empty space?' she asked as Harry stepped on the back of his boot and pulled it from his foot.

'There'll be a few animals roaming around but no people.' He took the other boot and his socks off and stuffed one boot inside the other and stood them on the ground.

Emma glanced over her shoulder into the darkness around them. 'What sort of animals?'

'Cattle mostly—although they'll be sleeping. Rabbits, dingoes, maybe some wild pigs.'

'Are we safe out here?' Her voice caught in her throat, not from fear but because Harry had stepped out of his jeans and boxers and was standing naked in front of her.

'Perfectly safe. I've been sleeping out like this since I was a kid,' he said. Turning, he stepped down the embankment and into the billabong.

His body was darkly tanned with the exception of his buttocks, which shone white in the moonlight. His bottom was tight and round and muscular and the sight of his naked cheeks as he stepped into the water made the blood rush to her groin. She felt slightly dizzy but she didn't want to sit down, not when all sorts of creatures could be climbing over her in a matter of seconds. She wanted to hold onto Harry.

He called to her from the water. 'But if you're worried, come and join me. Most of the animals don't like to get their feet wet.'

She fully intended to join him but she was going to brave the creepy-crawlies for a few minutes while she made Harry beg.

She pulled her boots and socks off first, thinking as she

did so that there was a reason women didn't wear work-boots when they were doing a striptease.

'Put one boot inside the other, like I did with mine, and throw your clothes on the bike.'

'Why?'

'It stops the bugs from getting in.'

Obviously her disrobing wasn't erotic enough to stop him from thinking about bugs! She'd need to work on that but she did as he told her, stuffing her boots and then resisting the urge to sprint to the water once her feet were bare.

She forced herself to go slowly. He wasn't begging yet but he was watching her and she enjoyed drawing out the inevitable. She undid her jeans and turned her back to Harry before she bent forward and slid her trousers down her legs. Her efforts were rewarded with a 'Hurry up, woman, I'm dying here' from Harry.

She turned back to face him. 'Patience, patience. Good things come to those who wait.'

She reached behind her back and undid her bra so she could slip her shirt and bra off together. She pulled her shirt over her head, exposing her breasts, and heard Harry catch his breath. She was almost naked.

She threw her clothes onto the motorbike and stepped out of her underwear, looping them over the handlebars. She stood, naked in the warm night air, and pulled the elastic bands from the ends of her plaits and shook her hair out around her shoulders before she joined Harry in the billabong.

'It's warm!' she said as she slid into the water and into Harry's embrace.

'It's artesian water, straight out of the ground. It's just what I need for my aching muscles.'

'What's wrong with your muscles?'

'I'm out of practice. Not enough time in the saddle.'

'Is that right?' Emma grinned. 'Let me see if I can help you with that. Where are you sore?'

'Here.' He rolled his shoulders and Emma ran her hands up over his chest to knead the muscles in his arms and shoulders.

'And here.'

He moved her hands from his shoulders to his lower back and the movement brought her closer to him. Their groins were pressed together and she could feel his erection, thick and hard, against her stomach. She rubbed the palm of her hand against the small of his back and each thrust of her hand pressed him tighter against her.

She moved her hands lower and cupped his buttocks. They were firm and spherical under her palms. She slid her fingers into the cleft between his cheeks and watched as he closed his eyes. His lips parted as he panted softly.

Emma brought one hand to his groin and cupped his testes, rolling them between her fingers before she slid her hand up the length of his shaft and ran her fingers lightly over the tip. Harry moaned and lifted her off her feet, pressing her hard against him. She wrapped her legs around him and floated effortlessly in the water, pinned firmly against him.

He bent his head to her breast and took it in his mouth. His tongue was warm as it flicked over her nipple, making it peak. He moved his mouth higher and she tipped her head back, exposing her throat as he kissed her neck before moving to her lips.

She didn't want to wait any longer. It felt like she'd been ready for this for hours, she'd been in a state of arousal since she'd watched him riding in the gymkhana. He was ready too, she could feel his erection pressing into her stomach.

She wrapped her arms more firmly around his neck

and lifted herself up, before lowering herself onto him. She heard him gasp as she took him inside her and then he took control. His hands were on her hips as he raised and lowered her, penetrating deeper with every thrust. There were no words, they didn't need words, but she cried out as Harry took her to a peak of desire, bringing her to orgasm in the warm Outback waters. She felt him climax with her as she clung to his torso, coming together until they were both spent.

CHAPTER NINE

HARRY held her hand as they floated in the water, side by side, gazing up at the heavens while they caught their breaths. Even with the full moon Emma could still see a million stars.

'I feel like I'm in a parallel universe,' she said when she found her voice. 'It's magical out here, isn't it?'

'This is why I can never leave. I'm a part of this land, it's in my soul and in my blood.'

Emma knew why he would feel that way, she was starting to understand how hard it was going to be to leave here herself after only a few weeks. 'I think I know what you mean. This land is special. I don't feel it when I'm in town but when I'm out here under the stars I feel at peace.'

'I was hoping you'd feel a connection. This land is good for your spirit. If you can let go and relax, it will help to heal you.'

Emma laughed. 'If I was any more relaxed now, I'd drown.'

'Do you think you can be trusted not to drown while I get out and make a fire?'

'I'll do my best.'

Emma floated on her back and listened to Harry gathering sticks for the fire. She turned her head and watched as he set up their camp. He was focussed on his tasks and it was a good chance to ask the question that had been bothering her all afternoon.

'Why didn't you tell me you and Lucas were twins?'

'Why didn't you tell me you could ride?'

'That's not the same thing and you know it,' she protested. 'Riding never came up in conversation, Lucas did, and the way you talked about him made it sound as though he was years older than you, not minutes. It doesn't seem fair that he gets the station because of a few minutes.'

Harry put a billy of water onto the camp fire to boil. 'Twins or not, he's still the oldest son.'

'Does he know about your dream?'

'He knows. But what can he do? If he hadn't wanted to run the station, it would have come to me, but he does. And he should have it.'

'Why can't you both live there? Is it big enough for two of you?'

'It's plenty big enough,' he said as he unrolled the canvas swag and pulled a blanket out before rolling the swag back up again to use as a seat. 'But that never works. It only needs one chief and I don't want to be an Indian. My parents are still on the property too.' She'd forgotten that fact. 'That's too many Connors,' Harry continued. 'I think Lucas's wife might draw the line at having me there as well.'

The billy was boiling as she emerged from the billabong. The night air was cool after the heat of the water and Harry wrapped the blanket around her naked shoulders and sat her on the swag. He poured her a mug of tea and served it with biscuits as he finished explaining.

'I knew from an early age that I'd have to make my own way. I get an income from the station but I don't get to run it and that's what I really want. The trouble was Lucas wanted it too. So it's up to me to make my own future. And that's okay. One day I'll have what I want. I'm not going to let a matter of a few minutes ruin the relationship I have with Lucas. That's more important than anything else.'

She couldn't argue with that. She knew from experience that having a family was far more important than having a place to live. From her nomadic childhood years, when her father had been the only constant in her life, she knew how important family was. Harry was lucky to have such a strong relationship with his brother and she knew he wasn't the type of person to jeopardise that. He valued his friends and family far too much. And if he was okay with the situation, it wasn't her place to judge.

As she finished her tea Harry unrolled the swag beside the fire and they lay together on a sandy bed under the Southern Cross.

'Do we have to go back tomorrow?' Emma asked.

'I guess you don't, but I do. I'm expected at work on Monday.' He slid one arm underneath her shoulders, hugging her into his side. 'You know, you could always make some enquiries about extending your stay.'

'Make plans to stay longer?'

'Why not? There's nothing waiting for you at home that couldn't wait a bit longer, is there?'

Home. It seemed such an alien concept at the moment. Her old life seemed so long ago. But Harry was right, there was nothing waiting for her at home. 'I guess I could…' But staying longer would mean making plans, making a commitment, and she wasn't sure she was ready for that either.

'But? There's a but in there, isn't there?'

She nodded. 'But I don't know if it's what I want. And that's the trouble. I don't have any idea about what I want to do with my life. I need a passion.'

She tried to explain her feelings but it was difficult when she didn't understand them herself. The longer she spent in the Outback the more confused she was getting about what she did and didn't want. While she loved aspects of the life here, there were other parts—the dust, the flies, the remoteness—that she didn't know if she'd ever get used to.

'I envy you. You have your flying and your dreams. I know one day you'll achieve your goals. I'm still trying to work out what mine are.'

'Well, that's what you should use this time for. You're away from your old life, away from all the old expectations. Take some time to figure out what floats your boat. All I'm suggesting is that if you're not ready to go home in a few weeks, you could probably stay a bit longer.'

But that would take planning—she didn't imagine she'd be able to decide on her last day that she wasn't ready to leave and be able to stay. It was more than likely that she'd have to start thinking about it now and that was too daunting. Anything could happen in the next five weeks.

It was all too much to think about—what would be the point of making enquiries if she didn't know what she might want to do?

'So, tell me all about last night,' Sophie said as she lay across the foot of Emma's bed, desperately waiting to hear all the details.

Emma was exhilarated but exhausted. The past thirty-six hours had been non-stop and she was longing to put her head on her pillow and catch up on some sleep, but she knew she'd have to tell Sophie something. The trouble was she didn't know where to start, she wanted to keep parts of last night to herself. Some parts were not for sharing.

She could tell her about Russ's accident, about Sam's angina attack, about meeting Lucas, about sharing billy tea and toast by the campfire with Harry this morning before they'd ridden back into Innamincka, but she knew that wasn't what Sophie wanted to hear.

'I bet you weren't thinking about Jeremy.'

'Who?' she asked with a smile. 'I've barely thought about Jeremy since I got here.' She actually hadn't thought about him at all for the past two weeks, her head had been too full with thoughts of Harry.

Sophie laughed. 'Harry's been a good distraction, then?'

Emma grinned. 'You could say that.'

'I knew this trip would be the perfect pick-me-up for you. So, what are your plans?'

'No plans. You know me. Are you trying to get rid of me?'

'No, you're welcome to stay as long as you like. I love having you here and I know Grace doesn't mind having you in the house. It's easy with the spare room.'

'I'm sure you don't want me freeloading with you for ever. I'll stay until my visa expires. I've got five weeks left.'

'You could always get a real job and stay longer.'

'Not on a tourist visa I can't.'

'You're half-Australian, you could always ask. Wouldn't they have to let you stay?'

'I have no idea. They'd probably deport me.'

'I'm sure the flying doctor service would sponsor you. And what will you do when you get home? Where will you live? Where will you work?'

She had nowhere to go, nothing to go back for. First Harry and now Sophie had implied as much and she knew they were right. But England was her home. She couldn't stay here indefinitely.

'I don't know. Something will come up. It always does.' What would it be like to stay here? 'I'm not sure that this is the place for me. I've been here three weeks and I've survived a plane crash, being buried alive and seen other people sustain injuries I never imagined seeing. I'm not sure I'm cut out for Outback life.'

'Not even with the perks?'

Emma knew what, or who, Sophie was referring to. 'Not even then. You told me yourself he has a reputation as a ladies' man. That there are a string of broken-hearted women scattered across the country. It's a nice interlude but it's just a holiday fling. That's not a good enough reason to pack up my life and move halfway around the world.' She wondered if she sounded convincing.

'Your mother did it.'

'She wanted to marry my father. One of them had to move.' That wasn't the same thing at all.

'It started as a holiday romance, didn't it? What if you're not so different from your mum?'

'You're forgetting one thing,' Emma said. 'They were in love.'

Maybe she and her mum had more in common than just their looks. She knew she could easily fall in love with Harry, it was hard not to feel smitten by him, he was as close to perfect as it was possible to be, but she wasn't about to admit that to Sophie. She wasn't about to admit that to anyone. As far as she, and everyone else, was concerned, this was purely and simply a holiday fling. And it would come to an end sooner rather than later.

'I promise I'll come and visit again,' she said to placate her cousin. She knew that wasn't the same thing as living here permanently, but surely that was out of the question?

It was one of the quieter days Emma had had at the flying doctor base but years of working in hospital emergency departments meant that she knew better than to say so. Old superstitions existed through the ages for a reason.

She and Grace were sitting together, sorting supplies

and bundling medications to restock the emergency medical chests for the stations; it was simple work that involved cross-checking the requests with the records, showing what had been used and marking off the items as they were gathered. It didn't require huge concentration, not with two of them working, and Emma's thoughts drifted to the myriad discussions she'd had with Sophie over the past week. Her cousin had been like a dog with a bone, trying to convince her to stay in Australia.

In fact, she'd been bugging her so much that to keep the peace Emma had actually made some enquiries. As she'd suspected, she couldn't apply for a working visa while she was in the country on a tourist visa, but what had surprised her was that she also had to leave the country to apply for Australian citizenship.

She knew why she'd given in and made enquiries in the first place and she also knew her reasons were not that sensible. She wasn't ready to go home because she wasn't ready to leave Harry but that wasn't a good enough reason to stay so it was a relief to have an excuse not to take it any further. The more difficult it was, the more reason she had not to pursue it. It wasn't as if she had a good reason to stay.

She and Harry were nothing serious. It was just a holiday fling and just because she wasn't ready for it to be over it didn't make it a reason to move to the other side of the world. Sure, her mother had done it, as Sophie had pointed out, but she had been in love. It was a completely different situation.

Emma's gaze drifted away from the medications and across the room to Harry. He was sitting at another table, writing something in a logbook, but whenever he was nearby Emma was aware of his presence, and the more time they spent together the more aware of him she became. She knew her feelings about Harry were influencing her actions as much as anything.

Harry looked up from his paperwork and saw her watching him. He winked at her and smiled and her heart skipped a beat, just as it did whenever she had his undivided attention.

But just because her heart skipped a beat whenever he touched her, just because he made her happy, just because their sex life was amazing and just because she didn't want it to end, it didn't mean she should stay. No, her relationship with Harry wasn't the same thing as her parents' relationship at all. She wasn't her mother and she couldn't move to the other side of the world because of a man.

Not even when her heart was telling her that Harry wasn't just any man?

No. She shook her head, mentally admonishing herself. It was a ridiculous idea to entertain. She didn't have a job, she didn't have a visa and she wasn't making plans around men again, especially when the man in question hadn't even asked her to stay.

No, this whole thing was all Sophie's idea and Emma decided she'd be better off putting it right out of her mind. She wasn't going down that path.

'Can I see you in my office, Emma? I need to speak to you.'

Irene stuck her head into the common room and interrupted Emma as she was focussed on counting bandages and trying not to think of Harry. She made a note of where she was up to and pushed her chair back from the table. She felt Harry watching her and she could see the question in his eyes, but she had no idea why Irene needed to speak to her. She shrugged and followed Irene from the room.

Emma was surprised and a little stunned by the conversation that followed but when she returned to the com-

mon room she was still aware enough of her surroundings
to notice that Harry was still poring over his logbook and
Grace was on the phone, obviously dealing with an incident. Harry looked up but before they could speak Grace
interrupted.

'Harry, this call, it's Jess,' she said.

'What is it?'

'She's had a fall. Off a ladder.'

Emma thought Grace must be talking about Lucas's
wife. Her name was Jess and that would make her Harry's
sister-in-law, Harry's *pregnant* sister-in-law.

'What the hell was she doing up a ladder?' Harry's
voice was brusque and Emma knew that wasn't the question he'd meant to ask but worry made people ask unexpected things. She knew she'd ask the same irrelevant
question in his shoes.

'I didn't ask,' Grace replied.

'How bad is it?' Emma jumped in. That was what they
really needed to know and she hoped it was something
Grace could answer.

'She's conscious and she doesn't think she's broken anything but she's complaining of abdominal pain,' Grace
replied.

'The baby?' Harry asked and Emma could hear the
catch in his throat, the concern in his voice.

'She's not bleeding,' Grace told him, 'but she hasn't felt
the baby move since the fall.'

'How long?'

Grace glanced at her notes and then at the clock on the
wall. 'Fifteen minutes. I told Lucas we're leaving now.'

Harry was already standing. Emma hadn't yet sat down.

Grace put her hand out, stopping Harry as he was about
to race past her. 'Are you okay to fly? Do you want me to
call someone else in?'

'I'm fine.' Harry shook her hand off. 'We're wasting time.'

Emma and Grace exchanged glances. The other crew was down at Menindee; Emma knew it would be quicker to get to Connor's Corner from the base but they couldn't afford Harry to be distracted. Grace nodded at Emma and she relaxed; if Grace thought Harry wasn't up to it, she'd stop him. They grabbed what they needed and hurried to the plane.

Harry hadn't waited for them. He was already in the pilot's seat and he'd dumped his logbook and cap on the co-pilot's seat. Emma had got into the habit of sitting next to him when they had no patients but today he was sending a pretty clear message that he wanted to be alone.

His message hurt but Emma said nothing. What could she say? Harry was clearly preoccupied and concerned and if he wanted space she had to give it to him, but it stung to be shut out like this.

Emma took the seat in front of Grace. Grace attempted to start a conversation but soon gave up when Emma's responses were less than enthusiastic. Emma felt bad but she had a lot to think about and she wasn't in the mood for talking.

The two hours spent in flight were two of the longest hours of Emma's life, right up there with when she'd sat beside her father's bed and watched him succumb to cancer. She felt as helpless now as she had then. Normally, racing to the rescue made her feel useful, important even, but today she realised for the first time that, even with the flying doctors, people were still a long way from help in an emergency.

Emma felt the plane begin to lose altitude and she swivelled her seat to look out of the window. The land beneath them was streaked with green and red and to the north-east a muddy green ribbon of water wound its way across the earth.

Grace had turned to look out of the window too and this time when she spoke Emma was ready to listen.

'We're almost there. That's Cooper Creek,' Grace said as she pointed at the muddy green river. 'Can you see where it turns the corner, that almost ninety-degree bend? That's the south-eastern corner of the Connors' station, that's where the station got its name. The river turns west there and heads to Innamincka.'

Emma had been keen to see Connor's Corner but not this way. Not on an emergency flight to treat one of Harry's family.

'On the other side of the creek is Cooper Creek Station, Sam's place,' Grace said, giving Emma her bearings.

Emma watched out of the window as the plane followed the course of the river before banking left and flying over the homestead. She could see dozens of buildings, sheds and several houses plus cattle yards. It looked like a small town and not at all what she'd expected. How many people lived there?

Harry touched down smoothly on the dirt airstrip and taxied off the edge of the runway, stopping next to a four-wheel drive that was being driven by Harry and Lucas's dad, Andrew. Emma had forgotten that Harry's parents lived on the station too. It seemed everyone lived there except Harry.

Andrew was an older, heavier, shorter version of Harry and Lucas but he had the same bright blue eyes as his younger son.

Emma and Grace gathered the medical kits as Harry embraced his dad.

'How's she doing?' Harry asked.

'I don't know. Your mother won't let me near them.

Lucas is in there, the boys are with the governess. The only thing they think I can handle is meeting the plane.'

With Andrew's help they loaded their gear into the vehicle as Harry very quickly introduced Emma to his father before jumping into the front seat and continuing his questions.

'What was she doing up the ladder? Why didn't she ask for help?'

'Lucas and I were out in the machine shed. Jess wanted to get some baby clothes down from storage and she couldn't wait—you know what women are like,' he said as he pulled the car to a stop in front of a large house.

Lucas had heard them arrive and was standing on the wide veranda of a single-level house at the top of a short flight of steps. Andrew had barely switched the engine off before Grace grabbed the medical bags and leapt from the car. Emma hoisted the portable ultrasound machine from the boot and followed at a run across the lawn that separated the house from the dust.

Lucas nodded briefly before he turned and led the women into the house.

Jess was lying on a single bed in the boys' room. She had her knees drawn up in a protective posture and a sheen of sweat glistened across her forehead. An older woman Emma assumed was Harry's mum sat beside Jess. She had a damp facecloth in her hand and had obviously been wiping Jess's face. An overturned ladder lay by a wardrobe and baby clothes and linen were strewn across the carpet beneath an open overhead cupboard door.

'Lucas, can you see if you can calm Harry down? He's a bit jumpy. Leave Jess to us,' Grace said, coming up with a reason to shoo Lucas from the room. There were enough people in here already.

Emma pulled the sphygmomanometer from the bag

and started to take Jess's obs as Grace introduced her to the other women.

'How are you feeling, Jess? What's happening now?'

Jess put one hand over her stomach, just left of her belly button between her ribs and hip. 'I've got pain here.'

Grace lifted up Jess's shirt. Her abdomen was rounded with the pregnancy but there were no obvious bruises or marks to be seen.

'How did you land?'

'I fell sideways but I caught my back on the edge of Jack's bed.'

Harry's mother, Melissa, reached down to the floor and lifted up a bedpan. 'Jess needed the toilet, I thought you might need to see this,' she said as she held the pan out towards Grace. Emma could see urine in the pan but it was streaked with blood. Dark red blood. In sufficient quantities to be alarming.

'Can you roll onto your right side for me?' Grace instructed, and somehow Jess managed to comply.

There was a bruise already starting to show on the left of Jess's lower back.

'Blood pressure normal, heart rate a little elevated,' Emma reported.

'Have you felt the baby move since you called us?'

Jess shook her head.

Over two hours.

Emma hoped the baby had been moving and that Jess hadn't felt it because she'd had her mind on other things. Like pain. She moved the stethoscope onto Jess's tummy, listening for the baby's heartbeat.

'You're twenty weeks?' Grace confirmed. 'You've felt the baby move before?'

Jess nodded.

'Third pregnancy,' Melissa said. 'Everything happens earlier.'

'Got it.' Emma found the baby's heartbeat and made sure she told Jess immediately, assuming Jess would be thinking the worst. 'It's good and strong.' Emma looked at her watch as she timed the beats. 'One-twenty.' It was possibly a little slow but otherwise seemed okay.

'The baby's okay?' Jess's eyes welled with tears.

'As far as I can tell,' Emma said.

'I'll do an ultrasound to double-check. It's not as sophisticated as the ones you get in the hospitals but it might be useful,' Grace said as she palpated Jess's back.

'Where's the...' Harry's mother paused and glanced down at the floor where she'd put the bedpan '...pain coming from, then?'

Emma knew she'd been about to say blood before she'd stopped herself. She couldn't have told Jess that there was blood in her urine.

Emma was monitoring the baby's heartbeat while Grace checked Jess's ribs and spine, but Grace looked up when Melissa paused and Emma saw her register the comment.

Jess gasped as Grace's fingers pressed over her left kidney.

'I think you might have bruised a kidney,' Grace told her. 'That would fit with the mechanics of the fall and your symptoms,' she said as she nodded at Melissa.

'What do we do?'

Grace addressed Jess. 'Jess, there was some blood in your urine. It's more than likely to be from your kidneys. I'm pretty sure it's not from the baby, but I'm going to do the ultrasound just to check.'

Emma was setting up the portable ultrasound when there was a brief knock on the door and Harry stuck his head into the room.

'Grace, how are you going here? The base is on the radio, they need us over at Cooper Creek Station if it's at all possible.'

'What's happened?'

'It's Sam. He has chest pain that's not settling. Jo thinks it might be a heart attack.'

CHAPTER TEN

'EMMA, can you go to the radio and speak to Cooper Creek? Find out what's going on,' Grace said as she squeezed transducer gel onto the ultrasound head and prepared to scan Jess's abdomen. 'If we need to, I think we'll be able to get to Sam from here. I'm almost done.'

Emma didn't have the slightest idea of how to use the radio. It wasn't something she'd done before but Grace had already turned back to Jess and Emma couldn't bring herself to argue. To think that just a few hours ago she'd been thinking how quiet the day was.

Harry was waiting in the doorway. He picked up on her hesitation. 'Come, I'll operate the radio for you,' he said. 'You just need to ask the questions.'

Emma followed him out of the bedroom but they only got as far as the passage before she literally bumped into Lucas. Emma couldn't believe the difference in him. He looked ten years older than Harry; worry lines had etched themselves deep into his forehead and his eyes were flat and unfathomable.

'How's Jess? And the baby?' he asked.

He'd obviously been hovering outside the door, desperate for news, and Emma couldn't blame him. 'They're going to be okay,' she told him. 'We think Jess has a bruised kidney and Grace is doing an ultrasound on the baby now, but I've heard the heartbeat myself.'

Lucas visibly relaxed as Emma's words sank in but she had no time to tell him anything more, even if there'd been more to tell, as Harry had her by one hand and was pulling her away from the bedrooms.

He led her into a study and picked up the handset for the radio.

'Push this button in to talk, and when you've finished just say "Over" and then let the button go. I'll take notes for you—just get whatever details you need.

'Jo, are you there?' Harry spoke into the handset. 'I've got Emma with me, over.'

He passed the handset to her as Jo responded and when it was her turn to talk Emma pushed the button in as Harry had shown her. 'Can you describe Sam's symptoms to me, Jo? Over.'

'He's been complaining of chest pain on and off all day but it has settled with the spray. Until now. Over.'

'How many doses of the spray has he had?'

'Three lots over the past twenty minutes but the pain isn't going away.'

'Where is the pain?'

'Behind his breastbone.'

'Does he have any other symptoms? Is the pain radiating away from his chest? Is he short of breath?'

'The pain is only in his chest but he's a bit out of breath.'

'Has he been doing any strenuous activity today?'

'No. Less than normal even. He hasn't felt well enough.'

'Okay. Make sure he stays lying down and continue to give him the spray every five minutes. We're on our way from Connor's Corner. We'll be with you in…' Emma glanced up at Harry. She had no idea how long they'd be. Harry held up three fingers on one hand and made a fist with the other. 'Thirty minutes,' she said, and was pleased to see Harry confirm that with a nod as he reached out and took the handset from her.

'Jo, can you ask Jonno to organise lighting the airstrip? It's getting dark. Over.'

'Will do, Harry. Over.'

'Stay in touch on the radio, okay? Over and out.'

Emma's hands were shaking as she pushed the chair back from the desk and stood up. The chair wobbled as she pushed it back in.

'You okay?' Harry asked, seeing the tremor in her hands. 'You did well.' He rubbed her back. 'Is it serious?'

Emma nodded as Harry continued to rub her back.

'Let's hope we get to him in time, then,' he said.

Harry's praise made Emma feel more confident but she was still concerned. 'I'm pretty sure Grace will want to take Jess back to Broken Hill—do you think we'll be able to get to Sam as well?'

'Sam's not far away. We can get him first and come back for Jess if we need to. Let's see what Grace wants to do.'

Emma still wasn't used to the idea that a thirty-minute trip wasn't considered far out here. She hoped for Sam's sake that Harry was right.

Grace was packing the ultrasound away as they came into the room. She looked up. 'Heart attack?' she asked.

Emma nodded. 'He needs attention now. How is Jess doing?'

'I want to take her to Broken Hill for observation and complete bed rest—there's not much chance of that here,' she explained. 'But there's no urgency. Jess can handle the scenic route via Cooper Creek Station. The baby seems to be sleeping and treatment for the bruised kidney is simply bed rest until the bleeding resolves. We'll take them both back to the Hill together.'

Twenty-five minutes later they had successfully transferred Jess to the plane and were landing on Sam's airstrip.
Twenty minutes after that they were bound for Broken Hill
with their two patients. There was no time for Emma to
think about anything other than Jess and Sam as she and
Grace were kept busy monitoring their charges.

Jess had a drip in place and a foetal heart-rate monitor
strapped around her abdomen. Sam was attached to the
portable ECG, oxygen and IV fluids. The back of the plane
was full and there had been no room for Lucas or Jo to
accompany their respective spouses. They would have to
make their own way to Broken Hill tomorrow.

By the time Sam and Jess were safely transferred to
waiting ambulances for the trip to the hospital Emma was
exhausted. After a slow start to the day it was now way
past their scheduled finishing time and she was looking
forward to going home and putting her feet up, preferably
snuggled against Harry on the couch.

'Did you want to come back to my place?' she asked
him. 'I'll make us something to eat.'

To her surprise, Harry shook his head. 'Thanks, but I
won't. Once I get the plane put away for the night I'm going
to head to the hospital. Lucas and Jo won't be down until
tomorrow so I want to be there for Jess and Sam overnight.'

Emma had never assumed she was Harry's first priority but it still hurt to know that she was right. She wished
she knew where she did fit into his list of priorities. But
he hadn't told her and she wouldn't ask.

She couldn't be upset with him for staying at the hospital, of course he'd choose to take responsibility for his
brother's family, she would have been shocked if he hadn't.
His sense of loyalty to both his friends and family was one
of the things she loved about him. She loved his confidence
and she loved the way she felt around him.

He made the world seem a better place, a happier place, as though it was full of good things. She loved his laugh and his ruggedness. And she loved the way he treated her, the way he had of making her feel as if she belonged here. But she didn't belong and he hadn't asked her to stay.

She couldn't believe she'd been considering accepting the job offer because of a holiday romance. Even though she knew it was more than that—for her anyway. She'd never become so quickly and completely besotted by someone. If she'd thought that Jeremy had trampled on her heart, she'd been mistaken. Sure, the experience had left her homeless, unemployed and single, but all that had really been wounded in that experience had been her pride.

She had an ominous feeling that she was going to lose a lot more than that when she left Harry behind. But she needed a better reason to stay. The trouble was, she couldn't think of one.

Emma was awake early the next day and filled the morning with odd jobs, pretending she wasn't waiting for Harry to call. Eventually she decided to visit the hospital to see Sam and Jess, telling herself she wasn't looking for Harry, telling herself she was visiting Jess and Sam because she wanted to, and in an effort to convince herself she went to the coronary care unit and sought Sam out first, knowing that Harry would more than likely be keeping Jess company.

But she couldn't quell the disappointment that rose in her when she walked into Jess's ward and found it empty of all but the patients. Harry was nowhere to be seen.

She paused in the doorway, looking at each bed, looking for Jess but also looking for Harry.

'Emma?' Jess was in a bed to her left and Emma forced

herself to bite back her disappointment and leave the doorway. After all, wasn't Jess the person she'd come to see?

'I thought that was you,' Jess said. 'Sorry, I was a bit out of it yesterday. I was in agony, not even my labours were that painful.'

'Is it better today? What have the doctors said?' Emma made an effort to ask the right questions, to avoid asking Jess if she knew Harry's whereabouts.

'I'm much better. Grace was right—bed rest is all that's prescribed. That and a few mild painkillers but I've tried not to have them. There's less blood already and the doctors think I'll be able to go home tomorrow.'

'And the baby?'

'She's fine. They've done some more comprehensive scans and everything is good.'

'She?'

Jess was grinning. 'According to the scans, it's a girl. Lucas will be stoked. I can't wait to tell him.'

'He's coming to town today, isn't he?'

'Yes. He's bringing Jo down with him. They should be here after lunch. Do you know how Sam's doing?'

'I've just been to see him,' Emma told her. 'He's comfortable but he's going to be sent down to Adelaide for more tests with the next available flying doctor run.'

Emma stayed to chat to Jess for a few minutes, killing time and hoping that Harry would return, but when Jess began to stifle a yawn Emma knew it was time to let her rest. Walking out of the ward, she ran into Harry. He must have been home at some stage as he had changed out of his flight overalls into jeans and a T-shirt that hugged his chest and biceps and made Emma want to wrap herself around him.

'Hi.' A smile lit up his face. He looked genuinely pleased to see her and he greeted her with a kiss. He was behaving as if everything was normal and Emma realised that from his perspective it was.

It wasn't his fault that she felt left out. It wasn't his fault that she wanted to be higher up his list of priorities or that she wanted to be more than a holiday fling. It wasn't his fault that she'd fallen in love with him.

Oh, that wasn't supposed to happen. She wasn't supposed to fall in love with him. This was supposed to be a holiday romance. She was supposed to be putting herself back together, not complicating her life. But that's just what she'd done. Once again her life seemed to have a mind of its own. Falling in love with someone who was expecting a short-term fling was only going to lead to complications. How was she going to fix this?

'Have you been to see Jess?' he asked.

'And Sam,' she said. 'I'm just on my way home again.' She waited for him to say he'd come with her or to ask her to hang around and keep him company, but he just nodded.

She took a step away. And another, and she was several steps from him when she heard him say her name.

'Emma, wait.'

She turned around expectantly.

'I forgot to ask you what Irene wanted to talk to you about yesterday.'

It wasn't what she'd been hoping to hear him say but she supposed it was to be expected. Today looked like being one disappointment after another. 'She offered me a job.'

'Really!' Harry's answering smile was all she needed to lift her spirits. His blue eyes sparkled and he closed the gap between them and wrapped her in his arms. She was just where she wanted to be. 'Congratulations. When do you start?'

'I don't know if I'm going to take it.'

'Don't you want to stay?' She could hear the frown in his voice.

'I don't know really. It feels a bit surreal.' As did this conversation. Standing in the middle of a hospital corridor wasn't where she'd imagined having this discussion.

'What do you mean?'

'It's not real life, is it?'

'It is for some of us.'

She could hear the wounded tone in his voice. She hadn't meant to make it sound as if there were more important things to do or better places to be. That wasn't what she thought or how she felt.

'But not for me. This is a fantasy world for me.' She tried to explain. 'It's something Sophie and I talked about as kids. I never thought I'd actually be here, let alone that I'd stay.'

'Sophie's doing it, you could too.'

'But Sophie hasn't had to move halfway around the world and she's only here temporarily. She'll move back to Sydney eventually. It's a much bigger commitment for me.'

'When do you have to give Irene an answer?'

'Soon, I guess. My visa runs out in three weeks, I'd have to make a decision by then.'

'But you don't have to decide today,' Harry said. 'Have you spoken to Sophie?'

'I haven't seen her. I was exhausted last night and she's at work today,' Emma explained, but she didn't need to discuss the job offer with Sophie, she knew exactly what she'd say.

'I want to wait here for Lucas but when he arrives I'll come past your place and if you think it will help I'm happy to be your sounding board.'

Emma realised she'd hoped he'd tell her she *had* to stay. That he wanted her to stay. And she was annoyed when he didn't. But why would he tell her that? It would make no difference to him. It wasn't his life. It wasn't his decision. And it wasn't as if he'd fallen in love with her. His response was just another disappointment to add to her list for the day.

She was tempted to say she was busy, that she couldn't sit around and wait for him, that she didn't need a sounding board, but she'd already told him she was going home and she knew saying anything else would make her sound petty and ridiculous. Besides, she wanted to see him, it was really why she'd come to the hospital in the first place, so telling him not to bother would only punish her. She went home and waited.

She didn't have to wait long. Harry came to collect her, instructed her to change into jeans and borrow Sophie's riding boots and drove her to some stables on the edge of town. He led her to the saddling yard where two horses were standing, waiting for riders.

'We're not going riding?' He knew she hadn't been riding in months, not since her dad had died. In actual fact she hadn't ridden for over a year as her dad had been too sick to go with her.

'I saw what you were like with our horses in Innamincka. You said you hadn't been riding because you haven't had anyone to ride with. I'm offering my services,' he replied. 'You need some thinking time. This is the perfect way to clear your head, to give you a chance to get some perspective.'

Emma reached out a hand and let the horse sniff her before she rubbed its neck. It was warm and soft and the familiar scent was comforting. Harry had done this for her.

Tears welled in her eyes. She'd been grumpy and thinking mean thoughts when he'd been busy thinking of ways to help her. He might not be in love with her but he'd only ever tried to do the right thing by her. He'd only ever tried to take care of her. She added that to the list of things she loved about him.

Harry rubbed her back as she rubbed the horse. 'I'm here. All you need to do is come with me. You know I'll look after you.'

The horse whinnied softly and nudged her. She didn't need to go riding but she wanted to. Badly.

Emma put aside her bad mood. She knew Harry meant every word. He wouldn't deliberately hurt her, she knew that. He had done this for her and she appreciated the gesture. It was a typical Harry thing to do. He seemed to know more about what she needed than she did herself.

A riding hat was perched on the horse's saddle. Emma picked it up and fitted it to her head. Harry grinned and cupped his hands giving her a leg up onto her horse before he swung himself easily into his own saddle and slapped his cattleman's hat onto his head.

In single file they headed into the bush. They didn't talk, the only sounds being the sounds of the horses' feet as they trod on the occasional stone and the sounds of the bush—buzzing flies, chattering parrots and the odd small reptile scurrying through the undergrowth.

Emma found herself gradually relaxing as they rode in silence through the bush. It felt strange to be riding again but enjoyable, and she was glad she was doing this with Harry. It would be a nice memory to keep.

By the time Harry stopped his horse at the top of a rocky peak Emma had found her rhythm. She brought her horse to a stop alongside Harry. He dismounted before helping her down and leading her to a flat boulder. It was warm from the afternoon sun and made a perfect lookout. She could see across the plains to the north. The countryside stretched away from them, there was a large lake in the distance but nothing man-made. Nothing but what Mother Nature had created. There was nothing to distract her, except for Harry, of course.

'Are you ready to talk about it?'

She closed her eyes and leant back against his chest. He was solid and reassuring and she had that now familiar feeling that nothing would go wrong while he was in her life. He was a man who could be trusted. She knew that.

'Why don't you start with the negatives?' he said.

She sighed. There were a lot of those. 'It means moving half way around the world.'

'Yes. That might take some planning to pull off. Not your strong point.' She could hear Harry smiling. 'But if it's something you really want, it'd be worth it.'

'I've never stayed in one place for more than three years. It's a huge undertaking to move my entire life, especially if it's only temporary.'

'It doesn't need to be temporary.'

Could she make the commitment? She didn't know. 'I can't imagine staying somewhere for ever. I've never done that before. And my family is in the UK.'

'Not all of them,' he argued. 'You're half-Australian and Sophie is here. And her family, your mother's family, are in Sydney.'

'It's not just where the job is, it's what it is,' she tried to explain. 'I love nursing, and I'm glad that this has given me the opportunity to get back into it, but maybe I'm better suited to an emergency department.'

'Why do you say that?'

'Yesterday, with Jess and Sam, was really difficult. I know I don't know Sam well at all and I'd never met Jess but because of their connection to you it made it really personal. I imagine that after doing this job for a while you'd get to know a lot of people and I'm not sure how I'd cope if we lost someone. It really hit home how far people are from medical help and we can't expect to save everyone. I don't know if I could handle that side of the job.'

'You must have lost people in hospital emergency departments.'

'Yes, but it's so much more personal out here. We're talking about people's family or friends or neighbours. There's more at stake.'

'That's probably why you're such a fabulous nurse—because you care about people.'

'You think I'm a good nurse?'

'I do. You've coped brilliantly with this job. I know it's not easy. I also know I'm not the only one who thinks you've done well. You wouldn't have been offered the job if the doctors didn't think you were up to it.'

'What do you mean?'

'The doctors would have recommended you. You have to be highly skilled to work out here and they wouldn't put your name forward unless they thought you were up to it.'

'Thank you. That's good to know but even if I decide to stay I'd have to leave the country and then come back, and I think Irene wants me to start immediately. My tourist visa expires soon. I'd have to apply for a working visa or Australian citizenship but I can't do that from here.' Emma knew the technicalities were irrelevant. She had one decision to make. Stay or go.

What she needed to do was decide if she would stay if Harry wasn't around.

She knew the answer was no. He was the only reason she would stay. She got the sense that she belonged, not to Outback Australia but to him.

She was considering Irene's offer based on Harry but that was foolish. She was imagining he was the one for her but he'd given her no indication that she was the one for him. She needed a better reason than that to stay.

She didn't need to go riding to get her answer.

She didn't need to gaze into the distance to find it. She already had it.

Unless Harry asked her to stay, she would go home.

'I can think of another way you can stay,' he said.

'How?'

'You could get married.'

Emma laughed. 'To whom?'

'Me.'

Emma's heart leapt in her chest and she could feel it beating a rapid tattoo against her ribs. She was taken completely by surprise. This was not the sort of suggestion she would expect to hear from a meticulous man who loved to plan things. 'You want to get married?'

'Well, one day,' he replied.

'But not right now?'

'I wasn't planning on it but if it will help you...'

Emma's heart plummeted, colliding heavily with her stomach. This was not how she'd ever imagined being proposed to. She shook her head. A marriage of convenience was not her idea of matrimonial bliss.

'I appreciate the thought but marriage is about two people who are in love wanting to spend the rest of their lives together. That's the only way I'm going to get married.' She paused as she tried to squash the swell of disappointment that was rushing through her because his proposal wasn't what she needed. 'Just out of curiosity, "one day" means when exactly?'

'When I have something to offer.'

She frowned. 'Like what?'

'My cattle station.'

'So not when you find the right girl and fall madly in love?'

'Finding the right partner for station life is harder than you might imagine.'

'Lucas found Jess.'

'He didn't have to look far. The three of us grew up together. Jess was our head stockman's daughter and Lucas and I have known her all our lives. She's the perfect station wife.'

'And Lucas got her too.'

'I don't want Jess,' Harry protested. 'She's the perfect station wife *for Lucas*. She's like a sister to me. I admit I'd like to find someone with some of her qualities but I don't want her and until I have a station of my own there's not much point looking for a wife.'

'So why would you marry me?'

'I told you. It would solve your problem. You'd be able to stay.'

'Getting a visa is not my problem. Working out what I want is my problem. I have more idea about what I don't want than what I do.'

'What don't you want?'

'I don't want to get married so that I can work. And I don't want to ruin your plans. I know your goal is to work hard, save money and buy Cooper Creek Station, it's not to get married. I appreciate the offer but it's not what either of us need. I don't want to be responsible for making your plans go awry. I've done enough of that in my own life.'

She would marry him in a flash if he said he loved her. But he hadn't. And anyway what sort of person married someone they'd only known for five weeks? That would be crazy.

She couldn't marry him.

She was happier than she'd been for a long time, because

of Harry, but it was unfair to expect him to be responsible for her happiness. She needed to be happy on her own, she needed to find her own inner peace, that was why she'd come to Australia. To find what she needed. To find herself. But instead she'd found Harry.

But if he didn't feel the same way as her, she knew it couldn't last. If he didn't love her, it would all end in tears.

Her heart sat like a stone in her chest. She knew she'd left herself open to heartache. She'd known for weeks she was falling in love with him, despite knowing his reputation and despite her vows to herself not to get involved. She'd told herself it was just a holiday romance, not a relationship, but a proper relationship with Harry was her heart's true desire. She needed to put some distance between them before her heart was well and truly broken.

She couldn't marry him.

No matter how much she wanted to.

CHAPTER ELEVEN

Lucas nodded at the beer that was sitting on the bar in front of Harry. 'Are you going to drink that or wait till it evaporates?'

When things hadn't gone quite the way he'd envisaged with Emma, Harry had persuaded Lucas to meet for a beer and a meal as an alternative to the hospital cafeteria food. The idea of going home to an empty house hadn't appealed to him but now that they were at the pub Harry found he didn't really have much of an appetite. Not for a veal parmigiana and not for the beer.

He picked up his glass and had a half-hearted sip as Lucas asked, 'What's on your mind?'

'I proposed to Emma.'

Lucas almost choked on his drink. 'Hell, I didn't realise it was quite that serious between you. What did she say?'

'She said no.' Harry pushed a few chips around his plate. 'I can't say I blame her. It sort of came out of the blue.'

'How exactly do you propose to someone out of the blue?'

'She's been offered a job with the flying doctor service but she needs a working visa and to get that she has to leave the country. I thought if we got married she wouldn't need the visa and she wouldn't need to leave.'

'If that's how you worded your proposal, I'm not surprised she turned you down. Whatever happened to marrying for love? Women marry for love or money, you're offering her neither.' Lucas had finished his meal but he reached across and pinched some of Harry's chips as he asked. 'Do you love her?'

'I'm not ready to be in love.'

'What the hell is that supposed to mean? You can't plan falling in love. It just happens.'

'I always thought I'd be settled and *then* I'd get married.'

'Things don't always turn out how you planned. Did you propose because she wants to stay or because you want her to stay?'

'I think if she leaves it's very unlikely that she'll come back. And I don't want her to go.'

'But not wanting her to go isn't the same thing as wanting to marry her,' Lucas said. 'Ask yourself this. Can you imagine your life without Emma? Can you imagine her as the mother of your children? Can you imagine her by your side when you're eighty years old?'

Harry didn't know when he'd have a place to call his own but he knew that he wanted Emma with him whenever it was. He couldn't imagine his life without her in it. 'I can.'

'Just because your grand plan was to have Cooper Creek and then get married doesn't mean it has to happen that way. Don't let her go because of timing. You will get Cooper Creek one day and when you do you'll need the right woman by your side. Marriage isn't easy but I imagine it'd be a whole lot worse if you marry the wrong woman.'

Harry knew that Emma was the right woman for him. She was everything he'd imagined. She was everything he needed. She was beautiful, she was capable, she was intelligent and she was strong enough for Outback life. With Emma beside him he knew he could achieve anything.

'Propose because you can't bear the idea of her leaving,

not because it's easier for her to get a job this way. Don't pretend that's it's convenient, or that you're doing it as a favour to her.' Lucas was still giving advice.

'Ask her to marry you because you love her and you don't want to live without her. Be romantic. Be honest. Convince her that marrying you will be the best decision she'll ever make. Propose again but do it properly. What have you got to lose?'

For the first time in his life Harry felt like he had a lot to lose. He had *everything* to lose.

But Lucas was right. He had to do something because if he did nothing, Emma would leave.

He didn't know if he'd be able to convince her to stay but he had to try.

But what if he wasn't up to the challenge? Proposing to help her out was one thing. Proposing because he loved her was something else altogether. What if she left anyway?

Self-doubt was an unfamiliar experience for him. But he didn't know what he was more afraid of, admitting he loved her or having her leave. Which was more frightening?

The idea of her returning to the UK, of her leaving his life for ever was something he didn't want to contemplate.

And that realisation gave him his answer. He loved her. He didn't want to live without her. If he had to choose between Cooper Creek Station and Emma, he would choose Emma.

But he didn't expect to have to make that choice, and he certainly hadn't expected to make it now, but a phone call from Sam Cooper further complicated matters. And more complications were not what he needed.

Harry could sense his plans for the future unravelling. He had two problems, neither of which could be solved simply by good planning. Things were spiralling out of control. He had too many balls in the air and it was only a matter of time before some came crashing down.

He spent days looking at his options, but they were limited and he didn't have the luxury of time. Both problems came with deadlines that were fast approaching.

He needed help. He needed Lucas. He was reluctant to ask but he couldn't see another way out.

He got his chance when Lucas brought Jess back to town for a follow-up doctor's appointment. He invited them for dinner and as they ate he tried to put aside his feelings of guilt for what he was about to ask.

'I had a call from Sam Cooper a few days ago,' he said.

'How's he doing?' Jess asked. They all knew he was still in Adelaide, where he was recuperating from heart surgery.

'He's recovering well but he's talking about retiring,' Harry said. 'He's worried about coping with the physical side of the station and Jo's been in his ear about moving to Tamworth to be closer to their grandchildren.'

'He's ready to sell Cooper Creek?' Lucas asked.

'That's fantastic.' Jess was beaming. 'Congratulations.'

'How much?' Lucas asked.

That was the crux of the matter. The price. It was too much. Too much for him right now.

Harry told him and Lucas whistled in surprise. 'Have you got the money?'

Harry shook his head. 'Not enough to buy him out. Not yet. The bank will lend me some but there's still a shortfall.'

'Of?'

'Half a million.' Harry saw the raised eyebrows but he had to press on. He had to ask. 'What are the Connor's Corner finances like?'

'You're asking if I can lend you the money?'

Harry nodded. He hated asking but he needed Lucas. He couldn't do any of this without his help.

'Harry, there's nothing spare. You know we're restocking after three years of drought conditions. The money's gone. I'm sorry.'

He wasn't surprised. He'd known it was a long shot. It wasn't often they had spare cash floating around, it was almost always allocated to one project or another.

'Let me sleep on it,' Lucas said as Jess tried to stifle a yawn. 'We'll work something out,' he added as he hugged Harry goodnight.

But Harry wasn't sure there was anything Lucas could do. He either had the money or he didn't.

He was about to lose everything. Without Lucas's money Cooper Creek Station was out of reach and in a few days Emma would be gone. He didn't want her to go. He loved her. But he had no idea if she loved him. She'd been avoiding him since his disastrous proposal. She'd probably decided that he was completely mad and she'd do well to steer clear of him.

But what had Lucas said? Love or money. What if he could still offer both?

He could only think of one other option given his limited time frame. He'd have to talk to Sam but what if he could pull it off? The odds weren't greatly in his favour, but he had to try. He had one last chance.

He would talk to Sam. And then he'd talk to Emma. He just hoped she would listen.

Emma couldn't believe she had less than forty-eight hours left until she said goodbye to Broken Hill and the Australian Outback. To Grace and Irene. To Sophie and Mark. To Harry.

Somehow she'd made it through the past two weeks

when all she'd wanted to do was run away and hide. To go somewhere quiet and lick her wounds in private. To pretend she hadn't fallen in love. But she couldn't keep running away. Sophie had begged her to stay until her visa ran out and Emma knew that leaving early would leave the flying doctors short-staffed with Lisa still out of action so she agreed to stay. But she requested different shifts from Harry. She couldn't bear to see him daily and have a constant reminder of all she was about to lose.

She had made her decision to return to England, not because she couldn't live here but because she couldn't live here without Harry. She'd live anywhere if Harry was with her. If Harry loved her. But it didn't look like that would happen. Her flight home was booked and Harry had never asked her to stay. Not properly. At least, not the way she wanted.

Sophie's house was bursting at the seams with all the people Emma had met since she'd arrived in the Hill. So many of them, who she now called friends, but there was one person she'd miss above all.

The air around her vibrated. He was behind her. She could feel him. She could smell him. She wanted to turn around and bury her face in his chest but she held herself in check. She'd missed him terribly over the past two weeks and she couldn't imagine how she was going to feel when she was gone, when he was gone from her life and she knew she would never see him again. She wanted to turn around and throw her arms around his neck and kiss him senseless, but she couldn't give in. It was over even if it hadn't sunk in yet that this was the end.

'So, you're really leaving.' His deep voice resonated through her. She closed her eyes and let it wash over her before she turned round.

She nodded.

Harry reached for her. His hands brushed her upper arms, running from her shoulders to her elbows, sending little lightning bolts to her groin. She knew she should step away, out of reach, but lust and longing had her frozen in place.

His bright blue eyes locked with hers. 'I have a favour to ask you,' he said. 'Will you spend the day with me tomorrow?'

'It's my last day.'

'I know. And I can't quite believe you're leaving. I know you didn't want to marry me but I thought I might be able to persuade you to spend one last day together.'

'You never asked me to marry you.'

'Yes, I did.'

Emma shook her head. She could remember that conversation word for word. 'No, you didn't. You said we could get married, that's not the same thing at all.'

Harry gave her a half-smile. He looked sad. She couldn't remember him ever looking sad.

'We can argue about semantics tomorrow,' he told her. 'Please say you'll spend the day with me.'

Emma knew she should refuse. It would only make things worse. It would only make it harder to leave. But she couldn't do it. She couldn't deprive herself of the final moments. Lisa and Irene were heading towards her and she knew they were about to be interrupted. She also knew she'd probably regret the decision but she was nodding her head anyway. She would spend her final day with Harry.

It was almost like old times, Emma thought as she sat in the co-pilot's seat. As a favour to Sam, Harry had offered to fly out to Cooper Creek Station and check on the place, and Emma was going with him.

This time tomorrow she'd be on another plane, bound

for England, and she'd never see Harry again. She knew her heart would be breaking but there was nothing she could do. All she could do was make the most of today. She'd arrived in Australia miserable and she'd be leaving even more so, but at least she'd been happy while she'd been here.

The plane touched down on the dirt airstrip. As usual Harry pulled off a smooth landing but Emma was surprised to find that no one was waiting to greet them. She was used to seeing at least a few welcoming faces whenever they arrived on the cattle stations.

'Where is everyone?' she asked.

'There's a rodeo in Thargomindah,' he explained. 'Most of the staff have gone into town for the weekend.'

Harry took her hand as they walked down to the house. His fingers were warm and Emma felt the familiar flutter of excitement flow through her with his touch. She was going to miss him so much. Her life had been changed for ever since meeting him and she knew she wouldn't get over him in a hurry. If ever.

She let her gaze roam over the house as they got nearer. Last time she'd been here it had been to treat and evacuate Sam. It had been dark and, even if it hadn't, she'd been too busy to take note of the surroundings. The house was a sprawling building, constructed of weatherboard and elevated on stilts, encased by a wide veranda. A large expanse of lawn ran away from the house and sloped down to the edge of the Cooper Creek.

One of Sam's stockman was waiting at the bottom of the steps. Emma recognised him from the gymkhana at Innamincka.

'G'day, boss,' he greeted Harry as he shook his hand.

'Jonno,' Harry replied. 'You remember Emma?'

Jonno dipped his hat.

'How're things?' Harry asked.

'All good. No dramas. Everything's set.'

'Great. Thanks, mate.'

Harry still had hold of her hand and he led her up the steps as Jonno took off across the dirt.

'Boss?' Emma asked as Harry took her round to the front of the house. Jonno's greeting hadn't gone unnoticed by her but it made no sense.

Harry stopped in the middle of the veranda beside an enormous wooden table. It was set for two and there was a bottle of champagne chilling in a wine cooler in the centre. 'I'll explain,' he said as he pulled a chair out for her and waited for her to sit down.

'Sam and I have come to an arrangement. You are looking at the new owner of Cooper Creek Station.'

He was grinning from ear to ear and Emma thought her heart would explode with happiness for him. He'd done it. He'd made his dream come true.

'Harry! Congratulations!' She sprang from her chair and launched herself into his lap, throwing her arms around his neck. She kissed him. 'I'm so happy for you. I didn't realise your dream was this close. I thought you couldn't afford it yet.'

'I can't afford it on my own but I had to have it. Sam and I have formed a partnership. I'll make repayments and share profits with him until I've cleared the loan. But…' Harry checked his watch and gestured across the lawn towards the river '…as of half an hour ago, this is all mine.'

'So that's what the champagne is for? We're celebrating?' She hadn't thought she could feel like celebrating on today of all days but she was truly happy for Harry. This was everything he'd wanted.

'Almost.'

'What else is there? You've done it. You've achieved your dream.'

'Only part one.'

'What's part two?' she asked.

'Convincing you to stay. I want you to stay here. With me.'

'I don't know anything about working on a cattle station.'

'I'll teach you.'

Why had he left it until the last minute? To have him ask her to stay was what she'd been waiting for, hoping for. But she needed more. He hadn't said he loved her and she knew that was what she needed to hear. If he didn't love her, there was no point in staying.

'Harry, I leave tomorrow. My flight is booked. My visa is expiring. If I don't leave I'll be deported. I have to go.'

'But I want you to stay.'

'We've had this conversation.'

'Not exactly,' he said. 'Do you think you could live out here? You once told me that you thought it was beautiful out in the bush. Peaceful, idyllic. Do you think you could be happy here? We wouldn't be able to pack up and move every few years. You'd be here for the long haul.'

'What would I do?'

'I can teach you everything you need to know and if you wanted to you could still work for the flying doctor service. You could do a couple of shifts a week or a fortnight, stay in town overnight. You could have it all, Em. I can give it to you.'

'You've got it all figured out, haven't you?'

Harry shrugged and gave her a half-smile. 'I'm a planner. I figure one of us has to be. The only thing I haven't figured out is whether you'll agree to stay. Owning a cattle station is my dream. I know it's not yours, but I don't want to be here without you. I need you. What do you think?'

'I don't know—'

'Wait.' He put a finger on her lips, stopping her from finishing her sentence. He gathered her to his chest and stood up, placing her back onto his seat and kneeling in front of her on one knee.

He took her hands in his. 'Emma Matheson, this is me, asking you properly and as nicely as I know how, to be my wife. I want to share my dream with you. I want to share my future with you. I want to share my life with you. I love you, Em. Will you please marry me?'

Emma burst into tears. She tried to maintain her composure but it was all so overwhelming.

'Emma! What's wrong?'

'I can't remember the last time someone said they loved me,' she sniffed.

Harry laughed and the circumstances reminded her of the day she'd met him, the first time he'd laughed at her expense and how she hadn't minded a bit. How she'd thought he was gorgeous. To think that was only a few short weeks ago. She couldn't believe she'd only known him for a couple of months.

'If you agree to be my wife, I promise I will tell you I love you every day for the rest of our lives.'

Harry reached into his pocket and pulled out a small box. He opened the lid to reveal an opal nestled on black velvet. 'Tony found this when he was removing the rubble from the tunnel collapse. It turns out there was still some opal there after all. He polished it up and I bought it for you. This symbolises the moment I realised I couldn't lose you.'

'You've known for all that time? Why didn't you tell me then?'

'I knew I couldn't lose you that day but I didn't realise then I couldn't lose you for ever. For so long I'd been set on getting this station and when I finally managed to sort that out I realised that there was one thing more important to me than this land and that's you. And I was about to lose you for good. I don't want that to happen. My dream won't be complete without you. I love you, Emma. Do you love me?'

She nodded and she could feel more tears threatening to spill onto her cheeks but they were tears of joy. 'Yes. I do. I feel I belong with you. From the moment I first saw you I've been drawn to you. I feel like we are two opposite ends of a magnet. You're impossible for me to resist. I know I belong with you but I can't stay. I have to leave.'

Less than an hour earlier she'd thought it was going to be difficult to make herself get on the plane tomorrow, now it would be almost impossible.

'I know, believe me, I know. But you can come back. I'll be waiting for you. Please say you'll come back to me. Please say you'll be my wife.'

'Of course I'll come back and marry you,' she said as she pulled him to his feet and kissed him as if her life depended on it. 'You are the love of my life.'

EPILOGUE

EMMA was woken by squawking galahs in a tree outside her bedroom. She opened her eyes, momentarily disoriented before she remembered that she was back on Cooper Creek Station. She was home and today was her wedding day.

She'd been back in Australia for just over a month, living with Harry, but she was still amazed every day that this was her new home. Life was chaotic, there was so much to learn, but there was never a dull moment and she was happy, blissfully happy, with her new life and with Harry.

She wondered where he was right now, what he was doing. She'd made him sleep in another room last night, telling him it was wedding-eve protocol, but she'd missed him. The bed had felt too big and cold and lonely and she'd spent the night wishing she hadn't banished him. After today she planned on spending as many nights together as possible. If she was going to town to do shifts with the flying doctors, she planned on taking him with her. She smiled to herself. How things had changed. Not only was she now an Australian who was about to get married to the love of her life, she was now also planning on making plans.

Harry stuck his head into her room. Their room. 'Good morning.' He was smiling from ear to ear and she couldn't help but smile back at him. She was always happy when he was around.

'Hey, you're not supposed to see me before the wedding,' she teased.

'We're not getting married for hours. If you think I'm going to wait all day, you don't know me very well,' he said as he came into the room.

The fact that Harry was bucking tradition shouldn't have surprised her. Nothing about today was going to be traditional. The station was overflowing with wedding guests, people had been arriving for the past few days and many would be staying for a day or two after the wedding.

Sophie and her family were here and Sam and Jo were visiting from Tamworth. Emma wondered if they found it strange to have new people living in their house but they seemed happy with the changes, her stepmother and half-sisters had arrived from England and Emma was enjoying introducing them to Australian life. And Irene, Grace and the majority of the flying doctor team were due today.

'Can I steal you away for half an hour? There's something I want to show you.'

Emma dressed quickly, picking her hat up as she left the house. Slapping a hat on her head had become second nature out here under the harsh sun. She followed Harry outside, surprised at how quiet the house and yards were.

'Where is everyone?' she asked him.

'It's only six o'clock. Lots are still sleeping and the ones who are awake are in the staff kitchen.'

Emma could smell bacon frying as she followed Harry past the staff quarters. The cook would be kept busy for the next few days catering for the guests. Harry kept walking past the kitchen and up towards the stables.

'Where are we going?'

'You'll see.'

Harry stopped beside the railings in the mounting yard. A pretty chestnut mare with a white blaze was loose in the yard but she quickly came to Harry's side when she saw the apple in his hand.

Harry handed Emma the apple and she held it out to the mare, who took it gently from her hand with soft, velvet lips. Emma didn't recognise the horse. 'She's a beautiful horse, who does she belong to?'

'You. She's my wedding gift to you.'

'Really?' Emma threw her arms around Harry and kissed him. 'Thank you, she's gorgeous.'

'Shall we go for a ride?'

'I would love to but I'm not sure if I should.'

'I promise I'll have you back in plenty of time. I'm not going to miss my own wedding.'

'It's not that. I have a wedding present for you too.' Emma took Harry's hand and placed it on her stomach. His hand was warm and Emma felt the now familiar flutter of excitement in her belly at his touch. 'We're going to have a baby.'

'You're pregnant?'

Emma nodded.

'What? When?'

'I think it was that night out in the billabong, when we spent the weekend in Innamincka.' She grinned at him. 'I told you it was a magical spot.'

Harry scooped her up, lifting her off her feet. 'This is brilliant, the best day ever,' he said as he kissed her thoroughly.

'You're happy?' Emma asked as she wrapped her legs around his waist and held onto him.

'I couldn't be happier,' he replied, before he kissed her again. 'I have everything I want right here.'

The mare whinnied softly and Emma laughed. Her life was fabulous. 'I love you, Harry Connor, let's go and get married.'

* * * * *

THE RETURN
OF HER PAST

LINDSAY ARMSTRONG

PROLOGUE

MIA GARDINER WAS home alone and preparing dinner for her mother when the storm hit with very little warning.

One minute she was rolling pastry, the next she was racing around the big old house known as West Windward and home to the wealthy O'Connor family, closing windows and doors as raindrops hammered down on the roof like bullets.

It was when she came to close the front door that a dark, damp figure loomed through the outside gloom and staggered towards her.

For a moment her heart leapt into her throat in fright, then she recognised the figure.

'Carlos! It's you. What are you doing—Carlos, are you all right?' She stared up at him, taking in the fact that he had blood pouring down his temple from a nasty-looking cut. 'What happened?' she breathed and clutched him as he swayed where he stood.

'A branch came down as I was crossing from the garage to the house. Hit me on the head,' he said indistinctly. 'That's quite a storm,' he added.

'You're not wrong.' Mia put her hand on his arm. 'Come with me. I'll fix your head.'

'What I need is a strong drink!' But he swayed again as he said it.

'Come,' she said, and led him through the house to the housekeeper's sitting room. It opened off the kitchen and was small but comfortable.

Mia cleared her mother's knitting off the settee and Carlos O'Connor collapsed gratefully onto it. In fact he lay down and groaned and closed his eyes.

Mia was galvanised into action. Half an hour later she had cleaned and dressed the cut on his head whilst not only rain but hail teemed down outside.

Then the lights went off and she clicked her tongue, mainly because she should have expected it. They had frequent power failures in the district when the weather was stormy. Fortunately her mother kept some kerosene lamps handy but in the dark she tripped around until she located them. Then she lit a couple and brought one into the sitting room.

Carlos was lying unmoving, his eyes were closed and he looked very pale.

She stared down at him and felt a wave of tenderness flow through her because the truth of the matter was that Carlos O'Connor was gorgeous. All the lean six foot plus length of him, the dark hair, testament to his Spanish heritage, that he often pushed out of his eyes, those grey eyes that sometimes glinted wickedly at you…

She'd had a crush on Carlos since she was fifteen—how could you not? she sometimes wondered. How

LINDSAY ARMSTRONG 9

could anyone be immune to that devastatingly sexy
aura? He might be ten years older than her eighteen
years but surely she could catch up?

Not that she'd seen an awful lot of him over the past
five years. He didn't live on the property but she believed he'd grown up on it; he lived in Sydney, but he
did come back from time to time. Usually it was only
for a couple of days but he rode, not only horses but
quad bikes, and because Mia was allowed to stable her
horse on the property, and because she kept a weather
eye on his horses when she was home, they had a bit
in common.

She'd had some marvellous gallops with Carlos and
if he'd ever divined that sometimes he made her heartbeat triple he'd never given any sign of it.

At first her daydreams had been simple and girl-
ish but over the last couple of years she'd graduated
from alternating between telling herself to forget all
about Carlos O'Connor—he was a multi-millionaire,
she was only the housekeeper's daughter—and some
rather more sophisticated daydreams.

Still, he was way out of her league. What could she
offer him over the gorgeous beauties who sometimes
accompanied him on his visits?

'Mia?'

She came out of her daydream with a start and saw
that his eyes were open.

'How do you feel?' She knelt down beside him and
put the lamp down. 'Do you have a headache? Or double vision? Or any strange symptoms?'

'Yes.' He thought for a moment.

She waited, then, 'What? Tell me. I don't think I can get a doctor to come out in this—' she gestured up towards the cacophony on the roof above '—but—'

'I don't need a doctor,' he murmured and reached for her. 'Just this. You've grown up, Mia, grown up and grown gorgeous…'

Mia gasped as his arms closed about her and somehow, she wasn't sure how, she ended up lying beside him on the settee. 'Carlos!' she remonstrated and tried to sit up. 'What are you doing?'

'Relax,' he murmured.

'But—well, apart from anything else, you could have a fractured skull!'

'If I did, quiet and warmth and comfort would be recommended, don't you agree?' he suggested gravely.

'I…you…perhaps but—' Mia broke off helplessly.

'That's exactly what you could provide, Miss Gardiner. So would you mind not wriggling around like a trapped pilchard?'

'A trapped pilchard?' Mia repeated in outraged tones. 'How dare you, Carlos?'

'Sorry. Not the most complimentary analogy. How about a trapped siren? Yes, that's better, don't you agree?' And he ran his hands down her body, then cuddled her against him. 'Pilchard. I must be crazy!' he murmured.

Mia took a breath to tell him he was crazy but suddenly she was laughing. Then they were laughing together and it was the most wonderful thing that had ever happened to Mia.

So much so, she lay quietly in his arms and when he

started to kiss her, she didn't resist. She was powerless to be unaffected by the amazing rapture he brought to her as he kissed her and held her. As he told her she had the most luscious mouth, skin like silk and hair like midnight.

She was made conscious of her body in ways she'd never known before as delicious ripples of desire ran through her. She was deeply appreciative of his easy strength and his long clean lines, the width of his shoulders and the way his hands brought her so much pleasure.

In fact she started to kiss him back and, when it was over, once again she lay quietly against him, her arms around him and she was deeply affected by everything about him. Not only that but conscious that it wasn't impossible for him to be attracted to an eighteen-year-old—why else would he be doing this? Why else would he tell her she'd grown up and grown gorgeous?

Surely it couldn't be concussion?

Two days later Mia drove away from the O'Connor estate and set her course, so to speak, for Queensland, where she'd been offered a university place.

She'd said goodbye to her parents, who'd been proud but just a little sad, but she was secure in the knowledge that they loved their jobs. Her father had a great deal of respect for Frank O'Connor, who'd built his construction company into a multi-million dollar business, although he'd recently suffered a stroke and been confined to a wheelchair, leaving his son Carlos in charge.

It was Carlos's mother Arancha, a diminutive Spanish lady, a beauty in her earlier days but still the epitome of style, who had given her only son a Spanish name and it was she amongst the O'Connors who loved the Hunter Valley estate of West Windward passionately.

But it was Mia's mother who actually tended the homestead, with all its objets d'art, priceless carpets and exquisite linens and silks. And it was her father who looked after the extensive gardens.

To some extent Mia shared both her parents' talents. She loved to garden and the greatest compliment her father had given her was to tell her she had 'green fingers'. She also took after her mother in her eye for decorative detail and love of fine food.

Mia was conscious that she owed her parents a lot. They'd scrimped and saved to give her the best education at a private boarding school. That was why she always helped as much as she could when she was home with them and she knew she was fulfilling their dream by going to university.

But as she drove away two days after the storm, her thoughts were in chaos, her head was still spinning and she didn't look back.

CHAPTER ONE

'CARLOS O'CONNOR WILL be attending,' Mia Gardiner's assistant Gail announced in hushed, awed tones.

Mia's busy hands stilled for a moment—she was arranging a floral display. Then she carried on placing long-stemmed roses in a standard vase. 'He is the bride's brother,' she said casually.

Gail lowered the guest list and stared at her boss. 'How do you know that? They don't have the same surname.'

'Half-brother, actually,' Mia corrected herself. 'Same Spanish mother, different fathers. She's a couple of years older. I think she was about two when her father died and her mother remarried and had Carlos.'

'How do you know *that*?' Gail demanded.

Mia stood back, admired her handiwork but grimaced inwardly. 'Uh—there's not a lot that isn't known about the O'Connors, I would have thought.'

Gail pursed her lips but didn't disagree and studied the guest list instead. 'It says—it just says Carlos O'Connor and partner. It doesn't say who the partner is. I thought I read something about him and Nina

French.' Gail paused and shrugged. 'She's gorgeous. And wouldn't it be lovely to have all that money? I mean he's got a fortune, hasn't he? And he's gorgeous too, Carlos O'Connor. Don't you think so?'

'Undoubtedly,' Mia replied and frowned down at the tub of pink and blue hydrangeas at her feet. 'Now, what am I going to put these in? I know, the Wedgwood soup tureen—it sounds odd but they look good in it. How are *you* going, Gail?' she asked rather pointedly.

Gail awoke from her obviously pleasurable day-dream about Carlos O'Connor and sighed. 'I'm just about to lay the tables, Mia,' she said loftily and wafted away, pushing a cutlery trolley.

Mia grimaced and went to find the Wedgwood tureen.

Several hours later, the sun went down on Mount Wilson but Mia was still working. Not arranging flowers; she was in the little office that was the headquarters of the Bellbird Estate.

It was from this office in the grand old homestead, the main house on the estate, that she ran the reception function business, Bellbird Estate, a business that was becoming increasingly well-known.

Not only did the old house lend its presence to functions but its contents delighted Mia. It contained lovely pieces of old furniture, vases, lamps, linen and a beautiful china collection—including the Wedgwood tureen.

She catered for wedding receptions, iconic birthday parties—any kind of reception. The cuisine she provided was superb, the house and the gardens were lovely but perhaps the star of the show was Mount Wilson itself.

At the northern end of the Blue Mountains, west of Sydney, it had been surveyed in 1868 and had gradually acquired a similar reputation to an Indian 'hill station'—English-style homes with cool-climate English gardens in alien settings, this setting being bush and rainforest.

And anyone's first impression of Mount Wilson had to be how beautiful it was. Yes, the road was narrow and clung to the mountainside in tortuous zigzags in places but the trees in the village—plane trees, limes, elms, beeches and liquid ambers, were, especially when starting to wear their autumnal colours, glorious. There were also native eucalypts, straight, strong and reaching for the sky, and native tree ferns everywhere.

The glimpses of houses through impressive gateways and beyond sweeping driveways were tantalising, many old and stone with chimneys, some smothered in creepers like wisteria, others with magnificent gardens.

All in all, she'd thought often although she kept it to herself, Mount Wilson shouted money—new money or old money but *money*—and the resources to have acres of garden that you opened to the public occasionally. The resources to have an estate in the Blue Mountains, a retreat from the hurly-burly of Sydney or the heat of its summers....

And tomorrow Juanita Lombard, Carlos O'Connor's half-sister, was marrying Damien Miller on Mount Wilson—at Bellbird, to be precise. Damien Miller, whose mother, rather than the bride or her mother, had booked the venue without mentioning who the bride was until it was too late for Mia to pull out without damaging her business reputation.

Mia got up, stretched and rubbed her back and decided enough was enough; she'd call it a day.

She didn't live in the main house; she lived in the gardener's cottage, which was in fact a lot more modern, though unusual. It had been built as an artist's studio. The walls were rough brick, the plentiful woodwork was native timber and the floors were sandstone cobbles. It had a combustion stove for heating, a cook's delight kitchen and a sleeping loft accessible by ladder.

It was an interior that lent itself well to Mia's photography hobby, her images of native wildlife and restful landscapes, enlarged and framed, graced the walls. It also suited her South American poncho draped over a rail, her terracotta tubs full of plants and her chunky crockery.

It was also not far from the stables and that was where she went first, to bring her horse, Long John Silver, in from the paddock, to rug him and feed him.

Although it was summer, there were patches of mist clinging to the tree tops and the air was chilly enough to nip at your fingers and cheeks and turn the end of your nose pink. But the sunset was magical, a streaky symphony of pink and gold and she paused for a long moment with her arms around Long John's neck to wonder at life. Who would have thought Carlos O'Connor would cross her path again?

She shook her head and led Long John into his stall. She mixed his feed and poured it into his wall bin, checked his water, then, with a friendly pat and a flick of his mane through her fingers, she closed him in.

That was when she came to grief. She'd collected some wood for her stove and was taking a last look at the sunset when, seemingly from nowhere, what she'd kept at bay for hours enveloped her—the memories she'd refused to allow to surface ever since she'd known who would be at tomorrow's wedding flooded back to haunt her.

'Surely I can do this,' she whispered. 'I've come so far since those days—surely I can do this?'

She closed her eyes but nothing could stop those memories as she allowed herself the luxury of picturing Carlos O'Connor in her mind's eye. Luxury? Or was it a torment?

Whatever, how could she forget that night-dark hair that sometimes fell in his eyes? That olive skin his Spanish mother had bequeathed, yet the grey eyes that came from his Irish father and could be as cool as the North Sea or so penetrating his glance made you mentally sit up in a flurry and hope like mad you had your wits about you.

How could she forget the satanic edge to his looks that was so intriguing; irresistible but at the same time capable of making you feel you were playing with fire?

Or not remember the way he laughed sometimes and that wicked sense of humour?

Or the times when no one would have suspected he was at the helm of a multi-national construction company. Times when he exchanged his suit for jeans and T-shirt and indulged his favourite pastimes—sailing, riding, flying. In fact he was rarely formal when she thought about it. But above all how could she ever forget lying in Carlos O'Connor's arms?

She stood perfectly still for a long moment, then she reached into her pocket for a tissue and mopped herself up, determined that she would recover her equilibrium before tomorrow.

Mercifully, when she woke early the next morning, it was to see that at least the weather was fine; the sun had just started to climb into a cloudless sky. She had all sorts of contingency plans for wet weather but it was a relief not to have to resort to them.

She got up, dressed swiftly in jeans and an old shirt and brewed herself a cup of tea, which she took out into the garden. She loved the garden, all five acres of it, and although Bellbird employed a gardener it was Mia who supervised what went in and came out, something that led her into frequent discord with the gardener, Bill James, a man in his sixties who'd lived all his life on the mountain. Bill and his wife, Lucy, lived in another cottage on the property.

Lucy James was away at the moment. She made an annual pilgrimage to spend a month with her daughter and her six grandchildren in Cairns. To Mia's regret, Bill drove Lucy up to and back from Cairns but only ever stayed a couple of days with them.

That left Mia in the position of having to cope with Bill living on his own and hating it until Lucy returned. If he was cranky when his wife was present, he was ten times crankier when she wasn't.

Still, it had been a huge stroke of luck how she'd come to be able to start her reception business at Bellbird in the first place. She'd met the two old ladies, sisters and spinsters and now in their late eighties, who owned Bellbird, at Echo Point.

It had been her first visit to the Blue Mountains' premier tourist attraction, from which you could look over the Three Sisters and the Jamison Valley.

From the viewing platform she'd gazed out over the scenery and been enchanted by the wondrous views.

The elderly sisters had sat down on the bench beside her and struck up a conversation. Before long she'd learnt about the estate on Mount Wilson, the fact that the sisters now lived in a retirement home in Katoomba, which they hardly had a good word to say for. And the fact that they were looking for a use for their estate.

Mia had explained that she'd come up to the Blue Mountains with the idea of opening a function business—and things had progressed from there. Of course the sisters had had her vetted but what had started out as a business venture had blossomed into a friendship and Mia often visited them in their despised retirement home that was actually very luxurious and well-run. And she often took them bunches of flowers and snippets of gossip about the mountain because she could well imagine what it must be like living away from Bellbird.

If there was one area of concern for her regarding the estate it was that her lease was renewed annually and due for renewal shortly. Her two spinsters would be perfectly happy to renew it but had let drop that they

were under some pressure from their nephew, their closest relative and heir, to think of selling Bellbird and in-
vesting the money for a higher return than the estate
was earning them.

On the morning of the Lombard/Miller wedding, things
at Mount Wilson were looking pretty grand. The gardens were in spectacular form and so was the house,
Mia noted, as she reluctantly went indoors and did a
thorough inspection.

The ceremony was to be conducted by a marriage
celebrant in an elegant rotunda in the garden, whilst the
meal was to be served in the huge main dining room
that easily seated the estimated seventy-five guests. It
was a spectacular room with a pressed iron ceiling and
long glass doors that opened onto the terrace and the
main rose garden.

Dancing would be in the atrium with its cool tiled
floor, and tables and chairs were dotted around the
main lawn.

'Well, it all looks good,' Mia said to the newly arrived Gail—she lived on the mountain only a few minutes' drive away. 'And here come the caterers. OK!
Let's get started.' And she and Gail gave each other a
high five salute as was their custom.

In the time she had before the wedding party arrived
Mia took a last look into the wedding suite—where the
members of the bridal party would dress and be able to
retire to if need be. And, content that it was all spick

and span, she jogged to her own quarters, where she took a shower and dressed herself for the event.

She studied herself thoughtfully in the mirror when she was ready. She always contrived to look elegant enough to be a guest but a discreet one, and today she was wearing a slim short-sleeved jade-green Thai silk dress with fashionable but medium heels in matching leather and a string of glass beads on a gold chain. She also wore a hat, more of a fascinator, to be precise. A little cap made from the same Thai silk with feathers and a froth of dotted voile worn on the side of her head.

He probably won't recognise me, she reassured herself as she stood in front of her cheval mirror admiring her reflection, and particularly the lovely fascinator, which seemed to invest her with more sophistication than she usually exhibited.

But even without the hat she was a far cry from the kind of girl she'd been in those days. Always in jeans, always outdoors, always riding when she could get away with it. Her clothes—her hair alone must look different from how she used to wear it. She grimaced.

Her hair was a sore point with her. Nearly black, it was wild and curly, yet it never looked right when it was cut to be manageable. So she wore it severely tied back when she was being formal, something she'd not done when she was younger.

Nothing, she had to acknowledge, had changed about her eyes, though. They were green and Gail had once told her her eyelashes were utterly to die for and so was her mouth. She also possessed a pair of dimples that she wasn't a hundred per cent keen on—they didn't seem to go with the sophisticated woman of the world she liked to hope she resembled.

She turned away from the mirror with a shrug and discovered, to her horror, that she was trembling finely because she was scared to death all of a sudden.

No, not all of a sudden, she corrected herself. Ever since she'd realised who the bride was, she'd been pretending to herself that she was quite capable of dealing with the O'Connor family when, underneath that, she'd been filled with the desire to run, to put as much distance between them as she could.

Now it was too late. She was going to have to go through with it. She was going to have to be civil to Arancha O'Connor and her daughter Juanita. Somehow she was going to have to be normal with Carlos.

Unless they didn't recognise her.

She took a deep breath and put her shoulders back; she could do it.

But all her uncertainties resurfaced not much later when she moved the Wedgwood tureen with its lovely bounty of hydrangeas to what she thought was a better spot—her last act of preparation for the Lombard/ Miller wedding—and she dropped it.

It smashed on the tiled floor, soaking her feet in the process. She stared down at the mess helplessly.

'Mia?' Gail, alerted by the crash, ran up and surveyed the mess.

'I'm s-sorry,' Mia stammered, her hand to her mouth. 'Why did I do that? It was such a lovely tureen too.'

Gail looked up and frowned at her boss. At the same time it dawned on her that Mia had been different over the last few days, somehow less sure of herself, but why, she had no idea. 'Just an accident?' she suggested.

'Yes. Of course,' Mia agreed gratefully but still, apparently, rooted to the spot.

'Look, you go and change your shoes,' Gail recommended, 'and I'll clean up the mess. We haven't got much time.'

'Thank you! Maybe we could get it fixed?'

'Maybe,' Gail agreed. 'Off you go!'

Mia finally moved away and didn't see the strange look her assistant bestowed on her before she went to get the means to sweep up what was left of the Wedgwood tureen.

The wedding party arrived on time.

Mia watched through the French windows and saw the bride, the bridesmaids and the mother of the bride arrive. And for a moment she clutched the curtain with one hand and her knuckles were white, her face rigid as she watched the party, particularly the bride's mother, Arancha O'Connor. She took a deep breath, counted to ten and went out to greet them.

It was a hive of activity in the bridal suite. Mia provided a hairdresser, a make-up artist and a florist and in this flurry of dryers and hairspray, perfumes both bottled and from the bouquets and corsages, with the swish of petticoats and long dresses, laces and satins, it seemed safe to Mia to say that no one recognised her.

She was wrong.

The bridal party was almost ready when Arancha

O'Connor, the epitome of chic in lavender with a huge
hat, suddenly pointed at Mia and said, 'I know who you
are! Mia Gardiner.'

Mia turned to her after a frozen moment. 'Yes, Mrs
O'Connor. I didn't think you'd remember me.'

'Of course I remember you! My, my, Mia—' Arancha's dark gaze swept over her comprehensively
'—you've certainly acquired a bit of polish. Come up a
bit in the world, have we? Although—' Arancha looked
around '—I suppose this is just an upmarket version
of a housekeeping position, really! Juanita, do you remember Mia?' She turned to her daughter. 'Her parents
worked for us. Her mother in the kitchen, her father in
the gardens.'

Juanita looked absolutely splendid in white lace and
tulle but she frowned a little distractedly. 'Hi, Mia. I
do remember you now but I don't think we really knew
each other; I was probably before your time,' she said.
'Mum—' she looked down at the phone in her hand
'—Carlos is running late and he'll be coming on his
own.'

Arancha stiffened. 'Why?'

'No idea.' Juanita turned to Mia. 'Would you be able
to rearrange the bridal table so there's not an embar-
rassingly empty seat beside Carlos?'

'Of course,' Mia murmured and went to move away
but Arancha put a hand on her arm.

'Carlos,' she confided, 'has a beautiful partner.
She's a model but also the daughter of an ambassador. Nina—'

'Nina French,' Mia broke in dryly. 'Yes, I've heard of her, Mrs O'Connor.'

'Well, unfortunately something must have come up for Nina not to be able to make it, but—'

'Carlos is quite safe from me, Mrs O'Connor, even without Ms French to protect him,' Mia said wearily this time. 'Quite safe, believe me. And now, if you'll excuse me, I'll get back to work.' She turned away but not before she saw the glint of anger in Arancha's dark eyes.

'It's going quite well,' Gail whispered some time later as she and Mia happened to pass each other.

Mia nodded but frowned. Only 'quite well'? What was wrong? The truth was she was still trembling with suppressed anger after her encounter with Arancha O'Connor. And it was impossible to wrest her mind from it.

Her skill at blending the right music, her talent for drawing together a group of people, her adroit handling of guests had deserted her because Arancha had reduced her from seasoned professional to merely the housekeeper's daughter.

'But *he's* not here!' Gail added.

'He's running late, that's all.'

Gail tut-tutted and went on her way, leaving Mia in her post of discreet observer but feeling helpless and very conscious that she was losing her grip on this wedding. Not only that but she was possessed of a boiling sense of injustice.

She'd actually believed she could show Arancha that she'd achieved a minor miracle. That she'd begun and prospered a business that had the rich and famous flocking to her door. Moreover she could hold her own amongst them; her clothes bore designer labels, her taste in food and décor and the special little things she brought to each reception was being talked about with admiration.

But what had she proved? Nothing. With a few well chosen words Arancha had demolished her achievements and resurrected her inferiority complex so that it seemed to her she was once more sitting on the sidelines, looking in. She was no closer to entering Arancha and Juanita's circle than she'd ever been. Not to mention Carlos's…

She'd believed she could no longer be accused of being the housekeeper's daughter as if it were an invisible brand she was doomed to wear for ever, but, if anything, it had got worse.

From a dedicated cook, a person to whom the smooth running of the household—the scent of fresh clean linen, the perfume of flowers, the magic of herbs not only for cooking but infusions as well—from that dedicated person to whom all those things mattered, her mother had been downgraded to a 'kitchen' worker.

Her father, her delightfully vague father who cared passionately about not only what he grew but the birds and the bees and anything to do with gardens, had suffered a similar fate.

She shook her head, then clamped her teeth onto her bottom lip and forced herself to get a grip.

That was when the snarl of a powerful motor made itself heard, not to the guests but to Mia, whose hearing was attuned to most things that came and went from Bellbird, and she slipped outside.

The motor belonged to a sports car, a metallic yellow two-door coupé. The car pulled up to a stone-spitting halt on the gravel drive and a tall figure in jeans jumped out, reached in for a bag, then strode towards her.

'I'm late, I know,' he said. 'Who are you?'

'I...I'm running the show,' Mia replied a little uncertainly.

'Good, you can show me where to change. I'm Carlos O'Connor, by the way, and I'm in deep trouble. I'm sure I've missed the actual ceremony but please tell me I haven't missed the speeches!' he implored. 'They'll never talk to me again.' He took Mia's elbow and led her at a fast pace towards the house.

'No, not the speeches,' Mia said breathlessly, 'and now you're here I can delay them a little longer while you change. In here!' She gestured to a doorway on the veranda that led directly to the bridal suite.

Carlos turned away from her. 'Would you let them know I'm here?'

'Sure.'

'*Muchas gracias.*' He disappeared through the doorway.

Mia stared at the door with her lips parted and her eyes stunned. He hadn't recognised her!

Which was what she'd hoped for but the awful irony was she hated the thought of it because it had to be that she'd meant so little to him she must have been almost instantly forgettable...

She swallowed, then realised with a start that she

still had a wedding to run and a message to deliver. She straightened her hat and entered the dining room and discreetly approached the bridal table, where she bent down to tell the bride and the groom that Mr O'Connor had arrived and would be with them as soon as he'd changed.

'Thank heavens!' Juanita said fervently and her brand new husband Damien agreed with her.

'I know I didn't need anyone to give me away,' Juanita continued, 'but I do need Carlos to make the kind of speech only he can make. Not only—' she put a hand on Damien's arm and glinted him a wicked little look '—to extol all my virtues but to liven things up a bit!'

Mia flinched.

'Besides which, Mum is starting to have kittens,' Juanita added. 'She was sure he'd had an accident.'

'I'd have thought your mother would have stopped worrying about Carlos years ago,' Damien remarked.

This time Juanita cast him a speaking look. 'Never,' she declared. 'Nor will she ever rest until she's found him a suitable wife.'

Mia melted away at this point and she hovered outside the bridal suite to be able to direct the latecomer to the dining room through the maze of passages.

She would have much preferred to delegate this to Gail, not to mention really making Gail's day, no doubt, but she was not to be seen.

After about five minutes when Carlos O'Connor still had not appeared, she glanced at her watch with a frown and knocked softly on the door.

It was pulled open immediately and Carlos was

dressed in his morning suit and all present and correct—apart from his hair, which looked as if he'd been
dragging fingers through it, and his bow tie, which he
had in his hand.

'I can't tie the blasted thing,' he said through his
teeth. 'I never could. Tell you what, if I ever get married I will bar all monkey suits and bow ties. Here!' He
handed Mia the tie. 'If you're in charge of the show,
you do it.'

Typically Carlos at his most arrogant, Mia thought,
because she was still hurt to the quick.

She took the tie from him with a swift upward glance
that was about as cold as she was capable of and stood
up on her toes to briskly and efficiently tie the bow tie.

'There.' She patted it briefly. 'Now, *if* you wouldn't
mind and seeing as you're already late as it is, this wedding awaits you.'

'Wait a moment.' A frown grew in Carlos's grey eyes
as he put his hands on her hips—an entirely inappropriate gesture between guest and wedding reception
manager—and he said incredulously, 'Mia?'

She froze, then forced herself to respond, 'Yes. Hi,
Carlos!' she said casually. 'I didn't think you'd recognised me. Uh…Juanita really needs you so…' She went
to turn away but he detained her.

'What are you mad about, Mia?'

She had to bite her lip to stop herself from blurting
out the truth, the whole truth and nothing but the truth.
Chapter and verse, in other words, of every reason she
had for…well, being as mad as she could ever recall.

She swallowed several times. 'I'm having a little

trouble getting this wedding going,' she said carefully at last. 'That's all. So—' She tried to pull away.

He slipped his hands up to her waist and said authoritatively, 'Hang on. It must be—six—seven years—since you ran away, Mia.'

'I didn't…I…well, I suppose I did,' she corrected herself. 'And yes, about that. But look, Carlos, this wedding is really dragging its feet and it's going to be my reputation on the line if I don't get it going, so would you please come and make the kind of speech only you can make, apparently, to liven things up?'

'In a moment,' he drawled. 'Wow!' His lips twisted as he stood her away from him and admired her from her toes to the tip of her fascinator and all the curves in between. Not only that but he admired her legs, the slenderness of her waist, the smoothness of her skin, her sweeping lashes and delectable mouth. 'Pardon my boyish enthusiasm, but this time you've really grown up, Mia.'

She bit her lip. Dealing with Carlos could be difficult at the best of times but she well recognised him in this mood—there would be no moving him until he was ready to be moved.

She heaved an inward sigh and mentally gritted her teeth. All right, two could play this game…

'You're looking pretty fine yourself, Mr O'Connor,' she said lightly. 'Although I must say I'm surprised your mother hasn't found a wife for you yet.'

'The last person I would get to choose a wife for me is my mother,' he said dryly. 'What brought that up?'

Mia widened her eyes not entirely disingenuously but

in surprise as well. And found she had to think quickly.
'Probably the venue and what's going on here,' she said
with an ironic little glint. 'Mind you, things are about
to flop here if I don't pull something out of the hat!'
And she pulled away, successfully.

He stared at her for a long moment, then he started to
laugh and Mia felt her heart pound because she'd gone
for so long without Carlos, without his laugh, without
his arms around her…

'I don't know what you expect me to do,' he said
wryly.

'I don't care what you do, but if you don't come and
do *something*, Carlos,' she threatened through her teeth,
suddenly furious although she had no idea if it was
with him or with herself, or the situation, 'I'll scream
blue murder!'

CHAPTER TWO

'FEELING BETTER?'

Mia took another sip of brandy and looked around. Everyone had gone. The bridal party, the guests, the caterers, they'd all gone. The presents had all been loaded carefully into a station wagon and driven away.

Gail had gone home in seventh heaven because she'd not only seen Carlos, she'd spoken to him. And the wedding had been a success. It had livened up miraculously as soon as Carlos had made his speech and Juanita had thrown her arms around Mia and Gail and thanked them profusely for their contribution to her special day as she'd left.

Carlos had driven away in his metallic yellow car and Mia had kicked off her shoes and changed her Thai silk dress for a smock but, rather than doing any work, she'd sunk into an armchair in the foyer. Her hat sat on a chair beside her. She was perfectly dry-eyed but she felt as if she'd been run over by a bus.

It was quite normal to feel a bit flattened after a function—she put so much into each and every one of them—but this was different; this was an emotional flat liner of epic proportions. This was all to do with Carlos and the fact that she'd been kidding herself for years if she'd thought she'd gotten over him.

All to do with the fact that the feel of his hands on her hips and waist had awoken sensations throughout her body that had thrilled her, the fact that to think he hadn't recognised her had been like a knife through her heart.

That was when someone said her name and she looked up and moved convulsively to see him standing there only a foot or so away.

'But…but,' she stammered, 'you left. I saw you drive off.'

'I came back. I'm staying with friends just down the road. And you need a drink. Point me in the right direction.'

Mia hesitated, then gestured. He came back a few minutes later with a drinks trolley, poured a couple of brandies and now he was sitting opposite her in an armchair. He'd changed into khaki cargo trousers and a grey sweatshirt.

'Feeling better?' he asked again.

She nodded. 'Thanks.'

He frowned. 'Are you sure you're in the right job if it takes so much out of you, Mia?'

'It doesn't usually—' She stopped and bit her lip.

'Doesn't usually affect you like this?' he hazarded.

She looked down and pleated the material of her smock. 'Well, no.'

'So what was different about this one?'

'I don't know.' Mia shrugged. 'I suppose I didn't think any of you would recognise me.'

'Why the hell wouldn't we?' he countered.

She shrugged. 'I've changed.'

'Not that much.'

She bridled and looked daggers at him before swiftly veiling her eyes. 'That's what your mother tried to tell me. I'm just a souped-up version of the housekeeper's daughter, in other words.'

'I didn't say that,' he retorted. 'Since when did you get so thin-skinned, Mia?'

She took a very deep breath. 'I'm not,' she said stiffly.

'I can't work out whether you want us to think you have changed or not.'

'Don't worry about it, Carlos,' she advised coolly. 'In fact, thank you for getting me a drink but I'd be happy if you went back to your friends. I have a lot to do still.'

'Short of throwing me out,' he replied casually, 'which I doubt you could do, you're going to have to put up with me, Mia, until I'm ready to go. So, why don't you fill me in on the missing years? I'm talking about the years between the time you kissed me with considerable ardour then waltzed off to uni, and now.' His grey gaze rested on her sardonically.

Mia went white.

'I'm waiting,' he remarked.

She said something supremely uncomplimentary beneath her breath but she knew from the autocratic set of his jaw that he wouldn't let up until he got the answers he wanted.

'All right!' She said it through her teeth but he intervened.

'Hang on a moment.' He reached over and took her glass. 'Let's have another one.'

With the deepest reluctance, she told him about the intervening years. How her mother and father had retired and were living in the Northern Rivers district of New South Wales. How they'd started a small tea shop in a country town that was becoming well known, not only for the cakes her mother baked but the honey her father produced and the herbs he grew.

How she'd finished university, spent some months overseas; how a series of catering jobs had finally led her to taking the plunge and starting her own business.

'And that's me up to date,' she said bleakly and added with irony, 'how about you?'

He avoided the question. 'No romantic involvement?'

'Me?' Mia drew her finger around the rim of her glass. 'Not really. Not *seriously*. I haven't had the time. How about you?' she asked again.

'I'm...' He paused and grimaced. 'Actually, I'm currently unattached. Nina—I don't know if you've heard of Nina French?' He raised a dark eyebrow at her.

'Who hasn't?' Mia murmured impatiently. 'Top model, utterly gorgeous, daughter of an ambassador,' she added.

'Yes.' He nodded. 'We had a relationship. It fell through. Today, as a matter of fact.'

Mia choked on a sip of her drink. 'Today?'

He nodded.

'Is that why you were late?' she asked incredulously.

He nodded. 'We had a monumental row just before we were due to set out—to be here on time.' He shrugged. 'About fifty per cent of our relationship consisted of monumental rows, now I come to think of it.'

'Oh. I'm sorry,' Mia said. 'But that probably means a…a grand reunion.'

'Not this time,' he replied perfectly coolly, so coolly it sent a little shiver down Mia's spine.

He was quiet for a time, rolling his glass in his hands. 'Otherwise,' he continued, 'I've worked like a Trojan to fill my father's shoes since he had that stroke. He died a few months ago.'

'I read about that. I'm sorry.'

'Don't be. It was a release—for all of us, I guess. After the stroke he became embittered and extremely hard to live with. He was always a hard man. I never felt I was living up to his expectations before he became ill but even less so afterwards.'

He sat back and tasted his drink. 'I've even branched out in new directions, successfully, but—' he paused and shrugged '—I can't help feeling he wouldn't have approved or that he would have thought of a different way of doing things.'

'I didn't know him much,' Mia murmured.

'The thing is—' Carlos drained his drink and looked out into the sunset '—I don't know why I'm telling you this; maybe weddings generate a desire to understand things—or maybe monumental rows do it—' he shrugged '—but I don't know if it's thanks to him and his…lack of enthusiasm for most things, including me, that's given me a similar outlook on life.'

Mia frowned. 'What do you mean?'

'There's something missing. Hard to put my finger on it, though.'

'Maybe you'd like to take a year off and live amongst some primitive tribe for a change? Is it that kind of an itch?'

He grimaced. 'Not exactly.'

'Then it could be a wife and family you're lacking,' Mia said in a motherly sort of way and was completely unprepared for what came next.

He studied her for a long moment, his eyes narrowed and very intent. Then he said, 'You wouldn't like to take Nina's place?'

Mia's eyes widened and her mouth fell open. 'What do you mean?'

'You wouldn't like to get engaged to me? Not that I was engaged to Nina, but—' He gestured.

She swallowed, choked again on a sip of her drink and came up spluttering.

He eyed her quizzically. 'An unusual reaction,' he murmured.

'No. I mean yes. I mean…how could you?' She reached for a napkin from the trolley and patted her eyes and her mouth. 'I don't think that's funny,' she told him coldly.

He raised a dark eyebrow at her. 'It wasn't meant to be. I'm in rather desperate need of a—what should I call it?—a shield at the moment. From Nina and the whole damn caboodle of them.' He looked irritated to death.

'Them? Who?' Mia queried with a frown.

'The set she moves in, Juanita too, my mother and all

the rest of them.' He gestured. 'You saw them all today.'
He paused, then smiled suddenly. 'In comparison, the
housekeeper's daughter is like pure sweet spring water.'

Mia moved abruptly and went white to her lips. 'How
dare you?' she whispered. 'How dare you patronise me
with your ridiculous proposal and think you can make
me laugh about being the housekeeper's daughter?'

'Mia—' he sat up '—it may be seven years ago but
you and I set each other alight once—remember? Perhaps it didn't mean a great deal to you, but it happened.'

'M-may not have meant m-much to me?' Mia had
trouble getting the words out. 'What are you saying?'

'You ran away, remember?'

'I…Carlos, your mother warned me off,' Mia cried,
all her unspoken but good intentions not to rake up the
past forgotten. 'She told me I could never be the one
for you, no "housekeeper's daughter" would be good
enough to be your wife. She told me you were only
toying with me anyway and she threatened to sack my
parents without references if I didn't go away.'

'*What*?' he growled, looking so astounded Mia could
only stare at him wide-eyed.

'You didn't know.' It was a statement rather than a
question.

'I ended up in hospital that night, remember? When
I got home you'd gone. Listen, just tell me how it happened,' he ordered grimly.

Mia stared into the past. 'She came home first, your
mother,' she said slowly. 'The storm had passed but I
was still—' she hesitated a moment '—I was still lying
on the settee. I hadn't heard her. You were asleep. She

was…she was livid.' Mia swallowed and shivered. 'She banished me to the service quarters after I'd told her what had happened and she rang for a medevac helicopter. I don't know when you woke up. I don't know if you had concussion but the next day was when she warned me off.'

'What about your parents?'

'I never told them, not what had happened with you. But I had just received an offer of a place at a Queensland university. I hadn't been sure I'd take it—it would mean I'd be a long way from my parents—but that's what I told them—that I'd made up my mind to do it. I left two days later,' she said bleakly. 'You hadn't come back. I didn't even know if you would. But I couldn't risk them losing their jobs.' She looked at him long and steadily. 'Not both of them at the same time. I just couldn't.'

He closed his eyes briefly. 'I'm *sorry*. I had no idea. I must have been quite groggy because I don't remember much about the medevac. But I did go back to West Windward after all sorts of tests and scans and—' he shook his head impatiently '—palaver to determine whether I'd cracked my skull but you'd gone. That was when she told me you'd got a place at a Queensland university, that your parents were so proud of you and what an achievement it was for you. So I congratulated them and *they* told me they were so proud of you and there seemed to be no trauma attached to it.'

Mia patted her eyes again with the napkin. 'They were proud of me.' She shrugged. 'Did you never…' she paused, then looked at him directly '...did you never consider looking for me to check it out?'

He held her gaze for a long moment, then he said, 'No.'

'Why not?' she whispered.

He looked away and rubbed his jaw. Then he looked directly into her eyes. 'Mia, it occurred to me I could only mess up your life. I wasn't ready for a relationship so all I could offer you was an on/off affair, especially if you were up in Queensland. I'd only just taken over from my father so my life was in the process of being completely reorganised.'

He shrugged. 'I could have kicked myself for doing it—' He stopped abruptly as she flinched visibly.

'Hell,' he said. 'I'm *sorry* but—'

But Mia had had enough. She jumped up precipitately. 'So, if your mother hadn't warned me off, *you would have*?'

'No.' He said it decisively and he got to his feet and reached for her. 'No.'

As she jumped away she tripped and would have fallen if he hadn't grabbed her. 'Listen to me,' he ordered as he wound his arms around her. 'Just listen.'

Mia ignored him and struggled to free herself.

'Mia,' he warned, 'since when did you think you could beat me in a damn fight? Be still and listen.'

'There's nothing you can say I want to hear,' she gasped.

He eyed her narrowly, her flushed cheeks and her eyes dark with pain, her hair coming loose. 'OK.' He shrugged. 'Then how about this?'

And before she had a chance to identify what he was leading up to, he bent his head and claimed her mouth with a kiss.

She went limp in his arms, from sheer surprise about the way he did it, the way he moved his hands on her body. The feel of him, steel-hard against her softness, was mesmerising. And her lips parted beneath his because she simply couldn't help herself.

When it was over her head was resting on his arm, her hair flowing over it, her eyes huge, very green and stunned, her lips parted in sheer shock—shock that he had done it, shock that she had responded after his news of what had to amount to a betrayal.

'Don't look like that,' he said.

'Why did you do it?' she whispered.

'It's a traditional way to stop a fight between a man and a woman,' he said dryly. 'Didn't you know?'

Her lashes fell and it occurred to him that he'd hurt her again—like some ham-fisted clod, he thought with distaste. 'Mia, I would never have warned you off because you were the housekeeper's daughter.'

'Oh, Carlos, you may be able to deceive yourself but—'

'Listen,' he broke in savagely, 'yes, I'd have told you there was no future for us *then* but it had nothing to do with who you were. I have never,' he said through his teeth, 'shared my mother's delusions of grandeur.'

It flashed through Mia's mind, an image of herself during the day and how, once again, she'd keenly felt her position on the sidelines, despite her designer clothes and her undoubted skills. How she'd proven to herself today that she still had a long way to go in the self-confidence stakes, how she might always be a fringe-dweller compared to the O'Connors and the ubiquitous Nina French.

But above all how much it *hurt* to know that Carlos would have warned her off himself…

As for his proposal?

'I think you must be mad,' she said with bitter candour, 'if you really believe I'd want to get engaged to you. After all that—have you any idea how cheap your mother made me feel?'

He closed his eyes briefly, then released her and handed her her glass. She blinked and took a sip of brandy.

Carlos stared at her for an eternity, then he said abruptly, 'How old are you now?'

She narrowed her eyes. 'Why?'

'Why not—twenty-five?'

She nodded.

'Has there been *anyone*?'

Two spots of colour entered her cheeks and she put her glass down on the trolley with a snap. 'That's none of your business, Carlos.'

'I think it is. I think it must have been a ghastly experience. My mother—' He gestured and shrugged.

'I'm a little surprised you believe me,' Mia broke in.

'My mother,' he repeated dryly, 'has persistently meddled in all our lives but not in a way that's actually hurt anyone like this before. What happened to my father came as a big shock to her too and may have made her…may have unbalanced her a bit.' He paused and grimaced. 'Whatever, I can't let this go.'

'There's nothing you can do. I…one…gets over these things.'

'That's the problem, I don't think you have. I strongly suspect you're a twenty-five-year-old virgin, Mia.'

Mia gasped and jumped up. 'Will you…will you just go away?' she flung at him. 'To…to think,' she stammered, 'that *I* thought you were the nicest of the O'Connors.'

He lifted a wry eyebrow. 'The best of a bad bunch?'

'Yes! No. Oh!' Mia clenched her fists and ground her teeth and suddenly it was all too much for her again and she kicked her shoes off and ran out onto the veranda, onto the lawn and down towards her cottage.

Of course she came to grief—it was that kind of day.

She didn't see the sliver of glass she stepped onto although she yelped in pain.

Carlos was right behind her, and he said her name on a harsh breath and simply picked her up and turned as if to take her back to the big house.

'No, no,' she said raggedly. 'I don't want to bleed all over the house.'

'Where then?'

'Down there, my cottage. I've got a first aid kit. Oh, I'm bleeding all over *you*.'

'Don't worry about it. Here we are. Stand on one foot while I open the door and get the lights.'

A few minutes later Mia was sitting lengthwise on her settee with a towel under her foot. Carlos had turned all the lights on and, following her instructions, had found the first aid kit in the bathroom.

'I'm a good doctor, by the way,' he said as he laid out tweezers, a bowl of antiseptic, cotton wool and dressings.

'How do you know?' Mia peeled off her stocking.

'I've had no complaints to date.'

'How many people have you actually "doctored"?' she asked. 'Is it deep?'

He studied her heel. 'Deep enough. But I can't see anything in it and we should be able to keep it from bleeding until tomorrow when we can get you to a proper doctor. It might need a couple of stitches. You'll have to keep off it for a while.'

He dabbed it liberally with cotton wool dipped in antiseptic, then he dried it and applied a dressing.

'There.' He sat back. Then he reached for her and took her in his arms. 'And you're a good patient,' he said into her hair. 'Feeling OK?' He held her away and studied her face. 'You look a bit pale.'

Mia grimaced and, without giving it a second thought, laid her head against his shoulder. 'I'll be OK. I feel a bit stupid. I always check the lawn for broken glass; when people drink you never know what they can end up doing with their glasses. I *never* sprint across it barefoot.'

'Why did you?' He kissed the top of her head and it felt like the most natural thing in the world to Mia.

But she sighed. 'I was running away from you, Carlos.' She lifted her head and looked him in the eye. 'For a few minutes I really hated you. And thinking back makes me feel that way again.'

'Then don't think back,' he advised and traced the outline of her mouth. 'It always was one of the most delicious mouths I've ever seen.'

Mia was conscious of a growing clamour in her nerve-endings, delicious but at the same time disturbing, as her awareness of him grew. Awareness of how surprisingly strong he was; he'd carried her with ease. Awareness of all the old sensations being in his arms could arouse, the feel of his body against hers, the pure male scent she used to love so much when they rode together, of the cotton of his shirt mingled with a hint of musk.

Awareness and memories of his hands, so sure when he'd kissed and touched her tonight and once before, even if he was suffering from a concussion on that occasion.

It was that last thought that brought her up with a start. She had to remember that Carlos was dangerous to her mental health!

Correspondingly, she pushed herself away from him and changed tack deliberately and completely. 'This accident couldn't have happened at a worse time. I've got wall-to-wall functions over the next week. I really need to be on my feet!'

'Tomorrow?' he queried.

'No, not tomorrow but from the day after.'

He looked at her with some irony. 'Don't you have any contingency plans? Are yours the only pair of feet available?'

Mia sank back. 'Well, no. There's Gail.'

'Ah, Gail,' Carlos murmured with a sudden glint of amusement in his grey eyes. 'Now, I met Gail. She very kindly introduced herself to me and offered me any assistance I might need.'

Mia looked briefly heavenward.

Carlos noted this with a twist to his lips. 'I did form the impression, however, that, despite being young and impressionable, Gail is a fairly practical person. Possibly a hard worker as well.'

Mia closed her eyes on her inward irritation, then opened them to say honestly, 'You're right. Forgive me, Gail,' she added in an aside.

'So you can give the orders and Gail can carry them out. Problem solved.'

Mia cast him a glance liberally laced with a mixture of frustration and exasperation and, in lieu of being able to trust her voice, merely nodded.

Carlos contemplated her for a long moment, then he said, 'I see.'

Mia blinked. 'What? What do you see?'

'It's not visible to the naked eye.'

She blinked again. 'How do you see it then?'

'It wasn't that kind of an "I see".' He stood up and gathered the first aid accoutrements together and took them to the bathroom. 'It denoted understanding,' he said, coming back.

Mia made a kittenish sound of frustration. '*Understanding of what*?'

'Your state of mind. I get the impression mine is the last advice you'd want to take,' he said with a flourish. 'That kind of understanding.' He moved into the kitchen area. 'Would there be anything to eat in your establishment, Miss Gardiner?'

Mia, who didn't at that moment know whether to laugh or cry—laugh because he could be so crazy at times, cry because he read her so well—said faintly, 'Look in the fridge,' and swallowed a lump in her throat. 'Uh…I'm sorry, I did bleed all over you but cold water is good for getting blood out.'

'You don't say?' He looked down at himself and swore softly. 'I see what you mean. OK, I'll scrub what I can.'

She had to laugh when, after he'd washed the bloodstains away, he found her apron hanging on a hook on the wall and donned it.

'There.' He smoothed it down. 'Presentable.' He opened the fridge door and apparently approved of what he saw. He withdrew a bowl of pasta marinara already prepared and just requiring heating up. There was a small salad also made and under cling wrap.

Lastly he took out a bottle of white wine with a shrug. 'Is there any point in being virtuous *and* sober at this end of the day?'

'Virtuous?' she queried.

'You could hardly call us decadent.'

'Well, no.' Mia paused as Carlos put the pasta in the microwave and set out some cutlery on her little round kitchen table.

Within minutes they were eating and sharing some of the wine.

Mia ate from a tray on her knees; she was still ensconced on the settee with her feet up. They talked desultorily—he was the one who'd promoted the conversation by asking her some questions about the reception business.

'So,' he said at one point, helping himself to more pasta, 'in the case of a bridal party like today, you actually provide a hairdresser and a make-up person so all the dressing et cetera takes place up here—very sensible. It'd be a long drive all kitted out in a wedding dress. But how do the brides cope with a strange hairdresser? I had a girlfriend once who left me to follow her hairdresser to Townsville.'

Mia wound her last mouthful of pasta around her fork and couldn't help grinning. 'The hairdressers and make-up girls work in salons in Sydney, so the bridal party have a couple of appointments with them *before* the big day to work out hairstyles and so on.'

He looked at her with admiration. 'That's pretty inspired, Miss Gardiner.'

She shrugged. 'It's just a question of—' she paused and looked thoughtful '—of helping Mount Wilson to work its magic, I guess.'

'Mmm…' He pushed his bowl away and got up to take the tray from her. 'Who owns the place?'

She told him and then, unwittingly, voiced her concern. 'They're in their eighties now,' she said slowly, 'and they seem to be going downhill a bit. They're getting forgetful and—I guess it's only natural but I think they're worried about Bellbird. They have a nephew who's their heir. He wants them to sell it and invest the money where they'd get a higher return. Of course—'

she gestured '—it's entirely up to them but I might be looking for somewhere else one day. Which would be a pity but—we'll see.'

'Are you attached to the property?' he asked after a moment. 'It's not only a business proposition for you?'

Mia sighed and reached for her wine glass. 'I love it,' she said dreamily and with a faraway look in her eyes. 'I'd love to own it. I'd love to pretend I was a lady from another era who had this summer residence in the hills and a garden I could open to the public if the whim took me. I'd love to call this place home.' She looked at Carlos, smiling. 'Mount Wilson residents can because they have roots here; they have a bit of history behind them.' She smiled at her glass and drained her wine. 'Yes, I think I'd love to play ladies up here at Bellbird. I'd also love to have ten kids.'

He blinked at her. 'Ten?'

She waved a hand. 'No, not really, but some. I love kids.'

She paused and recalled one of her early fantasies—having Carlos's children. She grimaced inwardly but, as had happened to her before, she couldn't help wondering if she ever would have kids now, if she couldn't fall in love again.

'I think maybe it was because I was an only child—that's why a large family appeals. It shouldn't,' she said humorously. 'The last picnic day I had nearly ruined me.'

'Picnic day?' he queried.

'Twice a year I invite some kids from a youth club in an inner city area up for a picnic—well, a sausage sizzle really. Eight- to ten-year-olds. The last lot were especially spirited. They…um…ran riot, you could say. That's what Bill said, anyway.' Her eyes glinted with laughter. 'He also said if he'd ever seen a bunch of hoodlums in the making they were it.'

'Bill?'

'Oh, didn't I mention him? He's the gardener. He and I have a…difficult relationship, although he's a wonderful gardener. It's just that I rather fancy myself as a gardener too.' She shrugged. 'At least my father thought I had green fingers and if anyone should have known, he would have.'

Carlos was sitting in one of her ladder-back kitchen chairs. He had his hands behind his head and was tilting the chair. 'That's…quite a daydream,' he said after a long moment.

Mia dimpled. 'Daydream being the operative word. But I guess we all have daydreams.'

'Yes.' He sounded distracted and almost as if he was examining his daydreams and not finding them satisfactory or perhaps not finding any at all.

'Do you have any…well, ambitions or future plans, if not daydreams?' Mia heard herself asking curiously.

He thought for a long moment with a frown in his eyes. 'I have one,' he said at last. 'Not so much an ambition but one thing I keep a long-term eye on, you could say. Someone I would hate to see steal a march on me.'

'That sounds more like a vendetta than an ambition,' Mia commented. 'Who?'

'Talbot Spencer.'

She blinked. '*The* Talbot Spencer?'

He looked at her dryly. 'Is there another? Yes, him.'

'But he's a builder, like you. I mean…I don't mean
you actually build things with your hands these days
but his is also a multi-million dollar construction company, isn't it?'

'It is and we've been competing against each other
for contracts for years. He's also tried to buy me out a
couple of times. That's one reason why I have a thing
about him.'

'He's a playboy, isn't he?' Mia frowned as she ran
through her mental resources on the subject of Talbot
Spencer. Then her eyes widened. 'I suppose you could
be called one too, though.'

'Thank you, Mia,' he said sardonically.

'Well—' she gestured '—cars, boats, planes, horses
and women. You both seem to qualify.' She paused and
pictured Talbot Spencer in her mind's eye, not that she'd
ever met him but she'd seen him pictured. Not quite as
tall as Carlos and fair-haired, he was still interesting-
looking.

'So what was the real needle between the two of
you? The cut-throat world of business?'

Carlos leant his chin on his hand and he took so long
about it she thought he wasn't going to answer, then he
said, 'A woman.'

Mia's lips parted. 'He stole a…a girlfriend from you?'

Carlos shook his head. 'Not from me; it was my best
friend's girl. Talbot's a few years older. My friend and
I were still at university, whereas he was a seasoned
bachelor. She was at uni too. She fell for him and gave
my friend his marching orders.' He fiddled with the

tablecloth. 'She was a country, convent-schooled girl. Anyway, to cut a long story short, Talbot got her pregnant, paid for her abortion and turned his back on her.'

'Oh, no,' Mia murmured.

'Oh, yes. She was devastated and guilt-ridden over the abortion and she tried to end it all. It took years for her mental scars to heal and my friend went through the mill with her. For which I will never forgive Talbot and he knows it and he knows why. That's why he'd like to grind O'Connor Construction into the ground… Why the hell am I telling you this, Mia?'

She had to smile. 'I don't know. It's been quite a day, one way and another. Maybe that's why.'

'You're not wrong. Uh…where's the bedroom?'

Mia waved a hand in the direction of the loft. 'Up there.'

He stood up. 'That's the only one?'

She nodded.

'Mind if I take a look?'

Mia tried to remember how tidy she'd left her loft, then shrugged. 'Go ahead.'

Five minutes later he looked down at her. 'It's going to be me up here, you down there, Miss Gardiner. Tell me what you need and I'll bring it down.'

Mia sat bolt upright. 'What do you mean? You can't be serious!'

'But I am.'

'Carlos—'

'Mia—' he interrupted firmly '—you cannot honestly expect me to abandon you up here on the top of a mountain with not a soul within reach. How come

you live so alone like this in the first place?' he asked
irritably.

'I don't. There's another cottage where Bill and his
wife live, but she's away at the mo…' She broke off
and bit her lip.

'Away at the moment?' he supplied.

Mia nodded.

'Then you're going to have to put up with me because
probably the furthest you'll be able to go is hop to the
bathroom. There's no way you're going to be able to
get up this ladder, for starters.'

And, so saying, he tossed down a pair of pyjamas
for her plus a pillow and a duvet.

Mia drew a deep breath as she gathered what he'd
thrown down. 'All right, maybe I couldn't do that but
otherwise I can manage. Thank you very much for the
offer, though; it's really kind of you but I don't need it.'

'Mia…' He came down the ladder and sat on the end
of the settee. 'Mia,' he repeated, 'I'm not going to rav-
ish you or even seduce you. Believe me.'

They stared at each other until she said tonelessly,
'I didn't think you were. I just don't like feeling be-
holden—to anyone.'

'Or are you afraid that even if we're not into ravish-
ment and seduction,' he said dryly, 'you might get to
liking me again?'

Mia opened her mouth but Long John Silver chose
that moment to make his presence felt. He neighed
shrilly several times.

Mia's hand flew to her mouth.

'Your horse?' Carlos queried.

'Yes. I forgot all about him! He hasn't been fed or rugged or put in his stall for the night. Oh!' She made to swing her legs down but sanity prevailed. 'I'm not going to be able to do it, am I?' she said hollowly.

'No.' Carlos got up. 'But I can. I can also get some more wood for the fire.'

'What about…aren't you staying with friends, though? Won't they be wondering where you are?'

He pulled a mobile from his pocket. 'I'll ring them. Any more objections?' he asked with sudden impatience.

She lay back with a sigh. 'No.' She sat up immediately, though, with anxiety etched into her expression. 'Be careful with Long John. He can bite.'

'Surely you don't put up with that?' Carlos raised an incredulous eyebrow at her.

'Oh, not me,' Mia assured him. 'Usually only strangers. Well, Bill, but I wouldn't be surprised if Bill provokes him.'

'Thanks for the warning,' he said dryly. 'Anything else I need to be warned about? Like killer cats or pet snakes in the loft?'

She had to laugh. 'No. Oh…' She grimaced and hesitated.

'Spill it,' he ordered briefly.

'Well, I didn't lock up. The main house, I mean. Not that we usually have any crime up here, but I don't like to leave it all open.'

'Just tell me what to do. Come to think of it, I left my car unlocked.'

Mia explained how to lock up the house.

'Wish me luck,' he said wryly and stepped out into the night.

Mia stared at the closed door and was conscious of never feeling more confused.

Bewitched, bothered and bewildered, she thought, and closed her eyes. How could she possibly kiss Carlos O'Connor when he had admitted there had never been a future for them?

A few minutes later she decided to take advantage of his absence and she got up painfully and hopped to the bathroom.

When she got back to the settee she was colourfully arrayed in her tartan pyjamas and she snuggled under the duvet.

Perhaps the wine on top of a couple of brandies was helping to dull the pain in her heel, she reflected, but it wasn't too bad.

Her last thought was that it certainly wasn't going to keep her awake and she fell asleep without intending to, without even realising it, on a day of mixed emotions like no other in her life.

Carlos came back eventually, all chores done, but Mia didn't even stir when he added some wood to the stove.

He stood looking down at her for a long time. At the almost ridiculously long lashes against her cheeks. At her thick dark hair that she'd braided, making her look younger, as did—he smiled—the tartan pyjamas. At her mouth—it *was* one of the most luscious mouths he'd seen and if he looked at it long enough it was hard not to want to kiss it.

What would happen if he did kiss that delicious mouth again right now? Lightly at first at the same time as he stroked her cheek.

Would she sigh a warm little puff of air, then reach out to wind her arms around his neck? Would she invite him to lie beside her and accept his hands on her body in all those softly rounded or slender places?

He moved restlessly and shoved his hands in his pockets as he was struck by the irony of it, this compulsion that came over him from time to time to have and to hold Mia.

He gritted his teeth but pulled up a kitchen chair and continued to watch her as she slept.

Truth be told, he was having trouble linking the two Mias—the one from his past and this one. Although he remembered clearly being aware of the shy schoolgirl crush she'd had on him he'd ignored it, quite sure it would go away but, before it had happened, a freak storm had intervened, he'd got clobbered on the head by a falling branch and when he wasn't sure what was what, he'd been beset by the certainty that all he wanted was to have and to hold Mia Gardiner.

Then sanity and reality had returned and he'd come back to West Windward kicking himself, although still not a hundred per cent sure what had actually happened between them.

Only to find the problem was solved. Mia apparently had accepted that he'd been concussed and gone on her way to a Queensland university, making her parents very proud.

But it hadn't happened like that, he reminded himself grimly.

How had she managed to throw off as much of the shadow of it all as she had?

He thought of his mother with grim forbearance. Arancha was—Arancha, fiercely loyal to her family, no matter the cost and no matter—he grimaced—how misplaced her sentiments might be.

It was a problem that had escalated with his father's death, one he'd inherited. It had struck him once or twice that maybe grandchildren would be the balm Arancha needed, only to wonder with a touch of black humour what kind of chaos his mother could create as an interfering grandmother.

Fortunately Juanita stood little nonsense from her mother but could Damien stand up to her? Come to that, Juanita stood little nonsense from Damien, he reflected wryly, and wondered if his new brother-in-law had understood what he was getting himself into.

None of which, it occurred to him, was of any help to him in this contretemps. How could he make it up to Mia for his mother's cruelty? Not only that, but *his* thoughtless declaration today that he could have kicked himself for what he'd done. And the admission that he would have deemed it right to warn her off too? Not only all that, but not checking out with her that she was all right seven years ago.

Yes, she might have made a success of her life but, beneath that, there obviously lurked the stigma of being branded 'the housekeeper's daughter'. And it was obvious that it still hurt.

What about the attraction there had been between them? Maybe only a teenage crush on her part and a concussion-fuelled moment of madness on his but there all the same. Yet, once again he'd held her and kissed her and she'd responded.

He studied her with a frown, sleeping so peacefully and looking quite unlike the high-powered executive she was in reality.

It must take considerable organisational skills and flair to hold receptions on Mount Wilson. The logistics alone—just about everything had to come from Sydney—were mind-boggling.

Not only that, the foresight to appreciate that the special magic of the mountain would make it irresistible to people for their special days. So, yes, it wasn't inappropriate to call her a high-powered executive.

Even though she slept in tartan pyjamas and looked about sixteen when she did.

He stretched and at the same time felt his mobile phone vibrate in his pocket. He took it out and studied it.

Nina…

He switched it off and put it back in his pocket.

Gorgeous, exotic Nina who ticked all the right boxes for his mother. Model looks, father an ex-politician rewarded for his services with an ambassadorship, uncle married to an Englishwoman who was a Lady in her own right.

Nina, who could be the essence of warmth and charm or cool and regal depending on how the mood took her. Nina, who aroused in most men the desire to bed her, yet who could be incredibly, screamingly insecure.

He stared at the flickering shadows on the wall behind the settee and listened to the crackle of the fire.

What was he going to do about Nina?

She was the one who'd called off their relationship in the middle of the row—he couldn't even remember how it had started now—they'd had before Juanita's wedding.

Well, yes, he could remember, he realised, not exactly how it had started but what it had been about. It was something that had been brewing through all of Juanita's wedding preparations. It all had to do with Nina's desire that *they* get married, something he'd not, for reasons all too clear, although belatedly to him, been willing to do.

And yet he'd allowed things between them to carry on when he'd known he shouldn't but his pride had got in the way.

He'd allowed the good times to define their relationship and he'd cut himself off from her when she was being impossible—she always came back to him as if he was the only spar she had to cling to in the storm-tossed sea of life. He had no doubt that was what she was ringing him for.

But could they go on like this?

He lowered his gaze to the girl sleeping so peacefully on her settee. And he was reminded suddenly of the ridiculous proposal he'd made to her—that she take Nina's place. What had prompted that? he wondered.

Could he blame her for being angry and insulted by it? No…

But what germ of an idea or perception had prompted him even to think it?

The feeling that Mia wouldn't cling, she wouldn't employ emotional blackmail to hold him? That she wouldn't be impossibly nice in between being a bundle of bizarre hang-ups?

If anyone should have some bizarre hang-ups, Mia Gardiner should, he reflected, directly due to the behaviour of himself and his mother.

CHAPTER THREE

MIA WOKE THE next morning to the sound of running water.

She moved under her duvet but she was so snug and comfortable, apart from a slight throbbing in her foot, she was reluctant to get up, reluctant even to open her eyes.

As for the water she was hearing, could it be rain? They had been forecasting rain for a few days...

But no, it didn't sound like rain on the roof, it sounded just like her shower.

Her lashes flew open and she sat up with a gasp as it all came tumbling back into her mind. It had to be Carlos in her shower.

Right on cue, she heard the bathroom door open and he padded through the kitchen wearing only his khaki trousers and drying his hair with a towel.

'Morning,' he said. 'Do you happen to have a razor I could borrow?'

She blinked. 'Only a tiny one. I get my legs waxed.'

He rubbed the dark shadows on his jaw. 'Then you'll

have to put up with me like this. What's your favourite tipple first thing in the morning?'

Her eyes widened. 'Tipple?'

'Champagne? Vodka and fresh orange juice? I personally subscribe to a Bloody Mary.'

He dropped the towel and reached for his shirt lying over a chair. 'You believed me, didn't you?' He shook his head. 'No wonder you're so suspicious if you harbour these dissipated views of me.'

Mia closed her mouth and tried to dampen her look of no doubt naive surprise. Then she confessed with a grimace that she had believed him for a moment. 'But I gather you meant tea or coffee? If so, tea, please, black, no sugar and one slice of raisin toast with butter.'

'Done,' he replied, pulling his shirt off after realising it was inside out. 'Mind you, there are times when champagne is a great way to toast in the morning.'

Foolishly, she realised too late, Mia raised an eyebrow at him. 'When?'

He studied her, his lips twisting. 'When a man and a woman have a night to remember, to celebrate.' His grey eyes flicked over her in a way that left her in no doubt he was visualising a night to remember with her.

Mia blushed—it felt as if from her toes to the top of her head. And hard as she tried to tear her gaze away from his, she couldn't do it as wave after wave of colour ran through her and her senses were alive and leaping. 'Oh.'

'That hadn't occurred to you, obviously,' he said with a glint of wicked amusement in his eyes now.

'No,' she said slowly, but her thoughts were running

riot. She had to get a grip on her responses to him! 'It may not be standard behaviour for housekeepers or their daughters,' she told him tartly.

He frowned. 'You really do have a chip on your shoulder, don't you, Mia?'

She bit her lip but decided she might as well soldier on. 'Yes,' she said starkly and pushed aside the duvet. 'But I don't want to discuss it, thank you, Carlos. I would *really* like to go to the bathroom.'

He put down his shirt again. 'Sure.' And, before she had time to resist, not that she would have been able to anyway, he came across, picked her up and deposited her outside the bathroom door.

Mia ground her teeth but was at a loss to be able to do anything about it.

He still didn't have his shirt on when she made her way out of the bathroom, but there was a steaming cup of black tea and a slice of raisin toast waiting for her on a tray. There was also a neat pile of clothes on the settee. A pair of jeans and a T-shirt as well as a selection of underwear.

'Don't,' he warned as he saw her eyeing the undies with a pink tinge of embarrassment creeping into her cheeks.

'Don't what?' she managed.

'Don't be embarrassed or go all prim and proper on me,' he elucidated. 'I've seen a few bras and panties in my time so I'm not going to become all excited and leap on you.'

'Ah.'

He eyed her. 'And there's still no way you could have gone up the ladder.'

Mia changed tack mentally and said sweetly, 'Thank you, Mr O'Connor.'

He looked surprised for a moment, then picked up his shirt but clicked his tongue as he stared at it.

'What?' Mia asked through a mouthful of toast.

'More blood on it!' He took it over to the sink and rinsed one of the sleeves.

'I'm doubly sorry,' Mia said, actually managing to sound quite contrite as she sipped her tea.

He looked across the kitchen at her with a spark of curiosity in his eyes. 'If that's what a sip of tea and a slice of toast can do for you I'm tempted to think a full breakfast could work miracles.'

Mia had to laugh. 'I don't know about that but I do love my first cuppa.'

He rinsed his shirt sleeve, squeezed it out and turned it right side out again.

That was when Mia frowned as she stared at his back. Her gaze had been drawn to it anyway because she'd suddenly been possessed of an irrational desire to be in a position to run her hands up and down the powerful lines and sleek muscles of it.

'Hang on,' she said slowly. 'What have *you* done to yourself? Your back—there's a black and blue patch on your back.'

'Ah.' He squinted over his shoulder. 'Can't see it but that wasn't me, that was your blasted horse.'

Mia's hand flew to her mouth. 'But I warned you.'

'And I told him I'd been forewarned and he'd be stupid to try anything.' He raked his hair with his fingers. 'We obviously don't speak the same language.'

Mia started to laugh helplessly. 'I'm sorry. I'm sorry,' she repeated. 'I know it's not funny—'

'You expect me to believe that?' he broke in politely.

'You know what I mean! But anyway, you'd better let me put something on it.'

He brought his own tea over and sat down on the coffee table. 'Don't worry about me. Let's see your foot.'

Mia was still shaken by giggles but she stuck her foot out obediently. He unwound the bandage and lifted the dressing off carefully.

'Hmm…still bleeding a bit. Look, I'm going to my friends' to get a change of clothes, then I'll be back and I'll take you to the nearest clinic.'

'You don't have to.'

He got up to fetch the first aid kit. 'Don't start, Mia,' he warned over his shoulder. 'By the way, it's raining.'

Mia glanced out of the window and rubbed her face as she noted the grey, gloomy view. 'I thought it was earlier. At least we don't have a function on today.'

'At least,' he agreed.

They were both silent while he redressed her foot until she said out of the blue, 'We always seem to be bandaging each other.'

He looked up. 'I was just thinking the same thing. History repeats itself.'

'What…what would your father have thought if you'd married someone like me?'

He frowned. 'What makes you ask that?'

'You said his influence was a sort of negative one. Do you know why he was like that?'

Carlos smiled, a tigerish little smile. 'I think it had something to do with the fact that he'd done all the hard work, he'd built the company up from the dirt, whereas I'd, to his mind, had it easy. The right schools, university, the means to—' he gestured '—do whatever I wanted.'

Mia thought for a moment. 'That doesn't mean to say you couldn't be an achiever. It looks as if you've nurtured his dreams and his company and taken them on to even greater heights.'

He shrugged. 'Yes, I have. I doubt if even that would have given him much pleasure.' He looked into space for a moment. 'I don't see why you're wondering about this in connection with us.' He searched her expression narrowly.

'I wondered if he'd disinherit you if he didn't approve of whoever you married.'

'I've no doubt he'd have found something to disapprove of, whoever it was.' He paused and looked into the distance with his eyes narrowed as if some chord had been struck with him but he didn't elaborate.

'Why do people get like that?' Mia asked.

He linked his fingers. 'I think it's the struggle. The almighty battle to pull yourself up by your bootstraps. Coupled probably with a sense of ambition that's like a living force.' He looked down at his hands. 'I could be wrong. But no, he wouldn't have disinherited me. That's the other thing that…weighed, you could say, with my father—my mother.'

Mia blinked. 'How do you mean?'

'She would never have stood by and let him disinherit me.' He grimaced. 'I'm not sure he entirely appreciated the fact that, while she would defend him with her dying breath, she would do the same for me. She's very strong on family loyalty.'

Mia stared into space and listened to the rain on the roof. Then she shivered.

'Mia, what exactly happened that night?'

Her startled gaze jerked back to his. 'You don't remember?' she breathed incredulously.

'I remember...feeling like hell and suddenly being possessed of the strongest urge to hold you in my arms. As if it would make me feel a whole lot better. It did.' His lips twisted. 'Then I remember laughing about something but not exactly what it was and—'

'You called me a pilchard,' she broke in.

He blinked. 'Why the hell would I do that?'

'You actually told me to stop wriggling around like a trapped pilchard.'

Mia said it seriously and her expression was grave but she couldn't maintain it as the expression in his grey eyes went from puzzled to incredulous then gleamed with laughter.

'I'm surprised you didn't find a pilchard to clobber me with! Hopefully I retrieved things?'

'You called me a siren next. Then you kissed me.'

'I remember that.' His gaze fell to her mouth and Mia trembled inwardly. 'But that's all,' he said after a long moment.

A moment when her fingertips tingled as if she was

actually touching them to his skin, as if she was running her fingers through the night-darkness of his hair and trailing them along the blue shadows of his jaw.

If she did that, would he grasp her wrist and kiss her knuckles, would he flick open the buttons of her tartan pyjama top and touch her breasts?

The mere thought of it made her nipples harden and a rush of heat run through her body. She moved restlessly and said hurriedly, 'That is all.'

'Nothing else?' he asked, scanning her pink cheeks with a frown.

'No. You fell asleep and I just stayed there. I didn't want to wake you.' She gestured. 'To be honest, I didn't want to move. I think I must have dozed too because I didn't hear your mother drive in.' She hesitated. 'Why do you ask?'

'So it was only a kiss and an embrace?'

She stared at him. 'Did you think there was…' her voice shook '…more?'

'Not as I remembered it, but…' He frowned. 'For you to be so upset and still so affected by it, I'm now wondering.'

Mia drew a vast agitated breath. 'You think I've made a mountain out of a molehill?'

'No.' He closed his eyes briefly and took her hands.

She wrested them free. 'You do. Oh, will you just go away and leave me in peace, Carlos O'Connor? To think that I once thought I had a crush on you—'

She broke off and her hand flew to her mouth.

'It's all right. I knew.' He stood up—and someone knocked on the door.

'You decent, Mia?' Bill James called out. 'I'm home, just thought to let you know—oh!' He stopped abruptly as Carlos swept open the door.

Bill was in his sixties, white-haired, stocky, tanned and with a distinctly roman nose. His bushy white eyebrows all but disappeared beneath his cap as he took in every detail of the scene before him.

Mia in her pyjamas, Carlos just starting to pull his sweatshirt on.

'Blimey,' he said. 'I'm sorry. I had no idea. I'll go.'

'I'll come with you,' Carlos said. 'I've just been given my marching orders. See you later, Mia. Think you can manage in the meantime?'

'Yes,' Mia said through her teeth, then was forced to back down somewhat. 'Uh…my horse. He needs a feed. Bill, would you mind? Just be careful—'

'Tell you what, Mia,' Bill broke in, 'it's time you got rid of that horse—he's a menace.'

'I couldn't agree with you more.' Carlos put out his hand and introduced himself to Bill, and they left together as if they were lifelong friends, closing the door behind them.

Mia stared after them, then picked up her pillow and hurled it at the door.

'I can't believe you've done all this,' Mia said later as the sports car nosed its way into Bellbird's driveway and pulled up at the main house. It was pouring.

'Taken you to the doctor?' Carlos raised a quizzical eyebrow. 'Would you rather I'd left you to bleed to death?'

Mia clicked her tongue. 'I wasn't going to!'

'The slightest pressure and it was still bleeding,' he commented.

Mia looked down at her bandaged foot. She now had three stitches in her heel and she had a crutch.

'No, not that. Thank you very much for that,' she said stiffly. 'I obviously couldn't have driven myself. No, I mean ringing Gail last night so—'

'Look, Mia,' he said evenly, 'when I came to lock up last night I noticed Gail's number in a prominent position on the wall in your study and I decided the sooner she knew you were incapacitated the better. I was going to tell you when I got back to the cottage but you were fast asleep. What's wrong with that?'

'Gail,' Mia said precisely, 'will be absolutely agog to think that you spent the night with me and will be imagining all sorts of wild and improbable things. You don't know her. She is also incapable of keeping things to herself so it will be all over the mountain. And Bill is just as bad,' she added forcefully.

'Who cares?' Carlos replied this time. 'You and I know the truth, that's all that matters, and anyway, in this day and age, nobody thinks twice about that kind of stuff. OK. I presume you will want to see Gail?'

Mia nodded.

'Then we'll do this the easy way.'

She looked questioningly at him but he simply got out of the car and came to open her door. He then scooped her out of the seat and carried her into the house. 'You know, if I owned this place,' he remarked at the same time, 'I'd add some undercover parking. Your office?' he asked.

'Yes. Oh, hi, Gail,' she added. 'And you remember Mr O'Connor?'

'Mia!' Gail said dramatically as she fluttered around them. 'Are you all right? Mr O'Connor, good to see you again. Bring her this way, Mr O'Connor—I've put a cushion under her desk for her to put her foot on and I've made some coffee. I'm sure we could all do with some!'

It was over lunch that Mia asked, 'Gail, are you sure you can handle all this? You'll have to do everything I normally do for the next few days as well as the stuff you usually do.'

Gail hesitated. 'There is my sister, Kylie. She's only fourteen but she's pretty good around the house. I'm sure she could help and she's on school holidays at the moment.'

'Kylie!' Mia sat up. 'That's brilliant. Will your mum mind?'

'No way. Anything to take Kylie's mind off boys at the moment will be very welcome.' Gail cast her gaze skywards as if she was at least forty with a boy-mad daughter of her own.

'All right.' Mia selected a smoked salmon sandwich. 'Thanks for making lunch, Gail.'

'No problemo.' Gail poured their tea. 'Uh—is Mr O'Connor coming back?'

'He didn't say—rather, all he said was, "I'll be back". By the way, Gail—' Mia took a sip of tea '—I misled you a bit yesterday. My parents used to work for the O'Connors, that's how I knew about Juanita and her family.'

Gail put the teapot down slowly. 'So you used to know him?' she said.

'Yes.' Mia flinched inwardly to see Gail staring at her with patent, revamped curiosity and regretted embarking on these tangled explanations. She'd only done so because she'd felt guilty about not precisely lying to Gail the day before but not being exactly honest and open either. Had she also thought it mightn't look so bad, the fact that Carlos had spent the night in the cottage with her, if they knew each other?

She bit her lip and could have kicked herself but decided she had to soldier on. 'I was only the housekeeper's daughter and I didn't think they'd recognise me. That's why——' She broke off and shrugged.

'So that's why he came back after the wedding was over,' Gail said slowly. 'How lucky was that? I mean your foot.'

I only cut my foot because he antagonised me enough to make me run away from him, Mia thought but did not say. 'Yes. Yes, it was lucky,' she murmured.

'You know what?' Gail rearranged her teacup and saucer, 'I think he'll keep coming back,' she confided.

Mia looked at her uneasily. 'Oh, I don't know about that.'

'I do.' Gail smiled mysteriously. 'But I won't say another word.'

'Gail!' Mia stared at her assistant with deep frustration written large into her expression. 'You can't just say things like that and leave them up in the air.'

'OK, if you want it spelt out.' Gail got up as if she thought she might have to take evasive action. 'There's chemistry,' she announced.

'What?' Mia frowned.

'There's a little crackle of tension in you when he's around and he enjoys picking you up and carrying you around. Not only that, he enjoys the fact that it annoys you. I can see a wicked little glint in his eye when he does it.'

Mia stared at her assistant open-mouthed.

'You did want to know, didn't you?' Gail enquired, looking the picture of injured innocence.

'Yes. No. You're quite wrong, Gail. I—'

But with a perky, 'We'll see!' over her shoulder, Gail left the office.

Mia glared after her. Next she glared at the last salmon sandwich on the plate but decided to eat it anyway. Then she sat back with a deep sigh, feeling moody and without grace.

Of course being confined to hopping around on one foot, even with a crutch—which was not that easy to manage—was enough to make her feel helpless but it was also an emotional helplessness. It was like a roller coaster ride.

What had she believed would happen between her and Carlos all those years ago?

At the time she'd had no expectations, it had all happened out of the blue and—yes, she had to concede, she'd wondered if it was all due to his concussion. But she'd also thought it wasn't impossible for him to be attracted to her.

Then had come the horrible confrontation with Arancha, and the weeks after she'd left West Windward when she'd cherished the little seed of hope in her heart that Carlos would find her and tell her his mother was wrong, he needed her, he wanted her, he loved her.

But as the weeks had grown into a month, then two, and she'd felt that fragile little seed die and she'd… hated him?

No, she thought, that was the funny part about it. If anything, she'd hated herself because she couldn't hate him, although she'd certainly hated his mother.

But the other funny thing was when she'd refused to allow herself to wallow in self-pity and started living again, socialising and dating and so on, it didn't happen for her. There had been no real attractions and the half-baked ones she'd thought might turn into the real thing never had. And that was down to Carlos.

'OK.' Gail came into the office, delving into her purse for her car keys.

Carlos had not returned after dropping Mia off from the doctor, although he'd said he'd be back and he'd stay the night. Consequently, Mia had asked Gail to make up two of the never used bedrooms in the main house.

Gail had cast her a narrowed look and said, 'Much snugger in the cottage, but it's up to you.'

'Yes,' Mia had replied with something of a snap.

'Look, I'm sorry I've got to go before he gets back,' Gail said now as she jangled her keys, 'but everything is under control and Bill is here. It's not such a big event tomorrow, only thirty for lunch, a garden club on their annual day out so they'll be raving about this garden—and I'll bring Kylie with me to lend a hand. Sure you'll be OK? I would stay until he comes but it's my Girl Guides night tonight so I can't be late.'

'I'm fine, promise, don't worry. And I've plenty of bookwork to occupy me.' Mia leant over her desk and touched Gail's hand. 'Thanks, pal. I don't know what I'd do without you!'

Gail beamed with pleasure.

Mia sat back and listened to her drive off, then smote her forehead with the heel of her hand because she'd been going to ask Gail to feed Long John Silver and put him away for the night but she'd forgotten. Gail was good with Long John.

Only a moment or so later, however, she heard a car drive up and assumed it would be Carlos, but frowned suddenly because his car had a distinctive engine note. She discovered she was right; it wasn't Carlos, it was her neighbour, Ginny Castle, and her twelve-year-old son Harry.

'Come in, Ginny,' Mia called in response to Ginny's knock. 'In the study.'

Ginny, a bustling redhead, came through, talking nineteen-to-the-dozen, as was her habit.

'Just heard you've got stitches in your foot, Mia, love—you really should be more careful!—but anyway, with Bill and Lucy away, how about if we took Long John home until you're up to scratch again? Harry can ride him over and I can bring all his clobber in the ute.'

'Ginny, you're a darling!' Mia said with very real gratitude. 'I was going to ask Gail to feed and rug him before she left but she was obviously in a hurry and anyway, I forgot. And actually Bill is home, but he and Long John don't get along.'

'Not a problem. Got anyone to feed and water *you*?' Ginny asked and laughed richly.

'Someone is coming, thanks all the same.'

'Then we'll get going before it gets dark.' And she shepherded Harry out in front of her.

'Just be careful, Harry,' Mia called. 'He can bite.'

Harry evaded his mama and stuck his head back round the office door. 'Not me, he doesn't!'

'How come?' Mia enquired.

'Because the last time he tried it I bit him back. See you, Mia.'

Mia was still laughing and experiencing a warm glow a few minutes later when the phone rang.

She answered it but when she put it down many minutes later she was pale and shaken-looking and she dropped her head into her hands.

'What's wrong?'

She jumped and realised Carlos must have driven in without her hearing him. It was raining again. He stood in the doorway in jeans and a tweed jacket and he was frowning down at her.

'Are you in pain?'

'No. Not much. Well, maybe a little heart-sore,' she said with an attempt to smile. 'I'm about to lose Bellbird. But I did know it might be on the cards so...' She shrugged.

He said nothing, then he reached for a cardigan lying over the back of a chair and handed it to her.

Her eyes widened. 'What's this? I'm not cold, not yet, anyway.'

'You could be. We're going out.'

'Where? No, I mean I don't feel like going out.' She regarded him with a frown and said something silly but she was feeling bruised and battered. 'Don't think you can call all the shots, Carlos.'

'Will you stop being tedious, Mia?' he shot back. 'We're going out to dinner whether you like it or not. Why you shouldn't like it is beyond me. You're not up to cooking and I'm still a P-plater when it comes to—'

'A *what*?' she interrupted.

'A pupil when it comes to cooking, like a learner driver.'

'Last night—'

'Oh, I can drive a microwave,' he said with a wave of his hand, 'but I don't happen to feel like anything microwaved tonight. I feel like something hearty, like an inch-thick steak with English mustard hot enough to make my eyes water. Like hot chips, crisp on the outside and soft and fluffy inside, like grilled mushrooms.'

He paused, then continued. 'Maybe a side salad, but not one with all those weird leaves—I'm very conventional when it comes to my salads. I like iceberg lettuce. And when I've finished that I'd like a nice piece of cheese, some cheddar, perhaps, and then something light and sweet but not too sweet, like lemon meringue and not a lot, just a slice followed by real coffee, Kona perhaps, from Hawaii.'

They stared at each other. He was resting his fists on the other side of her desk.

'Oh,' was all Mia could think of to say. But a moment later, 'My mother makes the best lemon meringue.'

He grinned fleetingly. 'The Northern Rivers might be a bit far to go. But we could try Blackheath.' He straightened. 'It's raining again. Would you like me to carry you to the car?'

'No,' she said hastily. 'I mean—' she got up and reached for her crutch, cast a quick upward glance at his expression—and there was a wicked little glint of pure amusement in his eyes, damn him! '—I mean I can manage.'

'Good.' He watched her for a moment more, then turned to lead the way and open the doors.

It was a small, dim little restaurant in Blackheath he took her to but when he asked what she'd like to order she could only stare blindly down at the menu in front of her.

'All right, I'll order for you,' he murmured.

A couple of minutes later she had a glass of golden wine and in due course his steak and a herb omelette for her arrived.

Good choice, she thought with the only part of her brain that seemed to be functioning, *I couldn't have coped with anything heavier*.

In the end she finished the omelette and ate her roll

before she finally sat back and said with a tinge of surprise, 'I didn't know I was hungry.'

He finished his steak.

'How was it?' she queried. 'As mouth-watering as you described it earlier?'

He grimaced. 'I got a bit carried away, but almost. So, they're not going to renew the lease?'

'No. My two lovely old ladies have handed over their affairs, including their enduring power of attorney, and they've signed Bellbird over as well, to their nephew.' She fiddled with her napkin. 'And he's decided to put it on the market.'

'I'm sorry.'

Mia lifted her glass and cupped the bowl of it in the palm of her hand, the stem between her fingers, as she watched the liquid swirling around. 'But that's not the only problem,' she said finally. 'I did have written into the lease should this happen that I needed at least six months' notice because I had to be able to take forward bookings.' She paused. 'Even six months is not very long; some people have wanted to book from year to year. Some weddings are planned nine—' she gestured '—twelve months in advance.'

'So you'll have to cancel some forward bookings you took over the six months mark?'

She shook her head. 'I didn't take any over the six months mark, although I have a lot under it. But the nephew wants to contest the six months' notice.'

Carlos narrowed his eyes. 'Does he have a leg to stand on?'

Mia sighed. 'I don't know. He's threatened me with

the fact that his aunts may not have been in their right minds when they signed the lease, that I may even have exerted undue influence on them. I think—' Mia twirled her glass and sighed '—I get the feeling he's in financial straits and he really needs to sell Bellbird.'

'*He* may have been the one who exerted undue influence,' Carlos said meditatively.

'I wondered about that, but the thought of going to court…' She shook her head. 'I may not have much choice, though. *I* could get sued for leaving some of the closer functions in the lurch.'

He sat back and placed his napkin on the table. 'Apart from that, are you confident you'll find somewhere else and be able to get a business up and going again?' he asked.

Mia shook her head. 'Not confident. I've got butterflies in my stomach—terrible fears would be more accurate—that I won't be able to, but I'll push on. Somehow.'

He said, as he pushed his plate away, 'Not a great couple of days.'

'No,' she agreed. She rubbed her forehead, then collected her loose hair in one hand and drew it in a thick rope over her shoulder.

'I like your hair loose.'

Mia looked up and their gazes caught and held across the table. And something in the way he was looking at her ignited a rush of awareness in her as well as sending her pulse racing.

Heavens above, she thought, it would be so easy to seek solace and comfort, from a cruel blow on top of everything else, in his arms. It would be not only that but something she craved, she acknowledged, still staring into his eyes and feeling herself drowning in their grey depths.

But she had to break this spell. She made herself look away and blink a couple of times.

'Mia.' He said her name very quietly.

'Tell me more about Nina.'

She bit her lip, then thought, why shouldn't she ask about her?

'I don't know why you're looking like that,' she said evenly.

He raised an eyebrow. 'Like what?'

'As if—' she paused '—as if I'm being ridiculous.'

His lips twisted. 'If I did, it was because I don't see the connection—thank you,' he said to the waitress delivering their coffee.

She blushed and tripped as she walked away.

This time it was Mia who expressed unspoken irony—she looked heavenward.

'We seem to be at cross purposes,' Carlos said lazily, sitting back and looking even more amused.

Mia controlled herself with difficulty. 'You don't see the connection? OK! Let's put it in black and white,' she said tartly. 'You've virtually come straight from Nina French's arms to being—to looking—to…' She stopped helplessly.

'To being possessed of the desire to have and to hold you?' he supplied and sat forward to rest his elbow on the table and his chin on his fist. 'You know, it's a funny thing but that desire seems to exist on its own.

It seems to have a life of its own. It doesn't seem to be susceptible to anything else that's going on all around it—if you know what I mean.'

'I…' Mia stopped, frowned at him, looked away, then looked back as if jerked on a string. 'I'm not sure what you do mean,' she said uncertainly.

'Simple. Since I got clobbered on the head by a falling branch, I only have to be in your company to want you. In my bed, in case there's any misunderstanding. Whatever the other circumstances of my life happen to be.'

Mia was dead still for a long moment, then she clicked her tongue in sheer frustration and stood up, ready to walk away. 'You're impossible! Actually you're crazy, Carlos O'Connor. What you're describing—the way you're describing us makes it sound as if we exist in a bubble. It doesn't sound *real*,' she said intensely.

There was silence for a long moment, then she said quietly, 'That's why I want to know about Nina. And if *she's* real for you.'

He stood up and it stunned her to see that he *was* suddenly grimly serious. 'Nina and I are washed up. I never should have let it go on for so long but my dearest wish is for her to find someone who understands her better than I did. Someone who anchors her and loves her even when the impossible things about her make it…almost impossible to do so.'

Mia blinked several times and sat down.

He stared down at her for a long moment and she was shocked by the harsh lines scored into his face, then he sat down himself.

'I'm sorry,' Mia said quietly but her throat worked. 'I didn't realise it was so painful for you.'

'Painful?' He picked up his glass and studied it. 'I wish to hell I knew what it actually was.'

Mia opened her mouth, then decided to keep her thoughts on that subject to herself. 'Shall we go?' she said tentatively. 'We're the only ones left and they might be wanting to close up. I'll just visit the powder room.'

'Sure.' He signalled for the bill and when she came back he helped her out to the car. It was still raining.

'Damn,' Mia said as they drove along.

He looked questioningly at her.

'I've got a garden club coming for lunch tomorrow. They're really keen to see the Bellbird gardens.'

'It could be a whole new world tomorrow,' he said wryly.

Mia smiled. 'It's what I need. But I doubt there'll be much change, although the sun may shine. By the way, Gail made up two beds in the main house for tonight—'

'Oh,' he interrupted, 'didn't I tell you? I've made different arrangements for tonight. Gail's coming to stay with you after her Girl Guides session ends.'

Mia's mouth fell open. 'No, you didn't tell me. Neither did Gail—she didn't say a word to me. Not about tonight.'

'She didn't know before she left work this afternoon. I didn't get around to making these other arrangements until quite late.' He looked across at her. 'I didn't think you'd mind.'

'I…well…' She stopped helplessly.

'You don't sound too sure and you look cross,' he

observed. 'In light of your extreme agitation on the subject last night, I'm surprised.'

Mia gritted her teeth. 'It's just that I like to know what's going on. When did you get in touch with Gail?'

'While you were in the powder room.'

'You...I...*how* did you get in touch with her?'

'I rang her last night, remember? So I've got her number in my mobile phone. Anything further you'd like to know, Sergeant Gardiner?' He turned into Bell-bird's driveway just after, as it happened, Gail did and they followed her tail-lights up the driveway.

'*Why*?'

'I've decided to go back to Sydney tonight—hell, I forgot about Long John. I'll drive down—'

'You don't have to,' Mia said.

'But you can't let him starve. That could make him worse than ever.'

'He won't starve—I've given him to someone to look after.'

'Someone he won't bite, I hope, but how do you know he won't bite *this* person?'

'Because *this* person bit him back,' Mia replied and dissolved into laughter. 'I'm sorry,' she said finally, still giggling, 'I think it's all been a bit much for me but it does have its funny side. And don't you dare carry me out of this car and inside. I can manage. Take care in Sydney.' She patted his arm, and struggled out with her crutch.

'What's so funny?' Gail asked as they met at the front door. 'Are you laughing or crying?'

'I don't know.' Mia rubbed her face. 'Well, yes, I do. You were right—it's much cosier down at the cottage, Gail, so shall we go down there and start a fire and have a drink? As someone once said, what's the point in being sober *and* virtuous at this end of the day?'

'Who said that? Shakespeare?'

'No—just someone I know.' Mia climbed into Gail's car and stowed her crutch. 'Not that I'm unsober. I've only had one glass of wine. Mind you, now I come to think of it, maybe I don't have anything to drink after last night.'

'Just as well it's me.' Gail climbed into the driver's side and she hauled a bottle of wine out of her bag. 'Don't know why but I thought to pop this in with my PJs.'

'Gail, you're a treasure.' Mia leant over to kiss her assistant on the cheek. 'You wouldn't believe the kind of day I've had. Or the last couple of hours, anyway. Oh, Gail, I've got some bad news.'

'Wait,' Gail advised as she drove down the track to the cottage. 'I know a bit of it, anyway.'

'How? Don't tell me Carlos told you!'

Gail nodded. 'He said you could be feeling a bit delicate so I was to take care of you on his behalf till he gets back.'

Mia stared at Gail in the gloom of the car. 'He said that?'

'Yep.' Gail coasted to a stop, switched off and doused the lights.

'He takes a lot upon himself,' Mia said indistinctly, in the grip of an emotion she found hard to name—

anger at his high-handed ways? Helplessness? Or the faintest whisper like a tiny echo in her heart that told her how wonderful it would be to have Carlos to turn to, for advice, for mental support? To help her to shore up her shaken defences?

'If I had Carlos O'Connor on my side,' Gail said with a certain militancy but almost as if she'd read Mia's mind, 'and thinking of me, I'd be a bit more gracious about it than you are, Mia. Now, will you come in and get warm and maybe a bit unsober?'

CHAPTER FOUR

THE SUN CHOSE to shine on the garden club lunch the next day and Gail, with the help of her sister Kylie, managed brilliantly.

Mia spent most of the day sitting in her office talking on the phone and working on the computer. She'd tossed and turned all night under the twin weights of losing Bellbird and what she thought of as the irrefutable knowledge that Carlos was still in love with Nina, much as he might wish otherwise.

Trying to seek legal advice as well as trying to find a venue she could transfer functions to did not do anything to cheer her up.

She had another twenty-four hours before she had to make a response to Bellbird's new owner but she couldn't make up her mind whether to go to court or not.

Finally, late afternoon, when all the guests had left, the clear air lured her out into the garden. She hopped over to a bench and sank down. The sunlight was warm on her skin; she was wearing a soft green summer dress that matched her eyes. And, because she'd not been on show, her hair was only lightly tied back.

The gardens were beautiful. The rain had freshened them up, there were bees and dragonflies hovering over the flowers, there were delicate scents on the air, there was the unique aura of Mount Wilson, and there were bellbirds calling.

Don't cry, she warned herself as she closed her eyes and gave herself over to the magic of the estate.

It was the roar of Carlos's car that roused her from her reverie.

She opened her eyes and watched it pull up at the main house. She saw Carlos get out and stretch, then walk inside.

Carlos, she thought with a sudden pang as well as an accelerated heartbeat. Despite all her own catastrophes, she'd not only tossed and turned overnight, she'd had Carlos and Nina French at the back of her mind all day.

It had sounded—from what he'd said last night— as if they couldn't live together but they couldn't live without each other. It had sounded like a relationship fraught with tearing, deep emotion, like a battlefield, but she got the feeling that while those tearing emotions might hurt deeply, the other side of the coin could be heights such as they'd never known with anyone else.

But, whatever it was, in comparison, her own romantic dealings with Carlos had sounded trivial.

She had to forget about him. He never was for her and he never would be.

It was the clink of glass that drew her out of her reverie this time and she opened her eyes again to see Carlos crossing the lawn towards her with a tray bearing a jug and a couple of glasses.

He was wearing jeans, boots and a blue-and-white striped shirt with the neck open and the sleeves rolled up. He looked impossibly attractive with his dark hair and olive skin, with his height and wide shoulders, his lean body...

'Hi!' she said, taking a very deep breath. 'Welcome back, but if that's alcohol I think I should abstain.'

He grinned. 'Gail told me you and she demolished a bottle of wine last night. No, it's fresh fruit juice, not at all spiked.'

He put the tray down on a wrought iron table and sat down next to her on the bench. 'How's the foot?'

'Not bad. I'm getting the hang of the crutches now—there's a bit of an art to it. I—' she hesitated '—I wasn't sure if you were coming back. You didn't need to. I'm being very well looked after.'

'Good.'

'Thank you all the same—' she interrupted '—for all your help. I don't want to seem ungracious.'

'Ungracious?' He looked quizzical.

'That's what Gail said I was.' She bit her lip.

'So Gail's giving you lessons in tact and diplomacy?' he hazarded. 'Should be interesting.'

Mia regarded him for a long moment with an expression of deep hostility. 'Between the two of you,' she said bitterly, 'it's not surprising I'm feeling like a nervous wreck. *I am not ungrateful for your help*, Carlos,' she said, emphasising each word. 'That's all I'm trying to say.'

'Good,' he replied comfortably and handed her a glass of fruit juice. 'Lovely out here, isn't it?' He looked around.

'Yes,' she said on a little sigh. 'Hear the bellbirds?'

He listened. 'Yes. How was your day?'

Mia sighed. 'Pretty disheartening. I haven't come up with an alternative yet and I can't make up my mind whether to go to court or not, but—' she gestured and squared her shoulders '—tomorrow's another day—I think it was Scarlett O'Hara who said something like that.'

'No doubt after Rhett told her he couldn't give a damn.' He looked amused. 'Uh…I have some better news for you. I've bought it.'

'Bought what?' she asked automatically.

'This place.' He waved a hand.

Mia choked. Even the bellbirds seemed to stop calling in the long moments before she could gather her wits to reply. Then she turned to him, her face suddenly pale, her eyes huge, dark and uncomprehending.

'What do you mean? What are you talking about?'

He put his hand along the back of the bench behind her. 'I bought Bellbird,' he said slowly and precisely.

'*Bought it*?' she echoed huskily, still looking stunned. 'Why?'

He withdrew his arm and sat forward with his hands between his knees. 'So you can stay on. You can lease it from me for as long as you want. But there were other reasons. I had this vision planted in my mind of a girl in a long white dress, carrying a big hat and playing ladies on a hill station. A girl with heavy, midnight-dark hair and green eyes. Wait,' he murmured as Mia stirred. 'Let me finish.'

He thought for a moment. 'A girl I admired and—'

'And felt sorry for,' Mia said out of a clogged throat. 'Please don't go on.'

He put a hand on her knee. 'No, I don't feel sorry for you, Mia. There's something about you that doesn't go with sickly sentimental stuff like that. But I do like to repay my debts.'

'You don't owe me anything.'

'Yes, I do,' he countered. 'Between myself and my mother, we must have created hell for you. I also—' he paused '—need to apologise for the possibly flippant way I described the effect you have on me from time to time.'

Mia blinked.

'Not that it doesn't happen,' he added dryly. 'But you're right, there's something a bit unreal about it.'

Mia flinched inwardly and immediately called herself a fool. Why did it hurt? She'd told herself only hours ago he wasn't the one for her; he'd never been. And her beleaguered mind turned to the fact that he'd bought Bellbird.

'I can't believe you bought it,' she said shakily.

He shrugged. 'It's a little bit of heaven. Who wouldn't want it if they could have it? Besides—' all of a sudden he sounded cold and grim '—there's not a lot I can do about a nephew exerting undue pressure on his elderly aunts but the details of the sale include

me taking over your lease and deducting a compensa-
tory amount from the sale price.'

Mia blinked. 'I don't know what to say. I wish you
hadn't.' It was a sentiment that slipped out unexpectedly
but it was true, she realised. Despite everything she felt
for the property and her business, she wished he hadn't.

'Why?'

She interlaced her fingers. 'It makes me feel be-
holden to you.'

He swore beneath his breath.

She hesitated and in the grip of a maelstrom of emotions, she rubbed her face distractedly. 'It also puts me
in an impossible position.'

'What does?' There was a distinct coolness in his
voice now.

Mia put a hand to her mouth. 'To think you bought
Bellbird because of me and therefore I should, out of
gratitude, do anything you want.'

'Perish the thought,' he said harshly. 'You don't really believe I'm going to blackmail you into anything,
do you?'

She was silent.

'But—' he paused '—if you didn't want to stay, you
could have your six months to get you out of any con-
tractual difficulties and then—' he grimaced, folded
his arms across his chest and stretched his legs out
'—we would come to our final parting of the ways,
Mia, at least with me knowing I'd done as much as
I was allowed to, to compensate for what happened
seven years ago.'

Mia jumped up, her eyes flashing, and fell over as her injured heel hit the ground.

Carlos was on his feet immediately and he picked her up and held her in his arms as she struggled.

'Whoa!' he admonished. 'What the hell do you think I'm going to do? Here.' He handed her the crutch and put his hands on her hips until she steadied.

Then, to her fury, he tidied her hair with his hands and pushed it back over one shoulder. 'I see what you mean about the crutch,' he said as he straightened the collar of her dress. 'Not only are you one-legged but you're one-handed—awkward.'

Mia breathed deeply and Carlos sat down again and drained his glass.

'Go on, I'm all ears,' he drawled.

'Look, please don't think I'm not grateful—'

'Here we go again,' he murmured. 'You're a good teacher, Gail.'

'All *right*,' she said through her teeth with sudden tears streaming down her face. 'I will *never* forgive your mother for what she did, how she made me feel. I will never forgive *you*—' she broke off and realised that it might have come seven years late but it was true '—for not checking up on me, even if it had been to come and say, "Mia, I *could only mess up your life.*"'

'Mia—'

But she waved him to silence. 'Nor will I ever forgive your mother for coming back into my life and patronising me all over again. This—' she gestured to take in Bellbird '—can't change that and if I did stay on I'd feel terrible because I'd still feel the same way. Don't you see?'

'All right.' He stood up and put the glasses back on the tray. 'But you'd be well advised to stay for the six months. Protracted legal dealings can cost a fortune. Don't worry.' He looked down at her sardonically. 'I won't trouble you at all.'

Mia discovered she was trembling all over and she still had tears rolling down her cheeks. 'Look, I'm sorry if I...if...'

'Forget it,' he said. 'Better to know where we stand. You hold your crutch.'

Mia looked up at him. 'What do you mean?'

'This, no doubt for the last time, Mia.' And he picked her up effortlessly and started to stride across the lawn with her.

Mia was struck dumb because, apart from kissing her, he couldn't have done anything that affected her senses more drastically. To feel herself cradled against his hard, toned body, to inhale that tantalising smell of sweat and fresh cotton sent ripples of desire and need through her.

Then he compounded it as they reached the house.

He set her carefully on her feet, waited until she was steady on her crutch, then he kissed her full on the mouth with his hand cupping her head.

'Take care, Miss Firebrand,' he advised with an ironic little glint in his eye. 'Take care.'

He made sure she was steady again and walked away to his car.

It was Gail who came out to stand beside Mia as Carlos accelerated down the drive. It was Gail who put her arm around Mia's shaking shoulders and led her inside.

CHAPTER FIVE

SIX WEEKS LATER Mia put down the phone and stared into space, her mind reeling.

She was still at Bellbird, having, after serious thought and some legal advice, written Carlos a stilted little note to the effect that she would be grateful to stay on for the six-month term of her original lease. She'd got a reply agreeing to her request, written and signed by his secretary.

Gail happened to be passing the office doorway with a pile of snowy tablecloths in her arms but she paused and raised an interrogative eyebrow at her boss.

'That was Carol Manning,' Mia said in a preoccupied manner.

Gail waited a moment, then, 'Do I know Carol Manning?'

'Uh...no, sorry.' Mia tapped her teeth with her pencil. 'She's Carlos O'Connor's secretary.'

Gail advanced into the office and dumped the tablecloths on a chair. 'What's he want?'

'A lunch for forty next week. They're holding some kind of a conference on the two preceding days and have decided to wrap things up with a lunch.'

'Not a great deal of notice,' Gail observed. 'He's lucky you had the day free.'

'He...' Mia paused. 'He had something else planned, a cruise on the harbour, but the long range forecast is for showers and high winds now—in Sydney, that is, it's only a coastal low pressure system, apparently. It should be OK up here. I can't help wondering why he didn't choose another venue, though.'

Gail grimaced. 'Why should he when he owns the best venue there is?'

Mia smiled dryly. 'In a nutshell,' she murmured. 'I still wish he'd gone somewhere else.'

'I can understand that.' Gail picked up her tablecloths. 'Considering the way things ended between you two. Not that I've asked any questions, but you only had to have eyes.'

'Gail, you've been a tower of strength and I really appreciate the fact that you haven't asked any questions,' Mia said warmly. 'I just...I'm just not sure how I'll be.'

'You'll be fine! At least you can walk on two feet now. OK—' she dumped the tablecloths on a chair again and sat down opposite Mia '—let's help you to be fine; let's slay 'em. Let's give them the best darn lunch they've ever had. Is there any kind of theme to the conference—did this Carol Manning mention anything pivotal?'

'Horses,' Mia said succinctly. 'O'Connor Construction is planning to build an equestrian centre that should accommodate stabling, tracks for thoroughbreds, tracks for trotters, dressage plus a vet hospital, swimming pools for horses, you name it. Thus, at the conference there'll be a variety of people from vets to trainers to owners to jockeys, but all horsey.'

'I'm quite a fan of horses,' Gail observed, looking thoughtful.

'I am too.' Mia chewed the end of her pencil this time. 'Gail, you're a genius. I've just had the most amazing idea.'

'I don't see how that makes *me* a genius.'

'It was your "pivotal" point that did it. You may not know it, but one of the most famous horse races in the world is the Kentucky Derby.'

'Well, I did know that.'

'Good.' Mia turned to her computer and her fingers flew over the keys as she did some research. 'The other thing about it is the fact that it's laden with tradition. You drink mint juleps at Churchill Downs on Kentucky Derby day, you eat burgoo—'

'I've heard of mint juleps but what on earth is burgoo?'

'It's a concoction of beef, chicken, pork and vegetables,' Mia read from her screen, 'and they play Stephen Foster's "My Old Kentucky Home" while you do. Then there are the roses.'

'We've got plenty of roses,' Gail put in.

'I know.' Mia thought of the rose gardens outside in full bloom. 'The tradition is that the winner, the horse, is draped in a blanket woven with five hundred and fifty-four roses. We probably—' she looked up at Gail '—don't have to use that many roses, then again we do need a horse.'

'Not a live one. Certainly not Long John—he could go about biting all manner of people,' Gail objected.

'Nooo—but I can't think what else to substitute. Apart from that, though, wouldn't it be something to serve a horsey crowd mint juleps and—' she pointed to her screen '—feed them burgoo from an authentic recipe—and have the waiters and waitresses dressed in jockey silks?'

Gail blinked. 'The mint juleps sound a bit danger-ous if you ask me.'

'The guests are coming by coach so we don't need to worry about drink-driving. A horse, a horse,' Mia said rapidly, 'my kingdom for a horse.'

'My mother's got one; it's a wooden rocking horse, it's nearly as big as the real thing and it's in beauti-ful condition for an antique. It's Mum's pride and joy.'

'Oh, Gail, do you think she'd lend it to us?'

'We can only ask. What else do we need?'

'Stephen Foster music, but I'm sure I can find that. All right.' Mia sat up. 'I won't have time to think straight.'

'Five hundred and fifty-four roses?' Bill James said incredulously. 'You must be mad, Mia. Clean off your rocker, more like it.'

'If you'd let me finish, Bill,' Mia said with a slight edge, 'I was just telling you that's the number they use in the actual Kentucky Derby to decorate the winner's blanket.'

'They, whoever they are, sound as nutty as fruitcakes

too, if you ask me,' Bill interjected. 'Five hundred and fifty-four. For a horse blanket!'

'Bill—' Mia breathed heavily '—we won't use *nearly* as many but we will use *some*—so be prepared.' She eyed him militantly.

Bill snorted and then eyed *her*. 'You're getting snippety, Mia. Not only that, you're looking peaky. If I were you, I'd get that boyfriend of yours back.'

Mia went to speak but choked instead and finally turned on her heel, the good one, and marched away.

To her dismay, she found herself tossing and turning in her loft the night before the O'Connor lunch, despite her earlier conviction that, with the forthcoming event to think about, she would be too busy to think of anything else.

Finally she got up, climbed down her ladder, put some more wood into the stove and brewed herself a cup of chocolate.

In the six weeks since she'd last seen Carlos, she'd had days when she was sure, quite convinced, in fact, that she'd done the right thing. Even accepting the six months had gone against the grain with her. It had made her feel like the recipient of charity. It made her, as unreasonable as it sounded, but she couldn't help it, feel like the housekeeper's daughter again.

But on other days she thought she must have been a little mad to have knocked back the opportunity to stay on at Bellbird.

Why couldn't she have buried her pride? After all, it had been her dream only a few weeks ago. Even now, as she resolutely looked for new premises to move to when her lease was up, it was tearing her apart to think of leaving.

But that's nonsense, she thought as she sipped her chocolate. It's only a place.

And he's only a man, but like it or not I've had a crush on Carlos for a long time, and probably always will....

She stared into the fire and shivered, not from cold, but from fear. She was feeling scared and young because she was confused, because she was sometimes tempted to think she could love Carlos much better than Nina French had.

In fact loving Carlos, or the thought of it, was something that plagued her waking hours as well as her dreams.

It was mad. No sooner had she told him she could never forgive him, no sooner had she told him she wished he hadn't bought Bellbird, than she'd started to feel bereft and in a particular way.

She missed him. She shook secretly with desire for him. She missed the way he charmed people, like Gail's mother. She desperately missed the way he forked back his hair, how his eyes could laugh at her while his expression was grave. The feel of him when he carried her in his arms...

The next morning Mia dressed carefully in a skirt and blouse.

She'd tied her hair back but used a lilac scarf to lessen the severity of the style.

Then, having checked with the caterers that everything was going well with the 'burgoo'—she gave it a taste test—she took a last tour of the dining room.

Pride of place on a dais was Gail's mother's rocking horse, looking spectacular under its 'rose blanket', which was a work of art, even if nothing like five hundred and fifty-four roses had been used. And in the centre of the room there was an ice carving of a mare with her foal at her foot.

'My Old Kentucky Home' was playing softly in the background and waitresses in jockey silks and caps were waiting to serve mint juleps.

Then the guests arrived and Mia held her breath as they filtered into the dining room but she was reassured by the gasps and delighted comments, and she sought out Gail across the room with her eyes and they gave each other the thumbs-up sign.

There was no sign of Carlos, although Carol Manning had introduced herself. 'He should be here any minute,' she said with some obvious frustration. 'He's often late.'

'I know, he was late for his sister's wedding,' Mia said and bit her lip. 'Uh…he didn't come by bus?'

'Bus! When you have the kind of car he drives, no,' Carol Manning responded and looked more closely at Mia. 'So you're Mia Gardiner? How do you do? I must say—' she looked around, wide-eyed '—I can understand why Mr O'Connor decided to have you do this lunch. It's inspired. Ah, here he is now.' And she nodded to the entrance of the dining room.

Carlos was standing in the doorway, looking around.

He wore a beautifully tailored grey suit, a pale blue shirt and a navy tie. Then, with a faint smile twisting his lips, he came across the room and, for an instant, Mia felt like fainting under the almost overpowering impact of his good looks, his masculinity and what he used to mean to her.

'Well done, Miss Gardiner,' he said. 'Very well done. How's the foot?'

'Fine now, thank you, Mr O'Connor,' she murmured. 'I'll leave you to it. Enjoy your lunch.' And she moved away smoothly.

'So here you are.'

Mia looked up with a start. She was in her cottage having seen, or so she thought, the last of the lunch guests off.

It had clearly been a highly successful function. Carlos had been nowhere to be seen, nor had his car.

'I thought you'd gone,' she said.

'Or hoped I had? Never mind. I actually went to see Gail's mother.' He sat down at the kitchen table.

'What on earth for?' Mia frowned.

'Gail told me she wove the rose blanket so I went to thank her.'

'That was nice,' Mia conceded.

'You sound surprised.'

'No, I've always known you can be nice.' Mia said flatly, then added on a rush of breath, 'What do you want, Carlos? We've got nothing more to say to each other.'

He raised an eyebrow. 'You may not have but it looks

to me as if you've lost weight. Finding it a bit hard to maintain a stance so full of righteous indignation, Mia?'

She gasped. 'How dare you? It's not that!'

'Then what is it?'

'I mean, I haven't lost weight,' she corrected herself belatedly, but it was a lie. She was not prepared to admit as much to Carlos, however.

'According to Bill, not only don't you look well but you're cranky and hard to work with.'

Mia opened her mouth, closed it, then, 'Hard to work with?' she repeated furiously. 'If anyone is hard to work with it's Bill. Have you any idea how I have to nurse him through Lucy's month with her grandkids?' She broke off, breathing heavily.

He watched the way her chest heaved beneath the black blouse, then looked into her eyes. 'If it's any comfort,' he said quietly, 'I'm like a bear with a sore head at times too.'

Her lips parted. 'Why?' she whispered.

'Whatever the rights and wrongs of it, I want you. I thought you might be in the same difficulty.'

She was transfixed as she turned pale then pink in a way that virtually shouted from the rooftops that she was.

'I...I...' she stammered and couldn't go on.

He moved a step closer but that was when her phone rang. It was lying on the kitchen table and she was all set to ignore it but she saw her mother's name on the screen and picked it up to answer.

Her tears were impossible to control when she ended the call and she was white to the lips.

'What?' he asked. 'What's happened?'

'My father. He's had a stroke. Oh, I've got to go but it could take me hours to get off the mountain, let alone up to Ballina.' She wrung her hands.

'No, it won't.' He pulled his own phone out and punched in some numbers.

Half an hour later Mia was on her way down the mountain beside him in his fast car and when they reached Sydney Airport she transferred to a waiting helicopter he'd organised.

'There'll be a car at the airport to take you to the hospital,' he told her just before she boarded the chopper.

'I can't thank you enough!'

'Don't worry about it,' he recommended.

She turned away to climb aboard, then turned back impulsively and kissed him swiftly. 'Thanks,' she said from the bottom of her heart.

A week later her father, who'd been moved to the Lismore Base Hospital, was recovering.

It was going to take some months of physiotherapy for him to be as mobile as he had been, but all the signs were good. And her mother had returned from the shell-shocked, frightened, trembling person she'd been at first to her usual practical and positive self.

'I think we'll lease the tea room out,' she'd told Mia. 'You know, apart from the birds and the bees and growing things, your father has always had another ambition—to drive around Australia. I think the time has come, when he's recovered, to buy a caravan and do it.'

'Why not?' Mia had responded.

Her mother had then looked at her critically and told her she looked as if she needed a break.

Mia agreed with her but didn't tell her she actually felt as if she'd been run over by a bus. Instead she mentioned that she planned to have a couple of days off before she returned to Mount Wilson, since Gail seemed to be coping well and now had Lucy James to help her out.

Mia's mother had looked unconvinced about the efficacy of 'a couple of days' but she'd urged Mia just to do it.

Mia took herself to Byron Bay, south of the Queensland border and the most easterly point of the Australian mainland.

She booked herself into a luxury motel just across the road from the beach and she slept for hours on her first day.

Then she took a stroll down the beach at sunset.

It was a beautiful scene, a pink cloud-streaked sky, the sheen of pewter laid across the placid low-tide water and the lighthouse an iridescent white on the dark green of Cape Byron.

She rolled her jeans up and splashed in the shallows. Her hair was loose and wild. She had a turquoise T-shirt on and she'd tied a beige jumper round her waist by its sleeves. On her way back she stopped to untie it and pull it on as the pink of the sunset slipped from the sky and the air cooled.

That was when she noticed a tall figure standing on the beach below the surf club.

A tall figure she could never mistake—Carlos.

She didn't hesitate. She pushed her arms into the sleeves of the jumper as she walked over to him.

'I didn't know you were here, Carlos.'

'I wasn't. I've only just arrived. Your mother told me you were here.'

'Oh, Carlos! You spoke to my mother?'

He nodded. 'And your father. I went to see them.'

'They would have loved that. Thanks a million. Where are you staying?'

He took her hand and touched the side of her face, then pushed her hair behind her ears. 'With you, Mia. With you if you'll have me.'

She took a breath and a faint smile curved her lips. 'Just as well it's only across the road then,' she said serenely.

'I like the way you do that,' Mia murmured.

She was lying naked across the king-sized bed and her body was afire with his touch as he left no part of her unexplored.

'But I think I need to be held before I…I don't know what, but something tempestuous is liable to happen to me, Carlos,' she went on with a distinct wobble in her voice.

He laughed a little wickedly and took her in his arms. 'How's that?'

'Oh, thanks.' She wound her arms round him and kissed the strong tanned column of his neck. 'You know, I can't believe this.'

'Believe what?' He cupped her bottom.

'How good it is to be here in bed with you,' she said on a genuine note of wonderment. She leant up on one elbow and looked at him seriously. 'It's not too tame for you, is it?'

'Tame?' he replied equally as seriously and removed his hands from her hips to cup her breasts. Her nipples hardened as he played with them and she took several ragged little breaths.

He looked into her eyes. 'Tame?' he repeated as she writhed against him and bit her bottom lip. 'It's the opposite, but are you ready for me, Mia?'

'More than that, dying, actually. Oh!' she gasped as he turned her onto her back and eased his body onto hers. And she was ready to welcome him so that in moments the rhythm of their lovemaking increased and there was absolutely nothing tame about the way they moved together and finally climaxed together—it was wild, wanton and wonderful.

In fact Mia couldn't speak for a few minutes afterwards as she lay cradled in his arms, her body slick with sweat, her hair a cloud of rough black silk on the pillow. And she made a tiny sound when he moved— a sound of protest.

'It's OK,' he reassured her and pulled the sheet up. 'I'm going nowhere.'

She relaxed.

Mia sat cross-legged on the beach early the next morning, sifting sand through her fingers as she watched Carlos body-surfing into the beach.

She'd given up on her hair and hadn't even bothered to pin it back. She wore short white shorts and her turquoise T-shirt, she was barefoot and, because of a playful breeze, she'd pulled on Carlos's sweatshirt.

It was miles too big for her but it not only made her feel warm, it was like having his arms around her.

She was smiling at absolutely nothing at all.

'Hi.' He stood in front of her, droplets of water still sliding down his sleek tanned body, and picked up his towel as he studied her dimples. 'Something funny?'

'No,' she assured him. 'Oh, you'll want your top.' She started to take his sweatshirt off.

'Keep it on,' he said. 'I'll use the towel—now you're laughing!' He looked around. 'What is it?' He sat down beside her.

'It's me,' she told him.

He grimaced. 'What's so funny about you?'

'You know those stereotyped women you see on TV and in the movies who float around radiantly on cloud nine after someone has made love to them?'

'Uh-huh.' He rubbed his hair with the towel and looked at her quizzically. 'Not…?' He didn't finish.

'Yep.' She nodded vigorously. 'That's who I remind myself of this morning. Or those smiley faces on computers.'

'The smiley trail?' He started to laugh and pulled her into his arms and lay back on the sand with her. 'You're crazy,' he teased.

'And you're wonderful,' she replied, sobering. 'There is something else your lovemaking has achieved, though.'

'I hesitate to ask,' he said ruefully.

'I could eat a horse,' she told him. 'I'm *starving*.'

'Ah—' he sat up with her still in his arms '—now there we are of the same mind. Let's go.'

They got back to their room and Mia showered while Carlos ordered breakfast.

When she emerged, breakfast had not arrived but a bottle of champagne stood in an ice bucket on the coffee table next to two flutes and a flask of orange juice.

'Oh,' she said, recalling their conversation about morning-after champagne celebrations. 'Dangerous and delightful.'

Carlos had showered at the beach and he wore khaki shorts and a white shirt. His hair was still damp and hanging in his eyes. His feet were bare but he was enough to make her heart beat faster and then, when he came and ran his hands down her body, over her colourful cotton sarong, all the fire he'd aroused in her the night before came back to her and she trembled and put her arms around his waist and laid her head on his chest.

'You shouldn't,' she said huskily.

He traced his fingers down the side of her neck and cupped the smooth curve of her shoulder. 'Shouldn't?' He said it barely audibly.

'Touch me. It sets off all sorts of chain reactions.'

She felt his slight jolt of laughter and he kissed the top of her head. 'You're not alone.'

There was a knock on the door.

They drew apart, both laughing.

* * *

It was a glorious day.

She spoke at length to her parents, then they drove up to the lighthouse after lunch and were rewarded as they gazed down at the wrinkled blue ocean to see a pod of humpback whales making their way back to the Southern Ocean after their sojourn in the tropical waters of Queensland.

'There's something about them that always makes me feel emotional,' she said of the whales as they sat on a bench from where they could see not only the ocean to the east of Cape Byron but the protected beaches to the west as well as Mount Warning, and Julian Rocks out in the bay.

'I think it's because they're so big and it's such an amazing journey.' He put his arm around her shoulders. 'Don't cry.'

She sniffed. 'I'm not crying, not really.'

'How about—' he stretched out his legs '—we go out for dinner tonight?'

'Uh…we could. Any special reason?'

He meditated for a moment. 'There's a band playing at the restaurant next door to the motel,' he said, 'so we could eat and dance.'

'Sounds good.'

'But I have an ulterior motive,' he went on. 'I think I would like to see a really glamorous version of you, all dressed and tizzied up, and be confident in the knowledge that when I got you back to our room I'd be able to undo it all.'

Mia choked. 'That's…diabolical.'

He took his arm from her shoulders and sat forward, taking her hand. 'You'd enjoy it, I promise.'

'I…possibly,' she conceded. 'Always assuming I could sit still and eat my dinner with that on my mind. However—' she paused dramatically '—there's one problem.'

He raised an eyebrow at her.

'I didn't bring any smart clothes with me.'

'Ah. Well, look, while I make some calls, why don't you undertake some retail therapy?'

Mia pursed her lips. 'You really think I should?'

'I really do. I've discovered that next to sex—and sometimes even over and above sex—retail therapy does wonders for girls.'

Mia almost went cross-eyed as she struggled not to make a thoroughly exasperated feminist retort to this.

'You don't agree?' he asked.

Mia looked at him. He was still in his khaki shorts and white shirt. The breeze was lifting his hair and the fine white cotton of his shirt.

He looked big, utterly relaxed and sinfully attractive with one dark eyebrow raised quizzically at her. As if he knew exactly what was going through her mind….

She shrugged. 'I don't mind a bit of retail therapy.' She waited for a moment but he said nothing. 'And of course Byron is not a bad spot for it,' she added.

'Bravo!'

Mia blinked. 'What for?'

'Not responding to the bait,' he drawled and put his arms around her.

Mia frowned, squinted, then gave way to laughter. 'How could I? Nothing on earth is going to stop me from going shopping now!'

He kissed her and they got up and strolled back to the car, hand in hand.

Byron Bay, with its village atmosphere and plethora of boutiques and restaurants, was a charming place for a spot of retail therapy.

It was in a glamorous little boutique that Mia found the dress. Chalk-blue in a crinkly fabric, the bodice was sleeveless and moulded to her figure, with tantalising cut-outs from under the arms to the waist. The skirt billowed down her legs with a long slit up one side. A pair of high blue suede sandals could have been made for the outfit so she bought them too.

Then she found a hairdresser and not only had her hair done but her finger and toenails painted a dark blue. It was the hairdresser who directed her to a lingerie shop where she purchased a pair of divine high-cut panties in blue satin and lace. The dress, on account of its cut-outs, had a built-in bra, but, because she was really on a roll, she also bought a sleek ivory silk nightgown that came with a black silk kimono embroidered with ivory birds of paradise that she fell in love with.

She took herself back to the motel, deeply satisfied with her session of 'retail therapy' but wondering how she was going to hide a certain glint in her eye from Carlos. Then she decided she didn't care. She was quite happy to share her euphoria with him.

He wasn't there.

There was a note on the table to the effect that he'd got a call from a business associate who'd found out they were both in Byron, and he'd gone to meet him for a drink. He was, the note said, ready for dinner and he'd meet her at the restaurant next door to the motel.

'It'll give you the time and privacy to do your own thing,' the note finished.

She stared at it and discovered she didn't want the time and privacy to do her own thing. She wanted nothing more than to sit down with him, maybe share a glass of champagne with him, and talk.

Yes, and show him her purchases, perhaps even model them for him, but anyway, she didn't want to be alone.

She dropped her carrier bags on the bed and sat down on it with a sudden sigh. So much to think about; when had this happened? How had she let it happen without any trace of a fight? Why did she hear something like warning bells ringing in her brain?

CHAPTER SIX

SHE WAS READY on the dot of seven.

She was not a hundred per cent happy about walking the short distance to the restaurant on her own. Not that she was afraid of being mugged or anything like that; she suddenly felt more dressed up than most people would be, an out of place sort of feeling. She turned to the kitchenette to pour herself a glass of water but a sound from the sliding glass door that led out to the garden and the pool arrested her, and she swung back on her beautiful new heels.

It was Carlos.

He wore a dark suit, a pale shirt and a navy tie.

He looked completely serious, even inscrutably so in a way that highlighted his dark looks.

And they stayed poised like that for what seemed like an eternity, staring at each other across the wide expanse of the bed.

It was an extraordinary moment for Mia. Not only the furnishings, the painting of orchids on the wall, the fall of the curtains seemed to be imprinted on her consciousness, but everything about Carlos too.

How wide his shoulders looked beneath the suit—
how different he looked in a suit, come to that, she
thought. Far more impressive than his father ever had.

But, at the same time, it registered with her that there
was an air of mystery about him. As if he was a man she
only knew a small part of, and she shivered suddenly.

He stirred at last and put out a hand.

She hesitated for a moment, then walked forward
to take it.

'You look sensational,' he said barely audibly as the
beautiful dress settled around her legs.

She moistened her lips. 'So do you.'

'I came to get you.'

'I'm glad you did.'

'So am I.' He pulled her a touch closer. 'Someone
on a white horse with wings could have whisked you
up and away over oceans and continents.'

A smile trembled on her lips.

He raised an eyebrow at her. 'Is that what you were
worried about?'

'Hardly,' she murmured. She looked down at herself.
'I felt a little out of place. And maybe a bit shy about
walking into a restaurant on my own. So that's why
I'm glad you came.'

'Good.' He drew her even closer then, right into his
arms. 'Am I allowed to kiss you?'

'That depends.' She brought her hands up against
his chest.

'On what?' he drawled.

'If it's a gentle salutation you have in mind, that's
permitted. I—'

But he interrupted her and bent her backwards over his arm with his other arm around her hips. 'How about this?'

Mia maintained her decorum with an effort. 'If you don't wreck my hair and my make-up, it's fine. If you do—'

'You'll never speak to me again? You'll scream blue murder?' he suggested with a wicked glint.

'No, I'll get changed and go for a jog along the beach. And I'll buy a hamburger for dinner.'

Surprise saw Carlos O'Connor straighten and Mia started to laugh.

'Is that what you really want to do?' he asked, looking startled.

'After all this?' She pushed herself a little away from him and gestured down her figure expressively. 'I wasn't really serious.'

His lips twisted. 'It would be fun, though. We could take a blanket. We could take some wine. It's a full moon tonight. It's mid-week, it's not school holidays, so there aren't many people on the beach and, anyway, I know of a secluded spot.'

Mia put her hands on her hips. 'You…are serious?'

He leant back against the door and folded his arms. '*You* were the one who brought it up.'

'I know, but—' she looked down at herself again '—all this!'

'You could wear it tomorrow night.' He straightened. 'We could just reverse things.'

'Are we staying another night, though? I didn't…I mean, I didn't know.' She broke off.

'I believe Gail is coping brilliantly,' he remarked, 'so why not?'

Mia shrugged. 'You're right. So much for believing I was indispensable.'

'How about it, then?'

She looked up at him. 'Why not? So long as you promise not to seduce me to some other venue tomorrow.'

'I promise we can dress up all over again tomorrow night.'

'Thank you.'

'This is rather lovely,' Mia pronounced as she snuggled up against Carlos in the depression they'd scooped in the sand against a bank and lined with a car rug he kept stored in the boot of his car.

They'd finished hamburgers with the lot: lettuce—iceberg specially requested—pineapple, beetroot, tomato, onion and cheese. There had also been chips. They'd bought a bottle of wine and some plastic glasses to drink it from.

The moon had cleared Cape Byron and was sending down a white light on the sea, and the stars looked within reach.

They were both dressed warmly against the night air.

'Be nice to put all this in a bottle,' she said suddenly.

'We wouldn't need to if we got married. We could do it time and again.'

Mia took an unexpected breath and tensed. 'Carlos, I don't know what to say.'

He picked up her hand and threaded his fingers

through hers. 'Look, it's a thought. What else did you have in mind? An affair?'

'If…I hadn't thought that far ahead. I don't really know what to think. It happened—' she pulled her hand free and gestured a little helplessly '—so out of the blue.'

'Really?' he said with an audible tinge of scepticism.

Mia bit her lip. She sat up suddenly and rested her chin on her knees. 'Maybe not,' she conceded, and paused as she suddenly recalled the horribly embarrassing fact that he'd known about her crush on him.

She grimaced. 'Look, all right, there was always some attraction but—' she hesitated, then said bleakly and honestly '—I've taken a bit of a battering lately.'

'You're not operating on full power, full mental capacity?' he suggested. 'Is that what you're trying to say?'

She shrugged. 'Something like that.'

'And that's why you fell into my arms without so much as a murmur of opposition?'

Mia glanced over her shoulder but she couldn't read his expression. A little shiver ran down her spine all the same. 'Well…'

'Not because you really wanted it, because you couldn't help yourself or anything like that? Not because it was *us* and nothing else was going to work?'

There was no doubting the mockery in his voice now.

Mia trembled within. 'I'm sorry if I've offended you,' she said slowly and carefully.

'Because—' he sat up abruptly '—you needed some space to lick your wounds? Is *that* it, Mia?' he shot at her.

She stumbled to her feet. 'Yes. Probably. I haven't had time to analyse it but you don't have to make it sound so awful.'

He stood up behind her. 'How would you put it?' he asked harshly, putting his hands on her shoulders and spinning her round to face him.

She tripped over her feet and had to cling to him for a moment. 'As…as needing some warmth, some consolation,' she stammered. 'What's wrong with that?'

'It's a lie,' he said and gripped her shoulders again. 'That's what's wrong with it. You need me, we need each other now and nothing else is going to make sense.'

Mia could feel her temper rising. 'You can't dictate to me like this, Carlos. I'll make up my own mind.' And she pulled away.

He reached for her but she warded him off and ran down the beach towards the water's edge. 'Stay away from me, Carlos,' she warned.

He took absolutely no notice of her and she ran a bit further, quite unaware the tide was coming in until a rogue wavelet broke around her ankles and her feet sank into the sand. She put out her hands to steady herself but fell over, just in time to be doused by another wavelet.

'Mia, be careful!' Carlos lifted her up and set her on her feet. 'You're all wet and sandy. What did you think I was going to do to you?'

'*Kiss me,*' she said through her teeth. 'Kiss me and hold me and touch me until I don't know if I'm on my head or my heels and then persuade me to elope! But that's not fair, Carlos. I don't want to marry you.'

'Sure?' He asked it quite casually as he lifted her

and set her down further up the beach and out of the way of the incoming tide.

'No, of course I'm not sure,' she said irritably as she looked down at the sodden mess she was. 'There'd be lots of quite nice things about being married to you. None of them are the real reason for marriage, though.'

'Quite nice things such as Bellbird, such as playing ladies and imagining yourself on an Indian hill station? Such as kids when you want them and as many as you want?'

She clicked her tongue. 'Those were dreams. I never really expected them to come true.'

'All right, how about this, then? Such satisfactory sex you can't stop smiling?'

Mia bit her lip and inwardly cursed Carlos.

He went on. 'As for those real reasons you quote— I imagine being madly in love for ever and ever is numero uno?' He raised a dark eyebrow at her.

She nodded reluctantly.

'How are you supposed to know it's going to happen?' he enquired.

Mia stared up at him. 'It can happen. You sound as if you don't believe in it, but it happened for my parents.'

'It happened for my parents,' he said dryly. 'But *I* happen to think it's something that grows between two people. Do you see it happening for you? Has anyone got as far as this with you, Mia?'

'This?' she said uncertainly.

'Yes, this. I'm going to take you back to the motel now. I'm going to strip off your wet sandy clothes and put you in a warm shower. When you come out I'm

going to put you into bed with an extra blanket to keep
you warm and heap up the pillows. Then I'm going to
brew some of the excellent coffee they've provided.'

Mia simply stared up at him.

'When we've had that,' he went on, 'if we feel like
it, we can make slow, exquisite love to each other. Or
the wild and wanton variety we had last night. Or we
can just go to sleep together.

'Incidentally,' he added, 'I love the way you curl up
in my arms and go to sleep. I love the way you even
smile in your sleep.'

'I don't…I do?' she said huskily.

'You do. Look—' he shoved his hands into his pockets '—you could catch cold like this.'

She shivered right on cue.

Fortunately they hadn't driven to the beach. They'd just
collected the rug from the car, so Mia didn't have to
worry about the mess she would make in his car; the
motel and the thought of shedding damp sand all over
the place was another matter.

'Put your shoulders back, tilt your chin and just do
it, Mia,' he advised. 'It probably happens all the time.
Besides which, they're bound to have vacuum cleaners.'

She cast him a look that told him he might pay her
funny little compliments but he needn't think he was
forgiven for anything. In fact she was in just the right
mood to do as he suggested, put her shoulders back and
tilt her chin—at him, though.

'All right. Not so bad?' he said as he unlocked their
door and she stepped into the room. 'Next step,' he said

as she nodded reluctantly. 'Straight into the shower. You can rinse yourself and your clothes off,' he recommended with just a hint of amusement.

Mia went to say something along the lines of it all being his fault anyway but she resisted the temptation and marched into the bathroom and closed the door pointedly.

He opened it immediately.

She whirled round, her eyes sparkling a furious green.

'I just wanted to apologise and assure you I now have no intention of laying a finger on you,' he drawled. 'As for marrying you, it was only a thought, not a threat.' And he closed the door gently.

Mia rinsed her clothes thoroughly before showering and washing her hair. By the time she'd done all this the bathroom was well and truly steamed up and her skin was rosy. The only problem that remained was the fact that she had nothing to wear; she'd not taken that into account in her high dudgeon.

Her shoulders slumped as she stared at herself in the steamy mirror. What was she fighting about anyway? she wondered disconsolately. No one could force her to marry them. All she had to do was remove herself.

But… She sighed suddenly and closed her eyes. She was inextricably tied up with Bellbird for the next few months, something Carlos well knew.

What would it really be like to be married to Carlos

O'Connor? Of course there was only one way to find out, wasn't there? And was he right—love grew?

She wrapped a thick white towel around herself and opened the bathroom door.

Carlos was lying on top of the bed wearing only his boxers, resting his head on his elbow. There was a tray with a coffee plunger and cups on the bedside table next to him. There were pencil-thin little packets of sugar in a brown pottery bowl on the tray and some locally made cookies in cellophane wrappings.

He said nothing, just watched her advance towards the bed and his expression was entirely unreadable.

Mia reached the foot of the bed before she spoke. 'I don't know what you're thinking, Carlos, but I hate this kind of bickering. I mean, I don't like myself for… for going along with it so I'll just say this. I'm not sure of anything anymore. I can't make any decisions right now…and—' she pointed towards her pillows '—would you mind passing me my nightgown? By the way,' she sniffed, 'your coffee smells wonderful.'

His expression softened suddenly and he sat up and held out a hand to her.

She hesitated, then walked round the bed and took it. 'Hop in,' he invited.

'This towel is wet.'

'Ah.' He reached under her pillows and withdrew her nightgown, not her new one but an unexceptional sky-blue silky one with shoestring straps and kites all over it.

She loosened the towel and he told her to lift up her arms.

She did so obediently and he slipped the nightgown over her head and smoothed it down her body.

'There, all present and correct,' he murmured and studied the kites. 'Could even be fairly topical.'

'What do you mean?' She looked down.

'Assuming you lift the embargo you placed on me—' he ran his fingers through her damp hair '—we—'

'I placed no embargo on you,' she broke in.

'You told me, through gritted teeth,' he contradicted, 'that I had a habit of kissing you and holding you and touching you until you didn't know if you were on your head or your heels.'

Mia drew an exasperated breath. 'All the same…I mean, that's not an embargo.'

'No,' he agreed. 'Still, no decent guy would fail to realise you disapproved of not knowing if you were on your head or your heels, and therefore desist.'

Mia stared at him almost cross-eyed as she tried to work out what he was getting at. 'What has this got to do with my nightgown?' she asked finally in a heavily frustrated voice.

'Kites,' he replied succinctly.

She blinked.

'I see you still don't understand.' He put his finger on her chin and smiled at her. 'We could reach for the sky like your kites—if we were friends and lovers. That's why it seemed topical.'

Mia stayed perfectly still for about half a minute. That was as long as she could maintain her sobriety and prevent a smile from curving her lips.

'You're quite mad, you know,' she told him.

'Maybe,' he agreed perfectly seriously, 'but am I forgiven?'

'Yes.'

'Come in then.'

She climbed into bed and said in a heartfelt way, 'That's much better.'

'Better?'

'Than fighting. Don't you think?'

'Yes.' He put his arms around her but she didn't see the faint frown in his eyes as he looked over her head.

A couple of hours later, Mia was fast asleep but once again Carlos found himself watching her as she slept.

They had made love, not the wild, wanton variety but it had been warm and sensuous all the same. She was generous and delicious as a lover and she came down from the heights in a way that aroused his protective instincts.

In fact, it occurred to him that he wouldn't like to think of her vulnerability at those times in another man's hands. Someone who didn't realise she gave it her all, like she did so much in her life.

He'd got up when he'd found he couldn't sleep and gone outside into the garden. He'd heard the surf pounding on the beach and the breeze sighing through the Norfolk pines that lined the road. He'd listened to it for a time before he'd come back inside and pulled on a sweatshirt and pushed an armchair over towards the bed.

And, as he watched, he thought back to her as a girl. A girl who'd loved nothing better than to ride like the wind whenever she came home. Almost as if, he mused, her horse and the breeze through that tangled mop of dark hair released her from the constraints of her boarding school.

She'd been a shy child—you wouldn't have known she was there until you caught glimpses of her on the estate.

Then, when she was about fifteen, he reckoned, they'd started riding together when he was home. It had happened quite coincidentally and not often but after a while he'd noticed on the odd occasion that she coloured slightly when he spoke to her.

He'd done nothing other than limiting his visits to West Windward if he knew she'd be home, said nothing and hoped it would go away for her.

Only to get hit on the head by a falling branch in a wild storm and to discover Mia Gardiner was no longer a kid. Not only that, but she was a luscious eighteen-year-old and eminently desirable.

She was still luscious and desirable but there was a lot more to it now. She was clever, she was spirited, she'd fashioned a successful career for herself that didn't depend on her looks—if his father had been alive to see Mia Gardiner now, he would approve of her much more than he'd ever approved of Nina French.

He grimaced as this thought came to him. Contrary to his wife's opinion on the matter, Frank O'Connor had deemed Nina French to be a lovely clothes horse

with an empty head and without the internal fortitude
to make a good wife and mother.

Not that his father's sentiments had surprised him.
But they had, unfortunately, he reflected, sent him
down a path he was now very much regretting. In fact
he was not only regretful but guilty, he thought sombrely.

Of course the irony of it all hadn't failed to strike
him either. Nina had very much wanted to marry him.
Mia did not.

He stared across the bed at a dim rim of light below
the bathroom door. Why had he brought marriage into
the equation like throwing a hat in the ring?

What kind of a marriage did he envisage with Mia,
anyway?

A peaceful one. A marriage to a woman who was
practical, clever, resourceful and artistic. Someone who
loved kids—his mother should appreciate that, always
assuming he could ever get his mother to appreciate
anything about Mia.

A marriage with her living at Bellbird and him coming and going as he saw fit. None of the highs and lows
of his relationship with Nina—none of the insidious
feelings that marriage to Nina would be like a never-
ending grand opera. And of course Mia being forever
grateful for the way he'd redeemed himself, and his
family.

He set his teeth because it was an unpleasant thought.
But there had to be something more to it all, he

reflected. The answer that came was not much help to him.

There was something about Mia Gardiner that got under his skin.

CHAPTER SEVEN

MIA WOKE THE next morning with no idea what to expect.

But, unaware that Carlos had been up half the night wrestling with his demons, she was surprised to find him fast asleep despite the sunlight filtering into the room, courtesy of the curtains they'd forgotten to close.

She watched him for a while and wondered why she should not exactly be uneasy about what today would bring but have a question mark in her mind.

Last night had ended well, she thought, and felt a rush of colour in her cheeks. *Ended well* was a strange phrase to use to describe an encounter that had left her on cloud nine and aware of her body in ever new and divinely sensual ways.

What if Carlos wanted to talk about marriage again? How would she respond in the cold light of day?

She shook her head and decided to go for a swim, thinking that maybe it would wash away all her uncertainties.

She slipped out of bed and padded to the bathroom, where she put on her black-and-white bikini and her white terry robe. When she came back into the room he was still fast asleep.

She blew him a kiss.

It was a fabulous morning. A high blue sky had followed the burnt orange of dawn as the sun rose and the surface of the water was glassy. It was about half tide and long gentle breakers were rolling in to the beach, perfect for body-surfing.

Mia dropped her robe, ran into the water and dived cleanly beneath the first breaker she came to.

Half an hour later, she emerged to find Carlos sitting on the beach wearing board shorts but looking moody.

'Hi.' She picked up her towel. 'The water is amazing. Don't you want to go in?'

'I do and I don't. Would you mind not dripping all over me?'

Mia clicked her tongue and hid a smile. 'Sorry.' She spread out her towel and sat down on it. 'I'll come with you if you like.'

'You think I might need my hand held?' he asked with some animosity. 'I've been surfing since I was six.'

She put her hand over his. 'Not that kind of a hand. The hand of friendship, I meant. Some days when you wake up feeling sour and cranky, it helps.'

She lifted his hand and kissed his palm, then folded his fingers over it and gave him his hand back. 'There!'

And she got up and ran down the beach and back into the water.

He wasn't far behind her.

* * *

'You're a genius,' Carlos said later, over breakfast. 'I got up fully prepared—' he paused and buttered his toast '—to be mean and miserable today. Now look what you've done.' He smoothed some marmalade onto the toast.

They were eating at a beachside café renowned for their breakfast. They both wore jeans and T-shirts. Mia had tied her hair back with a floral scarf.

'I'm glad,' she said, and smiled.

'Still on the smiley trail,' he commented.

'Still on the smiley trail,' she agreed but sobered. 'What are you doing today?'

'Why?'

'I thought I'd go up to Lismore and see my parents, but you don't need to come.'

'I would come but in fact I've got some guys to see this morning—you'd be amazed who ends up in Byron,' he said a shade ruefully. 'But they're actually involved with the equestrian centre, so it's a good opportunity. Take the car.'

'Oh, I thought I'd hire a car.' She poured some coffee and sniffed appreciatively. 'More delicious coffee.'

'This is grown in the area, around Newrybar, I believe. Take the car,' he repeated.

'I've never driven a sports car.'

'So long as you can drive a manual you'll be fine.' She hesitated.

'Mia, do you have any idea what an honour this is?'

'Honour?' She looked around bewilderedly, at the

wooden table and benches, at the other breakfasters and the beach over the railing.

'Not this place,' he told her. 'But I have never offered my car to a woman to drive.'

She stared at him with parted lips. Then she had to laugh. 'If you think that makes me feel any better about it, you're mistaken.' She paused. 'But thanks, anyway.'

'Don't forget we've got a date tonight,' were his last words to her before she set off for Lismore.

'I won't! Thanks again,' she called back and with a surge of exhilaration swung his beautiful little car into the street.

Mia arrived back late afternoon, safe and sound from her trip to Lismore and without putting so much as the tiniest scratch on his car.

She was happy with the state of mind she'd found her parents in and the news that her father would be leaving hospital shortly.

She was greeted on her return with the news that Carlos had gone to Queensland.

'Gone to Queensland?' she repeated to the receptionist who had waylaid her. 'Are you serious?'

'Just over the border by helicopter to look at an equestrian centre. Apparently he's developing one down south and he wanted to see if he could get any ideas from this one. He asked me to explain that to you, Miss Gardiner, and to assure you he'll be back in time for your dinner date this evening.'

'Oh. Well, thanks.'

* * *

That had been a few hours ago and Mia was now almost dressed for dinner, although there was still no sign of Carlos.

She was sitting at the dressing table contemplating her hair.

Whereas this time yesterday she'd had a most elegant and intricate style wrought by a hairdresser, she'd washed her hair twice lately, once last night after getting rolled over in the wet sand and once this morning after her swim. Therefore her hair was no longer sleek; it was wild and curly. With an inward sigh she decided there was only one solution—to tie it back severely.

But she stayed where she was when she'd finished, staring at her image unseeingly as she fiddled with her brush and recalled her parents' unspoken curiosity on the subject of her and Carlos.

Assuming she had to explain things to them, she thought, what would she say? *He actually asked me to marry him but I said no.* Why? *Because I still sense... I don't know...I can't forget what he said or how he looked when he talked about Nina in the restaurant at Blackheath that night.*

Why? Because it struck me—and he didn't so much ask me as suggest we get married—that it was a testing the waters sort of proposal. A thought, not a threat, maybe another unreal aspect of our relationship.

And, for all the happiness he's brought me, there's still a shadow of something in him, be it Nina or...

Her eyes widened suddenly as Carlos strolled in and stood behind her so she was looking at his reflection.

'Hi,' he said. 'Penny for them?'

'What do you mean?' she asked huskily.

'I was watching you from the doorway before you caught sight of me. You were deep in serious thought.'

Mia stood up and smoothed her dress down. 'I was beginning to think you'd forgotten about me.'

'No.' He caught her in his arms. 'I've been thinking about you all day, it so happens. And half the night,' he added a shade dryly.

She cupped his cheek. 'Is that why you woke up in a bad mood?' she asked wryly.

'It was myself I was cranky with. Hey—' he looked down at her '—what have you done to your hair?'

She explained.

'But I like it wild and curly.' He raised his hands and started to take out the clips.

'Carlos!' She stopped.

'Mia?' He raised an eyebrow at her and continued to take out the clips.

She grimaced. 'I guess it's a waste of time asking you to desist?'

'Yes. There.' He presented her with a little bundle of clips and ran his fingers through her loosened hair.

'Is there anything else you don't approve of?' she queried.

'About you?'

'Yes, me. I just thought I ought to be prepared in case you decide to wreak further havoc with my appearance.'

'No,' he said simply as he looked her up and down. 'Well, much as I am looking forward to removing your lovely blue dress and allowing myself the pleasure of parting your thighs, running my fingers over your breasts and round your hips, I'll wait.'

Mia all but choked. 'I'm glad to hear it,' she said with difficulty.

He raised an eyebrow again at her. 'You don't approve?'

'Oh—' she tossed her head '—I approve. That's the problem. But if you can wait, so can I.'

And she turned on her heel and walked away from him.

He caught her and turned her in his arms. 'On second thoughts,' he growled, 'I don't think I can. We've still got time.'

She took a ragged breath.

'We've—' he looked at his watch '—got nearly an hour. Half an hour until the table is booked, half an hour or a bit less to be fashionably late.'

'Carlos,' she breathed but she couldn't go on—for several reasons. She had no idea what she'd been going to say and it was impossible to think straight as he ran his hands from the rounded curves of her shoulders down her arms.

He still wore the jeans and shirt he'd put on after their swim, clothes he'd been wearing all day, and she was assaulted by the pure man smell she'd always loved about Carlos, musk and cotton and something that was so masculine she just loved it.

Then he found the zip of her dress and the material parted down her back and the dress pooled on the floor at her feet.

He made a husky sound of approval in his throat as

she stood before him wearing only her blue silk and lace panties and her beautiful high blue sandals. And his grey gaze lingered on her slim waist, on her thighs and on the smooth hollows at the base of her throat where a telltale nerve was beating a tattoo.

Then he moved forward and cupped her breasts and bent his head to tease her nipples with his tongue and teeth.

Mia went rigid as wave after wave of sensation and desire crashed through her body, and he picked her up and laid her on the bed.

This time there was no time for any more formalities, this time they were both ignited to a fever pitch and desperate for each other. This time it took Carlos as long to come down from the heights as it did Mia.

'That,' he said eventually and still breathing heavily, 'is a record. In as much as we could still shower, get dressed again and be on time for our reservation.'

Mia chuckled. 'We could also sit down and die at the table. I think I'd rather be late.'

He rearranged the pillows, then pulled her back into his arms. 'OK?'

She nodded.

He kissed the tip of her nose. Then he looked into her eyes wryly. 'Realistically, I suspect we're not going to make dinner.' He looked a question at her.

'You suspect right,' she told him. 'I don't feel like getting all done up again.' She snuggled up to him. 'I just feel like staying here.'

He smoothed some strands of hair from her cheek. 'Why not?'

So that was what they did—stayed in bed, with Carlos watching television with the sound turned down and Mia dozing next to him.

Then, at about eleven o'clock, they decided they were starving so they got up and dressed in jeans and sweaters and ran down the motel stairs to the ground floor, hand in hand, and out into the moonlight.

They found a small packed restaurant vibrating with blues music and serving late dinners.

Mia had pasta, Carlos had ocean-fresh prawns and they drank Chianti. Every now and then they got up and joined the crowd on the minuscule dance floor until last orders were called, then they walked to the beach.

'Still OK?' He swung her hand. 'Still on the smiley trail?'

She stopped walking and looked up at him. 'Yes.'

He responded to her rather intent look with a quizzical one of his own. 'You were going to say?' he hazarded.

Mia licked her lips. *I was going to say yes, I will marry you, Carlos. I couldn't not marry you. It would be like sentencing myself to purgatory. I almost got it out but I can't quite bring myself to say it. Why can't I?*

She said, 'What will we do tomorrow?' and inwardly called herself a coward.

He studied her expressionlessly for a long moment, then he shrugged and they started walking again. 'If you think Gail can spare you for another day we could drive up to the Goldie and have a look around.'

'You mean the Gold Coast?'

'Uh-huh.'

'All right. As for Gail—' she dimpled '—she is in seventh heaven—and she's doing marvellously well. She's got her mother helping and Bill's wife, Lucy. I'm proud of her.'

'You probably trained her well,' he commented. 'Ready for bed? Again?' he asked whimsically.

'Considering it's three o'clock in the morning, yes!'

But they didn't go anywhere the next day. Instead they swam and lazed around and enjoyed each other's company.

That evening they were seated at a table for two in the luxurious restaurant next door to their motel. Mia was wearing her new blue dress.

'Third time lucky,' she'd said to Carlos earlier, when she was dressed and ready to go.

He smiled down at her. 'You look marvellous. So does your hair.'

She'd left her hair loose and riotous. 'You know,' she said to him, 'you could make my life much simpler.' She paused and looked suddenly rueful.

'I have been trying to make that point,' he replied as he shrugged into the jacket of his navy suit, worn with a crisp white shirt and a navy tie. His dark hair was thick but orderly and secretly he took her breath away.

'I meant my hair. I wouldn't have to worry so much about it.'

He closed in on her and tilted her chin with his fingers. 'That should be the least of your worries,' he said softly, but scanned her significantly from head to toe.

'Now you've really got me seriously concerned,' she said with an anxious expression. 'Did I speak too soon?'

'About getting to dinner in your new blue dress?' He let his words hang in the air, then took her hand with a wicked little smile in his eyes. 'Get me out of here, Miss Gardiner, just to be on the safe side.'

They dined on lobster and they drank champagne.

Mia was just making up her mind whether to have dessert when she looked up from the menu to see Carlos staring past her, looking pale and with his expression as hard as a rock.

She didn't have to turn to see what had engaged his attention so dramatically. Nina French swept up to their table and there was no mistaking her or, after a startled moment, the man she was with—Talbot Spencer.

Nina was eminently photogenic but in the flesh she was breathtakingly beautiful, with the finest skin, velvety blue eyes and long smooth-flowing corn-gold hair. She was wearing a floral sheath dress that clung to her figure and was held up by shoestring straps so that it just covered her breasts. High nude platform shoes complemented her legs. Above all she had a tiny smile curving her lips, not of triumph or mockery, but a genuine smile.

Talbot wore a suit and Mia had to admit that, fair and freckled, he was also dangerously attractive, although in a way she couldn't quite put her finger on.

It was Nina who broke the startled silence. 'Hi there, Carlos. This is a surprise. I guess you know Talbot, but please introduce me to your friend.'

Carlos stood up and probably only Mia noticed that

his knuckles were white as he put his napkin on the table. 'Nina, Talbot,' he drawled. 'You're right, this is a surprise. Didn't know you two knew each other. Uh… this is Mia Gardiner. Mia,' he went on, 'and I are contemplating getting married, so wish us luck.'

The silence that crashed down around them was deafening.

Nina's expression spoke volumes although she said not a word. She looked horrified; her face actually crumpled and her beautiful blue eyes filled with tears.

It was Talbot who broke the silence. 'That's an interesting way of putting it. Do let us know the outcome of your contemplations. We're off back to Sydney tomorrow—maybe we could get together down there? Nice to meet you, Mia! Come, Nina.'

Nina swallowed, then turned obediently and followed him out of the restaurant.

Carlos sat down but immediately stood up. 'Let's get out of here,' he said tersely.

'Th-the bill,' Mia stammered.

'Don't worry about it, they know me. Ready?'

It wasn't to the beach he took her. They drove up to the lighthouse instead. In silence.

It was cool and dark, the moon hidden by a thick blanket of clouds.

'It's going to rain tomorrow, the end of our idyll, Mia. In more ways than one, I suspect.' He turned to her and slid his arm along the back of her seat. 'Go ahead, say it. I can guess anyway—how *could* you, Carlos?'

Mia cleared her throat. 'Yes,' she agreed huskily, 'I was, and I'm still going to say it. How could you?'

He raised a sardonic eyebrow at her. 'It isn't true? I've certainly been contemplating marrying you, Mia. I could have sworn you might even have been having second thoughts about it.'

Mia bit her lip and tried desperately to gather some remnants of sane rational composure around her. 'Carlos,' she said as she battled more tears, 'do you think linking up with Talbot Spencer was a calculated move on Nina's part to get back at you for breaking up with her?'

'Yes, I do,' he said dryly.

'Have you spoken to her since you broke up?'

'No.'

'Has she tried to speak to you?'

'Mia, she was the one who broke it off,' he said tersely. Then he shrugged. 'She's left messages,' he said sombrely, and added, 'I've been overseas most of the time.' He took a breath and said through his teeth. 'Anyone but Talbot!'

'I don't think so.' Mia closed her eyes and tried to concentrate. 'I think whoever it was, you'd hate the idea of it because—' she gestured helplessly '—there's still something between you two. From the way she looked, there certainly is for *her*. But whatever, none of this is about *me*, don't you see? I've been like a sideshow to the main attraction through all this and it's not something I care to be any more.'

Despite her tear streaks he could see the determination in her eyes and the set of her mouth, and he cursed inwardly.

'Mia...' he paused, and his tone was harsh as he continued '...there's something you don't understand. I will probably always feel guilty about Nina unless I can see her genuinely happy with another man.'

'Guilty?' Mia whispered. 'Why?'

'Because she quite inadvertently became a hostage in my war with my father.'

'You're right. I...I don't understand,' Mia stammered.

Carlos rubbed his face. 'He didn't approve of her.'

Mia did a double take. 'He must have been the only one!'

He grimaced. 'Possibly. But because I thought he was running true to form, finding fault with my choices simply on principle, I wanted to prove him wrong.

'But he was right. Well—' he shrugged '—I don't know if she'll ever make a good wife and mother, but underneath the initial attraction, and you'd have to be a block of wood not to be attracted to her,' he said with obvious bitterness, 'we were never really compatible, Nina and I, only I refused to admit it because I couldn't bear to think my father was right and I was wrong.'

Mia stared at him incredulously.

'And in the process,' he continued bleakly, 'I guess I gave Nina a false sense of security—if not that, I obviously led her to believe that whatever she did, I'd always be there for her. In a way she was entitled to think I'd marry her. And for that I will always feel guilty. And now she's fallen into Talbot's clutches.'

He raked a hand through his hair, then, as she shivered, he took his jacket off and put it round her shoulders.

Mia hugged herself beneath his jacket and came to a decision. 'I...I can't help thinking—I'm sorry but I still believe you haven't got over her and maybe you never will.'

'Mia—'

'No,' she interrupted. 'Please, you must listen to me. I can't be a party to breaking Nina French's heart, or taking you to a place you don't really want to go, not in *your* heart.'

There was a long silence as they looked painfully into each other's eyes. Then he said, 'It's been good, though?'

Mia thought back over the last few days and nodded. 'Yes, yes, it's been lovely.' She wiped her eyes on her wrists.

'Don't cry.' He slipped his jacket off her and pulled her into his arms. 'Don't cry, please.' He kissed the top of her head. 'I feel bad enough as it is.'

'You don't need to.'

'I can't leave you like this.'

'Carlos, you can—for once in my life I didn't bring a tissue or a hanky!' she exclaimed frustratedly.

'Here.' He pulled a clean navy hanky out of his trouser pocket.

She mopped up and blew her nose. 'What was I saying? Yes, you can.' Mia paused and dredged the very depths of her soul for the right words, the right key to handle this, to bring it to a closure that would release not only her, but Carlos without him realising how much she loved him.

'Have you ever seen the Three Sisters?'

Carlos blinked. 'At Echo Point?'

'Mmm-hmm…' She nodded.

'Well, yes.' But he looked mystified.

'I used to feel a bit like them.' Mia dabbed at her eyes again. 'Sort of frozen and petrified. As if I could never break the bonds of what happened at West Windward.'

She hesitated, still searching for the right words. She stared out to sea, but all she could see was a dark blue world.

'Now, thanks to you, I feel different,' she said slowly. 'I feel I can go ahead. It's funny because she'd absolutely hate the thought of it, but what you've done for me is remove the stamp your mother put on me that kept me trapped like that.'

He was silent. But the lines and angles of his face spoke volumes too; he looked harsh and forbidding but at the same time tortured.

'But—' Mia took a deep breath '—this is a real parting of the ways for us. You do see, don't you?' she pleaded.

'You don't believe you're sending me back to Nina, do you?' he asked roughly.

Mia put a finger to his lips. 'That's not for me to do,' she said huskily. 'Only you can work that out. But I think you *have* to work it out. I just want you to know you don't have to worry about me.'

He took her hand and kissed her palm and, as she had done only the day before, closed her fingers over her palm.

'I can only do this one way, Mia.'

She looked a question at him with silent tears slipping down her cheeks.

'Now, tonight. I'll take you back to the motel, then drive on to Sydney. I can organise transport back for you whenever you want it.'

She licked the tears off her lips. 'That's fine. Thanks.'

'Mia—'

'No, you mustn't worry about me.'

'You're crying again,' he said harshly.

'Most women probably have a man they remember with a tear and a smile. The one that got away,' she said whimsically. 'But, believe me, it's the way I want it.'

He stared into her eyes and found them unwavering. He closed his eyes briefly.

She leant over and brushed his lips with hers. 'Still—' she managed a brief but radiant smile '—we don't need to prolong things.'

They didn't.

Carlos drove them back to the motel, consulted over the bill, and it only took him ten minutes to pack. He changed into jeans and a tweed jacket.

Then it was all done and Mia stood straight and tearless in her lovely blue dress before him. 'Bye, now,' she said barely audibly. 'Please just go, but—*vaya con dios*.'

His face softened at the Spanish salutation and he hesitated, closed his eyes briefly and said, 'You too, Mia. You too.' Then he was gone.

Mia stayed where she was for a few minutes, too

scared to move in case she fractured and broke like glass. But of course it didn't happen.

You just go on, she thought as she lay down on the bed and pulled a pillow into her arms. You just go on and hope the pain goes away. You just know you couldn't go through the hoping and the dreaming—and the slamming back to earth again.

The Pacific Highway between Byron Bay and Sydney was at times narrow and tortuous, almost always busy. Not an easy drive at the best of times. Late at night in wet conditions behind the monotonous click of the windscreen wipers with spray coming up off the road from oncoming traffic, it required skill and concentration.

It didn't stop Carlos from thinking that he'd displayed little skill in his dealings with Mia. After the encounter with Nina and Talbot, who could blame her for withdrawing from the lists?

After revealing that Nina had known what she was doing in linking up with his enemy and after their tit-for-tat exchange and the way Nina had looked was enough to make anyone believe there was unfinished business between them.

Was there? he wondered suddenly. Other than the explanation he undoubtedly owed Nina? Could he ever go back to that emotional roller coaster he'd shared with Nina French?

It struck him suddenly that he might have if he hadn't run into Mia again. He might have allowed the familiarity of their routine to draw him back to her; the guilt he felt towards her might have made him do it.

The irony was that now he knew he couldn't go back to her, the reason for it—Mia, who smiled in her sleep—was apparently prepared to sleep with him but not to marry him.

Could he blame her? No. Her shock on hearing how he'd used Nina in the war with his father—had that recalled memories of the way she'd been treated back at West Windward?

Had those fears ever left her—that it could happen to her again in some way? Would they ever leave her? Yes, she'd slept with him, but had she ever really opened her heart to him?

She certainly hadn't shown any great excitement at the thought of racing to the altar with him.

But here he was, racing back to Sydney to stop Nina French from getting entangled with Talbot Spencer—why?

Because he had a guilt complex? No doubt about it.

Because he needed to exorcise himself of the demons that his father as well as Nina had left him with so he could go back to Mia without any baggage.

But how to do that? If she really meant it was over?

CHAPTER EIGHT

FOUR MONTHS LATER Mia sat at her desk on her last day at Bellbird.

She'd held her last function the day before and a van now stood outside the house, ready to remove all the equipment she'd hired on a year to year basis, tables, chairs, trolleys and linen. Another truck had removed the commercial kitchen equipment and all the crockery and cutlery.

Her office was unusually tidy. All her paperwork was filed and boxed, all her notes on the wall had gone.

All that was left, in fact, was her phone, a pen and a pad.

It had been a successful four months in that she'd managed to fulfil all her obligations. She had quite an extensive file of references for her next venture but, as it turned out, the glowing terms for her entertaining skills in those references were not going to be much help to her at all as things stood at the moment.

She'd neither seen nor heard from Carlos. All her dealings had been with his secretary, Carol Manning, and no more functions had been booked for O'Connor Construction.

She'd held her breath and felt like fainting for a moment when she'd been idly scanning a newspaper and seen an article entitled: O'Connor Wedding Goes Without Hitch Despite Weather.

Carlos and Nina, a voice of doom had said in her head. But when she'd opened her eyes and forced herself to read, it wasn't Carlos O'Connor who'd got married—it was his mother!

She'd read on, astounded. 'Arancha O'Connor, widow of construction billionaire Frank O'Connor, had remarried in an elegant ceremony despite highly inclement weather, with her son Carlos and her daughter Juanita by her side. Her new husband,' the article continued, 'was a chef, and he had made the wedding cake.'

Mia had choked on nothing to the extent that Gail heard her coughing and came and banged her on the back, then brought her a glass of water.

'What?'

'I don't believe it!'

'Don't believe what?' Gail asked.

'His mother has married a chef!'

'Always handy to have a chef in the house,' Gail had commented. 'Whose mother?'

Mia took a mouthful of water. 'Carlos.'

'Oh, him.' Gail had shrugged. Carlos had never regained his stellar status in her estimation. 'I remember her. Small, dark, big hat. Almost regal.' She'd looked at Mia curiously. 'Is there anything wrong with marrying a chef, though?'

'Yes. No, of course not, not in the normal course of events, but—' Mia had stopped, breathing heavily.

'That explains that. Yes and no. Clear as mud.'

Mia had to laugh. 'She…she could be quite snooty.'

Now, a few weeks after Arancha's wedding and the day before Mia left, not even Gail was with her.

She'd moved down to Sydney and taken up a position in a top hotel restaurant.

Bill and Lucy were staying on as caretakers and keepers of the garden; Bill was looking forward to having his autonomy handed back to him.

Not even Long John was with her; she'd given him to Harry Castle, the only person apart from her and Gail the horse didn't bite.

Now don't get maudlin, she warned herself as the last of the trucks drove off and she had the place more or less to herself. *What I'll do is—play ladies.*

She stood up and looked down at herself. She was wearing a long, full floral skirt with a white broderie anglaise blouse. Her hair was tied back in one thick, heavy bunch at the back. She even had a wide-brimmed lacy straw hat which a guest she hadn't been able to trace had left behind.

She also had a Royal Albert tea service, patterned with roses, one of Bellbird's heirlooms; she did have tea and a lemon on the tree beside the back door and she did have a kettle.

Ten minutes later, she'd pulled a wicker chair onto the front veranda, she had a small round wicker table beside her and a cup of lemon tea on it as she watched the late afternoon sun cast its lengthening shadows over the summer gardens of Bellbird and Mount Wilson. Her hat lay on a second chair.

She sipped her tea then put her cup down. Breathe this in, she told herself. *May some dim deep memory of the lovely peace of Bellbird always be with me.* She closed her eyes. *May the association it will always hold with Carlos bear no bitter memories for me.*

A car drove up.

She had to be dreaming, but didn't she know the sound of that engine off by heart? Didn't he *always* manage to kick up the gravel when he stopped?

She opened her eyes and it was Carlos.

Her hands flew to her mouth. 'It is you!' she whispered. 'I thought I must be dreaming.'

He propped a foot against the bottom step and leant against the rail. He wore cargo pants and a navy shirt. His dark hair was wind-blown; he must have had the car roof down at some stage. And, just at the sight of him, her heart started to beat heavily and her pulse raced. And for a moment she could smell the sea air, hear the surf and see in her mind's eye the wrinkled ocean below the lighthouse on Cape Byron....

He said, 'I couldn't let you go without making sure you were OK.'

He stopped and took in the lovely china on the wicker table beside her, the hat, and he half-smiled. 'Playing ladies?'

She grimaced. 'Being silly really, but yes.'

'Where are you going, Mia?'

'I...' She took a breath. 'To my parents for a while.'

'I thought they were driving around Australia.'

'They are. So their house is empty. I can stay as long as I like. But it'll only be until…' she plaited her fingers '…I get organised again.'

He watched her twining fingers as a faint frown grew in his eyes.

'So nothing definite in the pipeline at the moment?'

'Uh…one or two. These things take time to set up, though, Carlos.' She tried to look casual and unfazed as she said it but the truth of the matter was she had absolutely nothing in the pipeline.

Hard as she'd tried to get motivated and to move her life and her career forward, she hadn't succeeded—not something she was prepared to admit, however.

'By the way, I read about your mother!' she said in a bid to change the subject completely.

'She surprised the life out of us but they seem to be blissfully happy, even if he is only a chef, although—' he looked amused '—she insists he's a "celebrity" chef.' He rubbed his jaw ruefully. 'And she's like a different person. Much more contented.'

'I was going to say good,' Mia murmured with a tiny smile, 'but on second thoughts I won't say a word. Uh—how's Juanita?'

'She's fine. She's pregnant. Another cause for contentment in our mutual parent.'

Mia smiled. 'That's great news.'

'How are you getting to your parents' place?'

'I bought myself a four-wheel-drive station-wagon. I can fit all my stuff into it. I haven't got that much.'

He raised an eyebrow. 'Not Long John, though. Will you send him by horse transport?' He grinned suddenly. 'That should be jolly. Does he bite other horses as well as people?'

She dimpled and told him about Harry Castle.

'That's better,' he said.

Mia looked enquiringly at him. 'What?'

'I haven't seen those dimples for a while.'

'They…must come and go. Oh, by the way, I've left an inventory of all the china and stuff. You probably should go through it with me now.'

'No. It doesn't matter.'

'But there's some beautiful stuff.'

'Help yourself if you want any of it. And so can Bill and Lucy, for that matter, Gail's mother too.'

'That's nice but don't you…you don't care about it, do you?' she hazarded with a look of something like pain in her eyes at the thought of Bellbird being summarily stripped of its treasures, even if they were going to people she knew. Not that they were worth a fortune or anything like that, but they were old and they were lovely.

Carlos straightened and folded his arms. 'Mia, you didn't want Bellbird. You couldn't have made that plainer. So it's going on the market again. As soon as you leave.'

It was like an arrow going through her heart. She gasped and went white.

He swore under his breath. 'What did you think I'd do with it? What do you think I ought to do with it?' he asked harshly.

'You told me it was nice enough for that to be sufficient reason to buy it.'

'Not if you're not going to live on it.'

'Carlos, I thought it would be safe with you,' she said passionately. 'Safe from people who'd tear the house down and put up something modern. Safe from developers and sub-division. You never know when that can happen.'

'It's not going to happen up here in the foreseeable future, Mia.'

She subsided but started plaiting her fingers again.

'You're not having second thoughts, are you?'

She swallowed and turned her head away.

'Mia, look at me,' he commanded softly. 'Are you?'

'No.' She said it barely audibly but quite definitely.

'Then what are you so upset about? Just leaving here?'

'I...I was doing fine until you turned up. Indulging in a little gentle melancholy, perhaps—' she grimaced '—but mostly under control. Tell me about *you*.'

He came up the steps, lifted her hat off the chair and sat down, putting the hat on the floor beside him. 'Nina married Talbot.'

Mia moved convulsively. 'Why?' she whispered. 'Why did you let her? Why was there no publicity?'

'You'd have to ask her why,' he said dryly. 'As for letting her, how could I stop her? And, lastly, they tied the knot overseas; in fact, they've moved overseas.'

Mia stared at him. 'But she looked so devastated. That night at Byron.'

'Nina's good at that.'

'But she looked so...I can't put my finger on why,

but she looked so nice, I mean, as if she's a thoroughly nice person!'

'She is, most of the time. But buried under that is a too-beautiful-for-her-own-good girl who's been spoilt rotten.' He shrugged. 'You never know, Talbot may just be the one to cope with her. She may even be the one to bring out the best in him. Strangely, I saw them at the airport recently. They looked—' he gestured '—happy.'

'Are you sick at heart?' Mia asked. 'Surely you can tell me.'

He picked up her hat and twirled it around. 'To be honest, I'm relieved. I know I wasn't at first, but Talbot always brought out the worst in me.' He thought for a moment. 'I don't know if she was on the rebound, I probably will never know, but one thing I do know, *I* couldn't have made it work for us. If I hadn't known that intrinsically I wouldn't have held out against marrying her for so long.'

Not quite the same as saying he didn't love her, nor did it mean he didn't still love her, Mia thought, and wondered what would be worse—to know Nina was unhappy with Talbot, or happy?'

She got up and walked to the edge of the veranda. The hydrangeas that rimmed the veranda and had looked so good in the Wedgwood soup tureen were dying off now. In general, the gardens were on their last summer legs, as Bill put it.

She looked out and shaded her eyes against the sun and she could suddenly visualise the gardens being allowed to run wild, the property being sub-divided, the house being altered or simply neglected and she thought she couldn't bear it…

'Would you…w-would you…' her voice shook '…would you consider going into a business partnership with me, Carlos?'

She heard the startled hiss of his breath and steeled herself for rejection, scorn, anger or all three.

'What do you mean?' he said harshly.

She turned round slowly and swallowed twice as she tried to marshal her thoughts. 'I made a small success of the business I ran here, I guess you could say, but it was always a bit of a battle. I only managed to start it with a bank loan and I was always having to plough most of the profits into loan repayments and lease payments. But with a partner, especially one who owned the place, I could really—' she twisted her hands '—go onto bigger and better things.'

'Like what?'

'Like upgrading the furniture and fittings. They're starting to get shabby. Like live music, such as a classical quartet for functions, or live jazz or live modern, but really good stuff. Like children's birthday parties.' She paused.

He frowned.

'I mean special parties with a marquee, a carousel, castles, fairies or, for boys, cowboy themes and pony rides. We could set it up in the west paddock. I have a theory that real class attracts real money and I think I could make the Bellbird Estate more than pay its way for you by going really upmarket, but with imagination and…well…' she looked a bit embarrassed '…flair.'

All she could hear in the silence that followed were the bellbirds calling.

'Another thought I had was a honeymoon suite. There's a marvellous view from the east paddock. You could build a luxury cottage for the bride and groom to spend their first night in, with open fireplaces and gourmet meals. Is—' her eyes were wary '—there any point in me going on?'

'All right,' he said at last. 'If that's how you want it, so be it. I'll get the paperwork drawn up.' He stood up and handed her the hat. 'You can unpack, Miss Gardiner.'

Mia stared up at him with her heart in her mouth because something was radically different about him. It was as if a shutter had come down and she couldn't read him anymore except to see how cold his eyes were now.

'Carlos,' she said involuntarily, then stopped and bit her lip.

'Mia?' He raised an eyebrow. 'You were saying?'

'I…no, nothing,' she stammered.

'Nothing,' he repeated. He lifted a hand and touched his knuckles to the point of her chin. 'Nothing's changed, I guess. I'll be in touch. Or Carol will.' And he moved past her, jogged down the steps and, minutes later, his car roared away.

'What have I done?' Mia asked aloud. 'Oh, what have I done?'

CHAPTER NINE

Six months later Mia and Gail were engaged in a conference about an upcoming function—a christening.

Mia had not so much pinched Gail from her upmarket job, she'd welcomed her back with open arms. Gail had been miserable down in Sydney.

The first thing Mia had done, after gathering herself together following her encounter with Carlos on the day before she'd been supposed to leave, had been to advertise and send out flyers to previous customers to the effect that the Bellbird Estate was reopening shortly after some renovations and with some new attractions.

For the next couple of months her life had been spent on the redecorating trail and consulting with architects, designers and builders.

The house had been finished first and it was gratifying to find she was almost booked up for the first month.

Then the honeymoon suite had been completed and their first couple to spend the first night of their marriage in it were so impressed they'd wanted to stay on.

The children's party arena and marquee wasn't quite

finished but was on its way. They'd called it Noah's Ark and, as well as a wooden ark you could fit thirty kids into, there were all sorts of wooden and plush animals, teddies, rocking horses, wombats and koala bears and Mia's favourites, white unicorns, all two by two.

But through it all she hadn't laid eyes on Carlos.

He'd been as good as his word; he'd been, despite keeping an eye on all her ideas, good to work with, except she hadn't worked with him at all. It had been done entirely at second hand through his secretary, Carol, and a variety of construction staff.

Mia had wondered if she'd be expected to cater for any O'Connor Construction functions but she had not.

Now, though, she was about to be thrown in at the deep end, as she thought of it. She'd been asked to put on the christening party for Juanita's baby.

'Make that babies,' she said faintly to Gail when she put the phone down on Carlos's half-sister. 'She's had twins!'

Gail started to laugh. 'It's all right; I don't suppose they'll have to have twin parties. But tell me what she wants.'

'Well, the actual baptism is to take place in the local church. Then she wants a light luncheon here in the house or garden, depending on the weather. And then, because there'll be quite a few kids, she wants them to go down to Noah's Ark.'

'You've been wanting to give Noah a test run. Now's your chance. How long have we got to prepare for this bash?'

'A month. We don't have to worry about a christening cake—the twins' step-grandfather will make it.'

Gail grinned mischievously. 'I told you it was handy to have a chef in the family.'

'So you did.' Mia rotated her pencil between her fingers and fell silent.

'How about their uncle?' Gail asked after a time.

Mia looked up with her eyebrows raised.

'Carlos?' Gail elucidated somewhat sardonically. 'The guy you got yourself all tied up in knots about, remember?'

'I didn't,' Mia said mechanically.

Gail simply stared at her.

'Oh, all right!' Mia closed her eyes in patent irritation. 'There's no "how about it" at all. I haven't seen or heard from him for months. For all I know, he could have married a…an Eskimo.'

'Now that I very much doubt,' Gail pronounced and stood up. 'He's too tall for an igloo. But it could be best to shore up your defences well and truly.'

Mia stared up at her with her heart suddenly in her eyes. 'How do you do that?' she asked out of a dry throat. 'How do you do that?'

'Tell yourself that, whatever he might like to think, you had good reasons for what *you* did.'

'But…but if you're not sure you did?'

'Mia—' Gail planted her fists on the desk and leant on them '—you've got to go with your gut feeling. And if it tells you things are not right, they're not.' Gail straightened.

'How come you're so wise?' Mia asked with just the glint of a tear in her eye.

Gail shrugged. 'My mum says it's easy to be right about other people's problems. And now I'll leave you to design this christening.'

The weather forecast for the day of the christening was not that good—wet and windy.

Mia grumbled under her breath as she read the details the day before but made the usual decision not to take any chances with sodden food, sodden effects or sodden guests.

She'd already partially decorated the dining room to be on the safe side and decided she needed to finish it off.

Rather than going for pastel pinks and blues, she'd used stronger colours and silver ribbons in bunches. For the rest of it she'd relied on magnificent bunches of flowers.

But some of the ribbons were coming undone and she fetched the ladder and climbed up to retie them.

It was a labour intensive job, getting up and down the ladder and moving it around the room as well as stretching her neck. Which might have been why she came to grief opposite the doorway to the hall.

She must not have had the ladder properly balanced because, as she started to climb down, it wobbled, she lost her footing and, with a startled cry, began to fall.

At first she didn't recognise the pair of arms that caught her. It flashed through her mind that it must be Bill, for once in his life, where she was concerned, anyway, in the right place at the right time.

Then recognition seeped through her pores—Carlos.

'Mia,' he growled, 'you could have broken your back or your head—couldn't you be more careful?'

'Carlos—' she said faintly; he still had her in his arms '—that's funny, isn't it?'

'What's funny?'

'I haven't seen you for months but, once again, it's in an injury situation. Well, no.' She slipped out of his arms. 'I'm fine! Thanks to you. But what are you doing here? The christening isn't until tomorrow,' she said foolishly.

He cast her a frowning look. 'I know that. I came to see you.'

It was her turn to frown. 'Does that mean you're driving back to Sydney, then up again tomorrow?'

He shook his head. 'I'm staying here.'

Mia's mouth fell open.

'Oh, not in your loft,' he drawled, 'but, according to what Gail told Carol, not that Gail knew why Carol was asking, the honeymoon suite is vacant tonight so I thought I'd give it a try. I also thought it was time to have a guided tour of all the changes and improvements.'

'By all means,' Mia heard herself say. 'I was wondering when you would want to see what you'd paid for.'

They stood back and studied each other.

Mia's heart was still beating rapidly beneath the pink blouse she wore with jeans, her cheeks were flushed and her hair was coming loose.

She thought he was taller than she remembered, then realised it was because she was barefoot. She put her hands to her cheeks, then looked around for her shoes.

'I'm sorry I'm so disorganised,' she gabbled, finding herself in complete disarray. 'Actually, I'm not really disorganised. I'm just…' She stopped helplessly and put a hand to her throat. 'Why did you want to see me?'

'We don't need to talk here, do we?' he countered.

Mia licked her lips. 'Where would you like to go?'

'Show me Noah's Ark first.'

'It was only finished a week or so ago,' Mia said as he looked around. 'So I'm really looking forward to giving it a trial run.' She grimaced. 'That doesn't mean to say I'm experimenting with Juanita's guests; it's all safe and sound—I just hope the kids will like it.'

Carlos picked up a wooden giraffe and a smile twisted his lips. 'They will.'

'There are things for older children to do.'

'You've done well, Miss Gardiner.'

She looked up at him. 'Is something wrong?' she asked because he seemed like a stranger to her, because she seemed to be fluttering like a trapped butterfly around him, but there was no light in him, just a very different Carlos O'Connor.

'You could say so.'

'What?' Her eyes were wide and dark and supremely anxious. 'What is it?' She put a trembling hand on his sleeve. 'Tell me.'

He covered her hand with his briefly. 'Just tired, I guess. I only got home from a European trip this morning. OK, now for the much-vaunted honeymoon suite. Lead on.'

Mia hesitated, not entirely convinced he was being honest. 'All right. I'll have to get the keys from the main house, then we can drive your car down.'

Fortunately, Gail had gone into Katoomba on an errand, so as Mia collected the keys she didn't have to attempt any explanations. She did collect a small basket of dairy products, fresh rolls and fruit to take down to the honeymoon suite.

'So,' she said a few minutes later, 'this is it.'

Carlos looked around at the spacious, uncluttered sheer elegance and luxury of the suite, at the stone fireplace and the lovely art on the walls.

Mia moved over to the windows and swept back the curtains and had to smile because the magnificent view down Mount Wilson in the late afternoon sunlight always had that effect on her.

She turned to Carlos. 'It doesn't look like it at the moment, but there's rain predicted for tomorrow. Uh… you'll probably want to have a rest. If you want a snack I brought some fresh rolls, some cheese and other stuff but—' she moved into the galley-style kitchen and opened an iridium fridge '—there should be a gourmet pack here. Yes. Some smoked salmon, anchovies, olives. Uh…beer, wine and champagne as well as spirits.'

She opened another cupboard and revealed a coffee-maker. 'And there's tea and coffee, and here—' She stopped because he walked up to her and took her hand.

'You don't have to sell the place to me, Mia,' he said quietly.

'You did pay for it. And I haven't shown you the bedroom.'

He shrugged. 'Sit down. Glasses?'

Mia hesitated, then pointed to a cupboard.

'Champagne OK with you?' He raised an eyebrow at her.

'Well, one probably won't hurt,' she temporised, then, at the look of irony in his eyes, put her hands to her cheeks as she felt herself blush and, in disarray again, sat down on a stool at the breakfast bar after nearly knocking it over.

He said nothing as he removed the foil from the champagne cork and unwound the wire. It popped discreetly and he poured the bubbly golden liquid into two cut-glass flutes.

'Cheers.' He slid a glass towards her and sat down diagonally opposite her on another stool.

'Cheers!' Mia raised her glass, then took an urgent sip. 'Oh.' She started to slide off the stool. 'I can put together a snack, won't take a moment.'

'Mia, no.'

She stilled.

'Tell me something,' he went on. 'Are you happy?'

She stared at him. 'I…I'm doing fine.'

'Not quite the same thing,' he observed, then gestured, 'except that in your case it might be.'

'What do you mean?'

He looked down at his glass. 'Six months ago I came up here to ask you again to marry me.'

Her lips parted and her eyes were stunned.

'I was going to tell you about Nina—I did, but only part of it,' he went on. 'I was going to suggest we put all the past behind us, not only her but West Windward. I was going to remind you of Byron Bay if you still had reservations.' He stopped and studied her and she shivered for some reason

'Only to discover,' he went on, 'that the one thing that really affected you was the concept of Bellbird being sold. That shocked you to tears and spurred you into making a partnership offer, that's all. That's, incidentally, what made me wonder if "doing fine" in a career and business sense is all that matters to you.'

Mia made a small sound in her throat—a sound of protest.

'Or is it that you still can't forgive me for West Windward, Mia? And my mother? Is that why you could be the way you were at Byron but then all you had to offer me was a business proposition?'

She licked her lips. 'Carlos, did you think all *you* had to do was tell me about Nina and Talbot and I'd fall into your arms? Is that what you're trying to say? I hadn't seen or heard a word from you for *four* months.'

He rubbed his jaw. 'No,' he said at last. 'But I couldn't find the words to tell you that I did try to stop her going off with Talbot. I did try to explain to her what had happened with my father—she was justifiably horrified. She asked me—' he paused, looking tortured '—what I was going to do to wreck *your* life. I don't know if she had any inkling that I'd already damaged it or if it was simply a shot in the dark, but it had a powerful effect on me.'

Mia stared at him, transfixed. 'What do you mean?'

'It made me think maybe my best bet was to avoid you. It made me doubt my judgement, even my sanity. She may never realise it, she may never have intended it as such, but she completely destabilised me with that one little question.'

'So you stayed away?'

'I stayed away—it was also what you wanted,' he reminded her. 'But the day before you were due to leave I knew I couldn't live with myself if I didn't see how you were. But that,' he said with palpable irony, 'led me down the rocky road to hell.'

Mia blinked. 'I was upset to think of Bellbird being sold,' she whispered, 'but I still believed it wasn't over between you and Nina. I couldn't decide what would be worse for you, to see her happy with Talbot or unhappy.'

'No,' he said, 'it is over, it is done with. I'm happy to see her happy, at last.'

Mia closed her eyes. And a surge of something she'd never known before ran through her, a powerful urge to clear her soul of all its secrets.

Her lashes flew up. 'There's one thing you don't understand about me, Carlos. Yes, I may be single-minded in a business sense. Yes, it means a lot to me to succeed because the more I do the fainter the memory of being branded the housekeeper's daughter grows. But it doesn't stop there.'

'What about Byron?' he asked tautly.

'Byron was lovely,' she said with the first sign of

tears in her eyes. 'But you got the shock of your life that night. So did Nina.' She drained her glass. 'I can't forget it.'

He made an involuntary movement towards her, then stilled and poured more champagne.

'Thanks,' she said huskily. 'I told you once I wasn't going to be used to break Nina's heart. Well, I'll never know about that but—' she stopped and drew a deep breath, then trembled as the shutters of her mind fell away and for the first time she really understood her own secrets '—you mean far too much to me to s-see you—' her voice broke '—tied to someone you don't love deeply.'

'Mia,' he said roughly.

But she held up her hand. 'The other thing is—' She stopped and sighed and soldiered on. 'The other thing is…I have an enormous inferiority complex.' Her eyes were wet and dark. 'I didn't really understand it myself, but Juanita is so sure of herself, for example. And Nina, that night. She was so poised—until you told her we were getting married. Poised and classy. It's not how I see myself, not around you. It's something that holds me back without me realising it.'

She rubbed her face. 'So you see, Nina is not the only one with complexes.'

He stared at her incredulously. 'Say that again?'

'No, Carlos—' she sniffed '—you heard.'

'I may have but it's hard to believe.'

'It shouldn't be, you—'

'I caused it?' he broke in.

'It might just be the way I'm made,' she said miserably.

He studied her for a long moment, her wet spiky lashes, that luscious mouth, her wayward hair, the lovely trim figure, and knew he had to pull out all the stops because he'd made all sorts of mistakes with this woman and it was killing him. Killing him to think Bellbird meant more to her than he did.... But how to right those mistakes? If only he could get her to laugh with him. Maybe the simple truth? It had all the makings of comedy. Well, a farce anyway...

'These have been the hardest six months of my life,' he said.

She looked at him with a faint frown.

'I've fulfilled one of my father's dreams, to have construction sites on the four corners of a major city intersection, to have O'Connor Construction billboards plastered on all four corners.'

'Oh. Congratulations.' But she looked at him uncertainly, not sure what his tone meant or where this was leading.

'Thanks.' He shrugged. 'It didn't help.'

'What do you mean?'

'It didn't help me to view him more affectionately. If anything I was more annoyed than ever. And it's a nightmare scenario, traffic-wise. Then there's my mother.'

Mia's frown grew.

'Yep.' He moved his glass. 'I've always taken her with a grain of salt.' He grimaced. 'What I mean to say is, I've recognised what motivates her, family loyalty above all, and I've dealt with the consequences without too much angst. Except in your case and then it was too late.' He studied his glass and pushed it away, as if it was annoying him too. 'But lately she and her "celebrity" chef husband have been irritating the life out of me. Turns out he's as much of a raving snob as she is, hard as that is to imagine.'

Mia blinked. 'A chef?'

A crooked grin twisted his lips. 'You're as bad as she is, as he is. Yes. He cannot remain silent on any topic relating to food and beverage. He's positively painful on the subject of what wines go with this, that and the other. On what is the correct way to cook this, that and the other, on the best restaurants, not—' he shook his forefinger '—only in Australia but the whole world.'

'Oh, dear.'

He eyed her keenly. 'As you say. Then there's Juanita. As a single half-sister she always had quite a bracing personality but she could be a lot of fun. As a married matron and mother of twins she's insufferably smug, another snob and—' He broke off and gestured. 'I don't know how Damien puts up with her.'

Mia put her hands on the island bench. 'Carlos—'

But he waved her to silence. 'Hang on. Then there's the construction industry in general. Now, I may have had issues with my father but I'm actually a passionate engineer and builder—or I was.' He looked supremely sombre.

'Not anymore?' Mia hazarded.

'I couldn't give a damn if I never built another thing.'

'Carlos—' she paused '—I'm not a hundred per cent sure you're serious.'

'I am, and there's more. I've lived like a monk ever since Byron Bay because I haven't been able to have you, Mia.'

Mia took an unexpected breath.

He waited a moment, then he slid his hand across the island bench and touched her fingers with his.

For a moment she was frozen, hardly even breathing, her eyes huge.

'Really?' she said at last.

He nodded.

'You…you tried?'

He nodded again. 'A couple of times. With disastrous consequences. How about you?'

'Oh, I didn't want to so I didn't even think of trying,' she assured him, then she broke off and bit her lip.

The pressure of his fingers increased on hers. 'Do you think that means…anything?'

'Carlos…' She took a breath.

'Mia, I can't live without you,' he said. 'It's killing me. All the mistakes I made are killing me. As for your complexes—' he closed his eyes briefly '—please throw them away because they mean nothing to me. And please take me on—you can redecorate me, renegotiate me but if you don't restore me I'm in serious trouble. And that's the plain, unvarnished truth.'

Her lips trembled and, hard as she tried, she couldn't stop herself from starting to smile.

Carlos got up cautiously and came round the island

bench. He stopped in front of Mia and tilted her chin up gently. And there was a question in his eyes.

'Oh, look,' Mia whispered. 'I'm not sure why, but I think I've always loved you, Carlos, and I always will.'

'Is there anything wrong with that?' he queried.

'No. Not anymore. I don't seem to have any fight left in me,' she conceded. 'I've missed you so much.'

He pulled her into his arms. 'Same here. More than you could ever know. Mia—will you marry me?'

'Yes. Yes, I will,' she said and found she couldn't stop smiling.

'They're back, your dimples,' he said unsteadily.

'That can only be because you're back,' she told him.

'Thanks for that.' And he started to kiss her.

Quite some time later they stirred in each other's arms. They'd moved from the island bench to a settee in the lounge area, one that overlooked the view—a view that was dominated by some magnificent purple thunderheads.

'I told you rain was forecast,' she said as she nuzzled into his shoulder.

He stroked her hair. 'Juanita will be upset—upset that she can't control the weather.'

Mia gave a spurt of laughter although she said, 'Now that's unkind. She's not that bossy. Is she?'

He shrugged and traced the line of her jaw with his finger. 'She has actually run into one spot of bother with Damien. Over naming the twins.'

'Oh, tell me about it, and about them! All I know is that it's a boy and a girl.'

His fingers traced a path down her neck to the little hollows at the base of her throat. 'True. And Juanita wants to name them Charlotte and Henry—if that isn't aspiring to the aristocracy I don't know what is. But Damien wants to call them Barbara and Banjo. His grandmother who he's very fond of is a Barbara—I don't know where he got Banjo from—apart from Banjo Paterson. Up until I last saw them yesterday, the issue was still to be decided.'

Mia had to laugh. 'They're leaving it a bit late.'

'Mmm,' he said, sounding preoccupied and his fingers slid down to the top button of her blouse. 'I'm a godfather, by the way. You'll probably have to help me out a bit there.'

But Mia had other things on her mind as he flicked open the button, and then the next and the next and slipped his hands around her back and released her bra.

She took several ragged breaths but didn't protest as he drew her blouse off and then helped her out of her bra.

Nor did she protest when he said, 'What we need is a bed.'

'This might be a good place to remedy that.' Her dimples appeared. 'You ain't seen nothing yet, Mr O'Connor,' she teased. 'Not until you see the bedroom.'

'OK, lead on.' He picked her up.

What he said next was somewhat different.

'Holy…mackerel!' He looked around the honeymoon suite bedroom, a symphony of white and green with a huge bed piled with cushions, an exquisite original painting of flowers taking up almost all of one wall, deep pile carpet, a padded velvet headboard and a beautiful crystal chandelier.

Mia laughed softly. 'Think I might have gone overboard?'

'Not at all.' He put her down on the bed and together they tossed aside all the silken cushions, then they shed their clothes and Mia could not doubt his desperate hunger for her, nor hers for him.

And when they crashed back to earth, he held her and helped her down from the heights in such a way that caused her to say with real gratitude, 'You make me feel as if I've come home.'

He cradled her to him. 'You make me feel the same. When will you marry me?'

'Whenever we can.'

He rubbed his jaw. 'I've got this damn christening tomorrow. I don't suppose I can get out of that.'

'Oh, no, you shouldn't! Anyway, we couldn't do it tomorrow, could we?'

He leant up on his elbow. 'No. I don't know how long it takes.' He tidied some damp wayward strands of her hair and pulled a silk coverlet over them. 'Will you come to the christening with me?'

'Carlos, I'll be working at it,' she reminded him.

'No,' he replied firmly. 'Get Gail and her mother and anyone else you can raise—Bill and Lucy—you've done it before. I need you with me, otherwise my family might prompt me into…being rude or unkind to them.'

Mia giggled but she soon sobered. 'Your mother will

be livid. Perhaps an occasion like a christening isn't the right time to break the news to her.'

'My mother is not nearly as interfering as she was, Mia, but, whatever, there's no point in hiding it.'

Mia thought for a moment, then, 'No. Anyway, I think we have to break the news to Gail. She'll be wondering where on earth I've got to.'

He stretched and looked disinclined to move.

'She could even come looking for me,' Mia said gravely, 'and we didn't lock the door.'

Carlos swore beneath his breath, then rolled over and enveloped her in a bear hug. 'All right. I get the message. I don't suppose we could shower together?'

'Ah.' Mia looked mischievous. 'We sure can. Come and have a look. This is the bathroom to beat all bathrooms.'

'There you are, Mia!' Gail said as Mia walked into her office to find Gail behind the desk fielding the phone. 'I've been looking for you. There's—oh, no,' she added as Carlos walked in behind Mia. 'Not you again.'

Carlos looked briefly startled, then amused. 'Sorry, Gail. I didn't realise I was on your blacklist. Why am I?'

Mia cleared her throat and started to speak but Gail overrode her. 'Why are you? You come and you go, Mr O'Connor, and every time you go I'm left to pick up the pieces.'

'*Gail*!' Mia protested.

Gail swung towards her. 'It's true. You've been devastated every time it's happened and—'

'Gail—' it was Carlos who intervened and he took

Mia's hand '—there won't be any more of that. Mia's
agreed to marry me, we're very much in love and we've
smoothed out all our problems. But I'd just like to say
I can't thank you enough for being such a good friend
to Mia.'

Gail stood stock-still then she ran round the desk to
embrace Mia and then Carlos

'Oh, I'm so happy,' she cried tearfully. 'I don't know
if I'm coming or going. When? When's the wedding?
Are you having it up here? You could leave it all to
me, you know.'

Mia was also mopping up some tears as she said,
'We haven't made any plans yet but, Gail, you'll have
to handle the christening tomorrow because I'm going
as a guest.'

'With pleasure.' Gail struck a nonchalant pose. 'I
could do it in my sleep.'

Mia and Carlos were still chuckling as they walked into
the garden as the sun set but he stopped suddenly and
put his arms around her.

'I feel terrible,' he said, looking down at her.

'Why?'

'For leaving you devastated up here. I'm not sure
why you've forgiven me.'

She slipped her arms around his neck. 'What Gail
doesn't realise is that I sent you away.' She stood on
her toes and kissed him.

'Even if it devastated you?'

She nodded and laid her head on his shoulder. 'What
about you?'

'Angry, incredulous, bloody-minded probably says it well, every time I drove down this blasted mountain. Sick to think it meant more to you than I did, this place. All in all, a mess.'

'Well—' Mia stirred '—since it seems we've both been to hell and back, let's go to heaven.'

He lifted his head, his grey eyes amused. 'I hope you don't mean that literally?'

'Depends! Let's go back to the honeymoon suite—'

'You're not worried about putting the cart before the horse?' he broke in gravely.

'Not in the least. I was thinking of cooking you dinner, you see—an inch-thick steak, chips that are crisp on the outside and fluffy inside—oh, some English mustard hot enough to make your eyes water, some salad, but only iceberg lettuce, of course, maybe some mushrooms. I just have to collect the ingredients from the house.'

'Now that,' he drawled, 'is an offer I can't refuse.'

'Good.' She dimpled. 'Then we can worry about putting the cart before the horse.'

He grinned down at her. 'I can see you're going to be a right handful, Miss Gardiner.'

'It's my aim,' she said pertly.

CHAPTER TEN

THE DAY JUANITA'S twins were christened was a day to remember. It was cool and showery, as predicted.

Mia drove to her cottage and collected her clothes.

As she was about to climb back into the car, Bill intercepted her with a particularly Bill James-like salutation. He was driving the property utility, laden with bags of fertiliser, and he drew up beside her and leant out of his window.

'Hi, Mia! Heard the news, by the way—you'll be much happier as a married woman, believe me.'

Mia drew a deep breath and cautioned herself not to lose her temper. 'Thank you, Bill. I...I will try to be.'

'And you give Carlos my best wishes. I guess he must know what he's getting into, although not many of us guys do!' And, laughing cheerfully, he drove on.

Mia contemplated kicking something but refrained.

She must have still been wearing the remnants of a militant expression when she arrived back at the honeymoon suite, however, because Carlos immediately said to her, 'What's wrong?'

'Nothing.' She put down her clothes. 'How do you know anything's wrong, anyway?

'You look—' he meditated '—as if you'd like to kick the cat.'

Mia grimaced, then had to laugh ruefully and she told him about Bill.

'Of course I wouldn't dare to agree with him,' he replied with utter false gravity.

Mia clicked her tongue. 'You men are all the same.' She paused and fiddled with her cosmetic purse before putting it down beside her clothes and starting to plait her fingers.

'Carlos, I'm nervous. I'm really nervous. I don't think I can do this.'

'Mia—' he linked his arms around her waist '—yes, you can. Anyway, they all know now.'

She put her hands on his chest, her eyes wide. 'Your mother? Did she have a fit?'

'No. She told me it was about time I settled down. Juanita said the same. Mind you—' he frowned faintly '—I got the feeling something else was going on. They both seemed preoccupied, if not to say tense, and that was before I broke our news.'

Mia relaxed a bit. 'I hope so. I mean…all I mean is I'd rather not be the headline news.'

He bent his head and kissed her. 'You were my headline news last night. You have a unique way of putting the cart before the horse.'

A tingle ran through Mia at the memory of their night. 'It was lovely, wasn't it?' she said softly.

This time he hugged her, then, with an obvious effort, put her away from him. 'Maybe we should get dressed,' he suggested. 'We have been known to—' there was a wicked little glint in his grey eyes '—get carried away when we should be on our way out.'

Mia laughed and stood on her toes and kissed him. 'I remember. I'm going.'

He groaned but didn't try to stop her.

Mia changed into a figure-hugging yellow dress and a smoky grey-blue jacket belted at the waist. She'd decided not to wear any kind of hat for this christening and saw no reason to change her mind now she was a guest so she left her hair wild and riotous, just as he liked it.

But she drew an unexpected breath at the sight of Carlos in a pinstriped charcoal suit, pale green shirt and darker green tie.

'You look seriously handsome,' she told him.

He came to stand right in front of her. 'Good enough to be a godfather?'

'Oh, definitely!'

'Well, you look gorgeous, Mia, darling.' He took her hand. 'Ready?'

She hesitated, then nodded. 'Ready,' she said quietly.

It stopped raining as the baptism proceeded.

There was even some sunlight bringing rays of colour into the church through the stained glass windows, violet and topaz, jade and ruby.

Arancha was arrayed in ivory shantung: an exqui-sitely tailored suit and a poppy-pink hat. She had ac-knowledged Mia with an almost non-existent kiss on the cheek but she'd said, 'Let's be friends, Mia, let's be friends.'

And Mia, who had searched her heart and known she could never altogether forgive Arancha, had con-trived to reply warmly, for Carlos's sake, 'Yes, let's.'

She'd then been introduced to Arancha's celebrity chef, who'd told her he could probably give her some pretty good tips on cuisine and all sorts of things to do with the catering business.

Mia had felt Carlos tense beside her so she'd smiled brilliantly and replied that she'd love to hear them.

Juanita wore violet linen and Damien wore a dark suit. They both looked a little shell-shocked for some reason and each carried a sleeping baby garbed in a sumptuous lacy gown.

It wasn't until the naming of the babies came about that most of the mysteries of the morning were ex-plained. The girl was baptised Alegria Arancha and the boy Benito Francis.

'Good Spanish names,' Arancha said quite audibly, 'and why not include the mother's mother?'

Mia heard Carlos suck in a breath but it wasn't until the baptism was over and they were in the car head-ing back to Bellbird that they were able to give way to their mirth.

'For crying out loud,' Carlos said. 'She must have

bulldozed away at both of them to get them to change their minds.'

'I thought you told me she didn't interfere anymore?' Mia had to dab carefully at her eyes so as not to smudge her mascara.

'I didn't think she did! Something about Charlotte or Barbara, Henry or Banjo must have really riled her.'

'Well, I thought Juanita could stand up to her.'

'I thought she could. I was wrong. Mind you, the fight over names between Juanita and Damien was beginning to assume epic proportions so it could even have been a stroke of genius.'

Mia put her hanky away but she was still chuckling.

'You were good with my mother and her chef,' Carlos said as he swung into Bellbird's drive.

'I intend to stay good with her.' Mia put a hand on his arm. 'I don't know why but I feel different all of a sudden.'

'Different?' He looked comically apprehensive for a moment. 'How so?'

Mia drew a deep breath. 'I don't feel like the housekeeper's daughter any more. I wonder why?'

'Could it be because you're about to become—and willingly—the padrone's wife?' he suggested.

But Mia shook her head although she acknowledged his rueful look with the glint of a smile. 'No, I think it's because suddenly you all seem so normal.'

'I would have thought we were all bordering on insanity,' he objected and pulled up in front of the house.

'Not really. You have your fights, your ups and downs, your loyalties, your crazy times, just like everyone else. Look—' she shook her head and her expression was wry '—I know it sounds ridiculous to you for me to say I hadn't seen you all like that before, but it's true. And it makes me feel different.'

He turned to her and put an arm along the back of her seat. 'Are you serious?'

'Uh-huh!'

'Well—' he paused '—I've had a thought. It's occurred to me that I've neglected them for a time. It's occurred to me I ought to undertake some fence-mending exercises, like somehow getting Damien to forgive my mother for insisting he call his son Benito. Ditto Juanita. And it looked to me as if Damien and Juanita are feeling just about as hostile towards each other as it's possible to be, wouldn't you agree?'

'Oh, I do! They didn't even look at each other.'

'Right. I must say, I don't know what I can do about the celebrity chef who's popped up in our midst but— do you remember the wedding you had here that was about to flop unless you were able to pull something out of the hat?'

Mia's eyes widened. 'Yes…'

'From memory, you actually exhorted me to make the kind of speech only I could make to liven things up or you'd scream blue murder?'

Mia's lips twitched. 'I do,' she said solemnly.

'Can you promise me, though, that if I do stop this christening from flopping and manage to turn it into a

happy, even joyful occasion, you won't go back to feeling like the housekeeper's daughter?'

'I won't, I promise,' she said huskily. 'Please do it.
I love you,' she told him, smiling through the tears in
her eyes. 'I love you, Carlos O'Connor.'

* * * * *

LET'S TALK
Romance

For exclusive extracts, competitions
and special offers, find us online:

f facebook.com/millsandboon

 @millsandboonuk

 @millsandboon

Or get in touch on 0844 844 1351*

For all the latest titles coming soon, visit
millsandboon.co.uk/nextmonth

*Calls cost 7p per minute plus your phone company's price per minute access charge